# Hearts and Hellfire

# The Dragon Empress Chronicles
# Book One

Ashlen Jordan

Published by Ashlen Jordan (Independently published)

First Edition

ISBN: 979-8-9987896-0-1 (Paperback)
ISBN: 979-8-9987896-1-8 (Hardcover)
ISBN: 979-8-9987896-2-5 (eBook)

Developmental editing by Danica Reynoso
Copy and line editing by Nevvie Gane and Toni Rakestraw
Proofreading and formatting by Samantha Pico
Cover design by Chelsea, Rocksauce Creative
Map illustration by Sarah Jones

This is a work of fiction. Names, characters, places, and incidents are either the product of the author's imagination or used fictitiously. Any resemblance to actual persons, living or dead, events, or locales is entirely coincidental.

Printed in the United States of America

For more information, visit: www.ashlenjordan.com
Contact: heybestie@ashlenjordan.com

For those who begged life to be more forgiving, knowing death
seemed easier—and chose to fight on anyway.
I'm proud of you. Keep rising.

# Author's Note

Hey, Bestie! Thanks a million for picking up this book—it means the world to me! You're a huge part of making my dream a reality. Just as a heads-up, this is going to start HEAVY and dark, but don't worry, it will get better! Will there be a happy ending? Well . . . I promise it'll leave you wanting more, and the story is just getting started!

**Trigger Warning:** Hearts and Hellfire may be intense. If you are sensitive to heavy themes (domestic violence, sexual assault, manipulation, suicidal ideation, etc.), please take care of yourself first. I'm here to chat if you want to know more about the content. Feel free to shoot me an email, and I will do my best to talk to you about the content without spoiling.

Okay, about the smut . . . Get ready for a wild ride, from steamy scenes to some darker kinks—maybe a threesome with some vampires and blood play. Thanks again for diving into this mess with me! <3

# Hearts and Hellfire

THE DRAGON EMPRESS CHRONICLES
BOOK 1

ASHLEN JORDAN

# Reading Playlist

"V.A.N" - Bad Omens - Prologue
"The Love You Want" - Sleep Token - Ch. 3
"Wonderland" - Neoni - Ch. 5
"Cotton Eye Joe" (Medieval Version) - Bardcore - Ch. 9
"Daylight" - David Kushner - Ch. 10
"I Can Do It With A Broken Heart" - Taylor Swift - Ch. 11
"Labour" - Paris Paloma - Ch. 12
"Queen of Kings" - Alessandra - Ch. 13
"Give" - Sleep Token - Ch. 16
"Castles" - Raizhell - Ch. 19
"Gravity" - Matt Hansen - Ch. 22
"Take Me Back To Eden" - Sleep Token - Ch. 23
"River" - Bishop Briggs - Ch. 24
"Devil Inside Me" - KSHMR - Ch. 24
"Pretty Little Devil" - Shaya Zamora - Ch. 25
"Burning Down" - Alex Warren - Ch. 27
"Royalty" - Egzod - Ch. 28
"Strike Back" (From *Fairy Tail*) - AmaLee - Ch. 29
"Indian Summer" - Jai Wolf - Ch. 30
"Abyss" (From *Kaiju No. 8*) - Yungblud

TERRA DRAC
Bellator
Batt
VITAENDARA

num
Cat's Paw
Otium
REXARIUS
Oppida Prima
rent Sea
onsfrick
Manor House
Carcer
MORDRYL

# Lady Death

*A* new world? We were not flesh and bone, not entirely, walking the line between all things from this new little place in the vast nothingness we had existed in for over millennia. The nothingness was peaceful, with steady magic all around us. Many different worlds and places we had traveled in our time, but this little place of blue and green? It was where my opposite and I found an elevated purpose in our existence.

This little place was creating its own space in this universe. We did not interfere with it, just observed as the magic seemed to work tirelessly to create. We watched as things in this place began to wither and fade; the magic of each of those little things faded into the vast nothing. Some sank deep below this little place, and some rose high above it. We gazed from our place in the universe, observing what would happen. More worlds, perhaps?

As this place grew, so did the Above and the Below, magic rising and sinking with each thing that was alive, eventually dying.

The magic pulled itself back and forth over this little cluster of blue and green, always an equal exchange.

"We have watched long enough; we should go experience now," my opposite said in a raspy voice.

I nodded. I had wanted more of this place; it was strange, new, and beautiful.

We made our descent to the little blue-and-green sphere, finding that this place of wonder and free-flowing magic and dust in the universe was also running with chaos. Things crawled over the earth, while others were falling from above into this place, and then as something fell, something else would rise, always in opposite. These little beings were so lost and confused. Suffering was apparent, as their magic would be trapped in these little bodies, confused as to why it was suddenly contained.

"We know the way. We should guide it back," I said to my opposite, only to note he was no longer by my side. My opposite was dashing to a falling orb of panicked magic, gripping the orb to throw it back to the space above this little world. The orb took hold of my opposite. It was too heavy to throw back. My opposite placed that orb into a being of flesh after giving it a warm embrace. It relaxed and lived.

I saw one orb fall away from another kind of being, and I went to grab hold of it. It was so light and airy that it began to pull me upward to the space above. I pushed it toward the Above and watched as it faded into it, with no panic. I looked at my opposite. We were both confused by this exchange but curious, and we kept guiding bits of magic, comforting it as it rose and fell time and time again. We never tired of this, bringing comfort to the newly created or newly departed beings.

They began to call us Lady Death and Lord Life. We watched over them and guided them. Some maintained their magic as they departed into the other spaces of Above and Below, sending their experiences back to the little blue-and-green place. The beings then began to litter the land and would call those who kept their magic in the beyond of that place gods; they would call their magic souls, and we were the carriers of souls. The beings began to fear me when I appeared. Their magic was being sent to another place while they cherished Life. They would beg me to leave them, but their magic, their souls, needed to be escorted to where they belonged. While my opposite, Life, would bring them here, only to see them forget about him as the magic entered its new flesh.

Life and Death, the carriers of souls, were feared and loved by the beings. We tried to stop, fearing we would upset the balance. The magic would erupt, and the chaos would start over, leaving the little place only to restart time and time again. Even in opposition, we knew we had a duty to this place we found. We would guide the magic and calm it, so we did, until their gods made monstrous beings out of their leftover magic, giving some of these beings' wings, talons, fangs, fur, and so much more. With our love and admiration, this place became our home, and we became its guides.

That was until these monstrous beings found a way to touch souls and warp magic, tormenting the creature it was harnessed in. Soon, beings began trapping my opposite, Life, to beings that should have been my duty to escort out of this place and into the next. I was feared. Life was loved and coveted. Yet. LIFE WAS MINE. He had always been MY opposite.

We raged against these beings; the so-called gods of our little place made these monsters too powerful. Why would they create such a thing? I couldn't fathom the creation of things, let alone things this wicked. The magic should be unbound, and the beings of this little place should be free to live and die as they please. We raged; I stripped life from things, while my opposite gave it to smaller and lesser beings. Until we saw their cruelty was not limited to us and bending our little world to their will. The dragons were merciless.

That was when I found her. Her magic was true and kind; she did not waver when she saw me, and her last words, even in a massive amount of torment, were a plea to my opposite.

"Life, let me stay."

Hearing her plea, I made a decision. I was Lady Death; I would submit to no one. I stayed with her, only bringing her comfort, and it was she who chose to cling to Life. This one, I would let her choose when she left this place. This little broken thing wanted to stay in this place. She was a fighter; she would help others. I would bless her, allowing her to fight and stain her heart so that others may also learn to embrace life.

I would make a god, maybe even gods, to send into the next place, gods who knew of the terror their creations caused. Gods who would demand balance among the beings and allow them to live and die on their terms. Looking at her, I knew my work had just begun. She would need my help, not just my blessing. I would give her magic and a lover to soothe her burning heart.

# CHAPTER ONE

## *Elsie*

Running, I was running through the dying orchard on small human legs. I dared a glance back. The manor house was engulfed in flames, smoke filling the air. I could barely breathe. I kept running away from the manor, from my home. I screamed and sobbed, "Why?"

Everything and everyone I loved was dead, burning in my precious home. I kept running, reaching the end of the orchard, the magic around me dying faster. I could see it leaving this place. *Take me with you.* Sobbing in desperation, breathless from the mile-long run, approaching the unicorn stable, shock hit me. I dropped to my already bleeding, burnt knees. A dragon's roar escaped my throat. My family's prized possessions, our main source of income and my joy, the unicorns, were gone. Not a body or a trace of their magic to be found.

My own magic faltered, and as another roar escaped me, I was ripped from that small body into my true form. Searing, burning, agonizing pain ripped through me, the human form a mask from the true horror that I had escaped. Bleeding in human form should have been enough to warn me of this. Still small, still weak, and now it was unbearable, and I crumpled. My wings shot out, ripping from my back, splayed out, one at a bent, unnatural angle, scales and flesh missing down to bone, the webbing ripped to shreds.

As I lay on the ground, the pain subsided; this was death.

"Life, let me stay." My pleas only fell around me, and the black mist consumed my vision.

As the mist dissipated, I began to survey the damage, finding a gaping wound on my long, slender neck, leaking and pooling my violet blood, Dragon blood. The blood was dark, and it shimmered in the full moon's light. I realized then I was only seeing this clearly through one eye. The other a red haze. Crippled and half blind, my wings splayed around me without the energy or magic to flick my tail or move one of my four limbs. I felt myself hovering above my body, looking down at the mutilated mess of a once-beautiful young dragon, my matte black scales absorbing the moonlight, tinged nearly nose to tail with the violet iridescence of my blood. A blood-curdling scream radiated through me, a dragon's dying scream nearly the same as my brother's when his wings had been ripped off.

I sobbed. "Why? What did we do to deserve this?" Footsteps approached behind me, coming from the manor. I heard the leaves crunch under their feet. Who were they? How many? At least this would be the end. *Death may be swifter than I thought.* Then she appeared in my line of sight, a dragon girl not much older than myself, subadult, in a human form. Why human? Her hair was long, and the ringlets fell past her shoulders, a mixture of blonde, amber, and light blue. The Mors Kingdom girl. She had been here, visiting with her father a few days prior. Had she done this? Mor's kingdom was a no man's land, the land of death; kill or be killed was their way, and it all made sense.

It all fell tragically into place. My mother insulted the Mordryl's when she refused them the sale of her prized stallion. She then set the unicorns free while her own family was slaughtered.

The sobs increased, the sounds escaping as more dying screams. Two more figures came into view—fairies, this girl's guards, perhaps? In a blinding movement, the sounds stopped, my sobs and screams now just the heaving of air exiting my lungs in pain, terror, and despair. The warmth of my blood pooled at my neck, flowing down to my chest and into the grass. At least I would not be cold as I died.

"Oh, look at this, the missing child from the manor, the female child," one of the fairies crooned and taunted. "Whatever shall we do? Kill her? Keep her?"

It was the girl who spoke next. "I want to keep her. She will be my new pet!" she whined. She placed her hand on my head, and the bleeding stopped; magic coursed through me, the wounds closing.

"Miss Cliantha!" the fairy exclaimed. "Don't burn up your magic. We have many who are injured, and your father would be very displeased if you used all of it on a pet," the other faerie warned.

With the tongue of a viper, venom leaching from her words, the girl replied, "Daddy will let me have anything I want, Luis. You know that better than anyone. Just ask your wife." I saw right through her the day she came to our home; nothing but a cold, spoiled brat. "You, Luis, will not tell me how to use MY magic. I will heal the injured if I please, or you can kill them. It is much easier and far less to clean up." The magic stopped flowing. "I can't fix this amount of damage, anyway." Anger crept into her voice. But I COULD MOVE. I jolted up, attempting to run, only to be slammed down headfirst. I felt cold hands at the base of my skull, right behind my crest of scales and horns. Still so small and weak, but the bleeding had stopped, and all the blood lost was back in my body. I twitched the broken wing; it was now intact but horrendously scarred. What had she done to me? The look in my eye must have been enough.

"You ungrateful dragon shit. Miss Cliantha has nearly healed you, and you repay her by attempting to run?" *Thud, crack,* my head bounced off the hard, dead soil. "If the young miss wants you as a pet, that is what she shall get!" Slammed back into the dirt, I felt some teeth shatter. I was no match for a strong Fae, too young, too inexperienced, too weak. I stopped fighting. The ice-cold chain met the scales of my neck; I knew enough to recognize a dragon tamer's chain. I roared, but no sound came out. Shocked, I looked at the girl.

A shy but cruel smile came over her young, delicate features. "Sorry, pet, your voice is nonessential and rather annoying. Wings, however, you will need those later. I would do anything to fly. When we get home, you can take me flying." There was a hint of longing in her voice as her guards stiffened. She continued, "Daddy took my wings when I was little, but that's fine. He needs me to stay home, fix the bodies, and I would do anything for Daddy."

*"Stop tormenting yourself! WAKE UP."*

* * *

Jolted awake, shaking and sobbing, I gazed around, the familiar black mist hovering in the corner with dead opaque eyes gazing at me. Then it hit me: just another nightmare from years past. Cliantha was crying, older now. At some point in my time here, I learned we had only been a few years apart in hatch dates. Now, we were both young adults; humans would say twenty-one and twenty-three years old. We were about one hundred and seventy years old, I think; I don't know how long I have been in this place. "I'm so sorry," she chanted over and over, her broken voice filling the air.

I blinked, and it came to me: Clia, my only friend, had suffered with me in this place for the last hundred and fifty years, at least. I was silently sobbing; still no voice. Years had passed since that day. She took me "home" to this hell as her pet, slave, and friend, but over the years, she had softened and hardened, switching between personalities, so it seemed. She was a victim of her father, the king of this land, who tormented her for his selfish agenda: make her the best dragon healer known to dragonkind. She had become that. Yet she was still unable to fully heal me from that day, mentally or physically. The king tormented her pet, her slave, and maybe even her friend, repeatedly, forcing her to improve her healing magic to save her pet—me. The first few years, she thought of it as a game until I suffered a near-death blow from the king—after I attacked him, protecting her from his magic. Then it was clear to her it was no longer a fun game she and her father were playing. She hardened more after that, shielding herself from the cruelty by meeting the world with her own. The princess of madness, she lost more light every day. Ignorance used to be her shield, but now she knew the wickedness of her own father and her brother.

Stuck, trapped, there was no light, no hope, just like this cell I was kept chained in. I was labeled a threat to the kingdom. The king was fearful I would snap and kill him. The black dragon was forged to be the greatest weapon in history at their disposal. So, I remained chained. A moment of freedom for me would send him to his grave. The chains only removed during battle or training, and even then, I was collared, and the Fae here made sure to set boundaries just like the battle bounds. Attempting to pass through the milky barrier they put in place was like being raked over hot coals. A form of torture I had endured for her. Taken her punishments time and time again.

I wrapped around her small, delicate human form, her blue-amber eyes glassy and soaked with tears. I tucked her in close and coiled my neck around her, laying my head in her lap, her long hair draped around her, being sure to keep my weight off her and not crush her. I held her as she cried, and I stared at the chain that held me here in this dark cell, the same tamers' chain from that fateful day.

She closed her beautiful eyes, slowly covering the amber, then the blue, and finally closing in on the most telling of dragon traits—the narrow vertical pupils. I think if you look hard enough, you could see the cracks in her soul. The eyes are the pathways to the soul, a sentiment my mother had told me once. I felt my mind and magic start to slip from reality. Seeing the tears streaming down her face enraged me. I curled my lips over my dagger-sharp teeth. Two rows of nine-inch daggers on my upper and lower jaws—one of my unique qualities. Death would claim her quickly; I could end her suffering painlessly. Not even her magic could fix being ripped apart. I would have to be fast: uncoil, strike. I tensed; this seemed like a good idea. Anything, I would do anything to stop her tears.

Then, as if she could hear my thoughts—maybe she just knew me well enough—she mumbled, "Elsie, please don't" in a delicate, soft voice. I lost my resolve; how could I murder someone I thought of as a friend? She curled deeper into the space I had created for her within the coils of my neck. A voice echoed in my mind, a male's voice, saying, *That's right, Elsie, find the light.* I questioned my thoughts. Why was it always a male voice? I despise males for what they had done to me, what they had forced upon me.

My thoughts scattered. Oh, that's right, my name was Elsie, not Pet Elsie. It was all coming back now, slamming into my mind, climbing out of the darkness and insanity that plagued me. I was King Arthur Pax's daughter, hatched in Pax's peaceful kingdom. This kingdom killed my family, took my manor, scattered the unicorns, and tortured the only friend I had known all these years. Well, fuck that and fuck them.

I was ugly and covered in scars with no voice, and no one knew who or where I was. I was not only Elsie Pax, but I was also Elsie, the lost princess of Pax, also known as the Black Dragon Death and Darkness. I held no real identity; that had been stolen from me. Maybe this only made me more dangerous? How optimistic of me.

The tears stopped and turned to droplets of white fire, never hitting the ground, just going up in smoke. My magic, my fire, Hell's Fire—this is what I had learned to wield. A basic fire dragon turned into a weapon from Below. No dragon in five thousand years had ever been able to handle the burn of the magic. The last wielders of Hell's Fire burned themselves alive from the inside out after their soulmate was murdered in cold blood. Finding my hell here in this forsaken place allowed me to wield it. Hell's Fire had manifested fully during the battles of the last mating season. Rage was my magic's trigger. Under the full sun, with a strong male taunting Clia, it came into full bloom. Fire of blue, violet, white, and crimson, dripping off my wings, talons, and teeth. As I felt my body calling that magic, the burn was painful, almost all-consuming. Pain, I learned how to handle pain. I had adapted quickly during that season when I heard her cheering me on. While a flashback from the prior Hell's Fire wielder clouded my vision—her death, her sorrow—I shoved against that vision, where fury forced me to adapt and take this magic into every burning fiber of my being.

Dragon mating season comes once every five years and is nonnegotiable for females. Female dragons must present themselves at the battlegrounds, or males driven by desire and need for conquest could destroy the continent. Males are insufferable.

Being that I was her pet and slave, I could not fight for myself to be claimed; I was owned. But holding the magic of mass destruction, I fought on her behalf. She would never dirty her hands herself. I wouldn't allow it, nor could she fight, being a healer. I would not allow her to take a life; she was not born for that. The rage I had for that male, a lowly lord's son, taunting MY Cliantha. I killed him in one blow after Hell's Fire manifested. The other challengers backed down immediately. Males would only back down if a female could break them. I was good at that part. We may be smaller by nature, but our blessed female magic was more formidable. And mine? Well, it was deadly. And they all hated me as much as they feared me.

That memory of his death had my lips curled with a smile. I hadn't even learned his name when his blood splattered on the battle arena boundaries. The shock of the crowd, their stunned silence, and best of all, the smile on Cliantha's face. Who cared what this season would bring? I would fight for her as I had done the last two seasons. I fought and will fight on her behalf to remain in this disgusting place. Great. Risking my life for her. If I were to lose in battle, death was certain either by the male challenger, her father, King Mor—I would be put to death because of the refusal of the fight—or I could turn my magic on myself and die on my terms. But, anyway, why did I care again?

My thoughts were a mess—I was a mess. Seemed like no matter my options, I was doomed anyway: win, we stay in this place; lose and die, or end my own life. I mulled it over. Failure was not an option. Should I fail, I would be put to death in front of Clia, and she would be whisked off to another land. That would cause a war all on its own: her father's reckless mission to reclaim his daughter. Worse yet, she could end up with a lord within this land of death. I wonder if any of them were alive at this point. Nevertheless, she would be forced to continue her father's bidding, forced into her own slaveship by a male who won her.

Not failing was also just as grim. She would be owned by her father with his sick, perverted magic. Males kept us submissive and forced us into our bonds. Females had been deemed fragile since my magics last wielder was consumed by her own magic. The males kept us subservient to "protect" us from ourselves. To me, it just looked like fear disguised as bravado.

My thoughts raced as my internal monologue began to rush and collide. I could enjoy the battles this year; I could kill if I wanted. What was the consequence? My own death. I could attempt an escape, and if all went wrong, I could turn my magic on myself and allow Hell's Fire to burn my very soul to ash. That stupid male voice bounced in my mind again, almost pleading. *Come on, Els, look to the sky.* Whose voice was it? It was like the damn shadows could speak. Insanity. That had to be it. After all, insanity was all I knew: jumbled, racing thoughts of murder, rage, love, and lust.

I had been here way too long. I couldn't even remember my family's faces, but this voice did not belong to them. Annoyed that it always filled me with such hope and longing to be free again. The voice had been with me for years, always bringing a small bit of solace.

I glanced at the small window—the only one in this small gray cell—and looked up to the pale gray sky, the light barely peeking through. It was at last dawn, and somehow, I found some hope that maybe I could wriggle free. The Battle of Mates would be my best bet to gain some sort of freedom, whether that be Lady Death taking me or a grand escape.

Lady Death was kind and warm, a far better friend than Clia. Why did I even care about Clia at this point? Death was my fail-safe. I knew her well; we had met many times over the years of near-death experiences via the torture I received here. I had made peace with her over the many times she sat with me. She would welcome me. She had never forced me to go with her. I looked back at the hovering black mist in the corner of the cell, Lady Death herself coming to say hello yet again. I did not fear her; she was mute, just like myself, and always appeared as an ethereal black mist. I nodded toward her, knowing she had come like all the times before in my darkest hours. Lady Death always came to me; whether it was to usher me into the beyond or bring comfort, I could never tell. No one else ever saw her. A faint warmth crossed over the dead eyes that were consumed by the mist and then vanished as light crept into the cell from that small, taunting window. Oh shit, it was dawn.

Right on cue, Camron appeared at the cell door. He was a blond, blue-eyed ice wielder, and a weak one at that. In his human form, he was nothing to gawk at. Same with his dragon form, he was just an overall average-looking male. He was accompanied by his two usual Fae guards, their transparent dragonfly-type wings tucked back tight and in gray unmarked uniforms. I had never learned their names, yet they were always with Camron. The male fairies were just as average-looking as Camron, with brown eyes and hair, and plain thin features. They were sickly thin. The starvation of this kingdom was bad if the Fae looked like this. Next to dragons, the Fae had the most ability for magic; they were not only guards, but they were higher up the ladder.

They were the dragon's governing agency to keep kingdoms and males from ripping each other apart on a whim, their females contained. The Fae held the last say and would fight back if someone, even a Dragon King, stepped out of line. Their long lives often gifted us with their companionship for many years. The Fae understood our kind. They did their best to regulate the dragon kingdoms while not overstepping and trying not to force our kind against our flaws, even though some of them should be burned out for eternity. Why they allowed such behavior was still lost on me.

"Hey, PET, wake her up. Breakfast," he bellowed. "Also, you are to come. Father doesn't like repeating himself."

Cliantha jumped up and, with ice in her voice, said, "Thanks. Like we don't know that, useless prick."

I kept my smile inside, my dear immature, bratty, hateful little Cliantha. She was my voice. She was my everything. She was the only thing I had ever had in this place, and my moments of insanity would always tempt me to kill her. End her suffering. Ever since I took that male dragon's life, it was all too tempting. Ending lives, sending them with the kind black mist I loved so dearly. I loved Clia like you love toxic plants—gorgeous and captivating, but touch it incorrectly or take a bite, they would claim your life. I loved the danger in her, her fractured personality. The sudden change in her tone to soft and sweet as honey.

"I will come back and get you. I need to change, but I'll come get you. I promise."

Her blue-amber eyes met mine, and my own eyes reflected, black as night, cold, dead, one reflected with the red tinge from that horrid day, the black scales and curved horns with a pink scar running the length of my face over that red eye. I look exactly like what you would expect from a dragon called Death and Darkness.

Clia pushed past her brother, leaving the cell as he spat in my direction. I hissed back at him, letting the fire drip and feeling the burn of the dragon tamer chain searing my neck as I pushed my magic past it, erupting a small, contained fireball at the dishonorable prince. He scoffed as he put out the flame with ice.

"Bitch," he spat again.

"You would think, after all this time, you would learn, and you just keep burning around that collar. I hope it scars."

Little did he know or understand the chain had left its mark years ago, not only on my flesh but my soul as well.

The sudden strike of ice caught me off guard just enough for Camron to throw a Fae stone, lodging it right in between the collar and my skin, pinning it there. Fuck. I felt my magic waiver and then the ripping cold of the Fae magic. My dragon body was being pulled in, and the small, sickly, disgusting body of my human form appeared. As much as I loved magic, I hated it as well. The collar still snug, I looked down at this human sack of bone and skin. I didn't bother to cover myself. What was the point? I knew what Camron was doing next; I was defenseless in this form. I knew how to fight, but chained, starved, and beaten, I could not fight right now, so I bowed my head and looked at the floor through the red hue.

*"That's right, don't fight. Your time will come."*

Lady Death hovered by the wall, her dead eyes filled with hatred, but even the mist disappeared. Camron smiled a wicked grin.

"That's a good pet. Bow to me. Know your place." He spat on me again.

Remain still and keep my head down. Maybe he wouldn't do it this time. He grabbed my matted black hair and forced my head lower, now pressed into the stone floor.

"Ugly whore," he purred.

He took no time entering me from behind and began his messy, uncontrolled thrusting. Damn, he did, in fact, do it. Again. I focused my eyes on the wall and let all my thoughts fall away, feeling nothing, hearing nothing, only being held down and gagged by the chain. I did nothing, felt nothing. I was nothing but a tool for males to use as they pleased. Whatever use that may be. I have realized more and more that I do want to die, but I want to take them with me when I do. If there is an afterlife, I want to torment them in it. Make that place one of even more suffering than even I have endured. Unfortunately, I was stuck living here.

He turned on his heel and left as soon as his performance was done, pulling the Fae stone free as he left. I would kill him if given the chance; I just needed to live long enough to exact my revenge, and then I could walk with Death. This chain limited my power to near uselessness. The only time I gained some freedom over the magic was in battle. I let the rage I felt consume me and the fire leach out from every fiber of my being with the collar biting against my neck. I shut off the flow of magic as I felt the warmth of my blood spilling from around the collar and chain and my body clawing its way back to its dragon self. I may love Clia, but I love Death even more, and Camron pushes me closer to Lady Death each day.

Clia would take a few hours to get ready. I would still be called to the table. Waiting on her would mean I would not be getting a meal. Showing up without Clia was impossible. Gods, she was selfish, but I loved it. The way she would force anything to bend to her will. I loved that about her, even when I was the victim of her spiteful and selfish whims.

I lay down, looking out the window, and I found some peace in the silence. I would rage at battle and have a fail-safe. I would no longer be kept in this place. I would rather die at this point than be kept prisoner any longer. I would kill Clia if I was kept longer. However, I would not be able to live with myself for taking her life, so I would rage and end my suffering once and for all. Perhaps it was a coward's way out, but no coward would have kept living this long in this wretched place. *"Very cowardly."* Those damn shadows need to learn how to shut up and keep their disapproval to themselves.

I closed my eyes as hope filled me, the hope of getting one last battle, seeing a blue sky one last time, and exiting that battle arena with my best friend at my side as ghosts. Hopefully, I would find my peace as I walked with Death hand in hand with Clia. I started to fall asleep, only to find myself dreaming again, but this time, it was the manor house from when I was young. The orchard full and spilling with fruit and berries. I was on the back of a black unicorn, following swiftly after a white-haired boy. His laughter in my memories filled me with more peace than I thought I could find within myself. I loved this memory of the boy I did not know anymore. Maybe he was the voice in the shadows. Tired and broken, I let myself fall asleep.

## CHAPTER TWO

### Elsie

*I* woke up to Clia a few hours later, as expected. Her tardiness was going to cause problems for us. She had told the guards to retrieve the muzzle, collar, and wing bindings. I stayed still as she fixed it all into place. I looked at the dark metal we never had at the manor. There was no need—we didn't live in fear of anyone; peace and joy were all I knew from my family's rule in our land. This metal dragon tamer's chain, forged by the elves and Fae, was dark and ugly, not black but not gray; the hammer marks were not polished. The metal was as raw and ugly as my scars.

As I sat and waited for Clia to finish, my family's faces came to mind, smudged memories, clear enough to know who they were if you knew them. But if you had never seen my mother and father, these memories would not pick them out of a crowd. My brother was different somehow. I never could see him. He had been two years younger than me. Maybe it was only his echoing screams of death I could hold on to.

I shuddered thinking of him: a dying scream, wings ripped, and then I ran. Pathetic. Those sounds replayed in my head far too often. Last night was a reminder of how close I was to being insane, walking the all-too-thin line between life and death, and worse, acting out my insanity. All this time, I had held onto who I was, but now, forgetting part of their faces and having memories stained with violet blood, it seems as if I had begun to lose myself entirely. I almost killed the only person who had shown me one ounce of kindness in this place. She knew as well as I did this was increasing.

I'm amazed she still chose to sleep with her pet, knowing her pet's mind was failing and getting lost in the darkness. Unable to remember my past clearly, but I could remember every ounce of pain that had happened in this place. Every training session, both mine and hers. I was Elsie Pax—dammit, I would fight. My tail twitched, and Clia paused, then kept working on fitting the muzzle. I shouted my name in my mind, huffed, and twitched under her hands.

Elsie Pax. I still knew my name. At least I had that, my name-sake; at least if anyone ever found me here, I could say . . . Wait, no, I couldn't. I couldn't say anything. I couldn't call for help. I couldn't roar. I could do absolutely nothing to help my situa-tion. King Mor, I sneered in my mind, what an excellent game to play. Kidnap and torture a princess, make her a weapon of mass destruction, and take her voice so that, while in a fight, she can't plead with anyone to get her out. Leave her one ally, who was also trapped, not only by the confines of this hell hole of a castle but by her mind as well.

Clia danced between personalities based on her mood. My mind swayed with thoughts that could never be spoken aloud. Neither of us could leave without the other, nor could we sur-vive. She was defenseless, and I—well, I was her monster, bound by the love I held for her. So well crafted. I'm sure the entire Pax kingdom had looked for the royals. We all died that day. Who was still looking? No one was my answer. They surely would have come by now.

I twitched again. The insanity, the anger, the snap everyone feared. "Get it together, Elsie. You won't last past breakfast if you keep it up. Be still." Clia said this coldly as she snapped the last lock into place. This was a reminder that she knew me, who I was, knew my heart and my anger. She, however, also knew how close I was to becoming truly consumed by my dark desires for death. Were they truly dark desires or just something I had made peace with and could welcome? I was thankful no one could hear my thoughts. She took up the end of the leash and led me to the dining hall.

I was always amazed by the interiors of the castle, per usual cells and cages for all us beasties underneath, then the main floor and the bed chambers above that. This castle was only about as large as my family's manor house, the main floor of stone and rock, not a trace of woodwork found. The manor had been all cherrywood. Dragon castles mimicked human ones very closely, except for the size. The archways and doors were twenty-five feet tall to accommodate the tallest wings, and in this castle, the doors had to be wider than the average fifteen feet due to the king's sheer size in dragon form. Also, a joke, a disgrace to our kind to be that rotund. Kings could pack on the weight, sure, but while his entire kingdom was starved, he needed to have the castle reworked to accommodate his disgusting sins of gluttony and sloth.

I rolled my eyes and held my wings high. Even bound, I had enough pride left in me to not allow them to see my wings drag across the ground. We passed through the arch to the dining hall. This place amazed me because it was barren, with no art, not a single tapestry, nothing but gray, cold rock. And there, at the head of the table in his human form—why even rework the castle if you're hiding in that body anyway, I thought—was a stupid, ugly male, inside and out.

King Mordryl sat at the head, still a grossly round man but also greasy. His dark red hair with a greasy film of his last meal over it. His eyes, human bloodred, unsettling for most humans, but for dragons, this was a common color. Clia was rare; her magic, her eyes, everything about her was rare beauty. I watched as she walked ahead of me with a confident but swaying gait.

I was less mad about being led by her if this was the view I received. She led me to the far wall and clipped the leash to the stone. I lowered my head to the king and kneeled properly. Stifles and elbows on the floor, then curled my neck toward the king and kept my head on the cold stone floor. She took up her seat in front of me, her back toward me, and made sure she placed herself in my line of sight. I was grateful for it. Tracing her curves in the pink satin dress she wore, backless, only held by small satin ties, one quick move, and I could have it on the floor. I blinked. No, Elsie, this kind of behavior was not allowed, pet or not. *Not here*, I said to myself. I blinked the thoughts of her body away. Taboo was the least of my problems. I dared not move, and I listened to him speak, those thoughts exiting my mind entirely.

The king gasped for every breath as he spoke. He spoke of the great victories of war Camron had been leading. *Victories?* I questioned silently. One hundred and fifty years had passed since they took over the south of the Pax Kingdom. It's taken him a hundred and fifty years to claim a small portion of land from a country with no army. Pathetic Camron. Clia seemed to agree as I saw her shoulders shudder with a silent laugh at her brother's "victories."

A crack of thunder permeated the space. I flicked my eye back to the king to see he had brought his hand down on the stone table hard enough to crack it. I lay motionless on the ground. She had not been silent enough; this was going to get messy quickly.

"Do you have a joke to tell us, Cliantha?" the king wheezed. She wouldn't pass the opportunity, firing back with the ice in her heart that laced her voice.

"No, Father, no jokes. I just find it a tad amusing that Camron is getting praise about taking a few hundred miles of land after a hundred and fifty years from a kingdom that has no military. Where is the pri—"

Her voice was cut off by a muffled groan. I flicked my eye back to her, and I could see the fork sticking out of her shoulder. That disgusting cutlery was carved from bone, the bowls . . . skulls of humans, Fae, vampires, werewolves, really anything they could make out of bone they did in this forsaken place. The bone fork stuck out of her arm, and she flinched as she pulled it out and placed it neatly on the table. I recoiled and sighed a little too loud.

"Camron, the beast," the king said.

Without hesitation, Camron stood. His eyes did not meet me. *Shit.* He walked around the table behind his sister. She did not turn. I did not move as he kicked me square in the ribs. Even though he was in human form and I was in dragon form, the magic behind the kick was enough to force a hiss from me. He met my eye, and I saw what I could have sworn was remorse crossing his blue eyes. He ran a hand through his golden hair. He was thin, tall, and lanky. His father was eating everything in sight, and the young war commander just looked even more pathetic. He walked back and sat down, tucked his chair in close, picked up his fork, and returned to picking at the sorry excuse of a meal served.

"Thank you for passing the fork, Father." Clia plucked it from the table and licked her blood off it—a nice touch—the wound already healed with her magic flowing. It took everything in me not to laugh at the king. Hell, I wanted to pounce on her and lick her from head to toe right there on that wretched table, scattering the bones. I felt eyes on me; had I moved? *Oh, shit, yes.* By an inch, I had moved to the left, closer to her. She had been right. I was not going to make it through breakfast. I felt it before I saw it, the magic-wielding king with a bone-carved knife gliding along the pink scaleless section of my wing; then as the most sensitive spot had been found, the knife plunged into it and bounced off the bones in my wing. I flinched—also the wrong answer. It drove deeper. I held my breath, blocking out the pain and going as still as death. He always went for the same sensitive spot. The scar of that day, like the mental pain, was worse than the physical pain. The knife dropped to the ground, covered in my blood. Just great.

The king said, "Cliantha, darling, you cannot even make it to breakfast on time, and you mock your brother. Tell me, do you want the pet to suffer more?"

He paused. I saw Camron looking into his bowl as if he could escape into it, a pathetic, unchained young male, scared of an old bastard. Silence fell, and not the comfortable kind, a waiting and nerve-racking silence.

"I thought not."

Mordryl paused again, taking a long look at me as I met his eyes with my own, not moving and barely breathing. If I was not confined to chains, I would rip his throat out within seconds, then pour Hell's Fire down his floppy gullet. Watch him burn. He broke eye contact, probably sensing my malice.

"As I am sure the three of you are well aware, the season will be here in six months. After last season, I am confident you will remain in our home, Cliantha. Isn't that right, pet?"

I carefully shook my chain in acknowledgment, blood still dripping from my wing, but I did not look away; he would not see my fear or pain. He spoke to Clia directly now. His eyes burned with intensity at his daughter.

"Should you have failed in training your pet to defend you, I will be sure that it ceases to exist exactly one second after its defeat—that is, if somehow, it is still alive."

His eyes narrowed in on her, flashing with magic.

"It is not an option for you to leave this kingdom. You want for naught here. Meals, water, shelter, and wealth are all provided for you. Fail this year, and you could find yourself in some lord's home with hardly a fire. I hope six months of war training on the pet will be enough, dear daughter."

Clia went pale and gray. I almost rolled my eyes again; this was the same speech from last season: kill or be killed, got it . . . And this so-called king was just as delusional as I was: wealth? What wealth?

"Yes, Father. I will continue training with it, and we will succeed this season and stay grateful for all you provide," she said with not a drop of emotion.

A well-rehearsed response. His majesty attempted to shove a lamb leg into his mouth and began gnawing on it. *Pig.* I sat, chained to the wall, while they ate in utter silence. No one talked at this table about anything but season and war. I had not forgotten that, in my deepest moments of insanity, I could self-destruct.

*"COWARD,"* the voice that plagued my mind screamed.

No, I will do it; I will end it. I stared at the three of them sitting at the table: a glutton, a weak warrior, and a gifted girl . . . What a sad sight indeed, a family gathered at a table, sharing a meal, and no love to be found. This was a torture of its own. I would not endure it after this season. I am done with this; she would recover from my death.

The silence allowed my mind to start wandering again. My manor house was nothing like this. This place was the color of corpses. The walls, the wine, the clouds, and the sky . . . just lifeless gray. Trees were dead across this land. The only place that had a live tree was the courtyard where we sat, and that alone was only thanks to Cliantha's healing magic, just healing the earth around her by sitting there once a week. It was like this current king was leeching poison into the land and killing it.

My manor was full of life; it was like living in a never-ending sunset. The sky was always blues, pinks, oranges, and purples, the clouds vibrant white and puffy, the trees green and thriving, and orchards bearing fruit all year. The air was crisp but not cold. And that house, black and silver on everything. It was an average size only intended for human forms. I never even saw my parents in their true forms. My family of black dragons had presided over that land. We loved it like a member of the family, the last bit of land to host wild unicorns and wild Fae, allowing the wolves and vampires to run free as well. The laws were easy: Only take what you need to thrive and be happy. No one ever took more than their fair share. It was like the unspoken rule of our small kingdom; peace and freedom were the only things I knew. Music was always alive in the manor, and here I was, stuck in this lifeless place. With my own life and vibrance stripped from me, friends with Lady Death, attempting to ward off the voice in my mind. I'm sure Camron had stripped that same life from the lands I once called home.

My anger swelled, and I flicked my eye toward Camron, pathetic looking and . . . sad? A tear dripping from his face? My breath caught for him; if anyone saw that, he would be beaten. Why did I care? He just kicked me like some useless old dog that wandered in here, and yet he was crying over this meeting? What is happening? I was used to the cruelty, but the tears? From Camron, over us? Her? Me? Mordryl noticed my lack of breathing before his son's tears. *Shit.* Another knife, this one slicing downward, cutting the webbing of that wing into ribbons. Silence fell. Rage, panic, and grief washed over me as I allowed the fire to drip from my eyes and my outer exposed fangs.

"*TURN IT OFF!*" the voice commanded, and I obeyed. Every thought and emotion I had stilled.

My primal desires snapped into place. *Kill him.* My gaze fixed on Mor. I felt the fire welling, aching to be unleashed, the collar biting into my neck and all the other bindings burning my magic against my flesh. Mordryl let out a bellowing laugh and went into a coughing fit. *That's right, die, you old fuck. Choke to death on that lamb.*

"Wow, Cliantha, I'm impressed. That pet is about as volatile as it gets." His cough settled, and he rasped out, "This should be an excellent showing this year."

That was it; my last ounce of composure was gone. A showing? Like our lives were nothing but a game. I lunged, but the short chain did not give as I slammed into the collar and choked back. Clia stood, whirled, and plunged that bone fork into her spot in my neck. The bite of the fork was far better than the bite of her words. I didn't need to look at her to know her darkness had emerged.

"I am sick of this! You will behave. You will battle for me, and if I wish it, I will have you killed after. And you will be grateful!"

The fire faded from me, and I knelt back down and dared not move again. *That's right, Clia. Kill me, allow me the pleasure of walking with death; that's all I can hope for in this place.*

"*Allowing her to have a hand in your death is a waste.*" That damn voice . . . had a point.

# CHAPTER THREE

## Elsie

Clia threw me in the cell after breakfast, only partially healing me, enough for function only. As usual, more scars would remain. The following evening, she halted right at the cell door, her stance guarded, angry. She shook, her eyes glowing, the anger twisting her delicate face. I couldn't help but notice the dress she had chosen: a dark violet—blood violet—a plunging neckline leaving little of her perfectly round breasts and pointed nipples to the imagination. The dress hugged her hips so tight you could follow the curves of her body and make out the shape of her sex.

"You bitch." My attention went back to her eyes.

"You stupid bitch! How dare you embarrass me like that?"

I knew this personality of hers, sadistic and cruel. *Great.*

"You know damn well what he could have done. You're lucky I stepped in, you absolute idiot."

She strode across the room and grabbed the chain. I did not move; I just let her wrap the chain around my muzzle, crest, and horns. She was right, after all, and whatever her plan, I would let her exact her revenge. Fuck the battle; I could just have her kill me here. Death by her hand would be bliss. I had let myself falter, costing her more of her pride. Terrible mistake, and I was sorry for it. Wrapping more and more chains around my wings, she clipped those chains to the floor. The chain that held my mouth shut and my head in place was connected by six points on the floor and four points to each wing. While I could use some of my magic around it, it was still unpleasant. Like bolts of lightning if I pressed too hard into them.

"Guards!" she yelled.

Four small Fae males appeared, not daring to look or say a word. Perfect, a beating—well, that would be easy to endure, at least.

"Bring me a pillow and a blanket," she demanded, her voice unwavering.

My confusion permeated the air. As the guards ran, she sighed and let out a low, sinister laugh.

"You withstand physical torture too well, plus then, I would have to heal you. In the last two days, you thought of killing me, embarrassed me at breakfast, and worst of all, upset Daddy. If I did not know for a fact you were female, I would assume you are a male ready for the season, ready to fuck anything. I mean, hell, look at you! Black scales with pale pink skin where you can't hide the scars, not a trace of beauty left. Oh, poor once-pretty Elsie, never to be seen again. You will win wars for Daddy and me, destroy your homeland, all because I wish it. You are nothing without me."

She clapped her hands. Her smile was huge while she laughed, but she held a sinister look in her eyes. It hurt; it cut deep, but it also enraged me. She had slept with me night after night; for years, I held her; for years, she had cried and leaned against me; for years, she had healed me. This was more than some male-season desire I was feeling. Right? The shock must have been all over my face, and droplets of fire escaped my fangs and wing tips. She had never been so cruel to me; we had played, and I had flown her around the training wards, allowing her to feel the wind on her face. I fought for her, for fuck's sake, risking my life for the love I had for her. This soulless wretch talking to me now had to be just another fragmented version of her, right?

*"It's just her true nature being revealed. Still wanna die by her hand?"* the voice taunted.

"Win the season for me, Elsie. Win the whole damn thing. Use that rage. Use the rage that spills over to make yourself worthy of my love for you. Tonight is the first night we train you to control that primal rage you have for me and my body. Can't have you getting distracted in the ring now, can we?"

Was she insulted I found her beautiful? What could she expect me to do but love and lust after her with all the time we spent together? All the nights we had shared secrets. She snapped her fingers, and the guards came over and set her pillow and blanket on the floor. A mere five feet from the tip of my nose. My mind was racing; what the hell was she doing? Worthy? OF WHAT? Win the season? Wasn't that the plan? Pillow? I felt like the stone walls were closing in. It was getting hotter, and more fire dripped off me in sheer frustration. Why was she talking to me like this? What was she planning? No way she would kill herself before my eyes. She loved herself too much. My breath caught as she sat down and pulled the one tie holding that dress to her body. In one graceful movement, she was seated on the blanket, naked, leaning on one hip and elbow. The droplets of fire fizzled out. I stared at her and took a breath. I loved seeing her body, never tiring of her scent—light and clean, like rain mixed with sweet peas. I locked eyes with her. The world around me faded away; there was only her, hair draped around her shoulders, a queen in our bedroom. She looked at me through her long lashes and blinked slowly. Desire, pure desire, was pouring off me. She reached her hand out, and I leaned.

*Zap!* I would have shrieked as the chain bit into my face and wings. My desire shifted to rage. I needed to touch her, feel her, admire her, pleasure her, and here I was, trapped by a chain.

"Oh, Elsie, so predictable." She laughed. "You poor thing, so mutilated by this life and forced to fight for me. You might as well be a male. Gods, that's just terrible and disgusting, but what could be expected of you, Elsie?"

My head hurt. Here she was in all her naked glory, taunting me, calling me disgusting when she knew damn well all the nights we had shared. My mind mixed with rage and desire. The chains kept me still as clumps of fire fell from me.

"Oh, you think this is bad for you? You embarrassed me," she growled. "This will be your constant reminder. Never act out of line again. You will sit here, still, quiet, with not a drop of fire coming off you. You will not embarrass me ever again. You will win the season, be worthy, and be my slave till the day you fucking die."

Her voice was stern. She was angry, extremely angry with me, and she wanted to hurt me in the most intimate way possible: break my heart. She was going to drive me further into insanity by toying with the one thing I valued most in this hell hole, my only reprieve: her friendship and love. The one thing I held love for besides muddy, unreliable memories. Her entire self. Tears fell from my eyes. I began to cry, distraught, for the life I wished I could have had with her, and she laughed. Lady Death appeared behind her, a black mist with her dead, opaque eyes that only held what could be described as rage and disgust.

"All right, come here, boys." The same four Fae guards approached her and knelt before her. "Now, don't be nervous," she cooed to them.

My eyes fixed on this mess, unable to look away. Something was off with these males; they looked like each other, each sandy blond, thin, almond brown eyes, and each the same height, with a tan skin tone. Cliantha spoke and gave them instructions.

"One."

She had numbered them and did not even think to use their names for such a gathering. *Zap!* As I flinched into the chains, I let out a breath of frustration. This was an insane game she was attempting to play . . . And it was working well. She snapped her fingers.

"Get behind me and hold me up for your brothers."

*BROTHERS?* Death quivered. I shouted against my useless vocal cords.

*"She wants you angry, to break you. Don't allow her the satisfaction."* I shook the voice away.

The first fairy took a wide-legged seat behind Cliantha, allowing her to lean back on his chest. Another snap.

"Two." She clicked her teeth at him.

Another zap of the chains as I went forward. I felt the pain, the burning as the chain pulled tight. I shrank back. The second fairy, with a face equally distant, gently took her thigh and hip and brought her around so I had a full view of her glistening, swollen sex. I lunged. *Zap!* Smoke rose. I saw stars as my scales burned. Another snap with clicking teeth, grating on each one of my frayed nerves.

"Three."

I didn't even look at Fairy Three as he picked up and held her other leg, presenting me with an even better view of her. A dark, wicked smile bloomed across her face. I glanced at the men, not a trace of joy to be found on their faces; their delicate paper-thin wings sagged as if this was also torture for them. Fairy One caught my stare and adjusted his hand. I looked, and on his finger sat a silver-and-gold ring . . . He was mated to another and then the cruelty of what she was doing hit me. She was not only going to break my heart but force me to watch helplessly as she broke others as well. She was going to show me that all of us meant nothing to her.

The Fae, much like dragons, claimed mates for life, except their mates were rooted in love, not lust and conquest as our kind had been subjected to. The Fae loved deeply and wholly, often dying when their mate died. A love I envied, the type my parents shared.

I looked at the others, who tactfully adjusted their left hands, their long fingers partially webbed, and each of them had a silver-

and-gold band. Each of them mated to their loves, now forced to play this terrible game with their princess. Did their mates know? A tear slipped from Four. Cliantha snapped at him and, with the most toxic sneer I had ever heard from her, commanded the little male fairy.

"Four, on your knees and devour me."

I briefly allowed my gaze to meet Death. The mist was smaller, her eyes moist. I could never fully interpret her feelings, but she looked distraught, like torturing souls was something that pained her.

Cliantha adjusted her hard gaze to me.

"How do you hold on to any hope?" she taunted.

The male moved silently with such grace and elegance. On his knees in front of her, he lowered his head, turned, and glanced at me pleadingly, tears running from his eyes. He turned back and began to carefully lick her sex. Appalling—but beautiful? Her question left my mind quickly. She was forcing these males into turmoil. Their mating bonds could be broken due to this; souls could shatter. It was one thing to torment me as punishment, but why bring in innocents? Why torture them this way, such plea-sure, such pain, such suffering, to what end? I felt it then: the rage toward her, the injustice for these males. I hated males, and yet these males had no part in this, just average guards going about their work, only to be intercepted by this insane, game-playing princess. Death's eyes, hovering above her, glowed red.

Hell's Fire began to run wild. I felt the heat, the chains burning against my scales, not only in sick, twisted desire for her but in rage. I wanted to hurt her. I could not move. She gripped his sandy hair in her hand, shoved his head deeper into her, and ground her hips against his face, moaning with pleasure as her body twisted and shook under the other three. One had not moved; a motionless pale, hollow shell, holding her in place, looking straight at me, a hardness in his eyes. I tore my eyes from her body and met his stare. His eyes flashed with rage; he, too, felt the same as I. The heat poured from me, the air growing hot and thick, the scent of her filling the air.

She huffed out, "How does it feel knowing you will never feel this bliss again?"

She climaxed, the fairies struggling to keep her body in place, tears of sadness and anger flowing from their eyes. I felt my sadness for them overcome me, and the heat began to fade. Death was still full of rage and despair, with glowing red wet eyes, the mist trembling. I relaxed my body so the chains hung loose; no doubt they had left their marks against my scales. Cliantha snapped her fingers, and the males quickly stood; she adjusted herself on her makeshift throne, now covered in her own wet, sticky mess. It smelled divine. I was disgusted with myself. She snapped again, and the males left the cell. With hard eyes, I met her gaze. I was her slave. If it was pleasure she was after—look no further, and I would happily give her the love she craved, but she chose to hurt others. Even Death was far kinder than that.

"Oh, Elsie, did you not enjoy the little show?" she said softly, head cocked to the left. I just sighed.

"You know why I did this, right"? she asked softly, almost innocently.

No, I can't imagine why you would bring more suffering; isn't there enough suffering in this life?

She responded to my stare coldly, "After all this time, you cling to hope and life, but I know you. You crave freedom. You will never have freedom."

I growled; she didn't know me as well as I thought. My hope was rooted in ending suffering: mine, hers, now theirs.

"Can you have such a beautiful show in the afterlife? Would I be as beautiful then? Or would I look like the whore my brother uses as a place to sheath his cock? Already dead on the inside, at least I can still enjoy my life. I have lost a great deal. But I can still force men to their knees and come all over them and you. While you, on the other hand, are just a tool for me and a cock holder for Camron. Daddy is right. I have everything I could want here, and I'm free to do as I wish. That, Elsie, is freedom and power."

I just sighed, defeated. Whatever this new, far crueler and deranged side of Clia was surfacing, it was not one I would argue or win against. Just maybe I could show her.

I was Elsie Pax, wielder of Hell's Fire. I would burn this place down. We would be free one day, or I would die trying. I let the pure white molten fire drip from my fangs, the fire as white as the hope she wanted to take, as white as the boy in my dreams. Maybe reminding her of hope would do something, anything. She laughed.

"Elsie, we will never be free. Just enjoy what we can."

She lay down and whispered, "I'm sorry, Elsie, but just give up already. Make this easier for all of us."

She fell asleep instantly, leaving me in chains. I stared at her naked body, grief filling me. She was just as broken as I was, so she had chosen to hurt everyone and everything around her. I looked at Lady Death, her eyes hard as she met mine. I could feel her willing me to fight.

I was broken by my rage and desire to get out, broken by my refusal to accept what she had said, that we were trapped forever.

I cried all night, knowing that if this was how she chose to deal with her insanity, it would never end. I would never be caught in a human form in this place. I would never allow her that again. I would never know her against my body again because, no matter what, I was the strong one. I had to uphold her. I had to be her white knight, blinding hope, with pure white burning fire. For the rest of my days, I would be what she needed—not what she wanted, but needed—and right now, she needed someone to protect her from herself. I would stick by her and her abhorrent behavior because, one day, she would never do that again. I would fight for her.

I nodded to Death. I will fight. I screamed in my mind that I would live and fight for her and dismiss the promise of peace the Lady of Death had granted me many times.

Tears of anguish were the companions I slept with that night, and I clung to the idea of hope for Clia's redemption. If she wanted to die, she would see Lady Death, but she wanted life, so I had to fight for her.

*"Would you please stop fighting for anyone aside from yourself?"*

I turned my mind off, willing with everything I had for the damn voice to stop its relentless preaching.

***

Five months had passed since that day. This new brand of torment she was subjecting me never ended. Each day was a walk in the courtyard, flying laps, working my magic and my body, preparing for the battle of mates. Skeletal or not, I had to train to win. Pushing my body further and faster each day. Each night, new fairies, elves, vamps, wolves, or whatever lurked, were selected to bed her in my cell. After a few months of this, I was able to control myself. I was just numb, watching the torment, as well as her insatiable appetite for sex. Even with her beauty, some males would fall soft and then be executed should they fail to bring her to climax. She was insane. My love for Cliantha had faded. Her cruelty was such I had never seen. It waged war on her mind for so long. The love I held was turning into the need to kill her and end her madness along with my own. Bound so tightly, I couldn't kill her, but I wanted to most days; other days, I felt immensely sorry for her. It wasn't fair that she never got a chance at real life, never even knew of the peace I once had.

*"She lacks your resolve. You cannot blame yourself for her shortcomings."* The voice that had plagued my mind for years would remind me of that every so often, probably just my mind's way of trying to protect itself.

Death never left me; I wish I could understand her more. She never left, but she was angry. Not a soul could see her, and it seemed she could not simply pull the life from Clia, so she sat with me day after day, night after night. I was never close to dying, yet she stayed. She and the voice always stayed.

And all I could do was hold back. I had decided I would not give into this sick, twisted act of Clia's. I had not leaked one drop of fire in three months. I had mastered the control she was "training me" for, and yet each night, she continued with this perverted insanity. And each night, she would utter the words, "I am sorry, Elsie." And each night, I would find myself wanting to save her again.

I held on to those words. Sorry? Sorry for what? Tormenting the others? Sorry we were trapped here? Sorry you kidnapped me? Sorry you keep choosing to live and not just let me kill you? Sorry for what, exactly? If I ever got my voice back, those would be my first words to her. What on earth could she be sorry for and yet continue the same behavior? Maybe it was just something she said and did not mean; maybe she wasn't sorry. My mother's voice echoed in my mind. *When you say you are sorry and you do not change your actions, then you were never remorseful.* The echo of words I had not heard in years was gone as quickly as I heard her voice. *No. Please. Help me.*

The cold silence was deafening as tears of fire sprang to my face. Was my mother right? I shook with silent sobs. I held so much anger for my mother yet to cry over a simple echo of her voice. Had she just sold that damn unicorn, I would have never ended up here. The sunlight through the window was blocked by the clouds. I missed my sky and my mother more. The fire of anger and sorrow kept flowing. Death brushed beside me as if trying to comfort me.

A knock on the cell door snapped me out of it. Camron? Ugh, why?

He opened the door and walked in, looking worse off than I had ever seen him: thinner, paler, the whites of his eyes red, and his angular face stained by tears. He ran his hand through his hair as he looked around. His sobs broke free as he saw Clia's little play place. Trapped by chains and collars, I lifted my head and looked at him. He dropped to his knees, snapped his fingers, and battle barriers appeared around us. So, he was skilled in magic. Fae Magic? I paused. No. I looked around him and noticed six orange stones in a perfect circle. Oh, I see . . . an enchantment. Fae had magic cast onto the stones that he could use by using his own to power it. Clever. Did he come here to kill me and feel bad about it? I glanced at Death. She seemed passive and bored. I hate this place. I stiffened as he spoke.

"I'm going to talk. You just listen." Like I had a choice in the matter. His voice was raspy, broken by his sobs. He looked up from his knees, his hair wet and slicked back, with a couple of strands falling across his forehead.

"My sister, she's insane. She has been tormenting fallen warriors as well instead of healing them outright like she used to. Forming their broken bones into odd angles and snapping them to the correct position after, forcing their blood out of them and watching them go white till she resurrects them. She told me she seeks my father's throne. She wants to rule this place, for fuck's sake! She's been drunk every day and fucking whoever and whatever all night! My useless father only encourages her behavior by saying, 'Whatever makes you happy, dear daughter.'"

His voice went from wavering to sneering that last sentence.

"I came here today because I need to ask you for a favor."

I growled. What right did he have to ask me for a fucking favor? He paused and pressed his head to the ground, fully kneeling before me. I was shocked. I knew her behavior was bad but not to the point that her brother would come begging me for anything.

His voice was a whisper. "Please, Elsie, throw the battle to claim her. Let her be taken from this place. I'll make sure my father won't lay a hand on you. I'll end you quickly and painlessly. I promise. I won't let him use his magic on you."

He was asking me to sacrifice myself for her. As I shifted my head, he looked up and met my gaze. Unable to speak, I rolled my eyes and sighed. I hated him, but I hated what she had become more. And, really, in my current state, I would be lucky to make it out of that battle arena with my life anyway.

"You already considered this?" he asked.

I nodded.

"You have a way out?"

I knew he meant an escape. I shook my head and dripped fire from my fangs.

"You could destroy yourself with your magic?" He was shocked, but his face was cold.

I nodded.

"That is more insane than Cliantha! Wouldn't it hurt you?"

I shrugged indifferently, and using a front limb, I gestured to what surrounded me as if saying, *What is hurt?*

Death shimmered as if she was laughing.

He slumped back on his knees, resting on his heels.

"She said you had thought about killing her. Is that true?"

No point in lying; he clearly was trying to help his sister. For once, we shared a common goal.

I slumped down, showing I meant no harm, nodding as a tear slipped from my eye.

"I'm sorry for all this, Elsie. I'm so sorry for what my family has done to you, for what I have done to you countless times. I don't blame you for those thoughts. After all, it's the simplest way out for both of you: death. I would be lying if I said I hadn't considered it myself. Why haven't you done it?"

I blinked; how could I answer in a way he would understand? He waited, almost knowing I was looking for a way to tell him. I took a claw and scratched the only words that might make sense into the stone floor. He looked up at me and took it in with a shocked, shallow breath.

"Love? Hope?"

I nodded and gestured to the window. Extending my wings as much as the chains would allow, I dropped Hell's Fire from the claws on my wings and my fangs, allowing the bite of the collar to scar my neck even more as blood leaked around it. Camron barked out a laugh, tears staining his face.

"Pet." He laughed again. "You have more resolve than all my warriors and myself combined." A change in his tone let me know he was saying his thoughts out loud, as if to confirm we were on the same page. "Let us set Cliantha free, send her away, set your soul on fire. Let yourself have this last bit of freedom fight to the end, then end this suffering you have found yourself in, for freedom and peace." He stood and ran his hands over his arms in an uncomfortable gesture.

He smiled, dropped the barriers, turned on his heels, and walked out of the cell, shutting the door behind him. I stared at the door. He was not as pathetic as I thought, and I began to cry. The words echoed in my mind, setting Cliantha free. He had abused me for years, but this was the end of my torment. The end of my life was a month away.

I sighed and let my fire of anguish rain down upon me. Bliss, a painful, hot bliss of fire. I would end my existence for her. She would have a chance at a good life.

*"You are a fool. Have some pride; you cannot quit. Ask yourself why is he trying to kill you?"* I flinched at the words. True as they may be, it didn't matter. I would die at the Battle of Mates. At least it would be under a warm blue sky. I accepted my fate; I would at least die and be free after all this time.

*"You are not this weak! Get back up! I am coming! I will take you home! Please, do not give up like this!"* That voice railed against my mind in frantic begging. Why did he care so much? I would be at peace with this, promises to take me home? What a cruel joke. And as much as I hated to admit it, his voice begging brought me comfort. At least someone wanted me to stay alive. I shut these thoughts down quickly, reminding myself that, no matter how lovely the voice, it was just a figment of my imagination clinging to someone who didn't exist anymore. *"Shut me out all you like, Firebird, but I will never leave you."*

# CHAPTER FOUR

## *Elsie*

The next month passed faster than the previous five, mostly because I filled my time not only training my body but also laughing at Cliantha's desperate attempts to get a rise out of me. And then, for my twisted amusement, I would pass the time by tormenting the guards who cared for me in the cell. I would pretend to be sleeping and then lunge at them at random, laughing as they nearly pissed themselves; it never got old. Knowing what Camron and I had planned brought me so much peace that I was able to sleep. My thoughts of killing Cliantha had ceased to exist, and plotting Mor's death also escaped me. The flashbacks of the manor were quiet as well. I had found peace knowing that giving my life for her freedom would end our combined suffering. Camron had not come back after that day. The voice in my head would argue and try to dissuade this plan, but this was the most peace I'd had in years. Counting down to the day and hour I could end my life and send her away from her family, consequences be damned. I wasn't going to be around to see it anyway. Let wars be fought; let her be dragged back to her father. Maybe after experiencing freedom from him, she would fight for herself any way she could. But alas, why did I care about anything that would happen after I was gone? That was no longer my burden.

Today, finally, was the day we would leave for Vitaendara, the unclaimed lands in the east of the continent, neutral grounds and territories filled with vampires, wolves, humans, and whatever else lived in those lands. Villagers would flock to the dragon arena to watch the battles, not only to see the kingdom rulers' sons and daughters fight but also the lower dragons' magnificent battles to secure mates. Males would have to be crafty, powerful, and never falter to win a female. Our battle was sure to be the last and would be a show to be spoken of for ages, ended by the black dragon of darkness in suicide. Sweet Death, she would welcome me like a long-lost friend.

"Ready?" Cliantha's cold voice echoed against the walls of the cell. She hiccuped, clearly drunk as usual.

Sorrow filled me, but also sweet hope. I would die today, and she would be free as well, as free as she could get, anyway. My last act of kindness. Friend, slave, pet—anything she needed. Today, I would prove just how far I would go for her. I nodded. She walked over.

"You better not screw this up," she slurred.

As she grabbed my collar roughly, I smiled, exposing all my teeth. She slapped me.

"Ow!" she exclaimed as her hand connected with my nose. "Shit. Ugh. Fine."

She took up my leash and led me outside, where the guards attached my muzzle, Mordryl and Camron appeared. If only she had known me better, maybe this could be different.

"Where is the transport?" Mordryl coughed out. Cliantha and Camron shrugged.

"The Fae, always late."

A silver-and-gold door appeared out of thin air, and the High Fae Master, Orion, stepped forward.

"What was that, King Mordryl? I was sure I said eight a.m. Oh, look at the time . . . ah, eight," he said casually, glancing at a massive jewel-encrusted watch on his wrist.

Orion was a tall, imposing Fae male. His magic seemed limitless. The fine dark silks he wore sparkled with silver and gold. Jewels dangled from his pointed ears, and he had a large red-and-black stone pendant at his throat. His hair was tight, short curls of deep, rich brown with silver running through it. He was indeed old Fae; the small wrinkles around his mouth and eyes confirmed it. He was still in great shape, not a fat old male like Mor; no, this male held himself tall, his dark skin absorbing the sunlight, his emerald-green eyes reflecting it.

"Who is joining us at the arena, Mor?" Orion's deep voice was commanding.

"Myself, the prince and princess of these lands, and the beast, naturally," Mordryl scoffed.

"Very well." Orion waved toward the door. The three stepped toward it, the chain tugging at my neck.

Orion raised his hand. "Any chance you would be willing to shift into a human form, child? It will strain my magic to move an entire dragon, even a small one like yourself."

Liar. It would not strain him. I could feel his magic pouring off him in waves; he just wanted to know who I was. I shook my head and let out a growl. No one would see me; I would die a mystery, and I was no child.

"I see. Very well. Proceed." Orion seemed indifferent.

We entered the door, Orion bringing up the rear as he passed, and we stepped into the arena. Fae magic was so impressive.

I stood behind my three travel companions. Orion went to the center of the arena. I looked around at the many males and females gathered, some looking nervous, some ecstatic to brawl. I looked up to the stands, packed, a glorious audience. Arena? No, colosseum. The walls were covered in white stone, colorful banners dancing in the breeze. The seats were covered in red velvet and padded for the spectators. I looked toward the sky, that beautiful pale blue sky, and stretched my wings out, taking in the sunshine and the warm summer air. Oh, what a beautiful day to die. A sharp tug on the chain snapped me back to Cliantha. She was drunk, leaning against her father. Camron looked back at me and winked. I nodded. We knew the plan. It was a beautiful day to die, and I would dance in the sky at my funeral. But where was Death? Out of nowhere, another Fae door of gold and silver appeared on the far end and out walked the most gorgeous male dragon I had ever seen.

*"Do not trust him,"* the voice in my mind growled.

The male at the opposite end of the arena floor let out a bellowing laugh. "Sorry I'm late . . . my transport, you see . . . it's a long story."

I could not help but allow my eyes to trace over him. He was in human form, his wings exposed. A beautiful matte white, absorbing yet reflecting the sunlight, the webbing of the wings almost translucent. His hair, medium length, dancing in the warm breeze, was also a stark white, and a simple silver chain encrusted with so many colored jewels hung above his brow. His eyes were the most beautiful pale icy blue. Captivated, I took in his high-set cheekbones, narrow nose, and perfectly defined square jaw, with a pale skin tone and a healthy golden color to it.

Beautiful. He wore no shirt; only scales of pure white covered his chiseled pecs. Broad shoulders, his arms sporting veins pulsing over his skin, traveling across his forearms and biceps. His abdomen was exposed, so much cut muscle; every ounce of him was lean and cut. Brown trousers hung low on his hips, exposing a deep V, as if beckoning every female to glance down, searching for what surely was a well-endowed package. Not to mention, the magic that poured off him was like no other magic I had ever felt, yet so familiar and welcoming somehow. My own magic bubbled while I gazed at him. Who was this glorious male? And why did he feel so familiar? And why on earth was I so infatuated with him, mind, body, and spirit? I was being sucked into his very essence. I loathed males, yet his presence felt like an old wound being ripped open. Like a memory in the flesh stood before me. But the smaller male next to him ripped my heart out of my chest.

It was Orion who spoke next. "Boy King of Rexarius, thank you for gracing us with your presence."

The entire arena went silent. You could hear the feet of the patrons stop mid-step as they turned their attention to the center of the oval-shaped arena. Boy King? This was a clearly full-grown male standing before us. Camron stiffened. Mordryl coughed and gagged. And Clia, well, she could have caught flies with her mouth agape. The two other human-formed dragons next to him were a female and a smaller, familiar-looking male.

"Who accompanies you today, King Rexarius, and why have you chosen to make an appearance?" Orion smiled as he turned to face the young king.

The boy king stretched his wings and arms as five Fae males appeared behind the human-formed dragons. The small male stared directly at me in shock, and horror crossed his face. His hair was black, his eyes black like mine, his skin pale as snow. His face was so familiar and so different. A small scar ran across his cheek, but the rest of his face was flawless. The wings he wore were small and mechanical; they did not match the rest of him. He was smaller than the white one but just as defined; the wings he wore attached to him by way of a leather harness sat above his tight white tunic. A crafted set of Fae wings? A king before him. My mind dug deep for any memories, but my head hurt. Who were these dragons? The female was slight and wore a mating band identical to the male with crafted wings. Blonde hair hung past her waist. Her hazel eyes had begun to fill with tears and dripped off her round, delicate face, yet the downward curve of her mouth seemed forced.

*"Do not fall for it. Fight, Elsie, for love, hope, and the freedom you crave. Fight, dammit."* I really wished the voice would learn when to shut up.

"I have come to claim my mate. Why else would I come to this type of event?" His voice boomed with arrogant pride as he ran a hand through his hair.

Orion sighed and rubbed the bridge of his nose. "King Rexarius, you know plenty well that you, being a king now, are welcome to challenge for a mate, privately."

That booming voice sounded again, interrupting Orion.

"Sounds lame. This"—he waved a hand around the arena—"is the type of excitement I'm looking for."

Orion pulled his hand from his face, exasperation rolling from him. "Your parents are rolling in their graves, King Rexarius, but very well."

Oh, a king by inheritance. His parents died and left their kingdom to him. Kings did not have to participate but merely challenge to be mated, somehow expected to just be better and less primal. Fascinating that we would trust that. A boy king as if any of them could challenge without mass destruction. Let alone one of his youth and arrogance.

His booming voice grew cold and slightly wavered in uncertainty as he met my gaze.

"I have brought with me Axl and Juniper Pax. My commanding second and third-in-command of the Kingdom of Rexarius."

A glamor dropped from the king and over his heart, and my breath caught. PAX? A black engraving across the pure white scales of his kingdom crests, a left-facing unicorn with its head slightly bowed, and a capital cursive R facing the opposite direction.

I was frozen, Cliantha was pale, Camron a shade of green, and Mordryl glowed with rage. I looked at the male with crafted wings. Axl. And then I was hit by grief, shock, and awe. My brother, as if risen from the dead, had come to my funeral. My brother stood before me, and I had a sister-in-law. I could not stop the tears from flowing.

*"Would you, for once, just listen to me! Do not trust them!"* The voice in my mind roared while I swore the shadows quivered at the rage in its words.

I shrank down. Cliantha choked up on the chain, and I gagged. I was looking at my brother; his face was hard, the whites of his eyes red, teeth gritted, and he shook with rage at me. And there stood next to him, Lady Death, a black mist invisible to everyone but me, her opaque eyes just hovering as if I needed to decide: go with her, or escape with them? Or was she on their side? She always allowed me the choice, and she came after all. But what was she doing here now with an expression in her eyes I had never seen? Pity?

I glanced at Juniper. She was looking at her mate with an expression of sorrow and pain, as if she could feel her mate's pure, unrelenting rage and torment. He touched his king's arm, and the king's eyes went blank for a moment, then fury bloomed across his face.

"Orion," the king of Rexarius said in a cold, deadly voice.

"I will challenge outright. The Kingdom of Mordryl for the female dragon slave."

Orion grew stiff. "On what grounds?" his voice equally as cold and now guarded.

The entire arena was shocked; every mouth in the place was open, and jaws dropped on the floor. I raised my head. This is bad. The king's words sent a chill down my spine.

"What grounds?" he sneered. "To claim what is rightfully mine. That is my mate, promised to me long ago. That slave"—he choked on that word—"is none other than Elsie Pax, lost princess. She is mine to have. Whoever I need to battle to win her, so be it." His words were laced with ice and conviction.

*"YOU ARE NOT HIS TO OWN,"* the voice roared.

Everyone was frozen in horror. Orion snapped his fingers, and a massive barrier around the arena appeared.

Orion spoke slowly. "How do you know that is Elsie?"

It was my brother who spoke; his voice cracked like lightning. "You old fool! You think I would not recognize my sister?"

He lunged at Orion. King Rexarius, planting a hand across his chest, stopped him cold. Juniper ran in front of the king, grabbing my brother as he spat blood from his mouth. The impact of the king's hand had suddenly broken something in his chest. Anger filled me, and fire poured around my collar while a gold glow came off her, and my brother straightened and swallowed. She was a healer, and death shied away from her.

"Get your people under control, King," Orion said plainly. "Mor, how do you find the challenge?"

Orion spoke as if he were indifferent to the entire situation. Seconds passed with no answer.

"Mor!" Orion barked, and Mordryl stepped forward.

All the other dragons in the arena exited at that moment. Shadows trembled, then stilled. They all passed the barrier, taking place above the sunken area, not an open seat in sight. The weight of what had been said about me was sinking in. I had been promised to him. I was something for him to own. No. Not only no, but fuck no. If this is how today was going to shake out, I would unleash terror upon them, all of them. I was no one's own, whether my brother, parents, the Mors, or this king. I would go to Death rather than be owned a moment longer. I would live and die on my terms and my terms alone. That was my plan and my hope; no one was going to take that from me. Rage burning, fire slipped from my fangs. I gathered myself, and the white king smiled as if he were looking forward to trying to take me. I growled. Familiar as he might be, such an arrogant male would not own me. To challenge in such an open way is more bravado than skill. Must be full of himself by how he impresses every female with his body. Males were all the same, driven only by conquest, I reminded myself.

Mordryl was in the center of the arena. Cliantha, holding my chain, was shaking in fear. Camron was still a sour shade of green, his thin features only more pronounced by the morning sun.

"You say you will battle anyone?" Mordryl sneered and coughed.

The king of Rexarius stood a few feet before him, taller, much taller, and far more powerful, at least on these grounds.

"I did not stutter," he responded, cold and hard. His eyes, a steel cobalt blue, now held hard with a glowering gaze.

"Then, you will battle me, the prince, and it"—he gestured over his shoulder at me—"on behalf—"

The king of Rexarius roared, "Her! Not it! You worthless sack of flesh."

The crowd flinched but dared not move away from their viewpoints.

"Her, it, spawn of the Below itself, all the same to me. My daughter will be kept on the sidelines. The pet seems ready to take you on anyway. Something you said probably angered IT," Mordryl sneered, a cough rattling his lungs.

King Rexarius roared. It sounded familiar, like a lost memory. I shook my head to clear the thought away. Orion spoke quickly, tired of this game; he did not waver as he set out the rules of engagement.

"Very well. King Rexarius will battle Mor, Prince Camron, and lost princess Elsie Pax for her to be mated to King Rexarius and moved to the Kingdom of Rexarius following the battle. Due to the nature of this battle, I will remind you four that no deaths will be permitted. Only incapacitation or capture will be permitted. I feel like I need to state this clearly and plainly due to the volatile nature of you four combined. If someone is captured, you cannot kill them. If someone is incapacitated, you cannot kill them. This is not a war zone but a battle for mates. Nothing more, nothing less."

King Rexarius interrupted and spat on the ground. "And if I kill them, what then, Orion?"

With a smile on his face, Orion said, "You will be stripped of Kingship, and magic will be stripped of you by the Fae. End of discussion."

All right, well, no one was dying here today in battle, at least, but someone was getting knocked the fuck out, and it was that arrogant asshole dressed in white. I would be winning this for myself and ending this myself. Orion grabbed the bridge of his nose again.

"When the battle horns sound, you may begin."

The king of Rexarius nodded and spat, the saliva landing right on Mor's chest. Mordryl looked ready to end his life right there. "Sorry, I just couldn't hold back that sneeze. Allergies," the Rexarius king sneered, then turned and walked to his companions.

He touched my brother's arm, their eyes glossing for just a moment. What was that? My brother took his mate's hand and led her out of the arena. She looked at me with a pleading look in her eyes, as if to say *please don't hurt him*. I looked to Death hovering in the stands next to Juniper and Axl; she seemed indifferent. Probably just waiting to take me to whatever realm she resided in.

Mordryl approached, but I didn't look at him. He took up the chain and whipped me across the face with it.

"You, bitch, are going to stay collared. I don't need you stabbing me in the back, you utterly worthless—"

A scream from outside the arena. I looked and saw Juniper, her voice like razor wire.

"Don't lay your hand on her, you bastard!" My brother was holding her back.

*A healer with a fighting spirit. Well done, brother.* The king of Rexarius stood against the arena wall, hand in his hair, a foot propped against the wall. The picture of arrogance. He glowered at Mor, the ground around him glowing, beginning to frost over. Ice magic. Ha! Easy for me to take him out; ice magic was no match for Hell's Fire. I would not be owned. I would free myself by the end of this, and I would get to battle a king. If my options were to be owned by a kingdom of a boy king or sent back to the Mordryl kingdom, my choice was death. *Brother, forgive me.* Death glared at me, her eyes shimmering, and she vanished. Well, what the fuck was that supposed to mean?

*"It means fight to live, damn it! PLEASE!"*

# CHAPTER FIVE

## Elsie

ordryl unclipped my leash, and Camron undid my muzzle, exposing my fangs. I hissed at the king of Rexarius, and he smiled, welcoming the challenge. He knew who the actual opponent was. Good. Camron took his place beside me to the left and Mordryl to the right. The king at the other end did not move, just stared at what lay before him. Cliantha was dragged from the arena, calling for her father. Such a stupid but lovely girl. I hated her but loved her anyway. Three on one. He did not shift, his stance unchanged. When the horns blew, I exploded into the sky. Climbing in altitude, I looked for Camron—Mordryl was useless, especially in this place. I wouldn't waste time looking for him.

Where was Camron? I glanced down to the arena. The white king was now in the center, and frozen in the place I left them were Camron and Mordryl in mid-defensive stance. Encased in ice. Oh, he was fast; maybe he had some skill after all. No matter.

I slowed and turned, beating my wings midair, hovering, inviting an attack. He stood, unwavering.

"Elsie, come back down here. Don't make me come get you," he taunted.

From midair, I released a mass amount of Hell's Fire, raining down the most beautiful storm of white, blue, and crimson fire. The crowd was awed and cheered in amazement. The fire burning so hot under this forsaken collar had cauterized the wound but not without blood falling from the sky.

The boy king threw up an ice shield, but enough fire hit Camron's ice, melting it enough for him to break free, and the icy gold dragon awoke, soaring into the sky. He nodded at me, and we began circling like a pair of vultures, the king now sitting on the ground looking up at us with a look of pure delight.

"Get Daddy!" I heard Clia, attempting to command us, and I grinned.

No, this was my time to shine and let the chaos that was trapped in my mind run free. Fuck the collar. I broke the circle, climbing higher away from her, and found the top of the milk-white barrier. The welcoming sky, the warmth of the sun, the sound of a gentle breeze from my wings tickled across my body. Homing in on my target that now lay back against the arena's dirt floor, looking up to the sky as if watching the clouds pass him by. Again, the picture of arrogance.

Camron still circled below me, ready to intercept any long-range attack; even he knew this was my battle to fight. The king lay wide open—an easy target. Just knock him out, Elsie; die on your terms. They cannot take that from you; no one will own you. I began the dive.

Coated in Hell's Fire, I drove myself hard toward the earth and that arrogant king, tucking my limbs in tight, increasing my speed. The air and sun felt so good. I allowed my magic to do the work. Fire blew off me as I dove toward the earth; the sweet, oh, so sweet heat of the fire as it came off my fangs, talons, and wings. Bliss. Doing what I do best, burning and destroying. The release of the fire felt like home. The arrogant bastard was in full view, and the look on his face was of shock and delight when a wicked smile crossed his face. I did not notice he was standing now when he formed a massive bow and arrow set of ice. Quick as lightning, he fired off two arrows, pinning Camron to the barrier walls by his wings as I passed. Camron let out a cracking roar of pain. I did not stop my descent; fuck Camron. I beat my wings to pick up speed, not sure how this king pulled that off.

Mere feet from this king, I opened my mouth. Hell's Fire poured from my fangs like venom. Here it was, the moment of impact, the moment I would knock him flat on his ass. A cold wave hit me as I connected, and I was tossed sideways. The sting of the barrier wall sent pain down my entire left side as I impacted the wall. I gagged as the air was forced from my lungs on impact, and I fell to the ground below. I rushed to my feet. My neck snapped into a defensive S-shape. Standing before me, a massive pure white dragon easily double my size, his eyes shimmering, his crest and horns translucent like the webbing of his wings. I hissed. He grinned, exposing his set of four regular fangs. He was glorious in his true form.

*"Testing, testing, come in, Elsie,"* he taunted in my head.

His voice was so different from the one I usually heard. I launched for the sky again. I needed to get away from him. I heard his echoing laugh. I raced to the top, passing Camron, cocking my head back to look at this massive white male hot on my tail. *Shit.*

*"Oh, come now, don't be like that. Can't you respond?"* The white dragon's elegant voice clouded my senses.

I paused. What in the fuck was going on? Another voice in my mind. I was going to implode.

*"Elsie, for the love of all Above, can you hear me or not? Just speak, for crying out loud."*

I screamed into the void that was my mind while I hovered in front of him, *"I have no voice! They stole that from me, you arrogant prick!"*

*"Jeez, no need to yell."* A smile bloomed across his face, exposing his fangs once again.

*"Confused?"*

*"Yes,"* I snapped.

I began circling him, looking for an opening as he hovered passively. My voice echoed back to me; it was cold, hard, and venomous. It was my mature voice, like large silver bells.

*"We came to take you home—well, to Otium, a coastal city within our kingdom. This little trick of Axl's is transference magic, so I may speak to you."*

*"Home? I have no home. I was lost and forgotten that day they came to kill us. I will never have a home. My brother is better off without me. He has a mate and a kingdom, and I refuse to be won or owned by any one of you,"* I hissed, lunging for him. He darted to the side, narrowly escaping me.

*"Elsie, he lost a great deal that day. He has been looking for you, and since his wings were taken, he has dumped all his time into finding you. When we couldn't find your body, we knew you had to be somewhere."*

His voice was kind and soft. We hovered in front of each other.

*"We?"* I questioned.

*"Don't you recognize me? I mean, sure, I've grown into this most gorgeous piece of dragon meat you have ever seen, but for real, it's me, Elsie. It's me, Karma."* His voice shifted to pleading.

Karma. I froze, shocked. I hadn't heard that name or seen this face in years. The white-haired boy in my dreams, Karma. I began to free fall, stuck in a trance. Karma, he had come for me, with Axl.

*"Elsie!"* his voice screamed.

But I kept falling, losing myself in the memories, my mind bending past a breaking point with thoughts about our times at the manor. Frozen in shock, facing memories that had been long forgotten. Camron roared a distant fading sound as my fire fizzled out. I heard Clia's screams also, as I was in free-fell to the earth.

Memories flashed before my eyes. Karma, once Prince Karma. Our parents had been best friends. We played together as children at our manor while our parents drank and discussed trade deals. Karma, Axl, and I would spar in the orchard, flying around and landing soft blows on each other. Our laughter had filled that orchard. We would race on the backs of unicorns at full speed, narrowly missing the trees. We played and played, pretending that Karma and I would be married or Axl and Karma would marry, which usually happened when Axl felt left out of the games. We would have stables full of unicorns, the peace that filled our lands unified in marriage. We were not only mates but had an undying love, even as children. We played out meetings with other kingdoms, Axl pretending to be a foreign king bartering for trade deals with us, consisting of mud pies we had made in the courtyard. I would pretend to be a knight protecting them from invaders. Dressing up and going into town, sometimes playing tag across villages and cities. Karma, my first love, my first lover, my first kiss, he was my first everything, and I had never wanted anything but him back then. Our parents laughed at all our shenanigans. My father's voice was in my head. *"I think those two will make a lovely pair—and to think they will never have to battle for it, what joy they will have in their lives."* That had been spoken days before the tragedy. How was any of this fair? How had my life come to this? Why couldn't I just find peace and be happy? Why do I need to fight?

*"Elsie!"*

Karma's desperate roar snapped me back to the present. I was too close to the ground, and I braced for the impact. Karma dove past me, breaking my fall a bit. We rolled across the arena floor; I didn't feel the impact. He smiled, covered in dirt.

*"I knew you could remember."*

I lay on the ground, a crumpled mess, dirty and sobbing. The silver chain on his brow glowed and shifted back, his human form dirty but unchanged, still a gorgeous mix of man and dragon.

Axl was screaming, "Get up! RUN!"

Karma threw up a shield, encasing us in walls of thick ice. Death hovered above, and her eyes looked full of happiness as they shimmered. She wanted me to stay here. I nodded to her, and she vanished, allowing my view of Camron clawing at the shell that held Karma and me. Mordryl was still trapped in his original encasement. Camron's roars and claws shook the ice walls. Karma stood in front of me and placed a hand on my cheek. I flinched, and he withdrew.

*"Sorry, I should have asked. I just can't believe it's you."*

My tears stopped, and I looked at the gold dragon trying to claw its way toward us. Karma spoke into my mind.

*"If it wasn't for the whole death-for-death thing, I would have no problem encouraging you to kill them if you wanted."*

I stopped sobbing and got to my feet, talons sinking into the soil. A bit dazed, I noticed the coldness of his magic. I shook it off. I spoke clearly in my mind.

*"Karma?"*

*"Yes, my sweet?"*

*"I won't kill them. I want to scare them. Will you allow it?"*

*"Oh, my sweet Elsie, you need not ask me for permission. Put the fear of the Above and Below into them."*

He placed one hand over his heart and his kingdom's crest, my crest, and held one hand out to me. I pressed my cheek into him. He smiled a great, big, toothy smile.

*"For the record, I wield Heavenly Ice. We, together, will represent As Above So Below."*

I knew what this meant: We were equals, perfect opposites in unison. The so-called other worlds of Above and Below leaked magic into this realm we resided in, As Above and So Below; our love represented the unison of the two, the balance. Together, we would bring our childhood memories and goals to life, our childhood love of life itself and each other, now blooming before me, knowing that Lady Death would always side with me and allow me a choice.

I shouted in my mind, *"Let's get 'em."* with the most excitement I'd had in over a century.

Karma nodded and dropped the shields instantly; Camron came crashing down. I pounced on him, my fire dripping from every fang and talon. Camron grabbed my collar, gagging me, but I was not going to stop. Clawing my way upon his back, I tore at the nape of his neck, allowing the fire to seep into him, burning him, my talons ripping at his wing bases and webbing, blood pouring off him as he screamed and struggled against the burn. I felt pure delight mauling him. My unrelenting revenge for every kick, slap, and gag he had given me over a century forced my fangs and talons deeper. His flesh parted like warm butter under me. This was exactly what I needed to feel alive: his despair. He lurched forward, and I bounded off, letting him go, bloody and torn to shreds. I stood tall next to my mate.

*"Oh, I should mention, that Mordryl over there can see everything. He just can't do anything. Do what you will, my sweet girl."*

Without further encouragement, I spun and raced across the ground with four free limbs toward Mor, my mate protecting me from the now-enraged Camron with yet another encasement of ice around the poor bastard. Poor Camron's ice could not begin to measure up to Karma's. The crowd was cheering, raving with excitement at the turn of events. I reached Mor, blew hot air, and melted the ice around his fat face. The look in his eyes was pure terror. I pulled my lips back, dropping Hell's Fire from my fangs onto his head. He screamed in agony while Cliantha's shrill voice cut me like a knife. "You bitch! Don't you touch him!"

I found her and lunged myself in one quick sweeping motion right into the barrier walls, right where she stood. Hurt like hell, but I opened my mouth as if to roar but just allowed the fire to flow as unbridled as I could muster. Fire clinging to the walls, blood pouring from my neck. She shrank back, tears filling her eyes as she pissed herself in terror. What a sorry sight to behold, and it was magnificent. She tormented innocents; I would bring her to ruin on their behalf in front of everyone. She thought she was embarrassed before, *ha.* I turned my head back toward my mate, my hatred for males disappearing only for him. No, I still hated dragons, but for him and only for him, I shoved those feelings aside. He was cross-legged, sitting in the dirt, laughing so hard he was coughing and gagging on tears of delight. Camron clawed at the ice separating them, struggling to even create a scratch on its surface.

Orion's voice snapped, and his large dragonfly wings flexed. "All right, that's enough. As Above, so help us all."

With a quick beat of my wings, I returned to my mate's side. He had stopped laughing like a madman and stood up next to me. Orion approached. His hand gripped his nose.

Exasperated, he said, "Feel free to release them at any time." He waved a hand toward the defeated king and prince.

My exhaustion was setting in, the emotional highs and lows of this battle and the use of my magic forced out filtered against this damn collar taking its toll. My upright stance wavered, and my mate looked at me.

*"I will carry you home,"* echoed in my mind. I looked at him.

*"What form can you carry?"* I asked in response.

Karma paused, anger flashing on his face, and he sighed, probably understanding I would not show them a human form of myself. It would also prove challenging due to the specific type of magic I had not willingly wielded in a century. Fae stones would be needed for that, but it appeared Karma also required a Fae stone for transformation; at least I was not alone in that.

*"I understand, my sweet girl. I have a plan, trust me."* I nodded as my vision blurred around the edges. There had never been a time in my life when I did not trust him.

He unfroze Mordryl and Camron, who were shell-shocked.

"Axl and Juniper, I need them down here," Karma said to no one in particular.

Orion opened the barrier ever so slightly, and my brother raced down with his mate in tow. They wrapped their arms around my front legs, crying in sweet relief. I would not dare shed a tear again publicly. My brother was crying so hard he vomited.

He turned toward Mor, covered in my blood. "Get your fucking collar off my sister," he cried.

"I will do no such thing. My daughter can unchain that monster," Mordryl said coldly, his burns still fresh. The bastard smelled like burnt hog fat.

Orion was quicker than Karma. "Cliantha, get down here at once," the master lord of Fae commanded.

She descended into the arena with a key in hand. Her soiled clothes reeked of piss, wine, and fear. I could barely enjoy the sight. As I felt the strength in me fading, I knelt. Juniper placed a hand on me, and gold glowing light came over my whole body. My muscles felt lighter. My magic boiled under her hand, yet a darkness lingered.

She whispered, "I can't help with energy, but I can take away some of the discomfort."

Until that moment, I hadn't realized how much my body hurt and how much blood I lost, between the fire, the wound under the collar, and the impact of the wall. This was painful. She was truly kind and seemed willing to lend her magic freely. Unlike the wretch that stood before us now. I could never forgive her for the torment Camron had spoken about and what I had seen first-hand. Any love I felt for her was gone; that's what I had to tell myself right now. Deep down, I needed to save her, too. At least for now, I was free of them, and I had a home to go to.

"So, what, Prince Charming comes along, and you forget you loved me?" she hissed while I stiffened. What would Karma think?

*"I don't care what you did to survive them."* I nodded.

"Bitch, this means war," she hissed.

Karma spoke for me while I spoke into his mind.

"You stupid girl. Our kingdoms are already at war. Your pathetic excuse of a war commander has not claimed any significant land, and you, too busy lost in the sauce and fucking anything with a firm enough dick that walks to lend a hand on the front lines, while your sick excuse of a king takes food directly from the mouth of your people, I was willing to sacrifice myself for your freedom, burn it all to the ground for you."

Karma flinched as the words poured from his mouth. I had a voice. It may not be my own, but I had one; after a century and a half, I had some semblance of a voice.

"I just have one question for you, Cliantha. Why?"

She stiffened at the question, her face flushed red, and with a voice laced with venom, she said, "I don't answer to slaves." She tossed the key to Orion.

"If you dare release that beast, my family needs to leave the arena. It has tried to kill me. It has no self-control."

I rolled my eyes at her words while Karma spoke on his own.

"Call my mate a slave one more time in my presence, and I promise you she won't be the one killing you, princess." He hissed and flexed his wings, tightening all his muscles. While Clia just rolled her eyes.

Orion barked out, "Fine, get out so we can get on with the rest of the day."

The crowd was silent; it was a shocked and somber silence, as if they had ceased to exist. The Mors turned and exited the arena beaten, bloody, and soiled. Drops of violet followed them. Camron turned over his shoulder, winked, and grinned at us. I dipped my nose and hissed as he turned back and left the arena. *Prick.*

Orion held up the key. He paused as Karma adjusted himself in front of me.

"May I uncollar you?" His voice was soft.

I nodded, and Karma stepped to the side. I could feel Orion place a hand on my neck as he inserted the key. I flinched under his hand.

"Elsie, I'm going to turn the key. As the collar falls away, you may experience a surge as magic courses through you. It could be slightly painful due to the nature of your magic. Don't lash out. This is not my doing." He was kind. I nodded and braced.

The key twisted, and the collar dropped with a thud against the ground. Flames engulfed me. A hundred and fifty years of suppressed magic now unleashed, fully unleashed for the first time. I did not move; I had been trained to remain still in times of a near-death experience. It felt like I was being burned alive. I screamed, and the silence fell around me, darkness clouding my vision. Slight pain? Try torturous pain.

*"Elsie, it is your magic. Tame it,"* the voices in my mind commanded.

They eased the pain with their words, and I found my resolve: him. I fought to push my fire back down, so Below, it hurt. If this was my time to die, Death would be here, and she was not. Panting, I was no longer on fire and dropped to the ground. Orion's face was gray and filled with sorrow.

"I am so sorry, Elsie. Forgive me." I nodded. He had nothing to apologize for.

"Orion, will you give us a moment, please?" Karma asked somberly.

"Not a challenge, King Rexarius." Orion turned and bellowed out to the stands.

"Please clear the arena. We will be taking a short intermission considering recent events. I trust you all can understand the situation that has unfolded here today."

No one said a word, then the crowd began to clap as they stood. I closed my eyes, listening to the sweet harmony of them clapping for us, for my freedom; they knew what they saw. They not only saw a mate be claimed. They saw a slave set free and a family reunited. The darkness claimed me as I felt myself collapse against the earth.

# CHAPTER SIX

## Elsie

I woke up still in the arena. It was high noon, based on the sun's position, and my mate sat next to me, chatting with Juniper and Axl.

*"Oh, good. You're awake. Orion was getting impatient."*

*"Sorry,"* I thought back softly.

*"No need to apologize—it gave us time to figure out how to get home. Remember how I said it was a long story with transport? My Fae has been a tad busy keeping the borders secure. Don't fret. We have it worked out, if you're willing."*

That devilish grin came across Karma's face. I was confused and tilted my head. He spoke out loud now as a courtesy to the others. He pulled a silver headpiece, almost identical to his own, from his pocket.

"Juniper here is not only a healer but has studied Fae magic for years. She crafted this for you. I did not want you to wake up with it on you, though. It's a simple headpiece. It could act as your crown—"

Juniper cut in with an excited twinkling voice. "It is infused with Fae magic. It will allow you to shift into a human form without hardly touching your magic. It will clothe you in human form, and best of all, it will give you YOUR voice!"

Karma cleared his throat. "I was getting there, Juni. A couple things to note. You have more stones than needed. You can have those programmed as you wish. Also, until clothing is programmed like mine, well, you will be naked."

I shuddered. Juniper blushed, and Axl was green.

*"Why do I need to be in human form to go home?"*

"The Fae I have that must transport us are far less skilled than Orion. They, well, can't do it. The other option is to wait till your strength returns, and we fly home. It's up to you."

*"Up to me?"* I had a choice.

Karma spoke gently, "Of course you have a choice, my sweet. I will never force anything upon you. That horror is long past you now."

Tears slipped from my face. He was as kind as I remembered him to be; my best friend, now a king, a hero. I looked at Karma. *"Cover me,"* I pleaded within my mind.

"Already planned on that."

I bowed my head. He placed the long, dainty crown over my horns and brow and tapped the center and left-sided crimson stones that adorned the piece.

I felt myself growing smaller. The fire felt like a lid was being placed on it, not unreachable like the collar but rather just secured within me. Juni pulled out a small red silk robe from what appeared to be a small leather bag attached to her shoulder, her green sundress fluttering in the breeze as she moved and passed it to Karma. He stood and flared his wings as Axl and Juni turned their heads and closed their eyes. Smaller still, I felt legs, arms, fingers, and toes taking shape, my head and neck shrinking. Panic filled me.

"Shh, shh, shh, I got you," Karma cooed to me as he pulled me into his arms and shrouded us with his wings, now covered in snow, blocking any view.

I was bare, and in his arms, I curled into his chest with sweet relief. I felt so small against him, yet I was free and safe. He felt safe. His frigid magic was soothing in a foreign way. I looked up to meet his gaze and found his eyes closed. Would my voice work?

"Karma?" Tears sprang to my eyes. I had my voice, the same voice that was in my mind mere hours ago.

He slowly opened his eyes, and his breath caught in his chest as he gripped me tighter. I looked into his icy blues and reflected. I could see myself. My hair was long, waist length, pitch black, and knotted to my scalp, my skin a sickly pale white. This body was made up of tiny cut muscle and bone, and worst of all, my scars. My eye was red where it should have been black, the white of it a hazy blue like an overcast sky, with a massive scar from my hairline directly over it down to my chin. A single jagged pink line. The scar drew attention, shadowing my sharp, angular, feline feminine features and large eyes. I saw the scar across my throat: a clean line, raised and pink, with a divot that Clia had put there long ago, the second hard scar across my neck for years in the collar below hers. My arms and legs were covered in chain marks and slashes. And worst of all, my marred pelvis was covered in claw marks around my sex. Camron.

I caught Karma surveying the damage as well, rejecting me.

"I am so sorry. I didn't want it. I—"

He cut me off as I sobbed into his chest, closing my eyes.

"Elsie, I know."

He gripped me tighter and tucked my head under his chin. I could feel his smile and his breaths returning to deep and connected, slowing his pacing to relax my own breath, as if willing me to remember. Karma was my first lover, a kind and strong one at that. But would I ever be able to enjoy him? What did he expect of a mate? Surely not this.

"You are stunning, scars and all. I adore every bit of it. These scars only prove how much you overcame." His words were hushed in a heavy whispering.

I untucked my head and looked in his eyes once again, full of love, looking at me, true love, my soulmate.

"Please, never even think of sacrificing yourself for someone else ever, my sweet queen." I nodded and tucked my head back into him. He took his hand under my chin, withdrew his head, and tilted my chin up.

"I'm going to kiss you," he growled.

A bitter cold exploded over me against his full lips, tasting of salt and fruit. I closed my eyes and leaned into it, heat pouring into my mouth as his cold tongue swiped across my lips. He smelled of sea air. He gripped me tighter and moved his hand to the back of my neck, cradling my head and neck in his large, strong, smooth hands. It felt so divine, like home was calling me back. I slumped into him and felt a wetness pooling between my legs. I had forgotten all about how wonderful he was to me. I wanted to be able to enjoy him; I yearned for that.

"That's my good girl," Karma breathed into my ear. I was fading into bliss. He was safe. I could let go with him. I would be okay, I reminded myself. He desired a whole mate, and I was scared the memories would never fade. However, I could ignore them and force myself to be whole for him.

A cough and a throat clearing snapped me back to where we were.

"Way to go, Axl, killing the mood here," Karma joked and handed me the robe. I awkwardly shrugged it on and stood up, Karma keeping his hands and wings around me to steady me and cover me.

"Ready?" he asked softly.

After more than a century, I said out loud, "Yes!"

My voice broke as he pulled his wings away, and my brother stood before me. I leaped for Axl and embraced him.

"You're alive!" I said.

He laughed. "You're alive!" He cheered, his face wet.

He pulled back as if to get a good look at me and gripped my shoulders.

"I am so sorry it took so long," he said, full of remorse.

"Don't apologize, Axl. I could never be angry with you." He tensed as I brokenly sobbed.

Juniper grabbed in next, pulling me in close, and without hesitation, I wrapped my arms around her.

"I'm so happy I finally get to meet you! These boys have been insufferable without you. Oh, we really need to get you cleaned up," she murmured in my ear as she quickly pulled away. I nodded.

"Alright, let's go home. Hey, guys! Door!" Karma boomed.

His five small Fae guards appeared. They also wore faces stained with tears but held beaming smiles that reached their eyes.

"You got it, boss," one of them choked out.

They grabbed each other's hands, and a massive door appeared. Covered in beautiful rosy gold and silver with the kingdom crest splitting down the middle, the doors opened slowly. I was weightless and found myself in Karma's arms. He sighed with relief. Axl hugged Juniper close, and we proceeded through the door.

When we stepped out onto firm ground, I was met with the smells of summer and salty air, heard waves crashing, and the magnificent estate before me stood massive and timeless. The stone walls were a warm pink and tan, with not a speck of gray to be found. I knew this place; I had been here as a child. It was the estate house my parents would take us to when Axl and I had begged them enough to go visit the sprawling city, beaches, and cliffs we had dove off, letting our small wings carry us back to the top. The three of us would run amok in this city, Otium. The home I had been promised as a child. My mother's voice filled my mind as I stood before the magnificent doors. The Fae doors were a replica of these estate doors.

*'One day, this will be your home, my dear Elsie.'* The distant echoes of the past filled my head while Karma held me tighter, and the doors opened.

The inside was just as magnificent. All colors imaginable flowed across the interior walls, made up mostly by massive tapestries filling the circular foyer. The one in front was the crest of the kingdom, high above the others. Hung with care on the far wall, commanding your attention, was the white background with that same bold black outline. It was the two paintings below it, however, that caught my attention. They depicted each of our parents. My father wore a hard face and kind eyes with a smirk on his lips. His hair and eyes were black as night. My mother stood next to him, the same cold look on her face. It seemed almost forced, as you could see the life in her black eyes, her waist-length black hair straight as arrows partially covered her brow. They both wore black regal dress clothes. Their matching black-and-red pendants that sat hidden under the collars were missing in these paintings. Those pendants were one of the things I remembered very clearly in my haunted memories.

They had planned for these to be made to represent them. To the left hung Karma's parents. For every bit of black on my parents, his were white. Seeing their faces was not what shattered me in that instant; it was the words at the bottom of the paintings put together.

"Stars can't shine without darkness," Karma read aloud.

"They loved us, all of us, and they never would want us to live in total darkness. Those four were truly magnificent. I combined the family crests after my parents died. We are joined by the love we all share."

He spoke with sadness yet confidence and affirmation. I tapped his arm as he stared at the portraits. He looked down at me with tears in his eyes.

"Yes, dear?"

I looked down and wiggled in his arms.

"Ah, I see." And he set me down gently.

Axl spoke carefully. "Els, you have a voice now. Don't forget that," he said so tightly it pained me.

I nodded, half hearing him, and looked around. The foyer was a massive perfect circle, and the rest of the walls were covered in silver frames, the paintings showing the marvels of this land. Each painting also depicted one of the previous royal dragons from his bloodline, displaying some of the magical landscapes in Rexarius. From beaches and the mountains to the soaring seaside cliffs. The more inhabited areas such as the orchards, forests, villages, and the cities. The art looked like you could walk through the canvas and fall into that moment in time. Crown jewels of Rexarius, the territory governed by the white dragons.

Axl, Juni, and Karma all stood while I turned in wonder, taking in the color and magnificence of it all. I blinked, breaking my focus from the paintings, and noticed archways at three of the four compass points. To the east was a great room with ornate chairs and sofas, and a large cherrywood table across the massive windows gave an excellent view to the overflowing vibrant courtyard. To the west, a hallway with doors running down on either side. And to the north, the most massive kitchen and dining room combined into one space. The floors were all the same white marble, with black obsidian running through it like shadows. I never thought I would see this place again.

*"Let go."* The voice in my mind pleaded.

My mind was splintering at the revelation of it all. And why was the voice still following me? I had everything I ever could hope for, but Death—she was not here. I dropped to my knees in the center of the room and screamed. My hands found my face and hair, pulling, as my scream shattered the crystal vases filled with flowers. It was all so much, too much, far too much. My vision clouded, and I felt Karma's wings and hands around me as I slipped into the darkness.

# CHAPTER SEVEN

## *Magnus*

arma was at the Pax manor house as if coming back to this broken, once-beautiful place would give him new answers. "Where? Where is she?" he wondered aloud. Such an idiot; he couldn't be this dense, could he? Wandering the abandoned, moss-coated grounds. He came here for solace and silence mostly; this was the only place in Terra Draconum where he felt remotely close to her. She was his best friend, his other half, his soulmate. Those were his grand claims years ago and now.

My teeth snapped. Yeah, that's what they all wanted to be true. She was mine; she belonged to my kingdom.

Now, I had a whole damn kingdom to protect, along with my constant need to follow these damn royal families. I watched from the shadows, always watching. Back then, it was my only job to watch, lurk, and report. A bad business deal took her away, so they ALL said, and his family had been too far away to aid during the attack. Even with Fae gates and flying their hearts out, they had been too late. Me? Well, I was not old enough to act, so I had to watch the fall of Pax. Pax, the great, peaceful wish from the previous royal family in my empire. Young and easily controlled, back then, it was my sole duty to give my father play-by-plays of the carnage unfolding.

Karma walked the courtyard past the overgrown gardens. Axl had let this place go, but I understood why. Axl kept this place untouched because rebuilding without Elsie would be admitting she was lost forever, a fact neither Axl, Karma, nor I could accept. Karma had silently taken control as prince years before his parents' deaths, only being established as King Rexarius once they were gone from an apparent suicide. However, something did not sit right with that theory. Murder was far more likely, yet unable to be confirmed.

I was the lurking shadow, never to be seen, but always in plain sight; my power stretched over so many lands, allowing me to listen, gather, and strategize. No one investigated the darkness besides those who knew what monsters would hide within. And not even I could confirm their death for Orion. Only being able to see what you were looking at and hearing only what you could hear, the shadows lent a lot of intel but not enough to end wars, not yet.

Karma continued toward the orchards they used to play in. Long gone was the smell of sweet fruit trees in constant bloom. As a young prince, I envied how they were all allowed to be care-free. Like wars and bloodshed didn't exist. For them, it didn't.

When his family arrived at the manor that day, the tragedy was well underway. The manor was on fire. His father had leaped into the sky, pouring ice over the blaze. His mother ran toward the manor and the inferno, and all Karma could do was scream at the horror. The howls that escaped him were of death and torment; dragons' dying screams radiated through him as he tried gazed upon the fall of Pax.

I watched it unfold, only able to report but not fight at the time. Regret filled me. Queen Rexarius called to him from the steps. Laid out were Mr. and Mrs. Pax, who had been ripped apart and half-transformed into dragons. It was a sight that haunted me to this day. Worse yet, his mother held Axl, cradled in her arms, his wings missing, shaking, cold, and gray. Violet blood poured from him, and Karma was frozen in shock and terror, just staring at it all. His mother's sharp, commanding voice snapped him to attention and shook the shadows.

"KARMA, fly now to the nearest village and find a healer, any healer. GO, NOW!"

He had choked out a pathetic response. "Elsie."

"We will find her, but go, NOW!" the queen had snarled.

Karma leaped into the sky and returned with a healer, carrying him on his back. The healer had vomited when he saw the prince of Pax and did everything to stop the bleeding. Axl would sleep for fifty years in the capital city, only waking enough to eat and drink on occasion. Karma had sat with him day after day, year after year. To bide time, he would read anything he could get his hands on, reading to him as well. Willing him to cling to life.

Reading his facial expressions was like reading a child's bedtime story. He had no concern or idea that anyone could see his thoughts as they happened plainly across his face. Simple man. He was so loud that, sometimes, I had to pull back after listening to him; his voice grated my nerves.

Karma often came to the manor to feel close to Elsie, as if seeing the manor reminded him what he was fighting for, not only physically but politically, with Juniper's family backing them every step of the way to a brighter future—one he would build when Elsie was to return. I laughed to myself. That's the story and ideals they held. But the path they were taking was one that only brought suffering. And their end goals? Still unanswered. To defeat an enemy, you need to know them, and I still had too many questions, even after a hundred and fifty years of stalking them.

A rough, shaky voice came from the south, and a lanky, gold-haired male stood before Karma. Oh, what an interesting development, I thought as I sank deeper into my plush chair. A burning roll of herbs in my hand the other covering my eyes lending me more of the dark.

"King Rexarius?"

I watched as Karma surveyed him: blue eyes, diamond-shaped pupils, dragon, ice magic, thin, not a threat—well, not one Karma couldn't handle lying down. The prince of the Mordryl Kingdom. Oh, if I could only get so lucky to have them both die here and now.

"Yeah, that's me, King Rexarius, of whatever the fuck this place is now," he said with a false indifference, like being here looking at his failures wasn't painful.

The male laughed. "Nice to meet ya. I'm Prince Mor."

That caught his attention. He jumped to his feet and, with a quick wing beat, took the opposing prince to the ground with his hand on his throat.

"Whoa, relax. I just wanna talk. You'll wanna hear what I have to say, trust me," he stammered out.

Karma's grip tightened; he could kill him here and now and be down one enemy. For both of us. Maybe the dense ice user could be useful after all.

He snarled, his fangs unsheathed, barely inches from the prince's face.

"What makes you think I want to talk to trash like you? You see this place? Your kingdom took my family."

I scoffed; his family, as if. The Mordryl prince coughed. Rage-filled Karma, ice creeping out of his now curved black nails, choking the life from him. Interesting. I took a drag and exhaled the puffy white smoke.

The prince rasped out, "El-sie."

Karma dropped his grip and stepped back. "Speak, pile of dragon shit," he sneered.

This is what kept me lurking—information. For a male dragon with so much pent-up rage, I would expect a cold killer like myself, but Karma had not killed in a very long time.

"We—well, my sister has her. I have had her for the last century plus fifty. I am sure you are aware of this. The dragon known as Death and Darkness, who fought for my sister in the battle of mates in the past seasons. That dragon is Elsie Pax. She's fighting again tomorrow, and after, she will turn her magic on herself and end it."

Karma nodded coldly. My rage filled me instantly. Why was she so hell-bent on just taking her own life? Hadn't I just talked her off that ledge time and time again? Elsie was alive, fighting, and ending her life tomorrow; she had planned it out. She'd lost hope. Godsdammit. The prince just kept talking like a faucet that couldn't be turned off, words pouring from his mouth. Filling Karma in on every detail of her existence in their kingdom. I lit another joint and brought it to my lips, taking a desperate needy drag, allowing the smoke to fill my lungs. All of them, such a pain in my fucking ass.

When he finally stopped yammering, he looked at the white king and stammered, "I'm sorry."

Enraged, Karma's magic slipped, and he froze the entire orchard. Covered in thick ice, branches from the trees snapped, crashing down around them. The sky grew gray, so dark it was almost black with storm clouds. I leaned forward, my chair creaking under my frame, and with the joint in my lips, I silently laughed.

"Cut the shit, prince. If you want things to be different, change them," Karma spat.

The prince sat back on the icy ground and mumbled, "What in the Below do you think I'm doing right now? I can't very well walk into your lands, into your capital, without being killed. I have no way to get in touch with you, so here I've been every day for the past month, hoping you or the black-haired one would show up."

He covered his face with his hands and mumbled, "She has kept holding on to hope—for what, I don't know. She can't speak. She's hopelessly in love with my disgusting sister. It's a tragedy, but if there's a way out for her, I had to try."

Such big talk coming from a rapist; disgusting. If she didn't kill him, I would. Happily.

Karma, naturally, was too stunned to speak. Just lay back on the ice, allowing the bitter cold to seep out of him.

The boy king and idiot prince sat there for what seemed like hours. Karma discussed memories of Elsie and the Paxes flooding his mouth. They had no time to plan an invasion, no time to hire an assassin to wipe the Mors out, no time to do anything. He was trapped in the political nature of the issue and by his fear that she wouldn't even recognize him. The type of torture she had been holding in was meant to break a soul. Then, in sheer panic, he realized the solution to all their problems was alive. Gods, I could win his entire kingdom in a poker game.

White mist with icy blue and gold eyes appeared—the Lord of Life. He was cruel, unwavering, and fickle, but Karma, from what I could see, knew him well. We both noted the look in his eyes as he vanished: a reminder and a warning. Interesting. I clicked my tongue as I pulled the joint from my lips. Now, why would the Lord of Life be dealing with Karma fucking Rexarius?

"Do you have a plan, prince?" Karma said in a monotone.

The prince paused, and in measured words, he said, "If you challenge us tomorrow, bring the black-haired one to confirm it's her and let it play out in front of Master Fae Lord Orion. With any luck, everyone will be so on edge and shell-shocked, it will look like nothing ever took place, and for what it's worth, you can take a shot at me. I would deserve it after the hell I put her through at my hands."

Fuck, that had been my plan for this year's season. Gods, damn it all. The king chuckled. He actually laughed. I would kill both of them for this.

"Prince, you have yourself a deal," he replied.

Karma stuck out his hand. They shook on it, and both launched into the night sky, going their separate ways. Yeah, that Mordryl prince needed to suffer; that much was clear. I needed to be patient. She deserved to spill his blood more than I did. Males who use females, the lowest of the low, deserved a fate far worse than death. Never in my wicked cruelty nor in my lands or ranks was this behavior tolerated. I hated the outside world. I took another drag off my joint, the ash falling onto my boots.

I followed Karma with my shadows to his estate. He went to his room and shut the door, panting. He began to pace, flexing his wings with each step.

"As Above, so help me," he said as he buried his fist into the bedroom wall, shaking the entire estate and freezing the wall solid.

Pathetic; the least he could do would be to lash out at something deserving, not a fucking wall. A knock at the door was followed by Juniper's voice.

"Karma?" She opened the door, a look of shock crossing her face. "What's going on?"

Karma laughed a cackling, unhinged, deep laugh. It had me wondering why would he not be relieved she was alive, little ice dragon? Hmm? I let out the smoke that was burning my lungs.

"Nothing good, Juni, nothing good at all. Where's Axl?"

"Great room, at the table." Her words were clipped.

He growled, "Follow me."

He strode into the room and simply announced, "Axl, Juniper. Tomorrow morning, we will be attending the battle of mates. Get the Fae ready."

He turned on his heel and strode back to his room, ice coating everything as he passed it.

"Fuck!" he shouted, slamming his other fist into another unsuspecting wall, kicking the door frame as he slammed his bedroom door shut. Finding Life himself hovering with a disapproving look, Karma groaned and sank onto his bed, sitting with Life, an ethereal being Karma seemed to have some sort of attachment to. If they spoke, I was not able to hear their words, and that pissed me off. Elsie talking to Death was one thing, but I needed information on these fucks.

The morning had been a mass of confusion from Axl and Juni, the house servants of vamps, wolves, and elves desperately trying to clean the wrecked west wing of the house, then the poor Fae trying to find enough of them to pull off the gate spell to get the dragons to the arena. It was pitiful to watch; my house was far better run, even on short notice. But then again, my house was always prepared for war; they all knew it well and would never falter. They had peace; they knew peace, and they were all preparing for war. My Kingdom would never fall. It would be an act of the gods for my people to see pain and destruction.

Finally, they arrived. Karma threw on that kingly charm with as much arrogance as his voice allowed as they passed through the gate, trying to calm everyone's nerves. That proved to be futile as soon as Axl brushed his arm and screamed into his mind. Even in the confines of his mind, I could feel the wave of emotions falling over him from Axl; they were like clashing tides against the cliffs. Axl went from excitement, happiness, and relief to fear, then finally settled on rage after he had taken in the entire picture before him. Juniper picked up on the situation right away. Her carefully placed mask—unlike the other two—was a hard read; she was dark.

Karma was no longer holding back his rage at that point either, seeing and feeling Axl's and Juniper's . . . pain? No, anger? I was forced to keep a better distance; willing Els to fight was all I could do without being uncovered. Whatever her brother's magic, I knew he could probably hear me if I spoke to her. Fucking transference magic. I groaned; why must this always be so annoying? I hate these games.

Karma broke and let the fury flow. A slight look at Camron and his voice exploded into that arena after his aloof, arrogant performance. Everyone stopped cold, feeling the temperature change, except Elsie. His cold, unrelenting fury could only be calmed by her warmth. It was a fact I couldn't deny, and it fueled more of my rage. He needed her to see him—see him and know him—as she had in the years they spent as children and subadults when things were simple. When they would run and play and later find themselves tangled in each other's limbs in the tall grasses of the orchard. Life appeared behind her in that arena, winked at Karma, shimmered, and vanished.

Oh, I hated them all, except her. For her, I would watch and wait. She was too hardheaded to push. She still could hardly stand my existence in her head, shutting me out whenever she could.

To protect my people, she needed to come home, willing and ready to accept her vows. Good thing I was patient. Although no other twisted sort of monstrosity aside from myself would push his empress into another man's arms. All while sowing the seeds of doubt from within the confines of her mind. I had to laugh at myself a bit. I am a monster. If I had been born a kind man, I would leave them alone, but I was born with a ruthless tenacity and to a Kingdom waiting for their empress.

Karma knew her move before she made it. When the horns sounded, he sent ice to the males who had not prepared for that first long-range attack of his. A carefully crafted dance of spilled magic around him gave the illusion of a lack of control, also forming the notion it would be a direct blow striking them first.

Karma had trained with the top warriors in many kingdoms from across the seas and carefully picked out and crafted this bold defensive bluff, feeding off his arrogance. A trick I had taught him. As his attention turned to her, she was the picture of beauty soaring into that pale, welcoming sky. I wanted to take her right there; I did not care who was watching, my cock instantly hard for her. My primitive desire to just take what was his but rightfully mine right out of the sky was all-consuming, but they had a game to play, as did I. She did not know she was a player. She needed to find and know herself. As a free female. I would not take that growth from her.

When her fire was released, I came right there, spilling my seed over my throne against my will. She was perfect. I could find no words to describe the beauty of the storm she unleashed. I would call it magnificent, glorious, captivating, and mine; no words were enough.

It was like his magic knew he was a fool and threw up the shield on its own while he secured Camron to the walls. Karma lay back in the dirt, just looking at her, marveling at her diving like a meteor toward him, and he could feel the magic pulling at him to go to her. She came plummeting for him; maybe when she got close enough to see his face, she would stop. He'd been wrong about that and was forced to toss her aside in his dragon form. I laughed. Her strength in battle was a wonder to behold. As she rushed into the sky again, I chuckled. Magnificent. And he started to taunt her, which ended as quickly as it began.

Thanks to the Above, that dunce Juniper had enough foresight to bring her a crown, leaving the stones ready to be set and prepared for whatever Elsie might need at a moment's notice. As the words left that little wench's mouth, my eyes rolled. At least planting one for her to find was not on my list of issues so far. Karma had risked too much today. Kissing her was a risk, but he couldn't stop himself. If he knew I was watching, that kiss would not have happened. If he knew she was not promised to him but to me and my kingdom, he never would have gotten entangled in this mess. Fucker knew better than to cross me.

He gripped her tighter while forcing his male organ back down. I did not. I stroked myself. I loved this magic. I had learned it for more practical applications, but it also allowed me to get off in private while watching someone in their most intimate moments. Damn, I loved my life. I knew what was coming was going to be unpredictable and messy, just like her Hell Fire.

But for him, it was the last thing for anyone to see him bed her on this dirt-covered arena floor. He would take her properly like the "gentleman" he claimed to be. Laughable. I would make damn sure she at least enjoyed him; can't have my firebird fearful once I make her mine. Watching would have to be enough for me for now. I gripped my cock harder, thinking of the ways I would watch them, learn what she likes, and when this idiot fumbled with her heart, she would fall madly in love with me. I shuddered as more seed spilled and dripped down my shaft, coating my balls.

Bringing her home to the estate would surely be a sight for sore eyes as well as a massive shock to her. She did not need to be coddled. She was strong and clung to life. Karma would hold her when she needed or wanted. I doubt he would push her to greatness. If she was safe, I would not intervene. My time would come.

Just not yet. I watched her look around the foyer, taking in everything for what it was. A tribute to their families, the lands, and their bonds. He knew she might break at that moment and made sure it was him who held her. I couldn't help but cringe at his sorry performance. She was unconscious, and as he lifted her small, too-thin body to his chest, he turned to Axl and Juniper. His breath catching, he stuffed his emotions down, both the others sobbing and holding each other. A beautiful, heartfelt performance. They lied to themselves almost as well as they lied to other kingdoms.

Karma was the strong one, it seemed; he had to hold it together for them. This is what they all had fought so hard for and made so many sacrifices for. So many twisted lies. My most deep-seated spies hardly found anything wrong with them, and that was a warning in its own right.

Karma found his voice. "I will take her to my room to rest. I will sit with her till—"

Juniper cut in, "Me—"

He cut her off, his voice firm but kind. "Not now, Juni. We will wait for her to wake."

Smart call, Karma. Keep that bitch away from Elsie. He clutched her tighter, I saw, and he felt a tug on his trousers. He looked down to find his son had escaped his nanny. Their best-kept secret here in Rexarius looking up at him.

I laughed. "Good work, boy," I whispered from the shadows.

Tears filled Karma's eyes, his 'soulmate' in his arms, his son at his feet with white hair, emerald eyes, his delicate silver crown with one singular emerald set on his brow. Juniper, his son's mother, reached out her hand and placed it on his arm. I felt Karma's heart break open. This is what life is about: experiences that make your heart sing with joy. Axl scooped up Cosmos, propping him against his hip, and his son pointed, his voice clear as day.

"El-sie."

I watched pride fill Axl. Each of them had told Cosmos so much about her that he'd recognized her. Well, I had shown him Elsie, telling him we could trust her. Karma's voice caught as tears flooded his eyes. Juni spoke for him, reaching out and cradling their boy's round face in her delicate hand. She sniffed, laying it on a bit thick.

"That's right. Elsie."

Axl laughed, bouncing Cosmos to his other hip, and kissing his cheek, a father's pride overflowing from him. Cosmos was far too big to be held anymore, but he allowed it at my suggestion. Axl tossed Karma a sideways glance, laughing.

"At least this one will have no shortage of parents, aye, Karma."

Karma laughed, too, shaking his head. "What a mess," he said, half laughing but mostly crying.

Karma turned toward his room, and Juni, Axl, and Cosmos strode off to the kitchen. Cosmos looked directly into my shadow and smiled behind his mother's back. Such a smart boy, always hidden in plain sight.

Karma walked to the end of the hall. I was impressed with the house servants, as no trace of his outburst was left behind. He shut the door and gently tucked her into his—no, their bed. I sighed as he grabbed a book and took a seat by the window, waiting for her to wake. If only they knew what was lurking and that, soon enough, she would be mine, and they would be the ones to drive her to me. Surely, this happy family façade would crack. It was all a lie, after all. But what exactly was the lie? That was my main question. What were they really hiding? I rose from my throne after tucking my cock back into my trousers and pulling my shadows back to me. I sighed. I was going to have to get involved, at least be physically close enough to pull her out if needed. I was not going to allow my empire to lose its empress again.

As I was walked to the flight deck of our custom cathedral, I found my brother and father.

"Where are you going?"

I kept walking; I was going to my empress, my bride; watching in the shadows would just not be enough anymore. Not with her in the lion's den.

I clicked my teeth. "Out."

My brother reached out and gripped my shoulder. "If you dare come back under my rule, you will have to kill me to take the throne," he said simply.

I shook his hand off. "If you don't step back down upon my return, I will end your life, brother."

My father let out a sigh. He knew that day would come. We may have grown up together, but I hated my brother as much as he hated me. The skies of Bellator were too small for both of us. Right now, the shadows and the skies were calling me. I needed to be within earshot of her to hear the voice they gave her with my ears, see her beauty with my own eyes. Somehow, tip her off to their games. Crushing my joint under my boot on the flight deck, I looked at the color-filled skies of Bellator. The words of promise to return and bring Elsie home didn't need to be spoken. The land knew, the people knew, and I knew. I would bring her home.

# CHAPTER EIGHT

## Elsie

*I* found myself surrounded by white, fluffy fabric enveloping me. I still wore a red robe. I looked down and gasped, surprised I was in a human-formed body. It hadn't all been a dream? I marveled and looked around a massive four-post-bed, the canopy black and sparkling with beads and crystals; it looked like the night sky with pockets full of stars. The walls of this room were snow white, with all the furniture matching the canopy. A golden and pink glow came from the massive windows, and in the window seat sat Karma. He was relaxed, wings casting rainbows across the room, a book in one hand and a teacup in the other. Blue baggy trousers hung low on his hips, draping over every inch of him, confirming my suspicion. Well-endowed as ever, a thought crossed my mind: Would I enjoy it? Could it fit? He looked up from his book.

"Well, good evening, Elsie," he cooed and shut the book. "Tea?"

I nodded and he stood. I felt the redness in my cheeks as I tore my eyes from his outlined package. He walked the few steps to the massive bed, dragging his wings on the floor, still the utmost picture of relaxation with his confident gait, and handed me the purple teacup. I sniffed it, a habit mostly. He sighed and wrinkled his brow. He sighed again but took a seat on the edge of the bed, not saying a word about what he was thinking. He gazed out the window, taking in the fading sun. I took a sip of tea. It was delicious and fruity, like apples, peaches, and berries, all in one, flavors I hadn't gotten to experience since the manor. I stared into the tea, just wondering how, in all that time, I never thought of tea or remembered who Karma was to me. How had I forgotten? Has the pain been that unbearable?

"Elsie?" I snapped my head up; Karma's voice was soft, almost a whisper.

"Would you like a bath?" I nodded.

He stood up and walked across the room to a naturally black, crystal-encrusted door. He moved with such elegance, opening the door and disappearing into a smaller room, where I now heard water flowing. I looked back out the window and took another sip of tea. It was beautiful; the sky held all sorts of vibrant colors with the sunset. The other side of the room had an identical set of windows, and I realized from this room you could watch the sun rise and set. A master had crafted this room just for him, down to the crystals that bounced the light around like his own ice. Magic was a beautiful yet terrifying thing. Karma appeared next to the bed, moving so silently that I jumped when I saw how close he was.

"Sorry, love . . . may I?"

I was frozen. Looking up at him, he so tall I had to tilt my head back to meet his eyes, dark blue yet frosty. He took the cup from my hand and set it on the small side table. He extended his hand toward my face and held it just a few inches away. I pressed into him. He circled that hand around the base of my skull, slipping to my shoulders. He tucked his other arm beneath the back of my knees. Lifting me, he walked to the black door. He did not need me to use words.

What I had expected was a small room with a hole that held water. This was far more inviting. Everything in it was black and clear crystals and, again, massive windows. I looked away from them.

"Don't worry, it's just you and me. No one can see from the outside. It just appears as stone on the outer wall."

I nodded and gazed out, the sun dancing and reflecting off the water, the ocean. I could smell the salt in here, it seemed. The tub was massive and could easily fit Karma with his wings. It was carved from the same black and clear stone. He paused at the edge.

"Test it. Make sure it's warm enough."

I reached down, and he softly went to his knees. I stuck my hand in the water. It was warm but not warm enough. Could I heat it? Without effort, fire leaked from my fingers, and it grew hot. Without the collar, my magic was much easier to use. Karma giggled and set me down on the fluffy rug in front of the bath, making sure I was able to stand on my own. I stood with my back toward him, looking at my reflection in the water. How could he love something with so many scars, love something so ugly, so broken? He is surrounded by perfection in this house; how could he love me? He stayed on his knees.

"Should I stay or go?" he whispered.

I panicked; no, not alone. I spun, my eyes wide.

"Easy, I'll stay."

He gently turned me to face the water again. He ran his hands along my shoulders and lifted the robe. I let my body relax and took a deep breath. It did not matter; nothing of the past mattered; this was Karma, I reminded myself. He was safe, always had been. He scooped me up again and stepped into the tub. He had kept his trousers on. His arrogance was gone; he was going to do anything, including wear trousers in a bath, to help me feel safe. I laughed as we submerged in the bath, then remembered the gift that was my voice and laughed again at my idiocy.

"So Below, Elsie! This water is as hot as hell. Good spirits above, save me!"

He chuckled and leaned against the back of the tub, pulling me to his chest, only my head above the water.

He had to be a good foot and some taller than me.

"Sorry, I kind of forgot I could talk," I said meekly.

"That's all right, my dear. I have the rest of my life to hear your voice." He grabbed me tight. "I'm just so happy you are home."

His voice broke over those words. I tilted my head back and smiled.

"Me too."

*"Let him care for you but know you are not his to keep."*

I flinched at the voice. Karma was unbothered and just kept brushing out my hair. He didn't hear the voice that taunted me. I would heal; I would get over it and shut out the voice one day.

We sat in the bath in silence, looking at the sun slowly falling over the water, watching the sky change colors. The crystals of this room reflected every bit of light. He washed my hair and gently raked it out with his fingers over and over till no knots could be found. He rubbed soap over every inch of me, pausing over my scars and asking if he could touch. The male he had grown into was so much softer than I remembered, so much kinder. I remembered the play fighting, the joking, knocking each other out of the sky, tormenting Axl, burying him in mud while he and I laughed. This grown Karma was kind, respectful, every-thing good I could ask for, and far different from any other male I had met. As the water grew cold, I stood and stepped out. With swift grace, he excitedly grabbed a soft fabric from the wall and wrapped me in it. Grabbing another, he wrapped it around his waist and ditched his trousers. I walked back into the bedroom and saw the sunset three-quarters gone behind the horizon. On the cliffs sat many roaring fires.

"What's out there?" I said, not breaking my view.

Karma tore his eyes from me and chuckled. "Oh, Above, have mercy. I told Juni to keep it quiet. Guess that's her version."

He gestured to the event below. "That would be a party for us, in celebration of our victory in the battle of mates and your return home. That is a very minor celebration for Juni. She's normally all about big parties."

I stared out at the fires, amazed. I could see Fae, elves, humans, vamps, and wolf types, all gathering around. In the center, orchestrating it all, was Juni, sending the musicians into one section, servants with food on crystal tables next to them. Karma placed his hand on my shoulder, and I found him seated on the bed.

"You and I have two things to discuss before we even consider going down there." He was somber, his head hung low. I nodded. "Sorry."

I paused. "What is it?"

He spoke softly. "First off, if you ever feel uncomfortable, unsafe, troubled . . . in any way at all, at any time, the stone to the right on your crown, either channel some magic into it or tap it, and I will know instantly. Second . . ." His voice caught, and he cleared his throat.

"Second, this house keeps the most valuable secret in this entire kingdom, possibly the continent . . . our family, but in our family, we have a son."

I froze. When he mentioned secrets, I thought it may be some monster, a caged beast. But a son? I was shocked.

"Whose son?" I asked.

He looked up at me, took his hand from my shoulder, ran it through his hair, and met my eyes, his eyes full of pleading for understanding. Then he dropped his hand into his lap.

"Biologically . . . mine and Juni's," he rushed. "Axl is just as much a father to the boy as I am, probably a better one, truth be told." He sighed and dropped his gaze. "You are a part of this family. I would not keep that from you, but I can understand if you can't be here in the house with us, I mean—"

I cut him off. I did not care how, who, or why at this moment. I was free. I had gone home. I was not owned, and I was alive and, for the first time in a very long time, grateful I was alive.

That was a strange, very strange feeling. My brother was considered a father. What more could I want? Nothing, this was the dream; no matter how I got here, this was it. I was not going to let any ill feelings sway me from my new home.

"What's his name?" I asked softly, reaching for Karma's hands.

Tears spilled from his face. I pulled him to my chest, forgetting the hand holding together the fabric. It fell from me as I pulled him into my small but firm chest. He gripped my waist and looked up at me.

"Cosmos. The new order of the world, Cosmos Rexarius." He cried.

I held him as he shuddered and sniffled. "You want to meet him before the party?"

A voice came out of me that I had not expected. I squealed, "Yes, yes, a million times, yes!"

*"You are a kind, compassionate, beautiful woman. Revel in this joy while you can."*

I turned over my shoulder; this voice, it was in my head, just telling me what I wanted to hear, just my subconscious, nothing more.

Karma quickly found a set of less revealing black trousers in the drawers of the massive armoire and turned to look at me.

"Uh, dress?" he asked. I nodded.

He tossed me a shimmery pink dress that reached my knees and had a modest scooping neckline and capped sleeves. It cinched up in the back with silver crossing ties, lifting my small breasts but giving the illusion they were larger and that I had a healthy waist. Flowing off me, this dress also hid just how thin I was. Karma looked me up and down and bit his lip.

"Oh, we are saving that here," he said, tapping my silver band. "Don't forget. Center is the dragon, left is voice, right is me, your right-hand man."

He laughed at his lame joke, and I laughed at him for laughing.

"For now, this will be what you have while human. We can have Juni add more later."

"Can we go now? Your mate is growing impatient," I joked, covering, not about Cosmos, but the party. That fear could wait till after. Just be normal, Elsie, like when you were before it all happened, I chanted silently to myself. Karma smiled so big you could see his pointed fangs.

"Race ya!" he said, bolting for the door.

I shoved him out of the way and into the wall, knocking over a table in his wake. As he was gaining on me, I reached the foyer, where I saw Axl on the floor of the great room. In front of him was a white-haired boy with deep green eyes. Karma raced past me, and I caught his wing like I used to, knocking him off balance into the room's archway. I felt the smile blooming across my face as I heard Axl start to laugh a deep, booming, joyous laugh. I rushed toward them, Karma catching my waist and lifting me from the center, holding me against him. We both reached Axl and Cosmos, laughing hysterically. Family. This was my new family, and it felt like no time had passed between us. I could be happy here. I could learn how to be happy here.

I knelt on the floor next to my brother and reached my hand out to Cosmos. The boy exclaimed, "El-sie!" I touched his face, and he grabbed my hand.

The scars on my hand faded. I just stared in shock and looked at Axl, then at Karma.

"What? Magic? Already? How old is he?" I exclaimed and pulled him into my lap, a little dark-green glow coming off him.

The scars down my arms and legs faded. I stared out the window as the redness in my eye began to fade. The glow dimmed, and I looked down. He had fallen asleep in my arms, and I gripped him tight. Axl spoke in a plain voice, just stating facts, like the questions I had asked were deeper than he wanted to explain.

"Yes, restoration magic. He's technically a child. We have a lot of scholars on other continents studying this phenomenon and attempting to replicate it, the early development without the deficits, not the specific type of magic, obviously."

He said 'obviously' like I could understand anything he just said. We'd been considered early bloomers in our pre-subadult phase, with small fragments of magic appearing. Karma had accidentally frozen the fountain in the courtyard; I had burned a hole in the dining room table, and—well, Axl, he would randomly swap magics around when he got upset or steal ours. The whole thing drove our parents mad when we were all together.

They would have loved this boy. And I? Well, I would burn the world for this boy. I would ensure his life was better and fuller than ours. He would know no suffering. I did not care if that meant destroying it all. Time and time again, I would destroy it and allow him to restore it in his image if he asked me or needed me to. Anything, I would do anything for him. My magic danced beneath the lid I had capped on it. This was the peace I longed for, the hope I held on to for so long, to find my family, no matter what this family looked like. I had it. I would never let this boy fall into the tragedy my brother and I faced. I looked up, feeling a small chill, and found Lady Death. Her usually dull eyes were a tad brighter, and the mist was thicker and almost bounding. Joy, perhaps?

Cosmos awoke quickly and pointed to a book on the floor, a book from the days long past, a child's picture book. He pointed again and whined. Axl reached for it, and it was, as I thought, the bedtime story my parents read to Axl and me as children.

"The dragon's origin?" I asked. Axl shrugged and handed the book to Cosmos.

"He loves that damn book. I think it's just the pictures, though."

Cosmos looked up at me with a somehow new intensity and gripped the book tighter.

"Do you want me to read it to you?" Cosmos nodded rapidly and held the book out before us.

I took in a breath. This story was the Legends of Dragons, known for its hand-painted artwork on each page; each edition was made for each dragon child by the Fae. It was a nice way to give dragon children a sense of where their magic was coming from. Not that any of this was real, the monsters, the Above, the Below, who knew, but it was a tradition in dragon families to receive this book from the Fae. If Cosmos was such a secret, how did he end up with his own book? I kept the thought to myself. Cosmos whined again, drawing my attention to the words on the first page. I sighed and began reading. Lady Death hovered out of sight, only her chill noticeable. I opened the book and began turning the pages and reading.

"Once upon a time, there was nothing, but nothing held everything, endless magic. The magic ran wild. One day, the magic started to settle and separate into light and dark. The light magic was airy, the dark magic heavy. And so became the Above and the Below. The magic started to come alive with thoughts and feelings. The magic grew lonely and began to split, creating a world of sea, land, fire, sky, and more. It breathed into the land, but the dark magic sucked it out. The land would wither and fade, the seas would run dry, and the light magic would rise again. Life and Death. As the land lived and died, so did more creations, beings with bodies of their own. Humans and their champions came first. They would rise up and praise the magic so much that some humans ascended to the Above to become gods, while others sank to the Below, becoming demons." I sighed. This story always bored me, even as a child. Axl, however, would beg for this book for years to be read before we were sent to bed.

*"Keep going, I like hearing you talk."* I shook the voice off and continued.

"With gods above and demons below, they began to fight for power over the space the magic had created. The limitless magic in the Above and Below was used by the monsters and gods to make more beings of light and dark, fighting to control the little world they had all been a start in. They crafted souls from their magic and placed more beings into the world. Soon, they saw the land and its creatures suffering with so many creations fight-ing, light and dark, always at war. The gods and monsters came together to create a beast that would rule the skies, lead the lesser beings to safety, and wield the type of magic that called to that one's own soul. Light and dark did not matter to this beast. This was a beast capable of protecting the weak. It was noble, kind, strong, gifted, protective, and, above all, brave. They had created the dragons. The end."

The book was beautifully painted, each page a masterpiece filled with color. I hated the story's end. I always had found it to be untrue. Dragons noble and kind? What a joke. Cosmos shut the book and peered up at me with a burning intensity; something was off with him.

*"I very much like this so-called legend."* Damn voice; of course, it would like this damn book. Lady Death looked amused and vanished quickly.

"Oh, good, the sitter. Right on time," Karma said jokingly. Appearing before me was a silver-and-gold Fae gate, and stepping through it was no other than Lord Orion.

Well, that explained the book.

*"Trust him."*

He wore less impressive clothes and just looked like a normal older high Fae male. His jewelry was gone, and he shut the gate and pulled up a seat at the large table.

"Karma, Axl, Elsie, where's Juni?" he said, musing.

"Oh, you know exactly where she is, outside, controlling the masses and gearing up for this party. We told her to keep it tame," Axl said, shrugging, staring at his son in my lap. A single tear fell from his face.

Confused, I asked, "I thought he was a secret?" Why would a high Fae master know of Cosmos?

"Oh, my stars! You got your voice back. That's wonderful! Was it Juni or Cosmos?" Orion said with the most excitement I had heard from him.

Thankfully, Karma spoke next, coming to the center of the room and plopping down beside me. He reached out to stroke his son's hair.

"Juni did the voice—Fae stones. Cosmos, well, he just managed to smooth over some scars. Thank you again, Orion, for your continued dedication to our family's mission." I cleared my throat and realized Cosmos had done more than smooth over some scars. My vocal cords felt more intact, and the Fae stones, I was passing less magic through them. I squeezed Cosmos, and he flinched slightly. Odd, all of it.

As if hearing the echoing confusion in my mind, Karma looked at me.

"Think of Orion as, well, Grandpa?" Orion chucked a wooden coaster from the table at Karma, missing entirely.

"Fine, okay, a cool grandpa."

I snorted, Axl snickered, and Karma just grinned. Orion gripped his nose again.

"Quite a show you all put on today. Excellent work. All right, well, I'll take Cosmos. I think we shall travel up to Bellator for some camping and fishing."

I couldn't hold back the hiss that escaped my mouth. As my grip tightened on Cosmos, their shocked faces turned toward me.

"Bellator? That's your idea of a fun grandfatherly outing?"

Karma rested his hand on my cheek, and I turned my gaze to him. He spoke gently but was firm.

"Orion is the only one outside of this family who can understand who and what Cosmos is. He is also the only being in this world capable of keeping him completely hidden and safe. If anything at all were to go south, Orion would have no issue opening a small gate and running to another continent with Cosmos. Our son will never be in harm's way with Orion."

Another hiss escaped me as I retorted, "Bellator, the lands of paid warriors for hire, safe? Right." Sarcasm dripped from every word.

Karma giggled. "We have a house up there. Well, a cabin. It's free to use for us, and Orion, sometimes, the old guy gets grumpy and needs a mountain cabin to escape."

Axl cut in, "Els, it's fine. We go up there all the time. Plus, we'll see the little guy in a few weeks."

I whipped my head, keeping the rest of my body perfectly still, noting that, after all, it was a useful skill to have. I hissed out, "Few weeks?"

Death had mysteriously reappeared and seemed ready to pounce. All the males in the room simultaneously said, "Yes, we are at war."

Karma gripped my shoulder. "I know it's a lot. I will explain all of this to you in time, but first, let us celebrate. Juni will have a meltdown if we don't join before nightfall."

I nodded and looked into Karma's eyes, seeing myself. My scars had faded, still visible, but my eye was pitch black as it should be. I looked at Cosmos in my lap and stood up, keeping myself steady so as not to wake him. The little guy seemed to fade into sleep and wake all too swiftly. Karma and Axl kissed the sleeping babe. I brought him close and then handed him to Orion, keeping a grip. I stared into Orion's eyes.

"I will burn the world to ashes for him. For all of them, I will burn it."

I saw my fire reflect in his light green eyes, but that lid was secured tight by MY doing. Orion took Cosmos, turned toward the gate, and said as he passed through, "I am glad you found something worth fighting for, Elsie."

The door closed, and I found the hands of my brother and my mate gripping my shoulders as I stood up straight and wiped a hot tear from my eyes. I turned to the boys. There was no time for details. I trusted Karma to fill me in when the time was right. I reminded myself everything was okay here and shoved my unease deep down.

"All right. Before I lose it, what's this party thing Juni cooked up?" They threw their heads back, laughing, wings shaking.

"Don't worry. There will be plenty of wine," Axl jabbed.

# CHAPTER NINE

## Elsie

We walked to the foyer, and Axl grabbed my hand. With caution, he said, "This is not going to be like a manor party. You can drink wine, you can celebrate. Enjoy your freedom, sister. The only thing you don't talk about is what happens within the walls of THIS house. No other rules apply to you."

Karma cut in, and they had an awful time not talking over each other, all of them, all the time—and since when did Axl grow up? I thought.

"That goes for magic as well. If you feel the need to let it out, do it. I will cool your fire. Dance, drink, release magic, fly, do whatever your heart desires, my sweet, lovely Queen Elsie."

*"Enjoy yourself, but trust nothing."*

The voice cooed to me. While Krama tucked a strand of hair behind my ear and tapped the band as a reminder that if I needed him, he was there. Juni burst through the doors.

"As Above! Hurry up! You're going to miss the sunset!" She grabbed my hand, spun, and we sprinted toward the cliff, the boys gliding behind us with their wings.

We reached the cliffs, and all around us was food, drink, music, dancing, and fires. Everything had been perfectly arranged: the tables of crystal holding food of all kinds, the drinks including everything from blood to wine. The music was a mixture of fiddles, guitars, drums, horns, and an odd-looking bag-type instrument that had a pitchy whine to it. But they all flowed together in the most uplifting song. The sea breeze was crisp but warm for summer, and the sun dipped below the horizon, throwing the sky into the most ravishing sunset of orange and purple.

Juni grabbed a crystal glass and tapped it with her long nails. Everyone turned, looking at us. I found Karma next to me and Axl next to her as she yelled, "A TOAST TO OUR KING AND HIS QUEEN!"

Everyone erupted into great cheers. It seemed louder than the arena. I couldn't contain myself. I gripped Karma's hand and surged my magic to that center stone. I felt my wings unfold and my talons grip the earth. I looked up, feeling the length of my neck, and saw Karma already in the air, his breathtaking dragon form against the nearly dark sky. I let out a roar for the first time in over a century, and the sound drowned out the cheering. I leaped into the sky after Karma.

I felt powerful, my magic flowing freely, the wind on my body, no burn of a collar. I kept climbing and circled high above them. Soaring out above the water, I began to freefall, wings toward the water, and then a foot from the water, with a quick beat of my wings, I grazed the waves and rolled across them, soaring back into the sky and up the cliffs. Once far above the party, I released fire, lighting up the sky. Karma froze all the Hell's Fire that escaped me, and it turned to snow, falling on everyone, with fires still blazing on as he controlled each flake to avoid them and the food.

I roared again, and the cheers rang out. I flew back down to the cliff's edge, gripping it, and powered that stone and crown, putting myself back into the small little human form. I was actually growing fond of it. Earlier today, I was at my funeral, and now, I was dancing with tears in my eyes at my freedom. Karma had been right to tell me to enjoy this night. With undoubtedly more grace, he landed next to me, tears in his eyes and wings held high.

We walked hand in hand across the snow-covered ground, the gathering chanting, "Long Live." I would remember this moment and this day for the rest of my life.

"Go enjoy your party, sweet Elsie," was all he said as he let me run headlong in that pink dress sparkling against the snow, the cold stinging my bare feet. Thankful I had a crown, clothing and shifting was so much easier this way.

I went for the food first, totally confused by all the different types, but I found the raw fish I had been craving for ages. I ate most of the platter, then found a pitcher of warm, fruity wine. Importing delicacies was an easy commodity around here, it seemed.

*"Nothing comes easy to anyone."*

The music was fast-paced, and everyone was dancing around the fires. I found Juni and Axl dancing, with Karma laughing and enjoying their night of release as well. A tap on my shoulder sent me crouched and hissing.

"Ope, sorry. I just wanted to say the dragon dance you put on for us made my day." I straightened.

I was nervous, ready for whatever they may do next. The female before me was low Fae, dressed as a mushroom. Maybe she was part mushroom? She was charming. Next to her stood a male who seemed out of place. He had dark glasses covering his eyes and an ominous large stature, his face obscured by his long, high-collared cloak.

"Oh, forgive me," I said, bowing my head to them. "And, uh, thank you for the compliment."

She smiled and gripped the male. "Enjoy your party!" They walked off. It was such a small encounter. I found Karma with a forced smile beside me, his presence looming over me.

*"Good girl, always be wary. The shadows talk, ya know."* That male glanced back, hardly exposing his mouth, but a sly smirk danced across his lips. I was about to take off after him when I remembered Karma next to me. The last thing he needed to know was that the voice was real. His secrets were not safe with me. *Shit.*

"Do you remember when our parents spoke about all kinds being able to live together in peace?" I nodded, nearly unable to look at him. "We did it here in Otium," he said with pride.

*"Mmm, did he now?"*

I didn't have much time to process what he had said when the music changed to something slightly slower. Karma bowed to me.

"May I have this dance?" he asked with an outstretched hand. I smiled, felt my fangs peeking through, and nodded. Anything to distract me; this would be perfect.

With a wing beat, he took me close to the fire, and a space cleared for us instantly.

"Just like when we were kids," he said, probably feeling my nerves as I noticed everyone clapping in time to the fiddles.

He began to lead, and I fell into the rhythm with him—something I never imagined being possible ever again. He brought me in and sent me out. I allowed my body to do the work, shutting off my mind and just letting everything flow within me and out onto that icy floor. I noted a change of hand. It was Axl cutting in, bringing me in and out and round and round. Then he spun me out to Juni, who caught my hand and led the same way the boys had, just with shockingly more elegance than Karma. Tears ran down my face as I passed between them. Other males and females cutting in and out of our circle, all kinds, dancing together under a starry night sky with the royals. They had done it. I shut off all thoughts and just allowed myself to feel the music and the life of everything around me. I grew warm, and then the cold hands of my mate found me, and we kept dancing. We danced well into the night, only stopping when the sun started to rise.

Karma grabbed my hand, and we ran across the snow as it turned to grass, running to the cliff edge to the east. Out of breath, he sat down, and I sat with him, watching the sun rise over the horizon. A new day was beginning. My future and freedom were no longer a hope for one day, but rather, this was day one of freedom. Axl and Juni found us and handed us wine. We sat in silence, letting the sounds of waves crashing, birds singing, and the sounds of the not-so-distant city start to stir.

*"Shut my voice out again, and you will be punished."*

A shiver went up my spine at the threat. Axl set his hand on mine. Karma rested his hand on my thigh, and Juniper rested her hand on my free one. I broke the silence. Laughing, I said, "Well, not sure about you guys, but that was probably the best funeral I have ever been to."

And we kept laughing, wine-drunk, watching the sunrise as I shut out that fucking male's voice. I was not going to back down, not now; I had too much on the line.

*Magnus*

With her third bottle of cheap wine in hand, Cliantha sat in the cell, now cold without Elsie here to warm it by just existing. I couldn't help but laugh at the pathetic little bitch she was.

"That little shit, she left me," she scoffed to herself. She had called her a child in front of all the kingdoms and so much more. I loved every moment my firebird raked this bitch over the coals. When they returned, her father had beaten her and Camron till they could not stand.

"Embarrassing. She left me. For a male. I had her. I had everything I needed in her. She was the key I needed to ruin my father, to end his fucking life, and that key has been taken from me. All I had to do was keep her. It should have been easy," she muttered, sending the bottle flying. It shattered against the stone walls. Gods above, this was an angry wretch.

"What is so special about family, anyway? They torment, or they run away."

She hated her for the family she had been born into; her family stole her chance at a normal life. She was entitled to the life she did not get to have, and yet my Elsie had it all, she thought. Little did the bitch know Elsie had nothing yet.

"Useless little black fire dragon. So much power, and I was the one to unlock it for her, but she still left me. I wasted my time on her."

Still thinking out loud, she sneered, filled with rage.

"Who am I even talking to? The rats in the walls? Myself ?" Her voice was like claws ripping apart a school blackboard.

"If I could drive her to the brink and dangle what she wanted most in front of her, she would surely break. But she never did, that stupid hope and love she held onto, day in and day out."

Cliantha hated the strength Elsie possessed; it outshone her power and resolve, dismantling her façade of control. She would have been dead had I not stopped Elsie so many times. It was never the right time to rid this world of this brat. Her suffering was not anywhere near the pain of the people she had inflicted suffering upon. She did break Elsie, but it was the darkness that held her together and the monster within it. I smiled. This little shit thought she knew despair. I laughed, taking a drag of my joint. She knew nothing of suffering.

Screaming, her voice echoed off the walls, "I was barely a subadult when I stole my brother's army and burned that fucking manor, told that army to slaughter them all. No one questioned me! The princess of death! When I found that blood trail and found her alive, I knew right then she would be my servant, my weapon of chaos and destruction. All I had to do was break her like my father broke me before I could even understand what being broken meant."

She could have simply asked Elsie or, for fuck's sake, me. We would have freed her. But this little shit was so hell-bent on doing it her way. Royalty outside Bellator were idiotic, conceited, wealthy morons.

Her voice wavered and broke slightly over what her father had done. "She had it all, and I took it! I should have had it all!"

Rage was the only emotion Clia knew. She may be a healer, but her magic was fueled by fury, hungry to right wrongs on her behalf. But she was hungry for chaos, and I couldn't blame her, a victim of her circumstances. It was a feeling I also understood all too well. This world was cruel, the magic harsh, and we had been sent here by the gods to protect it from themselves.

I scoffed at my own thoughts. They use and abuse our kind without hardly a thought, just throwing magic at the world and hoping something worked. Magic was far deeper than that; beings with conscious thought were deeper than that. I understood why my bride held a soft spot for her; she shared a brokenness with Cliantha. However, I would not allow that softness to cloud my mind. Camron and Cliantha needed to die; this whole place needed to be burned and left desolate.

"My disgusting mother." She launched another bottle of wine at the wall. "Left her children here in this disgusting place with a disgusting male acting like a father."

Clia paced around, uttering all the thoughts she'd never let slip with Elsie around. Her mother had left the king and flew to Pax on a stormy night. They'd smuggled her from these lands, and she never returned. She hated her, too, for fleeing and leaving her behind. She was only a hatchling, and when her father learned she flew away from them, from him, he had Cliantha's wings cut off. I could understand why he did it—desperation—but he created a monster in that decision. One hell-bent on killing him. She tried to forge a weapon under her father's nose, bring her back after the battle and unchain her, probably dying in the process. In Elsie's condition, she would have fought and died trying.

She leaned back against those gray stone walls.

"I hate them, and the one tool at my disposal is gone. Had she returned with me, I would have unchained that bitch and let her burn it all down. All while thinking she was setting herself and me free."

Her claws came out, her magic slipping, and she gripped and tore at the stone and laughed, a mechanical, seething sound.

"She would be my slave till the end of her miserable life. With her love for me, she would have enjoyed it. I would have found my useless mother after exacting every bit of pain my father had put me through, ending her life as well."

The laughter stopped, and she straightened, contracting her magic back. Her actions did not match every hateful word that dripped from her. Behind it was love and admiration for Elsie, laced with jealousy of her newfound freedom. No wonder Elsie wanted to save her as well. The poor girl never had a chance. I flicked my joint and stepped on it as I came out of the alley, walking the streets of Otium. Behind the cover of my lenses, I kept watching Clia.

"We are at war, and I am going to take back what is mine. Elsie Pax is mine." She stopped, musing at herself. "I just need to find a way to get her back. Magic and family be damned, that little bitch is mine. I stole her and used everything at my disposal then to do so, and I will do it again."

*Over my dead body*, I thought as I watched Clia.

She took another swig of wine, pushed herself from the walls, and left the cell. She had a war to win; she was morally corrupt from a lifetime of abuse. The princess of death—except she was truly dead—had no concept of love, no ethics, and no morals. Everything in her experience had sucked the meaning of life from her, and she was going to serve herself and only herself. But not even Lady Death would come to take her. Guess that means she was my problem, after all. I groaned; what a pain.

She called out down the halls of cells in a soft, singing voice. "Oh, brother! It's time. If you would like to see your wife, I suggest you hear me out."

She skipped down the hallways of the castle to bring undoubtedly more pain to anything and everyone around her. The princess of Mordryl had just signed her death warrant. I laughed. No, damn it, Elsie was mine. But if it was Elsie's choice, Clia would make a fine pet in my kingdom. Pets always had a use.

# CHAPTER TEN

## Elsie

The four of us had sat in the sunlight for hours, just thankful to be with each other. My mind was quiet, not a word or thought out of place, just at peace around them. The sun was high in the sky. The servants had cleaned the party space, leaving the entire place looking untouched. I looked at the open sky before me and thought of Clia; she would have loved this sight. The thought ended there; I forced it to. I did not want to think of her. She was my past; this was my present. Here, with Karma, Axl, and Juni, and soon, we would add Cosmos back into this happy house. And I would make sure this was, in fact, a happy house, no matter what. No one was going to take my peace from me again.

Karma was the light, and I was the darkness. United, we had a war to end. I would end it and destroy it all. I silenced my mind again. I needed to stop and just lay back in the grass, take in the sunlight that surrounded me. I fell into a deep, much-needed sleep. Everything was going to be okay; it had to be.

When I woke up, I looked around. It was dark. I was in Karma's room, alone, and panic set in as I noticed his absence. I couldn't breathe; everything felt hot, my body shook, and I screamed. I heard glass breaking, things being toppled over in the house, and quick footsteps. More of this feeling of panic and dread set in.

*"He will come. You are okay. You are safe."* I screamed again, pulling the covers around me and feeling the tips of my fingers burning through the fabric they grasped, with fire streaming down my face as it burned. *Where is he?* I screamed again, but the words did not leave my mouth. The door flung open, and Karma was there, breathless, a look of terror and heartbreak across his face as he took in the scene before him.

*"Let him help you."*

"Elsie," Karma breathed.

He ran toward me, his magic coating mine, stopping the burning. He pulled me to him.

"It's all right, it's all right," he chanted in his thick, heavy voice.

I shuddered and leaned into his cold body, letting him soothe and cool me. After a few moments of panting and shaking in his arms, he lifted my chin to meet his eyes. They were less blue, darker and cloudy with what I could assume was grief.

"What troubles you?" he asked.

I did not break his gaze. It was like he was soothing my burning soul with that look of deep concern and compassion.

I broke again as I spoke, gasping, "I-I-I don't know! I was alone—"

He pressed his lips to mine, cool, lush, and peaceful. He pulled back, resting his head against mine. One hand circled up around the base of my skull, while the other tugged my waist toward him.

"I'm sorry, I should have known." He gently pressed another kiss on my lips.

I couldn't help but notice him, and my fear quickly changed to something else altogether. Even in the dark, he illuminated almost everything, casting rainbows even in the moonlight. My body felt cool, and I relaxed against him, the planes of his well-defined body soothing my soul. I could feel my magic wrapping around me, relaxing back into my body as I breathed him in.

*"Drink him in."* The voice coached from the darkness of my mind, and I did.

Tonight, he smelled of the sea but also of sugar cookies, sickly sweet. He did not loosen his grasp; he just held me while I took him in.

When I was wrapped in his arms, he was everything; no thoughts besides him. I would do anything for him. I loved him. I felt my core growing wet and full. I wanted him. I hadn't wanted any male since him, and yet, here he was, beautiful, and I needed him.

The deep male voice praised and comforted me, *"Such a good girl, listen to my voice. I will never lead you astray."*

I wanted him to soothe every ache and burn of my soul under his cold touch. I squeezed him, wrapping my arms at his waist, and spoke it aloud, "I love you."

He ran his hand over my hair, kissed my forehead, and whispered, "As I you. You are the fire that warms my heart and soul."

He tilted my head back and kissed me softly, then swept his tongue over my lips. I felt myself opening for him, surrendering. He gently pushed his tongue into my mouth, as if asking permission.

*"Take him, bend him, and break him."*

Following that voice's command, like a wild animal, I grabbed for the back of his neck, pushing him deeper into my mouth. His breath caught; he paused and withdrew, looking at me, confused by my bold approach. He tilted his head to the side and let out a deep sigh, as if trying to regain composure.

"Els, you have no idea how badly I want you, hearing you moaning my name, but I could have every inch of your body and still need more. I cannot say I can make love to you, not the way you deserve me to, not right now. Please understand."

*"Coward."* My inner demon scoffed.

There was sadness in his voice, like he was asking to be forgiven. I paused. He was worried about hurting me, and yet I could say the same. Would my magic and heat be too much for him? I never had considered this would be difficult. My brows knitted together as I looked at him. I didn't understand, but I also couldn't stand to see him sad, so I kissed him gently. I softly uttered the truth and my question.

"I don't understand, Karma. I feel loved and safe with you. Do you not feel the same?" He was shocked, as if my question was a surprise.

"Oh, sweet Els. No, it's not that." I breathed.

"Tell me." He sighed and pulled away.

"I don't know how. Are you up for a walk?"

I nodded.

We walked in silence, holding hands, out to the cliffs and down the carved path to the beach below. The only sounds were the waves crashing on the cliffs and of soil beneath our feet. It was peaceful; the sky was full of stars, and the moon cast brilliant rainbows against Karma's exposed wings onto the sand. A muted and moonlit rainbow of only blue, the color of tears. I smiled up at him, but he kept looking forward as we walked. I gathered myself and decided to repeat the question he asked me.

"What troubles you?"

He cracked a sullen smile while the sea breeze gently whipped his hair about his face. He dropped to the sand, pulling me into his lap as he stared at the ocean with heavy, dark eyes.

"I'm not sure where to even begin. Can you ask me something more specific?"

I paused, looking out at the water, and decided to open with something obvious. He was trying to be vulnerable but was sad, and I should be patient and kind. That was the decent thing to do, not demand answers or ask invasive questions right away. I was never very tactful, though; it took effort for me to try. And, being honest with myself, as much as I wanted to be happy, I had so many questions. Would their answers bring more pain? Blurting out something obvious about him would be a safer bet.

"Why do you have your wings out all the time?" He sighed as if I had just asked him something deep and personal. Crap.

"I can't put them away. Same with some of the scales that cover me. If it weren't for this crown funneling my magic, I fear I would never be able to walk among all kinds but rather be stuck trying to simply keep warm as a dragon."

*"Lies,"* the voice hissed. I felt my mind flinch, while I hid my physical reaction. Stillness, absolute stillness was my default.

Karma's words confused me. My fire was much easier to control with the crown but could still slip. What did he mean by trying to keep warm?

He continued, "Let me try to explain it better. Ice magic for dragons is hard enough to control. We are cold-blooded creatures, and this magic is a bitter, unrelenting chill to the bone. We need the warmth of the sun, we need heat, but our magic keeps us frozen in a way. Then, on top of that, the ice magic I wield is much more powerful than the average ice dragon as well. When I contain all my magic within me, it feels like I'm being frozen to death. It's peaceful, heavenly, to feel so close to death. However, I love life far too much to walk with death, so I keep as much magic flowing out and around me as possible so I don't become encased in my own ice."

He hung his head like he was ashamed, but this I could mostly understand. Yet something about the voice told me he was lying, and the dramatics Karma displayed seemed off.

"Can you freeze your soul?" I asked.

He nodded in response, like the realization was too heavy for him to admit. He could freeze his very essence of being, and I knew if he could do it, he had come close to having done it or had done it, but if he had done it, he wouldn't be here. So, why?

"I set my soul on fire. It's blissful. How did you learn?" The question came out suddenly and lacked the tact I was trying hard to muster.

I did not dare ask if he had met Lady Death. She was not here, and without her essence to define my next move, I would not ask about her.

*"Smart girl."*

Karma stiffened and whispered, "When I found my parents, I was frozen solid. Axl and Juni pulled me out of it by reminding me how much life there was to live."

I wanted to ask more prying questions. But I didn't need more than that, not right now. He was haunted by more than I knew, and this is why he refused me. He was worried about hurting me; sure, my body was thin and frail, but he was also worried the bliss would drive his magic to a breaking point. I should fear it as well; I had not considered this. Our passion could be our demise. I could almost feel my mind roll its eyes.

*"That's not it. There is something else. There must be more."* That damn voice is always the skeptic. I hated to admit it, but so was I in this case.

The silence was comfortable but needed to be filled.

"I found out when I killed that male. I'd let the rage boil over. I couldn't turn it off, and before I knew it, he was dead, splattered on the walls, his body melting and turning to ash."

The words kept pouring out of my mouth. "As much as I crave peace, I also crave violence. Maybe that's just the product of the last hundred and fifty years. Maybe I have always been this way. I've been lost in the darkness so deeply that I also loved seeing him die. He was disgusting, and it was a joy to watch. When I knew what I had done and that I had enjoyed it, my magic became all-consuming. I felt it burning deep within me. I hated myself but loved the feeling. Had it not been for Clia's cheering, I would have let it consume me. After that, the next years are kind of a blur. I know I stopped thinking of home and peace. I started to crave violence. My magic was constantly pour-ing, and I was hearing voices in my mind. I was always on fire in some way."

I paused. Karma was still looking at the water, a single tear running from his eye, so I continued. Maybe if he could under-stand me, he would see he didn't need to hide.

"It was so good, but also, the lack of control I had over it pushed my mind to the darkness. I debated killing her and myself, thinking that might be the best option. When I lost hope and decided to let my fire rage one last time, walking hand in hand with Death, I found myself again. I was happy, happier than I had been in years. So, I get it, Karma. Not trusting yourself—I understand that."

*Better than anyone*, I thought as I looked out to the waves. I knew insanity, sickness, being mentally unwell for so long; I knew it well. I understood it at a level I'm sure no one else could.

He gripped me tighter, and I felt his head rest on my shoulder, his tears cold, streaming down onto me. It confirmed he did not know Death the way I knew her. I gripped his hand.

"I love you," he said between broken breaths.

"I love you, too."

Thankful my voice did not betray me, I was firm and sure. I gripped his hands in my lap and leaned my head on his, sinking into him. As I relaxed, I felt the fire rise, and I let it. I could feel him relax into me, and I felt the bitter cold he had spoken about. Then I felt us melding together. Both of us had just admitted we had considered ending our lives, and in that, I felt more at peace with him. He knew me, and I knew him. I understood the sadness along with the happiness that ending your own life could bring. I also understood the resolve it took to not allow it. We may have found our way out of those thoughts in far different ways, with different motives, but we both knew what the thought, ability, and resolve to end your existence brought to you.

*"He lies."*

Karma composed himself and spoke softly.

"Promise me if those thoughts ever take hold, we tell each other—no matter how dark, we tell each other immediately. Whatever it is, you always need to tell me."

I nodded. His words reminded me of a simpler time, the promises we would make as kids. I held up my pinky finger and said, "I promise."

Karma let out a snorting laugh, gripping my pinky in his. "I promise," he said, laughing, and we came together, kissed each other's fingers, and turned as we locked eyes. He burned with desire, and I felt my desire growing against the warmth at my core.

*"Enjoy him while you can."*

Fuck it, we just admitted one of our deepest and darkest secrets, and with the heat rising, I needed him badly, so I kissed him hard and fast, not giving him a chance to pull away. I pulled him into me, rising to my knees in front of him. His breath caught, and I moved my hands into his hair as I wrapped my legs around his hips, seated in his lap. He let out a breath, and it was like frost coating the sand. I thought about it for a moment. I needed to show him I could match him. I let more heat escape me, melting his ice. His eyes grew wide, and the frost-covered sand was back. I released more heat, matching his unfolding desire, the perfect mixture of fire and ice. Melting him as he soothed my burning, steam rose from us. I let the hold of my magic go, with his tongue in my mouth burning for just a moment, and I heard him growl. He gripped me tight, washing out all the burning.

"Sweet Elsie."

I kept kissing him hard, messy, and fast, filled with passion in every movement. Spreading my legs wider around his waist, letting him hold me up in his arms, I purred into his mouth.

I felt his shaft against my dress through his trousers. It was firm. The length had me wondering once again if it would even fit, but he let his magic flow, dropping his guard, and I matched him, holding him as he held me. Then, as if he couldn't hold himself back any longer, he pushed up from the sand, and I found myself looking at the stars. I closed my eyes again, taking everything in. I felt his hands under my dress, gripping my hips and ripping my panties from my body as he came back to my mouth, breathing deeply as if he could regain control. I kissed him back, surrendering to him completely, mind, body, soul, and magic. I would be his peace; I would be the warmth he looked for. I gripped his hips and ground myself into him.

He whispered, "I need to hear you say it."

Without hesitation, I responded breathlessly, "Take me."

I needed him closer. I pulled his trousers to his thighs. Exposing his long, perfectly erect cock, I took it into my hand, slowly stroking it from the base, coated in white curls, to the now glistening tip. Allowing his fluid to coat my hand as I circled the tip and moved that slick fluid back down his shaft.

He let out a feral growl. I felt his tip rest on the entrance to my body. He bit my lip and moved down my neck. I shuddered; he was so close. I gripped his hip in one hand and his cock in the other and pulled him into me, abandoning all thought. He gasped, muttered, and purred into my neck.

"You are perfect, burning like wildfire," he ground out while settling himself in me, filling me.

He bit my neck and kissed my scars. He thrust into me, then sat back and rose to his knees, pulling me by my hips up to him, forcing himself deep into my core. I moaned, gripping his thighs. I felt my nails biting into his skin. I opened my eyes and found him looking at me, feral, full of desire, and ice white. His eyes reflected mine, which danced with flames.

*"Good girl. That's perfect, enjoy him."*

He drove himself deep and gripped my hips, thrusting deeper, each time moans of pleasure escaping him. He moved against my body, entering and exiting hard and fast. I couldn't breathe. This was pure, this was love, this was everything. It needed to be; this was it, and I needed it to be good. I needed to be good for him. I used the bits of muscle I had in this frail body to tighten around his cock, sending a new pleasure through him and myself.

He moved his hand over my sex and sent a new wave of pleasure through me as he played with the small, delicate bit of flesh. I cried out with a moan of his name broken by pleasure, "Kar-ma."

His thrusts quickened, and I could feel myself spilling all over him and felt him spill into me, my body shuddering as he let out a roar and collapsed, still pulsing within me. He gathered his breath, pulled back slowly, and lay down to the sand on his side, turning me and pulling me to his chest.

We lay still, breathless, sticky with sweat and sand. I turned to my back, looking at the night sky filled with stars. I knew I would spend the rest of my life trying to put into words what sex was like with Karma. No matter how brief it was, it was the kind of sex that not only took your breath but stilled your mind, in those moments existing only for him.

*"You will have better."* The voice chuckled in an odd breathy way.

But Karma was everything I didn't know I was missing. He was the ice to my blaze, the love to my hate; he was everything. Did Death know? Is this why she always offered me a choice? I turned to look at him. He also now lay on his back and, at some point, had tucked himself back into his trousers. I wondered what he was thinking and remembered I could ask.

"What's on your mind?"

He did not turn; instead, he stared up into the sky. "I will never stop falling in love with you."

I smiled. Karma sat up, got to his feet, and held out his hand. "We should get back home."

I nodded and took his hand. We walked back home the same way we had come down, hand in hand, in a peaceful silence with waves crashing in the distance and the sun starting to rise. I was thankful that Karma wasn't like some other kinds, just talking until your mind shuts them out. He allowed me to be one with silence.

# CHAPTER ELEVEN

## Elsie

We returned to the quiet estate. We went to Karma's room and bathed, washing away the grit of the sand.

I sat on the bed, looking at the rising sun, while Karma sprawled on the bed in utmost relaxation.

"Would you like to stay in this room? I figured you would want your own. I can take the guest room."

I paused. I did not want my own room. But this was Karma always asking for permission. "Can we make it our room?" I asked. Karma smiled toothily, his fangs peeking through.

"Absolutely, Els. I would love nothing more." His voice strained. I smiled and returned my gaze to the sun and water. It was beautiful watching the sunrise.

He lay back on the bed, stretching. "Juni will have breakfast soon. Does anything sound good?" I shook my head. Any food was food; it was not difficult.

"One day, you'll have preference. Just let me know when, or Juni, for that matter," he said kindly. It was his way of acknowledging the reasons I did not care what was prepared, just thankful someone was doing it. Then it dawned on me.

"Wait, Juni cooks?" I asked, kind of surprised.

"Oh, yes, it's something she loves to do, and she's very good at it. It's part of our routine. She makes all our meals most of the time. The house servants mainly clean, and for parties, she orders food."

*"Check for poison."*

I felt an odd emotion and frowned. She had given him a child. She lived in his house and planned parties. I mean, sure, she was family, but—

Karma's voice interrupted my thoughts.

"You're jealous, and that's fair, but what Juni and I have cannot hold even the smallest flame to what you and I have."

I felt myself darken at his words—have, not had. My voice did betray me this time.

"Have?" I asked coldly. As if I had summoned her, Death appeared right behind Karma, her gaze cold. For the love of Above, would she only show up to get gossip or what?

Karma bolted upright, and I faced him. His eyes told me this was going to be an interesting conversation.

His words were cautious. "Well, yes, have."

I felt myself wavering on the verge of rage and repeated myself slowly, with venom.

"Have?"

Karma met my eyes and spoke softly. "Have. What she and I HAVE is a very different type of love and lust, same with Axl."

I couldn't hold it back. Fire dripped from my emerging fangs. Even in human form, the crown could not hold back the rage spitting fire as I clapped back.

"Oh, so, what? You also have sex with my brother?" His response was firm. "Yes."

He never dropped my gaze. My fire seized up, and I coughed as my breath caught in my throat.

Death's gaze softened and appeared curious—if a mist with floating eyes could look that way. I stared at him, mouth agape, and blinked. That was not what I was expecting. My emotions had gone from jealousy to pure shock. This was more complicated than I could wrap my head and heart around, but it somehow hurt less than him just lying with Juni. I shut my mouth and turned back to the window. I could feel Karma's gaze, and I could feel Death vanish; she would leave at a time like this . . .

"I love you."

And just like that, with those three little words, I went from shock to calm. I reminded myself he did love me; I knew that.

"I love you, too," I said, a tad breathless.

I would love him, no matter what he did. That alone was terrifying, and the fire within me bubbled at that realization.

*"Breathe, this won't be your life. You do not have to accept this."* I shook that thought away, gathering myself, and shut myself down. I didn't need this voice in my mind playing tricks on me. I was just crazy, I knew that. I would continue to hide it. This was fine; I would accept it. It's fine. I could do this, broken heart and all. I could accept it. I can handle this.

He was the best I could hope for, and I got my wish for freedom; this would be fine . . . Karma continued after a deep sigh.

"I love you, but I also love them. We see love as appreciation, not possession. The capacity for love is limitless and comes in many forms. I love you; my love for them changes nothing about how deeply I can love you."

I was still, taking in his words. Love was limitless, but so was suffering, and he was not wrong.

But if that were true, he would not be able to pick between us, so I asked, "And if I gave you the choice between me or them, who would you choose?"

He took in a breath and stumbled over his next words quickly while reaching for my hand. I stayed still, my gaze locked out the window.

"I could never choose that way, Elsie. It's not a choice to love. It is, however, a way of life you choose to live and love within. I would never force anyone into this. If you truly cannot bear it, I would never force you to stay, and I would do everything I could to show you every day I love you. I would like you to at least see how we fit together, how we love, and be open to the idea. I'm sorry I didn't explain this better. I fucked that up miserably. I would ask you to give me the chance to prove to you that love is true and limitless. And it is my hope you will stay here, but you are never trapped here."

He gripped my hand. That was the best answer I could ask for in the face of this news; that answer told me all I needed to know. Karma was love, light, life, and peace. This would be fine and better than any alternative. This is who he was at his core, a broken heart after his parents died, and Juni and Axl pulled him from death because they loved him just as deeply and reminded him what it was like to be alive and choose life. They could have taken an entire kingdom to themselves, wealth, power, and glory, but they loved him. I wish someone had loved me that way; maybe that's why Death never forced me. Gods, she was confusing. If only I could talk to her, she knew me best.

Love is love. I could understand it. I had loved Clia, lusted after her, even. Karma loved my brother, another male. Yet another thing we had in common, a taboo form of affection born from love, was welcomed here; this place was for all kinds, all kinds of love and passion, as well as species.

Otium, the city of bliss. And even with the revelation, I still felt slightly numb. I understood what he was talking about; maybe I could grow to feel it the way he did. But I needed to break the tension. I was not going to run from this. This was a hard thing to accept for me, something I would need to grow into, and for him, for them, I could try to do that. No, I will do that.

*"You don't have to."*

"I love you, but I'm not having sex with Axl. That's just gross," I said casually. Karma roared with laughter.

"You are an idiot, though, for not telling me sooner." I giggled and gripped his hand.

"Oh, sweet Elsie, of course not! That ass is mine." He boomed with laughter and ripped me down to the bed, showering me with kisses. It was then a knock came on our bedroom door.

"What in the Above has you both at an unhinged volume at this hour?" Axl said through the door, and I burst out laughing again. Karma jumped from the bed and ran toward the door, stark naked. I rushed to cover myself in the blankets. He pulled the door open, and Axl turned white as a ghost. He had his hand still raised, knocking on it.

Karma gripped his face and boomed, "Elsie! She gets it!"

I didn't get it, but I could learn and try to understand.

Karma pulled Axl into his face, planting an excited, messy kiss on Axl, who just stood frozen with a look on his face of *what in the Below had just happened*. I laughed more at his expense. Karma pulled back and hugged Axl, who was turning a brilliant shade of pink across his cheeks. Karma let go, and Axl straightened himself out and sighed.

"It's far too early for this much excitement. I need coffee."

Karma laughed and threw an arm around him. "I could say the same!"

Axl pushed him off with an exasperated sigh and spoke in a voice I did not know he possessed. It was lighter, far less serious, and slightly feminine.

"Could you at least get dressed and, for the love of all Above, take a better shower. You smell like sex, and what's worse, sex with my sister, you—"

Karma cut him off with another sloppy kiss, pulling Axl into him by the back of his neck and hair, and growled, "Are you done talking yet, or should I shut you up myself?"

Axl turned bright red, and I couldn't contain my laughter. No wonder Juni had been grateful for another female around; these two were an absolute mess.

"Just put some fucking pants on!" Axl shrieked, breaking out of Karma's grasp, and slammed the door shut.

Karma sank to his knees, laughing hysterically, gripping his midsection.

"Looks like we found a new way to torment poor Axl," I said, out of breath. Karma locked eyes with me, knowing I meant the way we used to pick on him for fun as kids. He kept laughing.

"Oh, you have no idea how much joy I will get out of this moment for centuries." I kept a smile plastered to my face. It's fine; centuries of sharing Karma with Axl, and Juniper, and his son. *It's fine.*

We got dressed. Karma wore silk trousers that hung low and left nothing to the imagination, outlining his perfect sex. Even while flaccid, it was impressive to look at. He tossed me another dress from the drawers and gave a small frown at it. It was very floral and very pink.

"You and Juni should go shopping in town and pick out some things you like." I shrugged on the dress. It was very similar to the other one I wore. It did not shimmer, but it was soft.

"I don't have money for shopping, Karma." I said it like I had said it when we went out in town as kids. Just a fact, like our parents hadn't allotted us anything for the day, knowing full well we would have burned through it on sweets.

He spun and looked at me, puzzled. He stammered out, "Uh, you're a royal now? Yeah, so that means you just pick out what you want, and the treasury will handle the bill, Els."

Now, it was my turn to be puzzled. "Okay, so like a royal tab?"

He laughed. "Uh, sure, you can think of it like that."

I was still confused. Did money just exist? He sighed.

"Just go with Juni. She'll teach you. Axl and I need to handle some business in the capital after breakfast. Will you be all right?"

A day of shopping with Juni, my love's lover, my sister-in-law, my brother's lover. Fuck, that was a lot to wrap my head around. But I responded truthfully. "I think so."

Another ugly thought reared in my mind that, this time, escaped my mouth. "Why are Juni and I not going to the capital for business?"

Karma gave pause. "We will talk it over at the table."

Then he took my hand and kissed the back. He opened the door, and I could hear Juni singing in the kitchen, the smell of cooking food filling the air. My mouth began to water.

Karma held my hand as we walked down the hallway into the round foyer, still just as magnificent as when I first saw it. We turned into the kitchen, the space filled with everything someone who cooked could ask for. The windows were massive, filling the room with warm light that bounced off the polished cherry wood that covered everything. Axl sat at the table, leaning back, a cup of coffee in front of him, watching Juni cook. You could see by the way he looked at her he held a massive amount of love, respect, and appreciation for her. Karma let go of my hand as we entered. He went up behind Juni, pulled her waist toward him, uttered a thank you, and kissed her cheek. My brother's gaze never changed, perhaps only to get softer and fuller. I watched from the archway, still shocked, trying to process.

*"Just watch for now, form your own opinions of this situation."* For once, the voice had a good idea.

"Els, grab a chair. Sit," Axl said, breaking my trance on what was filling this room.

I grabbed the one against the only solid wall, still watching as Karma turned, came to the table, and sat at the head. Four seats—they had planned for me.

"Juni cooked for you every day," Axl said. "We could be drowning in leftovers, and she would still set a place for you, Els," Axl said while sipping his coffee.

It was a small statement, but I felt the weight behind it. I couldn't help but ask, "How long?"

Axl paused and looked into my eyes. "Since she joined us, about fifty years." His voice was steady, like he was waiting for me to implode, and I felt like I might.

Since Juni came to this home, she has always thought of me.

Juni said, "It's nothing, really." She sounded nervous and shy.

It was far more than nothing; she knew it, I knew it, and they knew it. I looked down at the table.

"Juni"—my head raised to meet her hazel eyes—"thank you. That is far more kindness than I could ask for."

Her eyes grew wet, but she blinked it away.

"You are most welcome."

She carried all three of our plates over at once. The plates were covered in meat and smelled delicious. She brought over cutlery made from crystal, and it was gorgeous. She sat down, and the boys began eating. I just stared at everything in awe. It was beautiful . . . simple, but gorgeous. But my stomach was turning.

"Do you not like it?" Karma asked with his mouth half full.

I looked at Juni, who seemed unbothered. I remembered to speak. "Oh, no, it's not that at all. I just—well, it's all so stunning."

Juni laughed. "It's just steak and eggs, love."

I responded, "It is so much more than that."

Axl nodded as if he understood. I picked up my fork, willing my body to just accept the food. Taking a piece of steak to my mouth, I moaned out loud. It was so good; she was a great cook. But this would not help my nausea. Small bites and just pushing it around on the plate would have to do for now.

Karma chuckled and said, "Told ya." Axl kicked him under the table at his remark.

"Oh, come now! She's not that delicate," he sneered. I laughed, thinking about how he gripped my hips on the beach. No, I was not delicate like a flower, more like delicate like wildfire. Contained, it brought warmth and rebirth; unleashed, destruction and chaos.

"I know she's not, but still." Axl sighed. All this seemed to put him on edge.

"Axl? What's on your mind?" I asked. Axl froze mid-bite and looked at Karma and Juni. They shrugged, and he lowered his hand and met my gaze, all his delicate features hardening along with his words.

"I worry about you, sister. We couldn't find you for years. It drove me mad. Juni cooked, Karma built a small empire for you to come back to, and I searched and searched. So, please forgive me if I walk on eggshells around you. I'm worried all of this could break you differently than what already has shattered you."

He never hid the truth, and I loved my brother for it. He always spoke his mind, even after we picked on him. He was tough. I knew I needed to reply and choose my words carefully. He would see through me.

"Axl, I cannot fathom what you all did. I will never be able to truly understand it, but I am grateful. I have never felt more at home in my life. And, yes, that includes the manor. You're not wrong to worry. I'm struggling to understand how your lives work, but I won't leave." Small lies laced between truths.

He wavered and nodded. I knew the depth of the manor house.

Axl said, "I love you. I'm happy you're home. I missed you." His eyes were watery.

I reached for his hand. "I missed you, too. I am so sorry you went through so much without me."

He gripped my forearm. I gripped his back and locked eyes with him.

"Never again," we vowed at the same time.

His voice changed to that light version from earlier. Not dropping the eye contact or the hold he had on my arm, he said, "Sex on the beach is a massive cliché. Do better."

Karma snorted in his coffee, and Juni let out a cackling laugh. I about fell out of my chair, laughing and holding Axl for support.

They cleaned their plates. It was an easy thing to do. Juni was a wonderful cook. Axl gathered them and placed them in the sink. My stomach began to roll—too much food, it seemed. Even just a few bites had been pushing it. I could shut that out, though; I had been through way worse than mild discomfort. *Maybe I should have checked for poison.* I shoved that dark thought down. No, she wouldn't do that.

"All right, Karma, you about ready to head out?" Axl asked as I stared out the windows, just marveling at the colors of the yard outside, the trees, flowers, grass, and sky. Karma's reply was what caught my attention.

"Yes, but no. Els needs clothes. Juni, would you take her shopping today?"

Axl was quick. "Elsie just got back. You don't think going into town could stir up—"

Karma cut him off. "I have thought about it—"

Axl spoke over him. "I don't think you understand."

Karma cut back in, and I snapped. I couldn't focus with them talking over each other.

"For the love of Above, can you talk one at a time?"

*"That's right, command them."* As the voice echoed in my mind, Axl's eyes slid to me, wide. Quickly regaining his composure, he looked away.

Juni giggled and sat back down. Axl and Karma leaned against the counter. The capital thing was still bugging me.

"Do you not want me to go with you today?" I looked at Karma, getting straight to the point. His eyes softened, and he gazed at the floor.

"It's not that we don't want you to come with us. It's just that being at the capital, we're not as we are here, and I would rather you have a few days to get used to us, rather than the politics in the capital."

Odd response noted.

Juni rolled her eyes. "Elsie."

I turned my gaze back to her, and I could feel the void look on my face as I met her eyes.

"Outside this house, only a handful of beings know how we run our family. No one knows how we all love, and most refuse to understand. Karma has been working on this since his rise to power, but changing the minds of long-living beings, such as dragons and Fae, must be done slowly and with care."

*"A weak mindset. Change can be accomplished with action."* Again, the voice, and this time I noted a shiver run up Axl's spine.

"The boys are worried that if they take you to the capital, it will only reopen the harsh reality that we had to keep going while you were lost." She shrugged like it was just hard facts, and it was the bitter truth.

Juni was more like Axl than I had given her credit for; she was kind but spoke with a harsh truth. Axl spoke next, somehow not interrupting her.

"In addition to that, who we must pretend to be at the capital is not the side of us we want you to know. Yet."

My head hurt, and I laid it on the table, exasperated. I didn't understand. I groaned, "Can one of you just tell me what the fuss is?"

All three of them spoke at once and in unison, "Cosmos." They fell silent.

I groaned again, burying my head in my arms, letting my hair cover my face. Politics? Really? How many skeletons were in this closet?

Juni broke the silence. "I have an idea. Karma is not going to like it, but what if we sealed your magic—"

Karma roared, "No!"

"*NO!*" the voice in my mind shouted in unison with Karma, filled with rage.

I paled at the realization while Juni continued, "—In the crown. If you feel like you need the magic, just strip the crown and fly up."

She spoke with confidence, like that could work. Axl shook his head. "No, if it's the magic we're worried about or something troubling her while you're in town, it's safer for everyone if I transfer some of your magic to one of us."

"I fail to see the issue, Axl. Karma will put on a tamers chain for us! For goddess's sake." Juni huffed. "At least she can lie with Karma without one. So, what is the issue?"

I realized it then; they were afraid of me, of what I could unleash if provoked or caught off guard. Even Karma would get put in chain to bed them, she was right what is my problem. I sighed against my arms, and I knew I was still going to be kept under lock and key. All of this was too good to be true. I felt Karma's cool embrace from behind me. He spoke softly but with a cold hardness I had not expected.

"We won't be doing any of that. Axl, Juniper, I understand your point of view. An immediate reaction from Elsie could set a blaze to the whole city. I am not blind to that, and neither is she. Elsie is family now, and we will not, under any circumstance, leave her with less power when she walks out this front door than when she entered. With that said, out of respect for your concern, Axl, grant me mind melding over Els to be able to feel anything amiss, and I will leave Oppida Prima and be back here within minutes. Think you can handle that?"

I sat up and looked at him. He straightened. He did not look like Karma at that moment but like King Rexarius commanding his second and third-in-command. The voice in my mind was snarling a deep, soul-ripping noise.

Axl looked at me, the word guilt could have been stamped on his forehead, while Juni tossed a sideways glance. I nodded. I could handle holding back.

*"I will be back,"* the voice gruffly stated.

They nodded, and everyone just let out a sigh of relief. Axl placed a hand on my head and on Karma, and I could hear Karma's thoughts within my head like I had in battle. It was a similar feeling to the voice that was living in my own mind. The realization hit me again. I didn't want to really believe it; this was not my voice or imagination, but someone. *Shit, I can't lose my family; I can't let them know.*

*"That was all uncalled for. I am sorry."* Karma said that only to me within the confines of the melding very softly, as if waiting for me to rip my brother's head off for threatening to take magic from me.

Juni, without missing a beat, said, "What do you like? Dresses?"

I nodded. I did not like dresses, but they were proper, and clearly, she was feminine in all the ways that mattered to Karma, so I should try to be like her.

She squealed, "Okay, let me get my purse, and we'll head out."

Karma kissed me, Axl hugged me, and they turned and walked out of the kitchen through the foyer. As soon as they hit the threshold, they kissed each other, almost like they were apologizing for what they just had to do and raced up into the sky. Axl could transform and fly with those wings, and that was beautiful.

# CHAPTER TWELVE

## Elsie

Juni came back to the kitchen with a leather bag over her shoulder, and I saw some beings walking in. They greeted us with a nod and started clean, so quietly, like they didn't exist. I wasn't sure how I felt about that. They should have a voice in their workplace, I thought, just sitting in the chair and looking out the window. At what, I didn't know; I was just looking.

"Would you like to sun before we go?" I nodded and stood up.

"I'm sorry for suggesting taking your magic. I hadn't thought that through very well," she said as we entered the foyer.

I nodded and held the door, following her to the cliffs. The conversation from earlier weighed on me. The voice's anger about being shut out, Karma's secrets, my brother's, and what were hers? Freedom, peace, and family were feeling a lot less sweet.

"Why don't they talk?"

I was tired of attempting to be tactful. It was bothering me. Juni dropped her warm smile.

"They can't, and they wish not to." I inclined my head in confusion.

"All our servants are refugees from Mordryl. It seems to be a common theme to cut the voice from someone, although we have not had a new one join us for a while with those wounds. Perhaps it can get better, after all." Juniper placed that warm smile back on her face. I wanted to like her, but something about her was just unlikeable.

Refugees? From Mordryl? That didn't make much sense. No one escaped that place, not with their life or soul, anyway. I was the only one with that so-called honor.

It was a short walk to the cliffs. She was so full of hope she bounced when she walked, a gold light, and she seemed pure of heart and wanted to see the best in everything. I should try to be more like her, more light-hearted, trying to see the better in everything. Maybe that's why I didn't like her; she was everything I should have been. A nice, quiet lady.

We sat on the cliffs, drinking the sunlight, letting it warm our bodies. The sea air cleansing our souls. My stomach had stopped rolling, and my head had stopped spinning, basking in the light of day. I had no thoughts. I wasn't even really looking at the water, just dissociating, when her voice snapped me back.

"Elsie?"

"Oh, sorry." I'm not even sure why I said it. I wasn't sorry for my silent mind and voice.

"It's okay. Are you okay?" she asked meekly, tucking some strands of hair behind an ear.

"I am all right, I guess. This is a lot to take in. I'm struggling to understand how this isn't just a dream," I said plainly. It felt more and more like a dream. Only a few days had passed, and the numb stillness was taking over, everything much more complicated than I'd anticipated.

Juni nodded. She whispered, "I understand that. When I came to live with the boys, I had been a servant for my parents for years. Truth be told, I didn't need to do a thing besides exist, and that was enough. It made me anxious, so I did what I knew best: cook, clean, party plan, heal, and repeat. I was waiting for the day they would be angry, but they never were, and then Axl asked me why I was cooking. I told him because it was expected of me. He told me to never cook another meal again unless I wanted to, that this life was not to be lived in servitude. So, I kept cooking but only out of love. That's how I show them each day that I love them."

I nodded, letting it sink in. She had been a servant to her parents. *Did every dragon have to endure horrible parents except us three? I* wondered. We sat in silence, Juni chewing on her lip. I found the silence welcoming. Maybe she found it unsettling.

"Do you not like the quiet?" I asked.

"No, I feel like you have so many questions, and I want to answer them all."

She turned to me with a look of desperation on her face. *Fine, it's fine.* I can at least hear her. I don't have to supply the conversation.

With a sigh, I asked, "All right." I glanced around. "Will you tell me about the boy?" I didn't waver, and my voice was not as soft as I had intended.

Juni nodded and, like a whispering wind, spoke so softly I had to strain to hear her while we gazed at the water, hearing it crash on the cliffs.

"He is the light of our lives. We met while Axl and Karma were touring my homeland. They came to greet my parents, as they are the King and Queen of Caelum Regandi. It was also war-torn for many years until they took power. I am the only heir left to their kingdom, and according to my father, a healer is incapable of defending a kingdom, so I could never be in power. They told me when I was subadult, if I ever wanted to make sure my home was safe, I would give them an heir or two and only use my magic for study and healing."

She sighed but continued without emotion. She sounded as if she had rehearsed these lines.

"When Karma and Axl visited, it was also for hunting down clues to find you. They spoke to my parents about you, this land, the wars, seeking out advice from another powerful king. Karma had been acting as Regent while his parents shattered under the weight of Rexarius. Karma spoke of grand plans to bring life back into the world, seeking peace. I was smitten with both men, Axl's courage, Karma's views, and their shared unending resolve to hunt down their sister and mate. We became friends after a few months as they studied war games with my father."

She took a breath and forced herself to pause but only for a moment.

"One night, after I had cleaned up dinner, I was on the way to the bed chambers with tea for us and found the boys hugging and crying, I caught them exchanging a kiss. They only noticed me when I gasped and dropped the tea tray. I had never heard of men exchanging such passions."

Juni tossed me a glance, and my eyes must have been begging to tell me more. I wasn't, yet she sighed and nodded again.

"When they saw me, Axl grabbed me, pushed me into one of the rooms, and began trying to explain it, while Karma just stood shell-shocked Axl rambled in sheer panic. I remember thinking, 'Take me with you, both of you. Show me the world, show me your ideas, teach me more.' I cut Axl off and begged to go. I told them all about how my parents were going to force me to bear an heir for the kingdom, that I was doomed to a life of servitude and study. Axl hugged me, and it was Karma who began plotting, ever the political strategist."

Juni rolled her eyes. "If Karma hates anything, it's forcing someone to do something with their life they do not wish to do. Only, none of us knew how twisted my parents were. Karma went to my father the next morning and told him that Axl was my soulmate and to deny that would be a travesty among kingdoms, claiming that it was love that bound us, and he, as ruling king, would see to his demands to take me to Rexarius. He offered trade, coin, metals. He was willing to topple a good bit of financial infrastructure to bring me back here. My father refused every offer, saying the only way I would leave his kingdom was if it were Karma who agreed to give them an heir."

Juni had tears in her eyes, but pressed on, like giving me this story was the only thing she was living for. I wasn't ready for this, the reason Cosmos existed. I expected a conversation about something all mothers gushed about—their kids' milestones, their strengths; I didn't need all this. I couldn't help but wonder why she was pouring all of this out.

"Karma told him he would have to think it over, and my father sweetened the deal by promising everything Karma had offered, in Karma's favor. My father wanted nothing more than to keep his bloodline in power in our lands and for the bloodline to become even more powerful. As far as power was concerned, King Rexarius was the obvious choice. Axl and I were listening to the exchange, and we formulated our own plan. We would just say the eventual child would be Karma's, but it would just be a secret between all of us, and Axl and I would conceive when we were ready." Juniper took a breath and tucked some hair behind her ear, and a small thin scar circled her neck.

"We thought the lie would be enough, so Axl and I strode into that meeting room and said we would agree to the terms. Karma looked stricken, and my father changed from the rather indifferent, hard-ruling man I knew into a power-hungry beast. He agreed to the terms, but then forced Karma to take me right then, in front of him, his guards holding me down with chains and knives. Axl was held back as well, more guards hovering around Karma. We were stripped of any power we thought we had within minutes."

I felt tears welling in my eyes. No wonder they had all fallen in love. They all went through something terrible together, bonded by their shared torment. That was something all too real I had experienced myself.

"This went on for weeks. We were detained and held each day. Karma would be forced upon me. Tamers chains to curb our magics." Juniper huffed, "Its degrading for him to still put one on to this day, even though that's the only way either Axl or I can be with him." I bit down on my lip, wondering where he hid his scars from the chains.

"He was always soft; he would cry and beg my father to end this. I kept reminding him it was okay and that I knew this was the only way out. He hated it all the same. It wasn't until months later when he finally came for me with an erection—I think to just end all our suffering—whispering Axl's name when he spilled his seed. My father knew my body would betray me, and we stayed until it was confirmed I was gravid. Then, he let us go. He's stayed true to his words and trades. Karma sent word to the family of his return and that he had news. When we returned, that's when he found his parents. After all our torment, dignity, and power stripped, and now his parents dead, Karma lost it. Everything was coated in ice. His body faded, and Axl and I clung to him, just willing him to live. He's never been the same since."

Her voice grew even softer, filled with grief. I felt for her. She was a tool of her father, passing along bloodlines and nothing more, securing more land. Her family had no care for her or for the boys—just Cosmos, just a continuation of a ruling power. I chuckled to myself. Maybe it was better I was captured; at least I never had to endure that brand of hell.

"Cosmos is a blessing, and I love him more than anything, but he's also a constant reminder of what we went through together. Some days are more painful than others for us, and I wish I could say it was love that brought Cosmos to us, but it wasn't. I love Karma, he set me free. I love Axl. He gave me courage, never fled, and never wavered, even as his best friend and lover was dying in our arms. When Karma came back to us, his magic even stronger, the three of us realized we were our own kind of family. We would love and lie with each other with no boundaries; we would show this child only love, and we would love harder than even the life bonds of the Fae. We had each other, we would find you, we would have a child, and we would do it together as a family. So, we did."

Juni smiled as she said those words, but it did not meet her eyes. I saw this woman in a very different light. She was still kind and giving, even after everything she had been forced into. She was fierce and strong; she was the holder of the family heart; she was the peacekeeper, my mate's savior, my brother's mate. I needed to try to like her.

"Thank you," I said quietly. She nodded, tears drying as she looked out to the water.

Now, I was the one uncomfortable with the silence. "I mean, you could have just told me what he likes for breakfast, but the story of his conception fills in a lot of gaps," I joked. She giggled and hugged me.

"I don't know how you do it, Elsie. You take all of this in such stride."

"Oh, I just don't think it's all hit me yet, or maybe all the years of torture have made me jaded, and these seem like small problems." I barked out an uncomfortable laugh.

These were small problems, for me, at least. Nothing changed other than my admiration for Juniper. I still had a family, I was free, and there was a war to win. And whether Juni, Axl, or Karma wanted me to or not, I would find her father and set him ablaze for what he did to them. First the Mors, then her father. No male should hold that power, and I would see to that. This world was filled with filthy, power-hungry males. I would be damned if I let this suffering continue for Cosmos to witness. I would make sure he was different. Lady Death appeared before me, winked, and vanished. I wish she would give me more information. Maybe that damn voice would pop back up.

Juni stood up and gripped my hand, pulling me to my feet.

"Let's go shopping!" she squealed.

I laughed, and this felt like a thing I could get used to.

We walked to the city arm in arm. We stopped in many shops, and Juni kept picking out summary flowing dresses of all colors for herself, her body filling out each one perfectly, elegantly, and defining her curvy figure. I attempted to stick to blacks. Juni always commented on my lack of color. "Be more expressive," she would say, or "How about this?" as she held up yet another horrendously poofy pink dress. That was, until I saw a beautiful red crystal-covered dress, but I cringed at the price. She knocked my hand away and threw it in the bags anyway.

"How do we pay for this?"

Juni laughed, and for the first time, I saw a sinister smile cross her face. "We don't. My father does, and I take great joy in sending him the bills to spoil the boys and even more joy spoiling you. It pains him to spend money, and I hate to admit I take great joy in his pain."

I laughed. Oh, thank Above, she was at least a little twisted. We went all over the city and filled shopping bags full of new clothes for us and Karma and Axl. We gossiped about the people who stared at us, making up little stories about them. We had an excellent lunch of sweets and tea, and wandered around the beautiful, pristine city. Everywhere we went, we were stared at with what I could assume to be admiration as their kingdom's royals fluttered about the city without a care in the world. As we headed toward the jewel shop Juniper wanted to go to, I tucked my head down, looking at the unsettling clean cobblestones.

I heard a cowbell, looked up from the ground, and saw what I could only describe as something I thought I would never lay my eyes on ever again. A woman, a human woman, being so boldly tortured.

She was at the end of the leash, being walked by what I assumed was her husband. I stopped and stared at the sorry sight, my mouth agape. I thought this was a place of peace, and yet a human woman in a gossip's bridle? Appalling. I reached out and spun Juniper to face me.

"What the fuck is that?" I asked.

Juniper looked at the scene in front of her and stiffened. Her words were cold. "Nothing she probably didn't deserve." Juniper spun on her heel and kept walking. I couldn't believe it. Had she no compassion? Human lives were short; any torture for them would last a lifetime. How was this permitted? The man at the end of the leash nodded and tipped his hat to me while dragging his wife as more men stopped and threw things at the woman. I felt my fire rising. This was exactly what Axl and Juniper feared. I turned my back, following Juniper to the jewel shop, ashamed of myself for not acting, but also conflicted by the new metaphorical chain I wore. This was not freedom. I was just in a much bigger cage. It's fine, I can change this place, it's fine. I chanted to myself.

Juni was looking at some jewels, and I found a small shop consisting of leather goods and weapons. Now, that piqued my interest. I went into the shop; a short, round elf was behind the counter, and his eyes lit up when he saw me.

"Elsie!"

Shocked, I stopped and stared at him. He jumped off his stool behind the wood counter.

"What can I help you with?"

I just looked at him. He was an elf, mostly harmless, but I was still wary.

"My apologies. I did not reintroduce myself. I am Mimic, and I own and craft everything in this shop. It's very nice to see you out enjoying the city again. It's been too long."

*Oh shit, Mimic!* He crafted in a small village outside the manor. For spirit's sake, would I ever remember everything I had forgotten?

"Mimic! Sorry, yes, it has been too long. I think I would like to get a set of leathers crafted for this body. Can you help me?" If I was going to change anything, I was going to need to fight, and to fight, I would need gear. If they were permitting such atrocities as a gossip's bridle, what else was going on here?

"It would be my honor, Elsie. Traditional, tight, fireproof, and black, yes?"

I smiled. "Exactly right."

Mimic ran to the back and returned with a box.

"Try it on," he whispered.

I went to the small changing room within the small, unimposing shop, and to my shock, the black pair of full leathers fit like a glove. Even the knee-high lace-up boots were perfect, the leather trousers tight and seamless, the blouse tight with a built-in armored corset hidden inside. I cinched it into place, the sleeves tight and full length with a scooping neckline. I looked in the small reflective glass. It all fit better than a glove, and it was perfect. I walked out to find Juni, and she looked impressed. She shook her head slightly, clearing her thoughts perhaps.

She spoke to Mimic. "We will need a hair dagger, sword, and combat daggers with a harness, and hip satchel for this as well, please, good sir."

Without skipping a beat, Mimic returned and fastened the accessory leathers to me, studded with silver. The seams were done in white thread, a black sword fitting for the queen, with a silver and crystal grip with four matching daggers. Juni picked up my hair and secured it in place in a low bun with the silver crown knotted into it, with the slender hair dagger, a last resort type of weapon.

I looked at myself, Warrior Queen, the queen to end a war for her family. I would be the queen of kings. I had two kings to dismantle and this place to change so far. The Dragon of Death and Darkness it was beautiful in a terrifically horrendous way. Pure malevolence poured off me, and I felt the fire dancing but secured within. This was me. I was finding myself, not who I was but who I am. Looking at myself, I felt more alive than I thought possible.

"Your king knows you well," Mimic whispered.

This is why Karma wanted me to go shopping. He wanted to allow me to explore and discover this on my own. He was my support, and he knew me well enough to have all this made and set aside for me when or if I would be ready. This was his way of inviting me to the table of war he sat at if I chose to join. He knew I would stand on my own, in my own time. I doubt he expected me to move so quickly. Juni tapped the small silver crown that sat on my brow, and the leathers glowed for a moment. I tapped the other stone, and my dress reappeared. As Above, I loved this, it was so easy. I still looked at the reflection of the stark difference between a Warrior Queen and a small, simple woman who was Karma's queen, which shocked me. How could I be both?

I saw Lady Death vibrating, but quickly, that changed when a man stepped into the shop. I could see through his glamor. I knew the dragon behind it. Camron. Fuck.

# CHAPTER THIRTEEN

## Elsie

No time to think, only react, do the one thing they were all terrified of, but like hell if I was going to let him out of here. I poured magic into the stones, my leathers making sure to avoid the dragon stone, and sending out a *"Sorry, he ends here,"* hopeful that Karma would understand. Let's hope my body would react the way I need it to. I had been trained as a dragon for years, but as a human, hopefully, it would all just transfer over. Surely, my body could just follow simple directions.

Mimic and Juniper were idly chatting when I struck. With my daggers and leathers on my person, I grabbed for the one secured near my chest in the harness. Quick, silent, deadly. Dagger in hand, I took three small steps and plowed into Camron, knocking him off balance. His glamor wavered as he pulled more magic. I took advantage of his stumble. I caught him off guard, perfect. Sweeping his legs out from under him, I circled behind him with a quick sidestep and threw my small frame on his back, knees digging into his hips. I curled one arm under his chin, threatening his airway, holding a dagger at the vein in his neck. My body knew the way and did not fail, thanks to the Above for that one. I could feel my muscles starting to coil and strain. I was a master of pain. This was nothing as I held myself up, on his back, holding his life in my hands. Kill him.

"Elsie!" Juni shrieked. "What are you doing to that man?"

Oh, for the love of it all, this fucking glamor. If they thought I would attack a random person, surely, I would be labeled a risk and prove my bother right.

"Drop it! Now!" I commanded Camron.

I clenched against him tighter, cutting off some of his air. He dropped further to the floor, struggling for a breath. I adjusted to his body without breaking my hold. It was effortless. Disgusted I had to be this close to him. The thought of his blood covering my knives and breaking in my leathers, I shuddered, my core tight and my thighs slick. Killing Camron Mordryl was going to bring me to the edge of climax. A hysterical giggle escaped me as Camron tapped my arm, begging to be let go.

"Now is not the time to beg, Camron. Drop. The. Fucking. Glamor."

My voice was hard, level, and armor-piercing. Juni gasped as he dropped it. I did not drop him, though. Kill. Him. Kill him. My blade twitched, and I saw the blood before I noticed my hand had done the work. Carried out my desire, the longing in my core placated only a little bit. I wanted more. I glanced at the mirror. Blood poured from his neck. I looked and saw myself, Death hovering with a gaze of satisfaction. This had been too easy. I felt nothing except elation and a small bit of release. One down.

Satisfied, I dropped him, stepped back, and looked at Juniper.

She dropped to the ground, and that gold light radiated off her. I watched as the blood was sent back into his body. She spoke as she worked on healing him.

"Elsie, what the fuck?"

"Oh, for fuck's sake, are you telling me you think I was out of line?"

She met my eyes; hers were hard, and her voice was firm. "You are way out of line for this. Karma will deal with you later."

I scoffed. "No, Juni, he won't deal with me. If you think I'm going to be kept under a thumb, you are sadly mistaken. Camron should not be here. He is the fucking prince of—"

She snapped, "I know who he is!"

I stepped back, rage filling me, and all my unspoken thoughts began to pour. That was where she was going to draw a line? Murder? Of Camron Mordryl? They allowed actual torture in the streets? But killing him was too far? Oh, fuck this.

"No, you three just don't fucking get it. You three just kept 'building.' You three dedicated yourselves to your so-called peace. It's noble, but it is idealistic and unattainable. All that fantasizing about the day I would be found! I spent over a century learning how cruel life was. You all spent months being tortured. Fuck, my brother had it the worst, sleeping for years and then waking up to find his wings gone, and yet! And yet! You all kept looking for me?" I sneered at her; my rage was unrelenting.

"Did you invade? Did you burn cities? Did you look under every rock and corner on this forsaken continent? NO! That's the difference—you all find peace in harmony. If it looks good, it's peaceful, while I just saw you turn your back on a human out there! It's maddening. I find peace in violence and death. Some beings should be dead. That prick and his family are at the top of my fucking list, and if you think you three will stop me from being who I am, I'll disappoint you now. You will not stop me. I will burn everything that stands in the way, and I will do it with a fucking smile on my face. Blessed are those who stain their hearts for others. And I will stain my heart black if I must!"

Those had been words from so long ago. I had forgotten, but this rage brought her words back to me: Blessed are those who stain their hearts for others. Those words were spoken to me when I died. I had thrown myself over Clia to protect her from her father's wrath, but my body couldn't hold out that time. That was the second time I met the Lady of Death. Fuck. Fuck. Fuck.

Where is she? I spun, saw Death hovered by the door, and bolted for her. She moved like the wind, and I kept on running after her. Panting and my legs on fire, I heard Juniper screaming my name, demanding me to come back and help her with Camron. If she wanted to be his hero, I was going to leave her with him. Death led me out of town, then stopped and gave me a pointed glare.

"Oh, for fuck's sake! How am I supposed to know what you want from me?" She rolled her eyes, and if a hovering mist could look enraged, well, she was. She moved, and I swear I saw wings.

"Wings?" She only nodded in response.

Okay, fine, dragon. I funneled my magic into the stones on my brow, and nothing happened.

"What now?"

She just made the motion for wings again. Fine, it's all fine, I repeated to myself as I ripped the crown off and shoved it in the pouch at my hip. I felt the magic rise, and I let it, ripping my body apart. The pain and burning were a welcome, familiar feeling. I launched into the sky, following Death. We passed the estate and kept flying south. I soared over the land and felt free; the silence a welcome reprieve. Only the sound of the wind drowned out anything else. Why are the three of them so stupid, so feckless?

Death slowed, and I kept following, just allowing my mind to go blank as we flew further south. It wasn't until I saw some villages and familiar landmarks that I noticed we were going to the manor house.

We touched down in the dead, barren courtyard. Death took the outline shape of a human. I focused my magic, closing my eyes. Surely, I could do this; obviously, she thought I could. I felt smaller, focusing on my shape the one I saw in the shop mirror, all the details I loved in those moments, smaller still. Then I felt the leather, hands, arms, and legs. I opened my eyes and looked down.

"Holy shit, I fucking did it!"

Death was still a mist, but not for long. She formed a dark silhouette, and a mouth appeared with bright, bloodred lips.

"Took you long enough."

I froze because her voice was raspy and ethereal.

"You could talk this whole time?"

"Would you shut up and focus? Gods, damn it all," Death barked out, waving one of her skeletal yet fleshy hands.

*He will die, I promise you that. Let the spirit talk. We will talk later.*" Well, at least my inner psychopath was on my side.

"I let you have a choice, and you have been a thorn in my side for over a fucking century."

I couldn't hold myself back; I threw myself into the mist. She could not return or feel the embrace, but I needed her.

"Thank you, thank you for staying with me. Thank you for giving me the choice."

"Don't thank me yet. I have much to discuss." She slipped out and was before me again.

"We don't have long, pulling the remnants of death to appear and speak. You need to pull it together, Elsie. You are not wrong for feeling the way you do. In fact, I agree with you. You are correct, and I was happy to see that ugly beast fall at your hand. They are misguided, but that's only due to your mate."

I balked, "Karma? What do you mean?"

"Shut it!" I knelt, looked at her, and promptly shut my mouth.

"I would have ushered that beast to the afterlife; any of them, I will still escort them to the beyond, and you know that. Life is a cruel experience and an even crueler lord. According to what I have found, Life has gifted your mate with a second chance at life, or so Karma says, to experience more life and learn what it means to live. But with that gift comes a great cost. Your mate cannot take a life or create another one. It is not his fault. Yes, your family should have broken it down for you step by step, but truth be told, they may not even fully understand. Lord Life does not give without taking. He feels the experience of life is worth living, and for most, it is, but you know and have experienced that there are times it is not."

I nodded. *Please tell me more,* I begged silently.

"Life is a difficult spirit, but it is easy to understand why. He brings souls to this world, and they live, laugh, and fall in love. Some have beautiful, full lives, and even at the end, it is me, his wife, who walks with them in their dark hours. When they don't call for him, he fails to understand why they would not cling to him."

Lady Death was always so kind to me; her voice was soft, and she was full of knowledge. I was lucky to have a friend like her. I would never have made it without her. I felt my eyes burning, holding back tears as she spoke.

"Even the fullest and happiest of lives must end. That is the balance of it all. Life and Death are intertwined. Every religion, cult, empire, and kingdom clings to life while they live, but when I show up, they almost always abandon him, begging me to spare them. They don't call for his favor. They only ask me not to take them, and that is out of fear of the unknown that lies beyond. This is how it is for the overwhelming majority."

She paused and sighed.

"He has spent years trying to resurrect his favored souls to give them more, but to keep balance, he must take something from them as well, something they will need in life, and even with their second chance at life, they almost always squander it because of what they lost for the gift. Life gifted a Dragon King life but only without the ability to take or create life. Truly, it's brilliant. He forced a veracious species—and a male king of that species, no less—to start playing by his ideals of never taking a life, only enhancing it, and all while that king had an upbringing filled with such love and promise and the ability to see the good in everything and that all of life was worth living, each being was worthy of existence. Only your mate would be able to cope with Life's gift, and he's doing it exceptionally well."

I could feel my mouth drying as it hung open.

*"I think there is more to this than even Lady Death knows."* The voice was right; something was still amiss.

"Shut your mouth. You will catch flies." She winked and continued, her voice dripping in dark kindness.

"You, my dear, are far different from being given the gift of life. When I came to usher you to an afterlife, you were not afraid. Life had been so cruel to you, and you were not allowed to make one singular choice in your life. When I saw that you had given your life to save a girl who, at her core, hated you, tormented you, and forced you to my doorstep, I felt so much compassion for you, and the least I could do was offer you the choice of going with me or allowing you to stay. Especially since your soul was still hovering over her as I appeared to take you. Protecting her, the weaker one. You see, my dear child, you are blessed by me, favored by me. The magic you wield is a gift I negotiated out of the afterlives of your ancestors to give you more choices, more freedom. No one deserves a life as you have experienced. When you did not beg and only asked to stay, you simply were at peace. You did not move to my side to follow, I saw in your soul you wanted to stay, you held onto life, had made peace with its cruelty, and chose him anyway. Even if he did not know you were clinging to him. I, as his wife, saw it, saw you wish for him but were at peace with me all the same. You were in perfect balance, so I wanted nothing more than to bless you with whatever I could without taking a single thing from you, so I gifted you choice. Then I worked to bring you a far more powerful magic; bit by bit, I gave you more. I am sorry you had to suffer more until your magic came into full bloom, child, but I am so thrilled you kept choosing my Lord Life. My love for him runs deep, with you the only other soul I can say I have ever loved. I know you will bring him some peace."

I spoke softly, "Blessed are those who stain their hearts for others."

Death nodded, and the cool mist stroked my cheek. I stood up to look her in the eyes.

"Please don't ever apologize to me. You did more for me than anyone in my life." I choked on the reality of my words. She was the only one I knew who had tried so hard for me, for years.

*"Harsh, I have been doing my best."* I rolled my eyes at the voice in my mind and thought, *Your best? Your best would be showing your damn face.*

Her voice dropped, and all light was gone.

"You are blessed by me, the Lady of Death. You know me better than anyone alive. When I tell you the Necromancer must be stopped, I mean it. You, my dear sweet child, can look Death in the face and not cower. You choose each day to live. You walk, speak, with Death herself. The Necromancer is tormenting souls. He has done so when even Life himself is not cruel enough to force that miserable fate on souls. Fracturing souls into pieces, his daughter helping him in whatever sick way she can, breaking anyone so her father can claim them, only to fill more bodies with enough souls to power a body but remain in his control. He is acting as a god, not as a dragon. You, my dear, are my warrior. You must stop him. Life is being broken by this magic to a point where he refuses to usher more souls to this realm in fear that only more pain will find the souls he brings here. As of now, souls are finding their way to this realm by wandering. Most are those that should not be here, like the demons. I don't have that choice. I must take them to their afterlife. I will always find a soul after death, but this Necromancer is bending and breaking Life. It needs to end, and I need you to end it."

I dropped to one knee swiftly.

"Say less. I will end the Mors. I will wipe out their magic, or I will walk with you after doing my damn best."

I looked up, and she smiled and pointed behind me. Karma stood with Axl, who was greener than grass, while Karma was frozen in fear. Orion, had terror marking his face. Juniper, with red, teary eyes, and Cosmos in hand, who seemed more amused than anything.

"They see me, but our time is up. I need to get back to work. Get some rest." Her voice grew louder, filled with pride as she began to fade.

"Rise." I stood and turned to my family.

"Death's Warrior, right the wrongs and find true peace as Life springs forth from Death."

I smiled and watched her vanish. *"Well, at least she's still reasonable,"* the voice scoffed.

# CHAPTER FOURTEEN

## Elsie

stood facing this family I had found, unwavering. I will fight, in my full leathers, unfazed by their stares. I felt a warm tug on my right hand. I looked down and found Cosmos, and more worrisome yet, across the skin on my hand, black and white swirling lines. I pushed my sleeve up and found these markings up my arm. I pulled at my blouse and found they led up to my shoulder. Black, white, and gray swirls, like water, air, and fire swirling together, only marked in black, seamless lines.

I gripped the boy's hand and met his innocent gaze. He had come to me while full-grown men shied away. Typical. I pulled him up onto my hip. He touched my new markings.

"El-sie prt-ty," he sounded out. I felt bad for him. He was too big for his age, missing out on the fun and wildness of child-hood. Far too delayed to have friends his age but too old to play with others. I would be his friend. Everyone deserved at least one friend. Lady Death taught me that.

I giggled. At least he liked the markings, and it seemed he knew more words than they gave him credit for. I walked toward the men, bouncing Cosmos on my hip. He was far too big for this. Had he grown again?

"Well, how much of that do I need to repeat?"

Axl promptly vomited. I wish he would find a stronger stomach. "I think I got it," he mumbled.

"I hope you can forgive me. I will take responsibility for my words to you, Juniper. I should not have said those things." I needed to make nice; I needed to figure out my next steps to burn the Mors down, and this family was going to be my best bet.

*"Or you could trust me?"* I shook the voice off. No, I wasn't about to trust anyone except Death herself.

Karma's voice broke. "What did she take?" There went some of my composure.

"Oh! So, you do know what your gift cost you, and yet I am the bad guy?" I felt my eyes roll as the mocking words left my mouth.

Cosmos squirmed, and I dropped to the dead grass and set him down. Cosmos went to Orion next, who was still filled with terror. And Juniper was clutching Orion with a death grip, looking like she may faint.

"What did she take?" Karma's voice was broken by sobs as his wings sagged.

"She took nothing, never has. She has only ever given me peace."

He looked up with tears running down his face. "That cannot be true."

I strode over to him and sighed.

"I have known her longer than anyone should. She has never taken from me. We have the same goal to save the men we love, the broken families, tortured souls, and I will, but I need you to let me."

Karma's eyes met mine. "No, I cannot allow you to kill for me."

"Oh, you sweet, stupid man. I'm not killing for you; I will be killing for her, returning souls to where they belong. You, Karma, are the reward. I will end it, whatever the cost, even if the cost is my family turning their backs on me."

*"And they will. Your power will shove them away."*

Axl froze, and Karma was stricken, dropping sobbing on the ground.

"What is the true nature of his magic, Empress?" I looked at Orion. He had regained some composure, but the title seemed strange.

"Necromancy. That is why Cliantha was trained to heal bodies and not souls. She can't heal them like Juniper, she—"

Axl cut in. "That's wretched."

"Oh, good, we agree," I said indifferently.

"We would never turn on you, but I can't stand by you, and I can't just send soldiers to battle without their leader backing them. What kind of king would I be if I stayed home and allowed everyone to fight for me?" Karma screamed and sobbed, his son clinging to him now.

*"The bastard really knows how to put on a show."* When I find out who this voice is, I'm going to give him hell.

I pulled Karma's head into my lap, stroking his hair.

"I can't have death on my hands."

I cut in firmly yet kindly, mimicking Axl as best I could. "But that's directly, isn't it? You can command an army. You gave Axl power to lead it. Death is a part of life, dear. I am not asking you to kill with me. I'm not asking you to give up your gift. Fuck, I want you to live, with all of us, for as long as possible, and I want it to end with you in one hand and Death holding my other as we cross into whatever lies beyond. I want to enjoy life with you, with Juniper, Axl, Cosmos, and even this grumpy fucking Grandpa Fae lord over here. Live with me; let me carry the burden you cannot. I can and will shoulder it."

Orion gripped his nose, tears in his eyes. Axl draped himself over Karma's body.

"I will carry it with you, sister. You are not alone, and Karma, don't you dare argue with us. You are just as key. You are everything we cannot be. Let us be what you cannot."

Karma stopped sobbing. "Okay, I will do what is right, and you will fight for what is right."

Juniper spoke softly and guardedly. "I will do what is right. We will build and heal and negotiate as we have done. Axl, Elsie, burn it down."

I looked at Juniper. She found her resolve and stood proud, wiping her wet, tearstained hands on her dress, looking at the decrepit manor we once called home. I stood and extended my hand to Karma.

"Come, my King. We have a war to end."

Axl rose next, Karma followed. Axl claimed a spot next to Juniper. I stood next to Orion, who held Cosmos. Karma gripped my hand, and we all looked at the manor house. We formed a line in front of this once-beautiful home, now a scar on this land. The decay only more evident by the untamed overgrowth. A war started here, and we would end it.

Fuck Life. We would make it worth living. We were going to make our own damn rules, gifts be damned. We would do what was right, and I would also get revenge; this could not be any better. I saw the white mist hovering next to Karma.

"Lord of Life, your lady sends her regards."

Karma flinched. "You can see him?"

"I can."

Life hovered in front of me now with accusatory eyes. I lifted my hand and rolled my sleeve.

"I chose you, clung to your essence without ever knowing your kindness, and yet she blessed me when you did not come."

If a mist could sob, it was sobbing and then vanished. Hopefully, going to Death and thanking her. I adjusted my gaze back to the manor house.

"Juniper, I agree. Let's burn it down," I said confidently.

Axl spoke up next, brimming with joy like he had just been untethered. "Burn it, destroy it. We will not be held back by our past any longer."

Cosmos added in his small, tiny voice, "Burn."

Juniper cried again, "We will make this place a southern point of rule in our kingdom, appoint a lord and lady to oversee it, and reclaim wealth and prosperity."

Karma said softly, clearly still shaken, "Burn it, build it, make it a southern powerhouse, reclaim it, open all trade, and bring peace to the villages that were so kind when we grew up beside them."

I nodded. It was a step we were going to take together. My patient violence was wearing out. I was fueled by rage and justice. This place needed to burn, the Mors needed to burn, and this family's stupid ideals and rules needed to be burned. It all needed to fall.

"Axl, transfer my magic between everyone. We burn it together, and we build it together."

Orion was moved and crying softly. I felt Axl's magic pulling on me, and I released it. I saw them all flinch as they felt the fire. I held up my hand, and everyone followed, including Cosmos and Orion.

"NOW!"

Each of us poured a crimson fire onto the remnants of what was and what could have been. Burning my feelings of sorrow and anguish over the life I would never get to have, the life that was taken from me. I loved her, but I would never forgive her for this. She would pay dearly.

*Cliantha, I will come for you. And I will give you the ultimate gift in your life: Death.*

"Els, you have to take it back," Axl said quickly.

I absorbed my magic back as Axl sent it back into me. The fire was angry, vindictive, burning hotter than ever before. I allowed it to rip free of my body, wings unfolding as I leaped into the sky and let it rain so hot it was turning the stone into liquid. The power of unleashed divine fury flowing through me grew even hotter for revenge. I gazed down, and all that remained was melted rock, ash, and my family covered in snow. This was the power females could wield. Rage.

I landed next to them, focused like I had done with Death, and returned to them in my leathers, feeling more like who I was supposed to be than ever before.

"Shall we fly home?" I asked as Orion opened a Fae gate.

"I will not. We are going back to the cabin." He stepped through the gate.

It was just the four of us again.

"I am so sorry." Juniper hugged me. I couldn't help but flinch as she wrapped her arms around me.

"It's all right. We all could have done better."

Karma pulled us in with his wings.

"I never want us to fight like this again. No running off, no cruel words. We are together, always. Yes. We fly home, we send a message to our kingdom, and their four ruling dragons soar in the sky. Far from home, they travel to protect the entire kingdom, not just Otium."

The other three of us nodded while I felt my eyes roll. It was going to take more than burning down an old house and kind words to get me back on their side. We all stepped back, each taking our forms.

Karma was brilliant as always, rainbows casting, towering over me. Juniper was elegant, with curved horns and delicate wings, a soft gold with a blue hue to her entire body. Axl was as menacing as I was dark as night; his crafted wings of metal and canvas decorated with silver studs complemented the silver-and-gold gears within the wings, and the black canvas matched his matte black scales; the pink slash across his face the only blemish. I saw my reflection in Karma's wings. I was far smaller, perhaps only standing at Karma's shoulders, whereas the others were at a far more mature height, also standing above me. I was small, but I was lethal. I carried the pink scars, the marks of chains and beatings, marks of who I was, and I could see the beauty of them, like fine jewelry that held a story. And now the gray and white swirls across my foreleg. A reminder that I was favored by Death. I was her warrior. I would be that warrior. I was done holding back. They perhaps had hoped I would recover my old self and be soft-spoken and sweet as I once had been, but that naive girl died on the grass of this manor, and in her place stood a monster comforted by the darkness and malice held deep within the hearts of those who had been scored.

I roared and launched into the sky. The others followed. We formed an arrowhead formation: Karma spearheading, I on the left, Juniper on the right, and Axl at the tail. We took the long way home, soaring over villages of humans and swooping down, exciting the children who looked into the sky. We flew over vampire territories that clapped as we flew past, over dens of werewolves who howled, elves beat their shields as we passed, the Fae sent up fireworks crafted from magic. The other dragon lords we passed looked surprised, not offering support, but this kingdom's people were ready to be united; they would support us. This was our proof that the rest of the kingdom was looking to us and Otium for the future.

Damn the dragons, damn the males. Our kind held control for too long, especially the insatiable power—hungry males. That would change whether they were willing or not, but first, war. The fleeting release I had with Camron's blood spilling . . . I needed more, the kill, bathing in blood, making them pay.

*"Bloodlust looks good on you, Empress."*

# CHAPTER FIFTEEN

## *Elsie*

We got home as the sun began to touch the water. Juni went straight inside and started dinner. Lamb. Okay, maybe I did have preferences after all. But I was not going to ask her to make another dish, not after the day we all just had. I took up my normal spot on the cliff and, this time, let my feet hang from it as I looked out to the water. What a fucking day. Karma and Axl went to the guest house. Why? Sex, maybe? Shit, where was Camron? I snickered to myself; they could have a threesome with him.

*"That would be hot."*

I was carefree about who was having sex with who at this point. None of that mattered. Why should I allow it to bother me? Axl had his wings ripped off. Karma played nursemaid to him for years; Axl had fallen for Karma, pretended to fall for Juniper to save her. Karma was forced to rape Juniper while Axl watched to bring Cosmos to life. Karma found his parents dead under the weight of their own guilt. The three of them found love in their torment, then only to have Life "gift" Karma with a second chance while also tying his hands behind his back. I was a prisoner of war for over a century. Lady Death had blessed me how? Negotiation with ancestors? Gods, that was enough to spin your head around a few times over. Who in the actual fuck cared who was having sex with who or what? Not me. I laughed out loud at the absurdity of it all.

*"It is quite the most ridiculous thing I have seen."*

I heard some heavy footfalls, no doubt Karma's. I turned with a smile. Oh, as Above, Camron. Wait, why? I scurried to my feet, thankful I was in leathers or he would have gotten a show.

*"Kill him again."*

"Death looked good on you," I said coldly.

He only nodded, walked past me, and took a seat on the edge of the cliff. He was still thin, lacking luster, and even his hair had lost its sheen. He ran his hand through it.

"Will you allow me the chance to speak with you, friend?"

I growled. NO, damn it. As much as I wanted to hate him, I had seen him waver from time to time, not just at that wretched table when tears fell from him.

"Your king said I could find you here."

"THE king, not mine. He belongs to his people just as much as he belongs to his family," I retorted, plopping down on the cliff, allowing my legs over the ledge again.

*"YOU OWE HIM NOTHING."*

I glanced out to the water and, looking down along the cliffs, saw some mermaids playing with humans in the tide pools below. I locked that voice deep in my mind where I was only bothered by its muffled groans.

"The king and his command are much more forgiving than you, you know," he said as he jabbed an elbow playfully into my ribs. I hissed and smacked his shoulder, making sure to drag claws over it and see the violet blood spring from the cuts.

"I was told you know far more about my family than even I did, courtesy of the friend you keep." He waved his hand toward my right hand, the markings of Death's Warrior streaking my skin. I pushed up my sleeve and held my arm up in the light.

"Yes, she's a good friend, gave me some pretty beautiful artwork."

Camron scoffed. "Elsie Pax, Lost Princess, the Dragon of Death and Darkness, Queen of Kingdom Rexarius, and Death's Warrior. How many titles do you need?"

I laughed and mused.

"I think Elsie, Death's Warrior, works just fine."

Camron laughed and lay back in the lush grass.

"All right, so what gives? Why are you here, and why is my family stupid enough to keep you out of chains?" I asked.

He shrugged. "No idea about that second part, but I did come here to try to track down Karma—or you, for that matter—and tell you, I want out."

I blinked. "Come again?"

He sighed. "I want out. I need out. I want—I need to stand with you all against Mordryl."

I fixed my gaze on the horizon.

"Why now?"

He sat up, and a single tear slipped from his face.

"They killed her. My mate, Aleah, they killed her. It sounds like they were attempting to fracture her soul, but Lady Death was swifter. You know when something dies, you can kind of feel a lingering? That didn't happen for Aleah—"

"You were there?"

"I was, in your chains. I had refused Cliantha control of the army. They turned on Aleah, an attempt to force my hand. She was in the cell across from you. I doubt you ever knew that's where she was, though. It was so swift. She was there, they stabbed her, and she was gone. It was hardly a lethal blow, but she must have run as soon as Death came for her. And I am thankful she won't suffer anymore." He sighed.

"I know Aleah would want me to live and avenge her. So, I escaped and mark my words I will avenge her."

It sounded good, but this was Camron. *Was this even true?* I wondered. My family may be blind, but I was not, and I wouldn't pretend I was, not anymore, not for anyone.

I broke my gaze from the water and turned to Camron, allowing my fiery gaze to meet him. I knew his games; this was certainly one of them.

"You are choosing Life. I hope he knows and can see it."

"You speak as if you know that spirit as well."

I shrugged and held up my arm. "I do."

Camron gasped. "Do you know what happens when we die?"

I laughed. "Death has only told me she takes souls to an afterlife. What that means, I don't know, but what I do know is we get one life here, and we should choose to live it. It's a gift, after all."

Camron sighed. "That's both disturbing and comforting."

I shrugged. Maybe it was for most, but I think those who could appreciate life and all it has to offer would find solace in that.

More footfalls. I turned to find Axl and Karma.

"You're welcome in our home, Camron." Axl ground out.

I gasped.

"Yes, Els, in our home. You can object if you wish," Axl said with borderline indifference. His true self was hidden from the rest of the world. That pissed me off, too; he shouldn't have to hide his love for Karma or Juniper. Hell, if he wanted to fuck a tree at this point, I wouldn't question it. It would certainly be less drama.

I looked at Camron, and he seemed shocked as well.

"Well, if you fuck this up, I'll just kill you. Again." I shrugged, stood up, and headed toward the estate doors.

Karma caught up quickly and whispered in my ear, "I don't trust this one, but he's good to sit at the war table in the morning, also . . ."

He pulled me into him, spinning me to face him. "You look like this in your leather, acting as the blade of a mighty sword for this kingdom. I don't think I have ever been this hard for you in my life," he breathed, growling into my ear.

My core went wet instantly. Whether it was my boiling anger for allowing Camron into the house, or just my depravity wanting to fuck Karma right there while Camron watched me come for Karma and never for him, I didn't know. It would be a lie if I said I did not enjoy the sight of him trying to hold back and keep his cock hidden; it must be uncomfortable. He deserved at least that. I swelled. I could feel everything igniting. He laughed.

"You will have to wait," I growled back, kissing Karma's cheek.

Dinner was idle chatter over the lamb Juniper prepared, talk of trade with Juniper's father, and how marvelous it was that they had fashioned such a great trade deal. Their acting was flawless. I kept my mouth shut. Karma lied flawlessly, saying he had given Juni to Axl since they had found love, and he was, after all, a merciful king. Axl's voice was deep and gruff, also a well-practiced show, while Juniper made sure she was taking her place as the female of the house and serving them, plate after plate, drink after drink. I almost felt the need to applaud their acting. They didn't want me to see this yet. But here it was, the act, an award-winning performance. All to protect what they held dear. Yeah, I would fight with daggers and spill blood, but then they were fighting just as hard, only differently. My way was far simpler and far more action-orientated.

*"Dinner and a show. My, my how intriguing."*

When the males had their fill, they retired to the great room, and I caught Juni at the sink. "Let me help."

She nodded.

We washed dishes in silence while the three suddenly alpha males started a game of three-sided chess, a game that seemed impossible for me to even begin to comprehend.

Juni whispered, "It's strategy, not only a game, they learn a lot about someone by the way they play." I nodded. Did she think I was dense?

I would not risk my voice; I could easily slip up. The boys were deep in battle over the game board. It was clear Axl was winning. Camron was disorganized, and Karma sat somewhere between the two. Just looking at the game made my head hurt.

Juni brought them more wine, and I settled at the long table and stared out the window. She set a glass down for me and took a seat next to me, also just gazing out at the moon and stars. As my gaze covered the garden, I saw what I could have sworn were two silver eyes looking at me, but as soon as I blinked, they were gone. It was a crystal-clear night. I felt a chill. Seated at the table of women now was Death.

I tipped my head down and flashed my eyes toward the boys. She blinked and vanished. Then it was another chill, for fuck's sake. I looked at the boys, and hovering next to Karma was Life. Karma tilted his head toward the game and took his hand to his shoulder, crossing his chest. He looked tired but acknowledged Life, who blinked and vanished. These damn spirits—sometimes, they could just get under your skin. Especially while I was stuck, impatiently waiting for Karma to take me to bed. I looked back at the window, watching him now in the reflection. I wasn't about to let the voice back in; it needed to chill out. I needed space for my own thoughts. Being able to shut it out, though, only con-firmed it was a magic user, and I was not crazy. That felt oddly refreshing, not being crazy. I resigned myself to this now: This was a being in my head, a sick, twisted one, who also happened to be supportive and a voice of reason most days. What was he? His goals? Why did he care about me?

Those were questions for another day, and I shifted all my attention back to Karma. He was beautiful, always shirtless, a male above all others, wings drooping slightly, his relaxed, arro-gant gaze on the board.

"Check," he said.

His voice rough and strained, he met my gaze in the reflec-tion, and the corner of his mouth twitched as he looked back toward the game. He stretched, his muscles tightening all over his body as he let out an indifferent, fake yawn. He took his hand to his trousers and pulled them away, smoothly covering his growing erection. How am I supposed to just sit here, growing hotter for him by the second?

"Tired, King?" Camron challenged.

Karma barked out a laugh. "After the day I had, I'm exhausted."

"Couldn't tell by the way you were eye-fucking my sister," Axl's gruff voice let out.

Juni snorted wine out of her nose as she choked. I met his gaze back in the reflection for less than a second.

"Can't help it, General. She just does it for me. I mean, like you're not eyeing my ex-wife all the same." I kept the amusement off my face, the fake titles, and lies pouring off them.

Camron blushed and coughed. "You lot are a wild bunch."

There it was; I could slide in. I will not be like Juniper, always a silent wallflower.

"You have no idea." I grinned warmly.

Camron made a move on the board, and Axl and Karma both jumped and yelled, "Checkmate!"

Karma grinned, clearly triumphant, I think? Camron sighed, tipped his glass to them, and downed the whole thing. Juni moved swiftly but unhurriedly to a cabinet by the foyer and took out a set of keys. She handed them to Axl. I was mesmerized, but this performance would all seem so natural to an outsider: just royals playing a game and drinking, things we often saw at our manor. Perfect hosts, minus the rabid black female dragon who wanted to end them all in one way or another.

Axl handed the keys to Camron.

"To the guest house. We fly out at eight a.m. Do you still want a seat at the table?"

Camron gripped the key, and I saw his eyes flash. It was brief, so brief I almost missed it; it was like he had just won something. It was not the look of sad, forlorn Camron, but something more. Camron stood.

"Of course I do. They need to pay for what they did to Aleah."

Sounded right, but something was still off. Only talking about Aleah, not souls overall. He used 'them,' not naming them, his father and sister. I couldn't tell why, but it did not sit right with me. I did not know this game very well, the one they called strategy, tact, or cleverness, so I kept my mouth shut and my gaze out the window.

Axl nodded and gestured for Camron to follow him. They reached the foyer, and Camron turned to me and Karma.

"Thank you, friends."

I growled at the use of his words but waved, watching the reflection, and they left. Juni began cleaning, and I watched Axl lead Camron to the door of the guest house. He shook his hand, a mistake on Camron's part. Axl turned back and caught my gaze with an evil smile gleaming across his face.

Axl entered the house and, in his regular higher voice, said, "Karma, wards, NOW!"

Karma snapped his fingers, and you wouldn't know it, but I could feel it. They were clear, not milky like battle barriers. Karma sank down into the chair and pulled out a flask from its underside.

"Well, that was unpleasant," he muttered, clearly annoyed as he gulped from the flask. Juni just dropped to the floor and let out a scream of frustration. It was loud and shrill. Karma groaned, and Axl also just started to scream into the void, joining Juni on the floor.

"What the fuck are you doing?" I asked. They didn't stop, and it was incredibly annoying.

"They do this. They say it helps them get it all out. Whatever. Whiskey?"

I nodded, and Karma tossed me the flask. I drank the liquid. It burned, but I welcomed it and drank again while my brother and Juniper just yelled and screamed. Karma sank to the floor, taking pillows from the chairs and hugging them to his head.

"Man, you guys really know how to kill a boner, don't ya?"

*"He is not wrong about that."*

Karma attempted to scream over them. I took another gulp of the whiskey.

"Well, if you can't beat 'em, join 'em, I guess."

"Oh, please fucking don't, Els."

I laughed and just started screaming. My brother and Juni stopped, looking me in the eyes. I dropped to my knees, lay back on the stone floor, and looked at them. They nodded and started up again, and I joined them. Yeah, they were right; it was nice to just let it out. Karma groaned and drank more, apparently from a second hidden stash. I laughed at his expense. And then we all just went quiet. I pulled my crown from my pouch and held the stone for that basic black dress, and it appeared. I looked at Karma. His eyes were hungry, and he adjusted his trousers again. Clearly, his killed erection didn't last long. I stood up and headed to the west wing.

"Night," I called over my shoulder as I passed Axl and Juni, still a crumpled mess on the floor. I stopped in the center of the foyer and looked at the paintings of our parents.

Karma joined me and looked at them. "What is it?"

I spoke without thinking, "I want to move them and place the four of us under the crest together, and it should read 'Blessed are those who stain their hearts for others.'"

Karma flexed his wings and scooped me up with a massive smile.

"I will commission that immediately." He turned and carried me to our room, our bed, in our house.

"Wards?" I asked.

Karma nudged the door with his foot and scoffed. "Please, you think I wasted time not learning defensive magic after my gift was given to me? Nothing in or out till I command it." He stepped into our room and set me down.

He snapped again. "And that one is for sound, so no one will hear how you scream my name."

I giggled, ran, and jumped onto the bed.

*"I can still hear you. Scream his name tonight, Firebird, while thinking of me, your monster sheathed in the darkness."*

Well, enjoy the show, you fucking creep. I shook off what the voice had said, not wanting to admit how much I was starting to love that voice. So, I allowed the whiskey to do its job and laid back into the mountain of fluffy white fabric.

# CHAPTER SIXTEEN

## Elsie

Karma came for me but hesitated, looking into my eyes. I ran my hands down the planes of his chest, his cut, and V-shaped midriff, up again, then down his arms, drinking in his cool, soothing touch. As much as I enjoyed looking at him, I caught myself searching for the scars. And I was unable to find a single one. His scent of pine and sea air filled my senses. His scent was ever-changing, but it always held that salty sea air. I would never get tired of him, touching him, letting him fill my soul with everything he had to offer. He sighed, his eyes soft and searching while he gazed into mine.

"Els, please don't be offended, but tell me how you want me tonight." I blinked, surprised. Was it not obvious?

*"Can't even read his mate, pathetic."*

I wanted to bend, break, shatter, and scream for him. I needed to escape into a place so far within my mind that no one could reach it except myself. He was mine. Damn this voice; it was wrong. I wanted him to give himself to me passionately, fully, deeply; so deep my body was already soaked and tightening for him at the mere thought of it. The whiskey blurred my vision and thoughts. I just needed him to send me to release so I could finally know some semblance of peace.

I wanted to be his; I wanted to not feel anything except him. I wanted him to drop me into a place where I could only feel the pleasure he could bring me, the weight of his body over mine, his cock filling me and taking its place within me. How was I supposed to admit to all that? How was I supposed to say I wanted to be his?

"I want you in a way the world no longer exists."

That was the best I could do. He nodded, and I tried not to be upset by his lack of words. He let out a breath, still smelling of whiskey, as he crashed his lips into mine. I welcomed his lips, soft and lush, then parted my lips for his tongue to invade past my teeth. He kept his mouth on mine, taking me in, softly biting my lower lip, dropping his hands, and running them over my body and up the skirt of my dress. I moaned against his mouth as his hands explored my body.

*"So vanilla. Come on, give me more than this."* Faceless asshole taunting me in my mind.

Karma groaned and pulled back, now looking at me.

"Well, am I going to ruin this dress or—"

I cut him off breathlessly. The voice wanted a show, didn't it? Fine. I'd give him one he wouldn't forget.

"Ruin it, and me."

Karma needed no more encouragement as he came back for my mouth harder, trailing his hands over my breasts and kissing down my neck. I heard the fabric rip. As he pulled it apart with his teeth and hands, I could see the hungry look in his eyes. A welcoming chill passed over me as all the fabric was tossed aside. I relaxed deeper into our bed and closed my eyes, just wanting to feel him. He took the hardened peak of my breast into his mouth, sucking and biting while he gripped the other and kneaded the flesh firmly, yet softly all the same. I sucked in a breath and sighed; his hands, his mouth—it was all-consuming.

*"My poor, starved empress. Just a little affection, and you crumple under him."*

Karma kissed and licked his way over to my other breast and drew up a long lick between them, then kissed the hollow of my throat, his hands trailing lower. Breathlessly, Karma spoke in unison with the voice, *"You are glowing, elegant, and captivating."*

The voice only mocked Karma as he spoke. How did the voice know Karma's words before he spoke them? Had the voice been watching Karma too?

Karma moaned against me as his hand slid down and brushed over my lower lip, parting my slit. He kept kissing my neck, biting, toying with a breast in his hand while using the other to further part my thighs, allowing him better access to the wet folds between them. His fingers gently circled that oh-so-sensitive ball of nerves. My breath caught, and he moved his hand away. I opened my eyes. He was pulling back. With a grin, he licked his fingers. His crown glimmered in the moonlight, and everything faded away as I looked at him.

I drank the sight of him, his male organ standing proudly erect as he stepped off the bed. When did he lose his trousers? Karma kept looking at me and, with a menacing smile, grabbed me by the back of my knees and hauled me effortlessly to the edge, dropping to his knees. On his knees, for me. Throwing my legs on his shoulders, he dove between my legs, sucking my firm small delicate flesh into his mouth.

I gasped and threw my hands over my head, gripping and clawing at the sheets. Looking above at the canopy, I saw the eyes from the garden. The voice was watching. I wasn't sure why I had not fully believed it before. Maybe I was still hoping for some insanity, not that I was being hunted by some psychopath who was starting to win me over—to the point that I missed the voice when I couldn't hear him. Embarrassing. I pushed it away, but I loved the way the eyes were hovering half closed. It seemed the silver was being eaten by the dark fabric, camouflaged in the jewels. The voice wanted a show; he wanted to see what Karma could do to me. Well, let me show you. Let me show this silver-eyed monster what I look like when it's not him tormenting me.

Shutting my eyes tight, I blocked out everything around me, save for Karma between my legs. I was writhing under his touch and his tongue. His hand gripped my hip, holding it in place while he took his fingers and plunged them into me, sending a new wave of pleasure through me. My hips bucked, and my core tightened around him, spilling over. I moaned in pleasure. He pulled back and kissed the front of my pubic bone.

"That's my sweet girl," he purred as he stood. I was panting. Fuck, so good. *More.*

"Karma," I whispered.

"Oh, sweet woman, say it again."

His tip rested at the entrance as he stroked the tip up and down, drawing breath after breath from me as it bushed over my clit.

"Karma," I moaned again.

His breath caught, and effortlessly, his beautiful cock disappeared inside of me. I couldn't help the words coming from my mouth.

"Oh, fuck, Karma, yes, please."

As I was begging for him, Karma dug his fingers into my hips and thrust in deeper, harder. I felt his shaft fill me, penetrating so deep that my body was coiling and clenching onto him. He hit the same place inside me, sending wave after wave of fluid around his cock and sending my muscles into vicious spasms. I clutched my legs around his hips, drawing him deeper than I thought possible. I opened my eyes as I reached for him. I wanted more, needed more.

He smiled and winked, grabbing my wrist and pinning it above my head as he leaned over me. Fuck, I love this and him. I closed my eyes and reached up blindly for his shoulder, following the curves of his well-defined muscles to the back of his neck, and pulled him into me. I needed him everywhere all at once. His kisses were hurried, and his thrusting came quicker as he pulled back just enough to slide the hand at my hip to my clit.

Oh. My. Fucking. Stars.

I bucked against him, the start of orgasm filling every part of my being. I saw stars, not just in the canopy above the bed, but behind my closed lids as well. His movement was deregulated for just a moment when he roared, and I could feel him emptying into me. He was breathless when I met his gaze.

"What?" I asked.

"Nothing, just looking at how perfect you are."

I felt my cheeks flush. Karma slid out and turned, walking to the bathroom. I sat up and looked out the window, hearing the water flowing from the bathroom. Disappointment and longing settled where he left me empty.

He returned and picked me up with grace, then carried me to the tub again like he had before, allowing me to test and heat the water to my ideal temperature. He stepped in and settled in behind me, pulling me to him. We sat in the silence, and I had no thoughts, just relaxed against him in the warm water, allowing him to wash me like he had before. Bliss.

*"Beautiful performance. Still vanilla."* What the fuck did 'vanilla' even mean? I was slightly annoyed at the voice and my lack of unconscious thought.

Once the water began to cool to the point I was catching a small chill, I got out, took the soft towel close to my body, and turned to look at him. He was nearly asleep.

"Karma?" I whispered softly.

"Mmm, yeah?" he muttered.

"Let's go to bed."

He groaned, "All right."

He got out of the tub, walked to the bed, and collapsed.

"Come here, please, Els."

I did, and I lay down facing him. He rolled to his side, and one wing and arm came around me as he pulled me into him while he intertwined his leg with mine, almost as if he needed every bit of him holding me. "What troubles you?" I asked softly.

He sighed. "When I saw you with Death at the manor, for a moment, I thought you had died. Then I thought you had made a deal with her, and I wouldn't blame you if you had. I felt like I had failed you, not only lost you but failed to bring you one ounce of life to hold on to, and that was some of the worst pain I have ever felt, that I failed to bring you joy."

He paused, let out a breath. "Tomorrow is going to be awful. I have an idea, but if you don't want to go, you do not have to."

I stopped him by bringing my hand to his face. He opened his eyes and met mine.

"I want to go."

He sighed. "I figured. I have much to tell you about what to expect, but I will not talk of politics in bed with you. We can save that for daybreak, for now." He pulled me closer. "Sleep."

I lay there for a few minutes, just watching his eyes grow heavy and fall. My poor Karma, exhausted by today's events and what lay ahead. As I faded into my sleep, checking the canopy and the window for those silver eyes, I found none and wished I had. With sleep claiming my mind, the only thoughts I had were how many lies had I been told, and how will I bring the world to its knees?

# CHAPTER SEVENTEEN

## Elsie

I awoke to Karma brushing his cool hand against my cheek.

"Good morning," he purred into my ear.

My body was a tad stiff as I came out of dreamless sleep. I don't think I had slept that well in ages. Less than a week with Karma and my entire world had changed. The prisoner-turned-warrior, a queen in a king's house, and that queen was about to learn how the king played his games. I would be lying to myself if I said I was not nervous about the way today would go. But it was just a day of observation.

*"Sure, milady, just observation,"* my invisible friend joked.

Karma pulled himself close and kissed me. It was soft and sweet, a morning-after kiss filled with admiration. It was a shame I was still disappointed and left wanting more.

"We need to get dressed, and I will fill you in over breakfast with Axl and Juni."

I just nodded and wiped my eyes, yawning and stretching. I looked down at myself, still not happy with the faint scars, small frame, and gaunt features. Would my chest fill out more, or my hips, for that matter? Could I be curvy and beautiful, or would I be stuck like this forever?

*"Stop that."*

Karma pulled himself from the bed, groaning and stretching, while I sat up, taking in the sight of him. I don't think I would ever tire of seeing him naked, always breathtaking, wings always casting rainbows over the room. He strode to the massive armoire, opened it, and pulled out some white fabric. His crown glowed as the fabric molded to his body, clothing I had never seen him wear. He was covered with a straight-lined jacket and collared shirt that hugged him perfectly, with the trousers pressed with perfect lines. The white was only broken with a black tie and the black thread holding it all together. In its usual space over his heart was the crest of the kingdom.

"I hate this fucking monkey suit, such an inconvenient thing to wear," he mumbled, stretching his wings out, a bit constricted at the base by the fabric. He looked older, more imposing.

"Then, why are you wearing it?" I was a bit mesmerized as he pulled his white hair back in a low-set bun with a solid black onyx dagger running through it, with only a small red stone embedded in the hilt.

Glumly, he explained, "The company we keep today are the royals from Fonsfrick." He let out a sigh. "And they are not like the kinds of our kingdom."

I nodded. "What do you want me to—"

He laughed, cutting me off.

"You, are the surprise. Your leathers will do just fine."

I grinned. Correction: Today was going to be an interesting day.

Breakfast was a combination of Axl and Karma giving me a rundown of the game to be played today. In essence, it was a bit like Karma was the ever-merciful king, allowing his lords and ladies to make deals among themselves. Even humans were allowed to partake in any negotiations they wished, yet husbands still ruled their wives; ladies were still second-class for now. It would be most likely that even though all his dragon lords were invited to this emergency meeting, they would not join except for one lord who seemed to understand and wished for change. The rules for this meeting were simple: Don't kill anyone, no magic, that would include Axl's magic; don't react until Karma gave the signal. Wait for Orion at the estate. I could handle four simple rules, right?

*"One more rule, Firebird, stay in the shadows, and know that if you need me, I will be there."*

Some day and soon, I needed to sit down and have a conversation with this damn voice and set some freaking rules. The voice laughed.

*"You can shut me out anytime you like, but I do love the chase."*

I cringed. Not at the voice but at the fact I was beginning to enjoy this game of voyeur and hunter, where I was the prey. It felt natural and easy. It was easy to be weak, and I wanted to lean into that side of me more and more. But outside my head, I had to be fierce and threatening while wearing pink to "tone it down a bit." "You don't want to scare everyone," Juniper had said over and over while shopping and at breakfast this morning. I did, though; I didn't want or need more onlookers. In leather, beings only glanced and tucked their heads back down; in a dress, they stared, the scars and ugliness of my body on display.

*"I told you to stop that."*

I walked out the front doors of the estate as Karma dropped the wards, Juni at my side. I wore a simple little pink sundress stolen from Juniper's closet. She filled it out much better with her full figure. Karma winked at me and had a smirk across his face as Camron approached.

Axl grunted, "Ready?"

Camron nodded, looking a sickly shade of gray, all emotion devoid from his eyes.

"Have a nice day, ladies," Karma said, bowing to Juni, and I stood still while Juni made a leg-sweeping gesture, to which Axl rolled his eyes behind Camron.

"Not very submissive, eh, Kar? Sorry my sister fucked that one up for ya," Camron attempted to joke, but Karma met his gaze.

"Why should MY mate be submissive?" He asked a question, but it did not sound like one. Camron shrugged, growing impatient. It was Axl who broke into the sky, surprising Camron that he would not be carried. The wings were not just for show, and now Camron knew that. If he kept that from Clia, I would kill him again just for that. She deserved to fly, just once. Camron followed.

"Pack extra daggers, my sweet. You may need them," Karma whispered and laughed, then exploded into the sky. I watched them fade into the east, Karma not only leading but lighting the way, casting rainbows over the ground.

"Shall we get some sun?" Juniper asked softly.

I giggled; Juni already knew me well. We walked to the cliffs, and I shifted my magic that would bring the leather to my body. Juni pulled her little brown bag to her center and pulled out six more pristine daggers for me. I smiled. We sat down, just enjoying the sea breeze and sunshine.

"You know it's going to be hard, right?"

*"For you, it won't be."*

I nodded, speaking slowly, allowing some of my worry to creep into my voice. A false worry, but I was not about to show any real emotions around anyone. I was living with a king, so would be looked at as a queen. However, the torture of women was still rampant. Were lesser beings also second-class? Who knows what other males do? Karma was kind, and Axl would step in should he try to hurt me.

"It's going to be more than hard, Juni. I must play a game I hardly know and maintain perfect control of myself. I barely knew I had slit Camron's throat until it was done." Lies, laced with truths. The best way to lie and hide in plain sight.

"Yes, but now you know the feelings and can control them. You don't lack control, Els. You may lack the political understanding, but you will be the one holding the most power in that room, and they will see it."

She had so much confidence in me to be on their side. I was on no one's side, not anymore. This meeting was to discuss trade among the kingdoms and secure an asset Karma wanted for himself from Fonsfrick. A pair of some sort of weapon that had been dormant for a hundred and fifty years. He said this weapon was the key to ending the Mors swiftly, and that I needed to keep my mouth shut about ending them. I stopped asking questions, annoyed with the state of things. We needed a weapon TO END THEM. Fine, I get it. I will obey. Karma said there would be all kinds in attendance, and most would speak freely. This was far from common or tolerated, so I needed to be on my best behavior.

"I wish you were joining us," I said quietly as she giggled and lay down across my lap. Without thinking, I started to play with her hair. I was finding the lies came easier; a bitter truth and symptom of the company I was keeping.

"I don't. I am so thankful I don't have to go and see those male dragons."

I laughed at her. "Aw, but wouldn't it be fun to see them shit their pants?"

She laughed loudly at my plans, and with the bell tower's chime, we ran back to the estate.

Orion stood with Cosmos, who was fast asleep. He handed him to Juniper, and I kissed his forehead. Juniper struggled with his size. He seemed to get bigger, yet he was still so childlike. Poor thing.

Orion snapped, and I felt the wards snap into place. It was unfortunate they would be cooped up all day, but Orion and Karma both had assured me that should anything besides him or Orion touch the wards, not only would they know, but the pain would be unbearable, sending even Bellator warriors to the ground.

*"Not for me,"* the voice reminded me.

I didn't ask how they knew that; kind of figured it had been tested a few times over.

Orion sighed and said with a deep voice, "Remember, Elsie, control."

*"Or put on another show for me. Really, whatever suits you. I'm bored."*

I nodded, and Orion opened the Fae gate. I bolted through it, finding the first shadow I could hide in.

Orion was crafty with his placement of the gate. It allowed me to find that shadow behind a pillar, looking at the scene before me.

*"My, my, what a good girl, already listening to the monster in the shadow."*

I hated this voice, but damn it all, calling me a good girl had my mouth contorted upward, and that low, gravelly 'good girl . . .' Yeah, I didn't hate the voice. Maybe I was annoyed my stalker wouldn't reveal himself, sure, but hate? No. Fucking invisible bastard. I had a fondness for him, whatever and whoever he might be.

The room was massive, the walls the same stone as the estate house, while the floors had a more formal feel of dark slate, matching the dark natural colors that ran over the pink sandstone of the walls. Tapestries hung on the walls, of dragon family crests, those in current stations. The Pax tapestry was a blank spot on the wall. Like it had just vanished and left a hole, and that was honestly a great representation of my former life. A gaping hole.

The windows let in the warm light of the sun with massive crystal doors to a balcony on the south. In the middle sat a table with a map of the entire continent sunken into its center, all made of a deep-colored wood, the center showing all the details of the continent down to even the smallest of human villages. We had a much smaller, condensed version of this at the manor that our parents would gather around. Orion pulled out a simple-looking chair at the center of the table and sat, while Karma sat at the north end with Axl standing at his back. I gazed around the massive room divided down the center. Seated directly across from Orion would be the Dragon King of Bellator, infamous for never calling a side in a war, only supplying warriors to whoever paid for them.

*"Shame that's not actually the king."* I felt my eyes roll while I recoiled at that information but ignored it. Karma was my mate. Following his lead—that was my only job right now.

*"Such a good girl. Doing as you're told."*

Fuck this guy. Correction: I wish I could fuck this guy that lived in my head. His voice alone was enough that the need, the craving in my core; that had yet to be truly satisfied and was driving me nuts, and this voice, well . . .

Karma's side of the table held empty chairs, no doubt for the dragon lords of this kingdom. On his right sat, presumably, Marcus, the one lord willing to attend, who was seething as he glared unashamedly at Camron sitting across from him. On the left of Marcus was his mate. I think her name was Holly. Both wore nice clothes. She was blonde and full-figured, while Marcus had dark brown hair with a lanky build, but not starved like Camron. Their eyes were a typical dragon color, red. Standing behind all the dragons on the north end were the different kinds of beings in this kingdom: a high lord of Fae, an alpha pair of wolves, a single elf, a clearly wealthy and ancient vampire, and some human pairs. They each seemed wary of each other but respectful. You could cut the tension between them, but they remained civil.

The southern end of the table was a far different situation, I noted. That was the end, where I needed to be. Cautiously, I began making my way to that end to stand behind the King of Fonsfrick, Alexander. He was older than us by a bit but not old enough to be dethroned by an heir. Yet. He was plain if you looked past his gaudy robes and fur adorned with jewels. Even the brown beard and hair he wore in a human form were nothing to gawk at. He was in good shape, medium build, with typical wealth and power and a stupid-looking gold crown on his head.

"What's the meaning of this, King Rexarius?" he glowered. "I will not hesitate to leave. You invited a meeting among kings. I count three kings, a pathetic-looking prince, and whatever all that is behind you."

Slowly, keeping to the shadows and out of sight, I listened, letting his voice cover the sound of my footfalls, and kept my gaze on the south. Two powerful Fae guards stood behind him, their magic pouring off in waves, only countered by the wall of invisible magic Orion had erected in the center, appearing uninterested, looking at the table before them. It was his mate who caught my attention next. She was fucking kneeling, even her with head dipped down, with a tamers collar and chain around her throat.

She was much prettier and, unlike her king, was worth the extended glance: deep blonde hair like gold, blue eyes, small, defined feminine features, full pink lips. You would say pure if you looked at her. The blue-and-green circle around her left eye told me a lot very quickly. First, I hated the King of Fonsfrick; second, he was now on my list of kings to conquer; third, he was right-handed. I was taking in information swiftly as I made my way behind them and their guards, blocking the voice and just putting myself into a deep trance of absolute focus.

Karma spoke cleanly. I could hear the grin in his voice. "I apologize, King Fonsfrick. You see, I run my kingdom a tad differently than yours. The lords and ladies here are always invited to my meetings—"

He was cut off by Fonsfrick's accusatory voice.

"So, it's true, then, the boy king does not lead." I smiled.

Fourth, I was good at this. I stood behind the king and his guards, still and silent. Oh, had the beatings taught me well, too well. Unnoticed even by Karma, I watched his every move and slyly glanced at Camron, whose head hung low, clearly asking for it to be lobbed off if I was given the chance.

"*Not now*," slammed into my mind. I gazed at a wall, only listening to the conversation, watching just slightly, ready to make my move.

*"Control it."*

"I would say my leadership style is different from yours, Sir. You see, if I am to lead these beings into wars forged by dragons, they should know full well what they are getting into."

Ugh, I loved him. He was noble and full of life, protecting life where he could. No one would fall because he ordered it, but because they were willing. A human woman spoke next, and I watched her, almost mesmerized.

"And we are truly grateful for the choice, King Rexarius. However, you know where my people stand. We will always come when called to battle for our clan and kin—"

She was cut off by fucking Fonsfrick again. My teeth ground silently.

"And you dare allow women to speak to you?" he nearly shouted as his mate recoiled slightly.

Yeah, I hated him. Karma's hard voice sent a chill down my spine.

"King Fonsfrick, you are in my kingdom. Mine. How I allow MY people to address me is none of your concern, women—"

The human woman was enraged by being spoken over or for by anyone. Human women were always kept in fluffy dresses, and meek, not this one. She was well-muscled, wore leather and an armored corset of dragon scales. Braided and knotted but groomed hair pulled back from her face with silver beads woven into it. A warrior in her own right, it seemed.

"Do not bow to men because they wish it. They earn it. We battle alongside our men." Her voice was hard like steel. Oh, I liked her.

"Thank you, Lagatha," Karma said sweetly.

"You are a joke, Rexarius, a harmless king. The rumors are true. You are incapable of violence, let alone action. You speak of peace. You don't even have control of your lowly human women in this kingdom," Alexander sneered.

I watched Karma closely; still no fucking signal. Let. Me. At. Him . . . For fuck's sake.

Magic bubbled. No, I was in control here; maintain it.

"I truly don't see your stance, King Fonsfrick, for my kingdom is prosperous. I have cities of all kinds that live in peace alongside each other."

*City, and it's not all that free, but fine,* I corrected mentally. He kicked his feet up on the table. Oh, I loved his arrogance.

"Perhaps I don't view control the same. Perhaps it's in my people's submission to me that I found the quote 'control' you speak of."

I drew my daggers, two in one hand and one in the other. Karma's voice was lower, like he was getting ready.

"Submission and control are one and the same, you arrogant boy. I heard, in the battle of mates, you never raised a hand to that little black dragon, just blocked her attacks and even took a hit from her yourself. The worthless bitch killed a male, and you didn't even strike her down. You submit to everything, even your own mate."

Alexander spat on the floor, some of it landing on his queen. She didn't flinch; she was trained like I had been. This was the submission we had been trained for, but this was far from the type of submission I was after.

Damn it, Karma, let me go.

"You didn't even dare to bring her with you. What was it? Hmm? Are you ashamed?"

Karma laughed loudly and kicked his feet to the floor, leaning forward, elbows on the table. I matched my own stance, ready to pounce on this fucking guy, still unnoticed by everyone. I laughed silently to myself. Karma gripped his nose and flared his wings. Thank fucking Above, finally!

I lurched forward from the shadows, quickly landing the butt end of my daggers at the base of the skull of one Fae guard, then at the other. They dropped instantly, knocked out. No deaths today—rule one. Flawless execution, just like I had practiced. I launched the two daggers from my hand, knowing they would hit their marks right in front of Karma. One perfectly at each elbow, tips embedded in the table, while I brought the last one in my hand to that pathetic king's throat. Brushing it over his veins, like a mistress's kiss. Control. That's what all of this was about. Control.

I leaned down to the king's ear and said with as much arrogance in my voice as Karma possessed, "How embarrassing, bested by a lowly, little black dragon. Tell me this, Alexandra," I sneered. Making his name feminine was a choice and a bold one. I pressed the dagger into his neck just a bit. "If our king had no control of his mate or his people, do you truly think you would be left alive right now?"

I could feel Karma's gaze on me, along with everyone else in the room, all stunned in silence.

*"So hot."*

"You would kill a king, knowing his heirs would come for you, little wench?" the gaudy Fonsfrick king scoffed.

"Yes, and then I would make sure to end your entire precious little bloodline."

His mate stiffened along with this king under my blade.

"Perhaps it is not his violence that controls me but my own," I scoffed. "And that should terrify you."

I growled into his ear; I couldn't hold back. I nipped it, sending home that message. I was not going to be the one to fuck with, not here, not today, not ever.

"Bitch!"

I laughed at the king. "But not your bitch," I hissed.

I looked at Karma, who sighed and looked at me like he did in our bedroom, hot with desire. Message received, and I withdrew.

"I prefer Death's Warrior, but if you insist, bitch works." I laughed.

*"I can't wait to have that venomous mouth around my cock. God damn."*

Exhausted by his words and horrendously turned on, I screamed into my mind, *"Would you please keep your stalker romance fantasies out of my head? I am trying to work here!"*

*"I think what you mean is, 'Don't stop.'"* Wait, he could hear me if I thought of an actual response to him directly? I groaned, trying to keep him at bay by imagining an invisible wall.

*"Oh, now that's a very naughty girl—"* Oh, sweet silence.

I returned to Karma, feeling the hateful gaze from that so-called king on my back. He would have to fly out of here now or hear us out with his Fae on the floor. All part of the plan. The boys kept their faces neutral, but I could see in their eyes clearly this had worked out better than expected. Everyone behind them looked shocked and horrified as I approached, except for Lagatha. She looked at me and saw me for what I was: a warrior with a smug grin across her face. As I approached, she stepped forward and planted a firm fist over my chest. She was a force to be reckoned with, even as a human.

"Valkyrie," she uttered confidently and stepped back. I had no idea what the hell that meant, but as she stepped back, I took my place next to Axl and glared down the table at the now-pale king.

"I will hear you, King Rexarius," Alexander said, devoid of all emotion.

# CHAPTER EIGHTEEN

## Elsie

Karma spoke to the king and moved many things around on the map, marking out new trade routes for all the people in both lands, showing where he intended to reinforce borders on our side as well as Fonsfrick's. He made it so simple that everyone in the room could understand what was taking place, stopping to answer questions about treaties in different provinces, allowing for safe passage, and even pulling out document after document of new treaties and laws that had been enacted on our side of things to ensure if anyone was to harm a Fonsfrick tradesmen, or suffered a loss of property, their punishment would be met by Axl or royal guard.

Karma, Axl, and even Juniper contributed to these documents, plotting, planning, and making sure that every small detail was ironed out, down to percentages of taxation. They fought for peace with tact, and negotiation, making each deal seem so good on all ends that it was impossible to refuse. The dragon lords may not have been in attendance, but they had all signed off on these treaties. It was all so mundane, like the threats I had so boldly made never existed in the first place. This was Karma's offer to Fonsfrick. Fonsfrick remained silent, watching as Karma mapped out all the new routes and showed the scum bag the benefits of working with us.

"Fine, boy, this is all fine, but there is still one thing I would like to know. What are you asking for in return?" the gaudy Fonsfrick king asked, crossing his hands over his chest, meeting Karma's gaze with caution.

It seemed the king of Fonsfrick was no slouch, unfortunately for us. The hope had been he would agree to whatever without question, knowing his nearly landlocked country would greatly benefit from the alliance. Karma sat down and kicked his feet back up on the table, tossing his hand arrogantly as he answered.

"Oh, yes. You get to have all this newfound trade and wealth for the simple exchange of Karrigan and Korrigan."

The king's jaw dropped, then rage crossed his face as he stood and slammed his hands onto the table, shaking all the pieces on the map, toppling the figurines of villages and mountains.

"Out of the question! Name a different price," he bellowed. His mate flinched.

Karma folded his hands in his lap, met Alexander's glare. "No."

"What do you mean, no, you arrogant, harmless brat! Those two belong in the Carcer for their entire immortal lives! Disgusting dragon-slaying vampire SCUM!"

I noted the wealthy vampire shifted his weight, upset by this, yet he spoke with confidence.

"Labeling them as vampires was unwarranted, King. Not even a fraction of our kind accepts them as vamps."

"Varian," Karma warned.

"No, Karri and Korri have been removed from every clan on this continent, and many others. They are the worst of the worst. To even suggest they be released is something not even I would stand for. You mentioned the release of two weapons. You did not say WHO," Varian sneered.

Karma stood, turning to the vamp and placing a hand on the rage-stricken Varian.

"I understand your hesitation. However, to ensure these trade deals and the defeat of Mordryl once and for all, I cannot think of two better beings for the job. Can you?"

Varian scoffed and rolled his shoulder, shaking Karma's hand from it.

"Your mate would be a better start. She can control herself under pressure. Karrigan is impulsive, a menace."

I looked at Axl, who was watching this unfold. His eyes held a look of desperation. Fine then, let's see if I can play.

*"Watch yourself."* Crap, the wall in my mind had slipped.

"King Fonsfrick?" His glowering gaze met mine.

"You dare open your mouth, bitch?"

I smiled. "I do. How about a wager, then? I am the lowly little black dragon, after all, so how's this: Your guards and way out of here are going to be down for at least the night. If I can break them out of the Carcer before the night's end, they belong to me. If I fail, I belong to you."

*"I should have known better than to encourage you."* How did he keep getting through? Ugh, men were infuriating.

The king of Fonsfrick looked smug as he sat back into the chair and patted his mate's head. In my peripheral vision, I saw everyone's jaws on our side of the table drop. Karma's face wore a look of horror, Axl radiated pure panic, and Camron had a flash of smugness, then changed his face to a grin of malice that no one noticed but me. If these vamps were the key to their downfall, or at the very least, a step in that direction, I would free them, whether anyone wanted me to or not. At least this way, it was legal; it was a challenge, after all.

Trapped in silence for years, only watching everything around me, gave me the upper hand in noticing all the finer details of everyone's body language simply by shifting my eyes ever so slightly. I was a weapon. I was death. I would bring the Mors down.

The king of Fonsfrick barked out a laugh. "If you fail, not only do you belong to me, but all the trade deals are enacted."

I nodded. "Deal."

I walked to the middle of the table and stuck out my hand. The gaudy king stood and met me in the middle once again, taller than me. I had to look up at him as he shook my hand.

"Deal. I can't wait for you to be mine. I will show you what a true king is like."

I shrugged and walked back to our end of the table. Karma and Axl had both regained some composure, but I could feel the room growing cold. Karma was about to snap. Maybe I overstepped a bit.

*"Oh, ya think? A bit?"* The voice was laughing maniacally, but it sounded so relaxed, like this was only a show for him.

"Well, then, where can my queen and I retire for the night?"

Karma stood, frost covering his seat. "Axl, show Anastasia and Alexander to the royal guest quarters."

Axl nodded and made his way to a door. The others began clearing out as well, some toward the balcony, some to the doors. There were quiet whispers, but most of the murmuring was filled with, "Did that just happen?" "Cocky bitch is going to get us killed." "And you think Karma really will allow this?"

I shrugged it off and took a chair, mocking Karma slightly by kicking my feet up onto the table. Orion gripped his nose as he dropped the barriers. Karma began pacing. I took out a dagger and began playing with my nails with the pointed end, not meeting his gaze. The frost began to cover the room. Only Orion was left.

"Go," Karma growled at Orion.

He nodded, made his way to the door, and tapped the wall. I felt wards snap into place. *Did he ever run out of magic?* I wondered. Why was Karma mad? He wanted the vamps, I wanted more assets; I would get them. Where was the harm?

Karma snapped his eyes to mine, filled with icy rage.

"What the fuck did you just do?"

I shrugged. Maybe some false bravado would help right now. Shit, I was in deep shit.

"Made a deal."

"Cut the shit, Els. Why the fuck would you offer yourself to another king? You would be so willing to leave this family . . . for what? Have we not been kind enough to show you we love you? Why would you voluntarily leave us?"

He had doubts about me, my strength, abilities, resolve, and my motives, it seemed. I would take out the Mors, and no one, not even Karma, would stand in my way of that. Not anymore.

"You think I want to leave?" I shouted the lie. Parts of me did want to leave, but go where? "You doubt me?" I know he did. He may know my strengths, but he also saw my weak points.

Karma flinched. "Yes, when it comes to running off, making unfounded deals, and a pair of bloodthirsty dragon slayers. Yes, I doubt your abilities."

My dagger nicked my finger as the weight of what he said slammed into me, and violet blood flowed down my hand.

"You don't know me at all, do you?" I whispered, hurt. "You think I am not capable? I know I can do this. I would die trying to get you and this family whatever is needed to win this war. If that's a pair of vampires, very well. Hiding Cosmos, killing Clia, killing Camron—I would do it all for you. I am a weapon of my own and the most dangerous one at your disposal, yet you DOUBT ME? And you allow Camron to stay in my home with my family!"

I screamed at him while my magic and rage bubbled. I was done playing nice; fuck the tact and pleasantries.

"I should be the one who doubts you! I was kept in a cell and turned into this monster that sits before you for over a century while you not only fucked my brother but had a CHILD! Where were you before your travels to Juniper's forsaken continent? None of you came for me! I only held onto myself through memories of you!"

"I thought you were dead, for fuck's sake!"

I stood up. "So, you lied? All of that never giving up hope? All a lie, and you lied to them, allowing them to keep the hope alive?"

I felt like I'd been hit with a knife to the heart. He had given up on me, a long time ago.

"Yes, Elsie, I lied. But only to protect you!" He sank to his knees. Oh, good, another show of emotion. I scoffed and crossed my arms.

"I lied because how could you love me if I admitted I gave up? Axl held faith. I didn't. I couldn't, so I chose to lie, shielding them from my thoughts, and I lied to you because I love you."

I shook my head. "That's pathetic, Karma. I wouldn't have blamed you, and to be perfectly honest, at least now I know why you never came."

I strode to the balcony.

"Where are you going?" Karma asked tearfully. "We are not done here."

"We are more than done here, Karma. I have till daybreak to obtain some vampires. Maybe it's Axl and Juni you need to speak with now."

I felt the wards. Yes, the magic holding them in place was powerful, and no doubt would drop someone to their knees, but I had a point to prove. I shrouded myself in fire and broke through the wards. I heard Karma suck in a breath. I turned my gaze back.

"You have no idea what I am capable of nor the lengths I will go to. I spent years, forced to train as a weapon to protect someone else I loved. That is what I am. That is all I am good for."

*Ugh, I was agreeing with you up to that point.*

Karma scrambled to his feet. "No, Els, that's not it. You're so much more." Such a pretty little liar.

I turned toward the sky, waiting for me to be one among the clouds. Fine. I spent enough time looking at the map on the table to know the way.

"Save it, Karma. We both know the girl you love died the day the manor was attacked. I'm just the monster that took her place."

I let my magic consume me and felt my dragon's body rip away from the husk of my human form. I launched into the sky, the wind and beats of my wings droning out Karma's screams.

*"You have been so naughty, haven't you, little Firebird? I think you will need to be punished for shutting me out."*

You are a huge pain in my ass, you know that?

*"Not yet, I'm not."*

Stop with the dirty jokes and just tell me who you are, I demanded.

*"No, I think I will play this game longer. Your performance in that war room, gods below, it made my cock throb for you. I thought I was going to rip it off, the way your words flung at them, my hand—"*

I threw the wall back up, stronger this time. I needed to keep it in place and hold him back if I was ever going to get a moment of peace. Fucker. I was hopeless; this voice tormented me in the best way. It made me feel seen. He was aroused by my wickedness. He wasn't afraid of it, yet I couldn't let him in. Not yet.

# CHAPTER NINETEEN

## Elsie

The flight was long, filled with annoying crosswinds. It was tiring. I hadn't thought this through very well, but I would die before I admitted that to Karma, damn liar. I wasn't any better. Although it made more sense to me: his lack of willingness to allocate resources to track me down, his family's guilt; it all made much more sense. They pretended to hope for Axl's sake; he'd been tormented enough. So, they lied, supporting him but using it as a ruse to get closer to their goals of peace without violence, only then to be crushed under the guilt when their son and their adopted son had been taken captive in Caelum. Did they know? Had they known about their relations?

As Above, it was all so fucked up. Karma was then "gifted" a second chance at living, only to never be able to do anything if he found me at Mors; that was a fight you would have to kill your way out of. I felt sorry for him. Kind of. Watching as his lover long for his dead sister, watched the woman he had been forced to lie with withhold such admiration for him and his lover, then add in a child.

I groaned as my talons sank into the earth in front of the Carcer. This world and this life were so fucked up. And I was supposed to right the wrongs on Death's behalf as well. Oh, and not to mention what I could assume was the silver-eyed voyeur. This was what I needed: a challenge. I was sick of holding back. I needed the burn, the pain; I needed to recenter. I was far from well, but I knew what needed to be done.

I stretched my wings, rolled my shoulders—a weak attempt to release tension—and looked at the entrance. Steel door, unguarded, recessed into a hill. Odd. I looked at the door. Fuck it. I gathered magic at the back of my throat and expelled fire with a roar, melting any magic and the door itself away. Even as a small dragon, I wasn't going to fit. Human form, it was. I groaned and stepped forward, allowing my body to shrink. *Gods, I hate you all.*

Walking into the Carcer past the molten steel, I was hit with the rancid smell of decay. I gagged. The walls had been carved into the hillside, just dirt walls and floor. It reminded me of a mine; maybe it used to be? Dimly lit Fae lights barely illuminated the long hallway. I felt her before I saw her.

"How nice of you to show up."

Death giggled. "Not sure why you're angry with me, but it's amusing."

I rolled my eyes and headed down the hallway, noting that not only could she talk here, but along the walls were cell doors, and inside were dead creatures, all painfully thin.

"They starve them to death here, don't they?" I asked.

"Yes" was her simple reply.

I glanced at her, her form more pronounced than I had ever seen it. Half bone and half flesh, perfectly split down the center, with a tattered black dress barely holding onto her body.

"Well, that's awful," I said as I passed the cells and corpses.

"You are such an odd soul, Elsie. You walk with Death in a place filled with torment, see my almost complete form, and still do not run."

I snickered. "Well, I am blessed by you, and you are my friend. Why should I run?"

I reached a staircase that went deeper and lower into the hillside. I groaned.

"You may be blessed by me and have a good bit of my favor, but I am not all-knowing, and that should scare you."

I laughed out loud this time, letting my voice fill the void.

"If you were all-knowing, that would terrify me more than this"—I waved my hand over her half-fleshed side—"because that would mean you lie. That's something I'm not sure I can forgive, and I can forgive a lot."

Death giggled. "I don't like lies myself. So, tell me, why do you keep lying to and for them?" I shut my mouth; she had a point.

We descended the steps. Death was so easy to be around. She didn't pry, lie, or expect conversation; she just existed.

"Thank you."

She stopped at the last stair, surprised, as her opaque eyes narrowed on me. "For what?"

I smiled. She knew what. "Just existing."

I looked around the Fae lights, fewer and farther in between, still not a guard in sight. I guess if you kill everyone in here, you don't really need guards. I looked around some more cells, but it was the one to the south that caught my attention. The door was open ever so slightly. I looked at Death. She shrugged, and we walked toward it. I let my hand hold some fire to illuminate the inside of the cell. My fire went out as soon as I saw the state of the cell. It was filled with dead animals and humans, and chained to the far wall lay crumpled a dreadfully thin, pale, barely clothed vampire. The rags were a mess of dirty patchwork. His only distinguishing feature was his fangs protruding into his lower lip. Even my captivity was not this cruel. Even if this wasn't Korrigan, I would free him. No one deserved this kind of agony, no matter their crime.

Gathering myself, I approached the body.

"Korrigan?" I asked softly.

I reached his body and nudged it with my foot. A faint groan came from him as he opened his eyes, investigating mine. He then looked to Death. He lifted a finger and pointed to another wall, where a female was chained, presumably Karrigan.

"Her first, take her first." His voice was rough and painful as he choked over the words.

Death laughed, and I snapped my head toward her.

"You know, I can't take either of you anywhere, Korri. That has been long off the table for both of you."

I felt my jaw drop, and I shook my head. "Y'all can explain your relationship to me later, but for now, I'm getting them out of here. No one should suffer like this." I went for his chains.

Korri snapped, "Her first," while Karri snapped back, "Him first."

I covered my face with my hand and sighed. How about neither? I gathered my fire and sent it to their chains, hoping they would melt off them, and sure enough, they did. They didn't move; they just sighed and fell to the floor. Clearly, I was not designed for rescue missions. This required an act of compassion. I didn't have that. I felt rage on their behalf. Death was a better sentence than a life of suffering. If you were going to treat something this way, locked away and tortured by starvation for gods know how long, Death should have been the one to take them, not a king.

I looked at Death. "Can you carry one out of here?"

Coldly, Death said, "I can't touch them, let alone carry them."

I groaned. Even skin and bone, they were probably more than I could manage in this pathetic human body, but I would have to try. I grabbed Korri and flung his extremely tall frame over one shoulder, securing one of his arms into my leathers, his feet dragging the ground. He was heavy but not near what he should be. I dragged myself to Karri. I gripped her wrist and shrugged her over the other shoulder. She was much smaller, only her toe tips barely scraping the stone floor.

She coughed out, "Hurry."

I secured her arm through my leathers. Hurry? Everything here is dead. Hurry for what, exactly?

Death spoke next. "We need to get them out of here."

I groaned under their weight. Combined, they outweighed me. Ugh, this human form was once again proving unworthy.

"Well, if I had some help, I would hurry, but I'm going to have to drag these two up those stairs, so hurry how, exactly?"

Death snapped back, "You're just going to have to figure it out."

My legs shook, not from the weight of Karri and Korri, but from the floor itself. I stopped.

"What was that?" Death's gaze grew cold as she met mine and faded into more of a mist now with just her bloodred lips and dead eyes.

Karri whispered, "Jorogumo."

"Who?" I asked as I placed one foot in front of the other, back to the door of the cell, now encased with some sort of white webbing. I knew this had been too easy.

Korri gagged out, "Not who, what."

For the love of all Above.

"Could the three of you stop talking in freaking riddles?" I hissed.

The vampires coughed dryly and groaned, trying to take their weight off me and onto their own feet but just could not muster it. The webbing over the cell door was fine like silk, but there was now so much of it that it was obscuring the view of the only exit in this place.

"Jorogumo, a shapeshifting spider. She feeds off anything that can be entangled in her web," Karri whispered.

I rolled my eyes. Great, a freaking spider. Well, spiders hated fire. "I'll burn it."

"No, you won't." Korri bit out.

I exhaled sharply. I was getting tired of everyone's doubt. "I can, and I will. Karri, Korri, I'm sorry, you're going to have to hold out."

Karri groaned and coughed. "Stop. Share blood with us, and we won't be as useless."

Death snapped, "Not a chance, Karri."

Karri lifted her head and spat in Death's direction. "It would be her choice, milady," she sneered.

"Wait, you can really see her?" I asked.

Korri cut in, "We know the lady well, and her husband. I will vow you this. If you share your blood with us, we will not take more than we need. Just please allow us to help you."

I caught the word choice before the words could come out of Death's mouth.

"What you need?" I sneered. "I may be young, ill-equipped, and foolish, but need? No, you need more than what I can give."

Korri chuckled and coughed. "Smart girl, aren't you, Empress?"

The ground shook again.

"She's getting angry, and patience does not suit the spider well," Karri rasped out.

Exasperated, I shrugged off the vampires at the threshold of their cell. They hit the floor with a thud.

"Cut it out. You know who I am? Princess of Pax, Queen of Rexarius, Warrior of Death herself, your only fucking chance at getting the hell out of here."

Korri's eyes opened, and he looked at me like Death.

Coughing on every word, he ground out, "Of course, we know who you are. It seems you don't know yourself. But fine, we will take what you can give, then we can get out of here. For what it's worth, your mother would be very proud of you."

All my thoughts left my mind.

My mother? No, not now. It's fine, later will come. It's fine.

I pulled a dagger from my leathers and dragged it vertically across my wrist and forearm, then switched to the other side. The bite of the cold blade didn't faze me. This was nothing. They knew my mom; I wouldn't let them suffer here, not a moment longer. I dropped to my knees and pressed the open wounds to their lips at the same time. I would not favor either of them. Death rolled her eyes, her mouth now gone.

"Really? At a time like this?" she just rolled her eyes again.

I felt the blood leaving my body. I would stop them once I felt cold. I looked down, and they were gaining color and some mass. I felt a shiver along my spine and ripped my arms from the vamps, surging fire to the wounds to seal them off. Great, more scars.

Karri and Korri looked still painfully thin but better, fuller. Their once dead eyes were now violet, hair that was gray now shades of blonde and violet. Korri was well-defined, and Karri was beautiful.

In unison, they said, "My love," as their lips met. I sighed.

Death rolled her eyes again.

"You know, if you keep rolling your eyes, they may get stuck in the back of your head." She just glared at me. She used her gaze to point to the spider webbing.

Ugh, right, monster spider woman. Great, grand even. What could be better?

"All right, let's get out of here," I said, turning toward the web. I stripped my crown from my head. I was going to need the raw power of my magic—control over myself. I felt my body was tired from the flight, the walking, the draining of blood; I shook it off. I would get them out, and I would go home. Well, to Otium, I amended.

I felt the magic rise when it was called, allowing it to burn. It started to roll off me. I formed it into a ball and hurled it at the webbing. It lit up instantly, and I surged more magic into the fire. I heard a scream and looked at Korri and Karri.

"It's her. RUN!" Karri screeched.

We sprinted from the cell, allowing my fire to burn everything in its path, the webbing smoldering around us until we reached the stairs, which were blocked with thicker webbing.

"Shit," I swore.

I coated myself in Hell's Fire. It burned a bit. My body was almost on the verge of giving out. I needed to be a dragon for this.

"Stay as close as you can," I called back to the vamps, burning everything along the way and scorching the walls. We ran up the stairs. I saw the entrance to the Carcer down the long hallway. There was no webbing. Instead, a gorgeous woman stood there. My fire faltered for a moment, and I saw the woman move at such a rate her nails had shot from her fingers, grazing the leather that now sizzled where she made contact. Venomous. Great. Recoated in Hell's Fire, I dove at her, abandoning all thought while I heard Karri scream, " Elsie, No!"

I plucked a dagger, flung it at the woman's head, and . . . missed? Damn, she was quick.

My breathing ragged; I was losing strength. No, not now. I growled, scanning the area, the shadows quivering.

Above me. I looked up and met the face of that woman, except now, she had many eyes and arms. Disgusting.

"Run," I snapped at Karri and Korri. Korri had enough common sense to bolt, dragging Karri with him as she screamed.

I quickly followed, surging every bit of fire I could from this small, pathetic body. The fire filled the hallway. The spider's screams would surely haunt my dreams later. The shadows faded as the light of the fire consumed everything, illuminating the burning woman.

It wasn't her fault; she was only doing what came naturally: hunting. It wasn't fair for her to die this way. I reached the doorway where Karri and Korri were on the ground. I turned back to the molten door. The webbing reformed, and the woman clawed her way toward the entrance. Not today. I allowed it to consume me, ripping from my body scales, wings, and raw power. I roared back, allowing all the magic and fire I could muster into that terrible place.

Burn.

Burn it down. Burn the sorrow and death that lingered in that place. The screams fell silent, and the hillside fell in on itself. I sighed, turning to Korri and Karri. Standing tall behind them, a cloaked figure headed into the forest, only a flick of his wrist as a wave over his head.

I was involuntarily silent. I knew he was the same one who haunted me. But the words fell short: come back, stay. I hit my knees, sinking into the ground. *"Don't go."* I begged him.

*"I have to, for now."*

# CHAPTER TWENTY

## Elsie

$\mathcal{D}$eath nodded at me and vanished. Clearly, the death of the spider woman wasn't enough for her to stick around. Karri and Korri had looked better but were now drained again. You could see their eyes dulling, their hair white. I was running on fumes myself. I looked at the sky; thankfully, it was only dusk. I looked at them, flared my wings, and nodded.

"You want us to ride on you?" Karri asked, shocked.

"Can you even fly at this point?" I growled at Korri, who rolled his eyes.

"It's an honest question. You can't tell me you're not feeling a bit drained."

I nodded, knowing he wasn't wrong. It still felt like defeat.

"We will fly to the forest of dreams, then. It's not far, and it's on the border of Fonsfrick and Rexarius. We should be able to rest there for the night without trouble." Korri's words were laced with exhaustion.

I growled and shook my head.

"Gods, you are exactly like your mother. Fine, till you can fly us the rest of the way, then?"

I nodded. I only needed a few hours' rest—not even sleep, just a few hours to lie still. I craned my neck and dipped my shoulder closer to the ground, an invitation to climb. The vamps knew their way around a dragon. Not many beings knew how to mount a dragon with grace and elegance, but they did, swift and soft.

"Well, go on now," Korri quipped. He was going to be insufferable; I just knew it.

I flared my wings and slowly took to the sky. I felt them gripping my sides. In this form, I knew they were there, but they were much easier to carry as a dragon than as a human. I was careful not to jostle them. Clia was the only one who had ridden me before. Carrying passengers was a mutual trust, for they relied on me not to drop them and not push them to extremes; a fall could kill them, I think. Surely having your body splattered across the soil would leave even the "undead" more dead. Right? And I was trusting them close to my wings, the most sensitive parts of my body with their thin scales. Mounting a dragon could be a suicide mission.

Missions to destroy dragons are filled with betrayal. To ride a dragon, allow us to trust them as a rider, then deliver a poisoned dagger into a wing, would end the lives of both dragon and rider. This was how dragon slayers got their name. Stories of legends.

"You are not the first dragon we have flown with. We need to get to the forest quickly, so fly like our lives depend on it."

I couldn't tell who said it over the sound of the wind, but nevertheless, I tucked up my legs and beat my wings harder, soaring over the landscape to the west to the forest of dreams. They were trusting me not to drop them, and I needed them to stay put.

This flight was fairly short, and the wind was calm. I saw the forest, the white trees, the dense fog, and started to descend.

"No, not yet. Cross the border by one mile, then when you see the single cherry blossom tree, dive."

I nodded, beating my wings harder, summoning all my strength. I saw an army on the ground. Fonsfrick, no doubt. I climbed higher into the night sky. As a black dragon, it was easy to stay hidden.

*"Smart girl. Use what the darkness has granted you."*

We soared over the army silently and crossed the border. I spotted the tree and dove for it. I felt them grip my scales harder. I broke through the fog . . . the ground appeared faster than I anticipated. I braced, flaring my wings back to slow the dive, and ripped into the soil with my talons right next to the tree and a small pond. The pond was so dark it reflected the stars on its surface. I lowered myself, and both vamps slid off and ran for the tree. I reached for my magic; it was tired, and my body was sore, so I just lay down and watched them.

"You took it too far," Karri called over her shoulder. I huffed at her.

Both spoke in unison, "Just like her mother." They nodded and began to dig at the base of the tree. I growled.

"Look, Empress, whatever you want from us, you have it. Wherever you go, we go," Korri ground out while digging into the soil with all his strength.

Ugh. I let out a sigh and rested my head on the ground, watching them dig. I was tired physically and more so mentally, tired of it all. Who knew the freedom I had been wishing for would be the thing that would slowly strangle me? My family was holding secrets from the world. Clearly, these two knew more than I did about my mother. Hell, they had ridden her, and I had never seen her in her natural body.

They dug for what seemed like ages, deep enough that I started to wonder if we were robbing a grave. Honestly, I broke two dragon slayers out of prison; grave robbing was the least of my concerns at the moment.

"Thank the gods it's all here, Karri," Korri called out.

Karri went to her knees, and they managed to pull out a massive trunk. After they'd gotten it to the surface, I noticed the crest on the front. It was my family's original crest: a left-facing unicorn. The trunk was black and red. I hissed.

"Nah, you're going to love this." Karri stood up and clapped excitedly. They opened the trunk, pulled out bags upon bags of preserved blood, and began pouring it into their mouths.

What the hell had my mother done for them? They changed in front of my eyes, their bodies becoming healthy, full, shapely, and beautiful, the violet hue in their white hair and eyes turning a deep shade of red, color even graced their skin.

With blood dripping from the corners of her mouth and fangs, Karri asked innocently, "Can you start a fire, Elsie?"

I rolled my eyes. I was tired, not useless. I flicked a talon, and a fire sprang from the ground.

Its warmth was welcoming, even if it was just my magic that held it. This was also reminiscent of winters in the cell, forced to keep myself warm. This was easy, even while exhausted.

They hauled the trunk closer to the fire, then pulled out a set of basic clothes each, as well as small leather-bound books, and more blood, which they happily drank. I just lay there watching them and their growing excitement, doing whatever they needed to do.

"These are your mother's journals," Karri said softly. I stiffened and forced myself back into my frail human body, my leathers damaged from the spider.

"Wouldn't happen to say in there why she released the unicorns but let her family die, would it?" I sneered.

Korri rolled his eyes and lay back into the fluffy grass.

"I knew that wasn't going to go over well."

"Care to fill me in?" I snapped.

Karri looked at me. "We can fill in some of the gaps with what we know, but her journals and letters to you and Axl will probably prove more useful."

I stared at her. Her now red siren eyes and high cheekbones burned with as much intensity as my fire. Korri seemed to be just as arrogant as Karma.

"Let me start by asking you, do you know why we are known as dragon slayers?"

I shook my head and looked at the pile of books and parchment labeled with Axl's and my names on them. Korri's voice was hard, laced with undisguised annoyance.

"That is because everyone holds on to legends of the past and thinks of them as current events. We stand accused of slaying the Mors queen, Camila, when we smuggled her out of that kingdom. What we did was take her to your manor. From there, your parents took her to another continent altogether. Your mother knew that, someday someone would figure it out and come for them, hence the letters. We stood by your family for years as spies and assassins. Always in the shadows and always adding to this trunk, for if the day ever came that you all died, we would hand the trunk over to whoever was left standing. No matter how many generations passed."

Korri never broke eye contact with me. I looked at Karri and sighed.

"Why?" I asked.

"To save her. Camila was being viciously attacked by Mordryl almost every day of her life. She had tried to run, to fly, anything she could do to escape, but she only wielded healing magic. She finally called a meeting disguised as a high tea with the other dragon women, hoping someone would see. A typical little women's party. It was your mother who saw the bruises and scars, on her old friend, she told the Rexarius and your father. Thus, the plan to free her was born."

I started to cry, bringing my knees to my chest. My mother had tried to help someone, and we paid for it with our blood.

"We never killed her, never even drank from her. What no one had predicted was the wrath of a husband and daughter.

"When your mother was slain, the magic left and they broke free. She didn't free them. The attack was swift and took years of planning."

I nodded. "You think Clia knew?" Desperation creeping into my voice.

Korri chimed in, "There is no way she didn't know or, planned it with her father."

I wiped my tears. "That means Camron knows. He's in my capital, and Fonsfrick thinks you killed her. That's why he smiled when I offered to go. He wants this to fail or to kill you both."

They both straightened, and Karri began packing the trunk.

"We take it with us; it should have all the proof we need to clear our names," Korri proclaimed. Karri and I nodded.

"Are you with me no matter what I plan to do?" I asked, staring at the trunk. There was a lot I needed to do, and being truly free from this hell was at the top of my list.

In unison, they said, "Our contract with your mother extends to her children. It is our sworn vow to stand by the black dragons, no matter the cost."

I nodded. A vow? That word struck me as odd. But we needed to act; they could fill me in later, and the journals could answer even more. First, I needed to secure my freedom—from Fonsfrick and from Karma. Politics, games—I wasn't interested. I wanted to change. And if that cost me the world, well, I was just going to have to burn it down.

"I have so many questions, but for now, we need to return." The vamps grinned and snapped the trunk shut.

"We have a few hours before daybreak. Let's stop at the estate to find something for you both to wear to the capitol and get some answers before I relive my entire life from in those journals."

They burst out laughing. "The estate in Otium?" Korri asked, and I nodded.

"Please, girl, we have a whole room at that estate." I shrugged. The twists and turns of my life were just beginning.

Korri and Karri cinched down two simple Fae bracelets to their wrists. I hadn't noticed them before. They were plain, just braided cord with a single black-and-red stone in the center. I raised an eyebrow, and they shrugged.

"Keys," they said in unison again.

*That is going to be very annoying.* " Oh, how right this voice was.

I shifted into my dragon form easier than before, the crown still tucked away. Maybe I didn't need it.

*"You don't. Trust yourself."*

Karri and Korri climbed up and settled in, heavier. They felt sturdier. I launched into the sky, driving myself forward with as much power as I could muster.

"You're faster than your mother!" Karri shouted over the wind.

I growled, beating my wings against the sky, flying due north; I had taken in every detail possible from that map of the lands in the capital. Faster still, tucking my limbs against me, I beat my wings harder, feeling the sting of the wind against my scars. We needed to be fast; we needed to get back on time. They needed to freshen up, and I needed to ask Juniper what in Below was her mother's name. Dragon healers may not be powerful fighters, but their magic was generally passed down between mothers and daughters. It was a pure type of magic, a nurturing kind, something divinely feminine.

And if she's who I think she is . . . That would make Juniper Cliantha's half-sister, and that would mean her mother was just as twisted as the kings she'd lain with and that Juniper was also a liar. I knew something was off. She was younger than the lot of us by a few years. Dragons were so hard to age once they were adults; you never really knew. We were timeless until about our fourth or fifth century. Kingdoms rarely fell in a dragon's lifetime; it could be a thousand years with only a father and son ruling a kingdom. The curse of long a lived monster. Five hundred years of war and governing kingdoms took their toll. No wonder it was only the first dragons that hold the ancient titles of gods. Their lifetimes had been even more impressive than our measly five century's, legend claims the first dragons would live and rule well into their one thousandth year.

Most of our reigning kingdoms were a few dragon generations in, minus Bellator. That land had been held by one clan of dragons for five thousand years. But in the last hundred and fifty years, massive changes have been made.

To what end? Wealth? Bloodline? It couldn't be that simple, yet maybe it was. Greed was the downfall of everything; why would this be any different? Was Juniper really that greedy? Did she have another motive?

I descended into the estate grounds, tossing Korri and Karri from me and dropping the trunk on the doorstep. Juni and Cosmos were probably asleep, but it didn't matter. Fuck tact and pleasantries. I kicked the door open as Korri and Karri strolled through the wards. Keys indeed; how interesting.

"Juniper!" I screamed into the foyer. Karri and Korri strode in behind me.

"Oh, I just love what they did to the place," Karri said breathlessly as she looked around. "Ah, that way." She headed toward the hallway, stopping short at a tapestry of the manor house. She pulled it aside and the wall was bare, but she held up her wrist, and a door appeared. How deep did these two have their claws in the dragon kingdoms before their fall?

Juniper came running from her room with Cosmos in her arms. Panic crossed her face while Cosmos looked unbothered; the kid was off as well. What had she done to him? I felt my lips curl. Something wasn't right. I may not have known this child long, but I could read beings like open books. When you spend your time in hell looking for holes and ways out, looking for anything to make someone else happy to end your suffering, you see others clearly, without detection. I was trained as a weapon, but I sharpened the deadliest weapon I had in silence, tucked away: perception.

As she almost ran straight into Karri, Juniper shrieked, and Karri smiled.

"You're going to get an ear full," Korri whispered as we approached their door.

"What the fuck, Elsie?" Juniper yelled as Cosmos wiggled, trying to escape her grasp.

"What? They have keys." I shrugged, keeping an innocent smile on my face. Juniper stopped and looked at them.

"This is Karrigan and Korrigan." I gestured to the vamps. Juniper shuddered.

"We're picking up some of their personal belongings from their room," I said nonchalantly. Juni did not let it slide.

"Uh, hello," she sneered, setting Cosmos on the ground. He ran for me, slamming into my legs. I struggled to pick him up and giggled.

"Hey, buddy, miss me?" He nodded, pressing a hand to my face. His green light filled the room, and my body instantly felt weightless. I loved this kid; he knew something. I needed to figure out what, and based on what I'd observed, he did not like his mother.

"Oh, look at that," Korri said, gazing at Cosmos.

"You're so much like your parents; it's unsettling," Juni whirled to Korri.

"What do you know about any of us? You think just because you had some secret room here, you can just come and go as you wish?" Juniper snapped.

Korri's gaze leaped up, and Karri stepped into their room.

"We know more about these families than the Fae, and I promise, I know what a dragon child with that ability means for you. What you need to know"—he tapped Juni on the nose with his index finger—"is that we are loyal to the black dragons entirely. Do not make me your enemy, girl."

He dipped into their room, the entrance going back to a normal wall after both had stepped through the door. I turned to make my way to the den with Cosmos now asleep in my arms— well, pretending to sleep. The voice chuckled in my mind. Juniper followed me, her anger palatable with every step.

"What the hell, Elsie?"

I snapped to meet her gaze, set Cosmos down in Karma's chair, and stepped in front of it, blocking the boy.

"What is your mother's name, Juniper?" I commanded.

Her face betrayed her for just a moment; she had a true fear creeping into her veins.

"Camila, why?" She crossed her arms over her chest. I could see it clear as day now: the slight, uncanny resemblance to Clia.

*"Ah, here we are."*

I laughed and sank into a crouch. Karma had hidden a flask in the folds of the chair. I pulled it out and took a swig, careful not to jostle Cosmos.

"I hated your father. I think I hate your mother and your sister even more. They will burn, Juniper. You will not stand in the way of that now."

My voice was colder than Karma's ice, and my gaze was unwavering as it held hers.

"I have a sister?" she asked, stunned, but the look in her eyes was different; she was cracking.

I barked out a laugh. "Oh, please, you didn't know?" Juniper dropped to her knees.

"I promise I didn't. Please, Elsie, you must believe me."

She begged. Why would she beg? I took another drink. The whiskey helped keep me warm, ready to strike, but dulling my nerves just enough with its bite to keep me focused. Live a life composed of only pain; soon, pain is the only thing tangible to keep your head.

"Cliantha is your sister, Camila your mother, Camron your brother, Cosmos your son. All C names except for you. Why?"

Juniper shook her head. "I don't know what you're saying, Els."

Karri and Korri stood in the doorway, glowering.

"I think she's asking you what your real name is and what your end game is."

Creepy that they still spoke in unison. Juniper's tears stopped flowing, and she got to her feet.

"Canna is my true name, but please, only call me Juniper."

*"Get away from her now! Take the boy. Run, now!"*

I snorted. "Why did you do it? Why hurt them like this? You trapped them, didn't you? The story you told me of the boys in your kingdom, you . . . you sold them out, didn't you?"

I slammed the flask against the table.

"They were my way out! You know my family is terrible!"

I yelled, "So, you used them!"

"At first, yes, but I do love the boys! I don't want my bloodline! If you want to burn them, I'll happily help." She sounded sincere, and whatever was left of my heart broke.

*"She's lying!"* I know, I saw it—there's more here. She was a victim in some capacity. The way she acted, her movements showed she was a liar through and through, but there was more to this. Someone had set her up to be the fall of them, and she played into it. The question remained: Was it willingly? Did she know what she had done, or had she been groomed for it?

"We need to go," Karri said plainly, but the venom in her voice was malleable. I stood straight and grabbed Cosmos, throwing him onto my back. Yeah, that's right, little guy, you know who to trust; he clung to me without hesitation. I began walking to the door through the archways, wishing I could trap her in a burning building. She sold them out. Betrayed their secret affair, but why?

"Where are you going? Give me Cosmos!" Juniper screamed. I turned to her. As Above, I could kill her right here and now, just for her betrayal. Cosmos gave a small tug to my hair, without putting too much thought into it I let his mother live.

"Over my dead body. Stay here. If you are gone by the time we are back, I will know where you stand. Stay here and face the boys yourself."

I clutched the child's arm as the vamps followed me out the door, passing through the wards with ease. I passed Cosmos to Karri, who nodded, took him to her chest, and wrapped him in her knee-length black wool cloak. She wore a red long-sleeved shirt underneath with black leather pants and boots. Korri was more intimidating now as he was dressed identically to Karri.

They were seamlessly put back together, a mystery for another time.

"Karma will come undone if you take him with you!" Juniper—or Canna, whatever her name was—shouted from the doorway.

I turned to her. "Karma will come undone knowing your true nature."

I forced my dragon self out, saw the trunk, and grabbed it in my mouth. I would be damned if I allowed my mother's words to stay within her reach. Just when I thought I could like her, I found out she had lied to them for years. Korri climbed up and settled in, taking Cosmos from Karri and allowing her to get situated.

"All set," Korri called out, and I took to the sky, allowing the wind to cover Juniper's cries of despair. I felt the fiery tears falling from my eyes. Karma had lied, Juniper lied. What about Axl? Had he lied? Would our family break over this? Who could I trust? I flew back toward the capital, knowing our time was limited.

*"I will come for you."* Fuck you, I don't even know who you are. And that voice went silent, leaving me with just my vamps, wandering back into this hell I was facing. I sent the wall back up; this was now going to be my problem, one that only I could solve. What was Juniper/Canna after? Did the boys know? What were their true goals? And who was I to them?

Thank Above for Cosmos and his magic, or the speed at which I could fly would be impossible. Racing against the setting moon and the rising sun, the capital was in view. Fuck the crown, no way to reach out to Karma telepathically. Shit. Everyone was going to hurt after today in more ways than one. I found Axl on the balcony, tears in his eyes. I landed more carefully for Cosmos than the vamps. They got off while I set the trunk down and pulled myself into a human. I looked at my brother, who ran to Karri and took Cosmos.

"Elsie, I am so sorry. I touched you before you left; it was sly. I felt so dirty for even doing it, but I didn't know if I could trust all of this."

I sighed. Out of all the betrayals today, this was the least problematic.

"So, you saw it all?"

Axl clutched Cosmos and nodded. "I transferred it to Karma as well on your way here. That voice in your head is a problem. We will need to figure out who that is."

I nodded—shit—and sat back against the balcony rail, crossing my legs, and my arms followed across my chest, holding myself together. They wanted to take the voice, too? Why?

Yeah, he was creepy, but he didn't do any harm, ever, and that voice was right. Time and time again, he was right. He was the only one aside from Death who hadn't abandoned me. He left me, and I would punish him for it. But abandon? No, he hadn't done that in a hundred and fifty years.

Karri and Korri exchanged a glance. "Transference?" they asked.

I nodded. Karri giggled.

"Well, damn it all. This group may just overthrow the world yet." Korri chuckled.

"And to think we may just be alive enough to see it all unfold after all." I raised my brow at them.

"You all might just be able to do it."

I rolled my hand in front of me. "And 'it' would be?"

They laughed.

"Establishing the intercontinental court of dragons."

Axl and I looked at each other and shrugged. I looked up, and standing in the doorway was Karma, ice falling, fury in his eyes.

"I am done," he said as he met my gaze. I nodded. Yep, this was going to be really, really bad.

# CHAPTER TWENTY-ONE

## Elsie

Karma stepped out onto the balcony, the sunrise casting his shadow far behind him while throwing shuddering rainbows against the stone building. Axl braced while the vamps sank to the ground cross-legged with Cosmos. Then I noticed Karma's gaze, no glare, pierced into my very bones.

"You want to tell me why my son is here?" I blinked, stunned. "Uh, Axl—"

Karma snapped, "He showed me everything with Juni! What I want to know is WHY. IS. MY. SON. HERE."

Yelling? He was actually yelling at me? For taking his son from his traitor bitch of a mother? My mind was spinning, confused, exhausted.

*No one talks down to you except me.*

I was quiet when I spoke, lowering my eyes to the ground.

"Do not raise your voice to me, Karma." I clenched my fists and felt the fire drip from the nails digging into my palms.

"YOU HAD NO RIGHT—"

I interrupted him again in a whisper. I looked up and met his stormy eyes. "To make sure YOUR son was away from a traitor? Is it not my right as queen to protect the innocent of this kingdom, no matter their bloodline? Is that not my duty? She admitted she sold you out! Did you know?"

I stood slowly, my rage boiling. I stepped toward him, glowering. "What exactly was not within my rights?" I growled out.

Axl stepped between us, sensing the rolling cold and exhaustive heat coming between Karma and me.

"Enough, we can argue as a family later. For now, I will take him. You guys need to act right. We will deal with the demon in your mind later as well."

He clapped a hand down on my shoulder. I shook it off, burning him and whatever magic he was trying to place on me, not breaking Karma's gaze.

"Do not dare infiltrate my mind again, Axl." I bit back all the harsh words I had for them. Karma's magic receded, grabbing his jawline and turned.

"You're right as usual, Axl." I dropped my magic and nodded. "So, plan?"

Karma's face contorted into an evil, menacing grin as he looked over his shoulder and dropped his wings, his mask of composure sliding back over him.

"Same as earlier. Wait for when the time is right. Only this time, Karrigan and Korrigan will handle his Fae. The queen is to remain untouched. Oh, and Elsie, one thing, don't you fucking dare act out—you will wait for my order."

At least in all his rage, he still had some sense to protect me. Korri stood taller and, to my surprise, was a touch taller than Karma, even broader. I imagined what that man would be as a dragon. Power—had he been a dragon, the only thing he could be was power.

"It would serve you well, King, to handle your blade with care," he said, almost scolding Karma, who simply nodded and walked inside.

*"The vamp is right; you are to be handled with care."*
The voice was cold; I could sense the rage in it now.

Karri, Korri, and I found ourselves under camouflage in the shadows as everyone began to fill the massive war room. The map now had a crushed figure where the Carcer once stood. So, the map was also infused with magic, updating structures as they formed or were dismantled, except for one area of the map, the gray section of Bellator, only showing the infamous mountain ranges, not a mark on it besides the spacey and far less detailed geography of the land.

Karma sat at the head, feet up on the table, looking bored but still full of malice. He glared at King Alexander while Anastasia knelt next to him with a new cut on her lip. The room was silent until Alexander boomed, "Well, well, well, looks like that little female stood no chance. I knew no little girl would be able to—"

Fuck it. I'm going now. What was Karma Rexarius really going to do about it? Korri and Karri were swifter than I ever could imagine, slitting the throats of the Fae guards as I passed between them, their bodies thudding on the stone. I took my blade back to that king's throat and angled another to his queen.

"Lady Rexarius!" Karma bellowed. I snapped my gaze to him. He was leaning forward with his feet now dropped to the floor, clicking his tongue.

"Untouched." He flicked a finger to the queen of Fonsfrick.

He had meant to leave her untouched, but me? What about me? I shook the thought from my mind. Fine, then. I wouldn't touch her; and I dropped the dagger into her lap. To my utter frozen surprise, she picked it up and very swiftly stood and drove it into Alexander's ribs, stunned. I straightened as she ripped the other dagger from my hand and drove it into his gut. I took a step back to find Karri and Korri, who both wrapped a hand around each of my arms.

Violet blood bubbled out of Alexander's mouth, terror in his eyes. The queen pushed the chair back and backhanded her king across his face, sending a spray of violet over the three of us and the walls.

She growled, "You wouldn't know the fury and strength of a woman forced to labor at your hand if she killed you herself." She gripped all the gaudy clothing on the king's body, and with a solid yank, she threw him out of the chair to the ground, face down, violet blood spilling all around as he lay there gagging and gasping. The queen kicked him in the ribs, and the king recoiled with a gasp as he exhaled his last breath. She ripped a key off his neck and plunged it into the collar at her throat. The metal fell to the floor with a resounding clank.

Karma clicked his tongue, and everyone's head snapped to him, away from the brutal murder scene that lay before us. Korri and Karri tightened their grasp on me.

"Lady Fonsfrick, was that satisfying enough, my dear?" Karma cooed, and I boiled. He never spoke to me like that, and I never heard him coo to Juniper like that either, not like this.

The queen smiled and took her seat. "Yes, my king," she said. She tucked her chin down.

"My lands are now lands of Rexarius." Her head snapped up. "I hereby relinquish my title as queen and accept the title of Lady. I will not disappoint you, my king, and *all* of my daughters will forever be grateful for the freedom you have granted us."

"*Fuck.*"

I swayed; it was all settling around me. Karri tightened her grip again and whispered to me, "Steady now. Show no weakness, just for now." Karri's voice was quieter than a mouse's breath, only for my ears.

I locked my gaze right above Karma, at the stone on the far wall, centered myself, and grew as still as death while everyone else had grown quiet, their eyes darting between the lady and our king. Panic filled the room, and Death was in the air. She looked confused but left as quickly as she had arrived.

I kept my gaze on the stone with Karri and Korri at my sides. I listened to them talk. This nearly had all been planned out, apart from the spider woman monster thing. Karma had planned on me offering to go and be successful in bringing them back . . .

I had been a pawn, and he had lied to me, and he had chastised me for doing so.

*"Only I am to use your body for my devilish desires,"* the voice growled.

The Fonsfrickians had abandoned the Carcer to save their already fading wealth. Anastasia knew her kingdom would fall, but to protect her daughters, she plotted against her king. For years, Karma had secret meetings and letters with the queen; for years, he helped a woman escape her tormentor while I sat in a cell. Anastasia had come to him for help, and in exchange, she would hand over her title. The sons the king had spoken of never existed, and Alexander had forced the queen to bear more and more offspring to continue a bloodline, beating her when she no longer could.

Females were still unable to rule without a king at their side. For a bloodline to continue, a male heir was nonnegotiable. Wasn't this what Karma was trying to end? This pointless power exchange of dragons? Kings, queens, lords, and ladies? Was he not trying to establish equality between us? All of the beings, for that matter? This should be the simplest thing to dismantle. Females held more magic. If it was power a king wanted, why not allow a queen to rule? When the weight of the exchange dawned on me, my rage was quick to bubble. He knew she was desperate and in trouble, so he cut her a deal. He was no hero; he was only fulfilling his end games. He saved her, abandoned me.

Desperate was the only word I could find for her. The only word I could find fitting for Karma was composed. He sat and talked with Anastasia, solidifying their plans as Alexander's body grew cold on the floor; no one dared move him. Karma had called this woman dear and darling; had he been with her as well? Juniper/Canna, Axl—who knew where else he had been?

He told me earlier he had given up on me; he thought I was dead, I shouldn't blame him. But if Juniper was the daughter of Camila, sister to Cliantha and Camron, surely, he had to have known where I was. Why did he never come? Was he as twisted as Life was? Was it his "gift" that twisted him in such ways? I felt a drop of fire leave my eye. I could handle Karma, Juniper, and Axl even, but more? Were there more women? Men? Lies? I lowered my gaze to the man I loved, surrounded by all kinds, going over every detail on the map, marking out new trade routes, discussing, talking, and there I stood next to the cooling body's. Ignored.

*"I am here. I will not lie to you."* The voice was pleading. I ignored it.

Karri and Korri were nearly holding me up by the end of the meeting. The beings whose deals were done funneled out. The only people left by the time things seemed to be settled was Anastasia, Orion, Camron, Karri, Korri, and myself. The room felt as large as it looked now, and a chill had settled over it.

"Orion, please escort Lady Fonsfrick back to her home." Karma spoke with authority. Orion nodded, took the lady's hand, opened a Fae gate, and left.

The room grew colder. Karma turned to Camron. "I think it best you return now. You have much to tell your sister and father of today's events."

Camron looked stunned, stuttering, "You, you, you know I can't return." Karma flared his wings, and frost covered every inch of the room and the map.

"You are a simpleminded one, aren't you?" Karma grabbed Camron by his chest.

"You will return. You will tell them what you saw. Information is the greatest weapon. You in turn will inform me of their next move. Do I make myself clear, prince?" Karma held Camron as he shrank down and nodded numbly.

My legs began to shake as Camron passed by me and leaped into the sky from the balcony. He was letting him go?

Karma turned to face me, still at the far end of the table. As he slammed his hands against the table, my knees buckled, and Karri and Korri lowered me to the floor. Karma strode toward us, the three bodies now encased in ice along with everything else. Maybe his inability to kill was a good thing. This was a side of him I never imagined. Karri stayed kneeling at my side while Korri stood.

"That's enough, King Rexarius, the bravado is un—"

Karma swung and caught Korri in the jaw, but Korri did not waiver; he only stood straighter and taller.

Karma snapped, "How would you know what's enough? She risked everything today! She acted outside the family! She could have died! She was cruel to—"

Korri, in a blinding movement, snaked around Karma, dropping him to his knees by sweeping his feet from under him. He gripped and twisted his wing, contorting it as his other hand gripped into his white hair and pulled his neck back to look Korri in the eyes.

Karma shrieked.

"I said that was enough, King Rexarius," Korri said. He let go and stepped back in front of me.

Karri wrapped her arm around my waist, and I slouched into her, my mind a garbled mess of emotions I had not felt since the cell: despair, confusion, panic, betrayal, anger, and sorrow. My freedom, it wasn't free. I wasn't free, not here. Karma sat back on his heels, and his wings dropped, crumpling the edges on the floor, his gaze locked on the floor.

"I've always known her name, Elsie. Foolish of you to think otherwise—"

Karri cut in just as venomously as she did with Juniper. "You are a fool, King Rexarius, an absolute fool. If you did not tell her, how could you expect her to know? You want her to read your mind? That's your lover's talent, not hers!"

Karri gripped me tighter protectively. How did she know so much so quickly?

"Elsie is my BLADE. She should have trust and faith I would wield her effectually. That's what they trained her for," Karma sneered as he stood.

Blade. I am his blade. What they trained me for? That's it? A weapon? Only a blade. That's what I am to him? Was that why

I spent years in a cell, training to be a weapon? To be his . . . weapon?

Korri chuckled. "Foolish king, a woman of her caliber requires a worthy wielder, one that can trust the blade will not shatter. You, foolish king, have not trusted in your blade," Korri mocked, "nor cared for her appropriately. Your BLADE"—he stretched out the word—"as you so callously called her, is not only your greatest weapon but a warrior, survivor, protector, and most importantly, your MATE. Treat her with any sliver of disrespect again, and I will make sure I become the blade she wields to cut you down with." Korri's words were like a knife. That was what Karma should have said to me, that he would cut anything down that stood in my way; he should have defended me, and he didn't. He used me.

I looked up at Korri and really saw him now. His eyes glowed a red hue, his white hair tousled and short, with faint hints of a bloody red, his face angular, broad, and defined, his fangs barely poking out over his full lip. My eyes traveled over him. Even past the modest black-and-red clothing, you could tell this vampire was the peak of fitness, almost as beautiful to look at as Karma. I shuddered into Karri. Yeah, he could have been raw power as a dragon; shame he was a vamp.

Karma scoffed, "Get rid of the bodies. I will see you all at home."

I was crumbling. A blade and body disposal, his love reduced to this: why? Because I didn't know what they didn't tell me? If Karma knew who she was, then Axl knew as well. The family I had so recently found lied to me. Lied. Tears of fire dripped from my face and fell onto Karri, who simply stoked my hair and pulled me into her chest.

Korri's voice cut through the ice. "We will be along when the queen is ready. A reminder, King, that was our home first."

I shook with silent sobs into Karri. I felt discarded. They knew I was alive, they knew, and they lied. I heard Karma's footsteps fade and felt Korri's hand on my back. My magic bubbled to his touch.

"May I?" I just nodded. I didn't care what he was going to do. I noted that I felt my magic being pulled from me but couldn't bring myself to care. It burned, but the pain was welcome, and the physical burn was a welcomed distraction from the war in my mind.

"Careful, Korri," Karri warned softly. My own burning stopped, and I smelled the burning of flesh. Darkness clouding the edges of my vision, I shut my eyes. I fell into the darkness and allowed it to consume me.

### *Magnus*

I sat in the tree line, ripping a branch from the nearest tree, selecting my switch. I played a game with her and miscalculated. I would punish myself for it. I should have just lured her away to start.

*Thwack.*

The sting of the limb was not enough, so I coated the limb in shadows and formed thorns along it.

I should have just stolen her away.

*Thwack.*

I should have been there for her.

*Thwack.*

I felt the blood welling over my back and wings, dripping down my legs. I deserved this; I should not have played this game with her.

*Thwack.*

I should have seen the depth of their lies.

*Thwack.*

I was sent to my knees from the blood loss. How could I have been so stupid, so careless? She was mine; I could have just taken her. Fuck. But she needed to see them in their true light as well. FUCK. Why did all of this need to be so fucking political?

I should just let the demonic thoughts take over.

*Thwack.*

I needed more information. I needed her. She needed to leave that kingdom, and I needed to get close to her. I needed to take her home, no matter the cost. If she was unwilling, so be it, but I would take her the fuck home. No one played with my firebird except me, and that arrogant prick, Karma, used her in a way that would break her mind. No, to play with my firebird was a sin I would not soon forget. He hurt my firebird; he hurt my girl.

*Thwack.*

And I was to blame.

*Thwack.*

I should have challenged them myself at the battle. I should have won her, showed her the truth, and hoped she would understand.

*Thwack. Thwack. Thwack.*

This was finally the year I was strong enough to prove to the world I should be the most feared being-not her, never her.

*Thwack.*

I sent my shadows out to the Mors, the pain of the switch not a high enough price to pay. I would push myself beyond that pain while incurring more to learn. Then I will go to her. I peered through the darkness into the Mordryl castle. My vision was blurry, my back and wings bleeding, my fur pulling and falling in black and violet clumps.

"Oh good, brother, you returned," Clia said, sipping her wine from the bottle. Camron nodded and sank back into his chair at their barren table.

"So, do tell. What did you see?" Clia leaned in. Camron motioned for a bottle while propping an elbow up on the table. He looked at his sister.

"Too much and not enough." Well, that was a statement I could relate to: always seeing, but understanding was a different problem altogether. A wolf appeared with a bottle for Camron, who chilled the wine instantly and popped the cork. Clia smiled but quickly shifted into a frown when Aleah walked in and took a seat, keeping her gaze lower than the princess's eyes. Ah, so that was a lie.

*Thwack.*

"What do you mean by that? Don't talk to me in riddles," she snapped.

Camron groaned and sipped. "They are stronger than we are capable of dealing with alone—"

Clia scoffed. "Still?" she jabbed.

"Yes, still, Clia," Camron barked.

"What I saw was fucking Elsie go into Fonsfrick territory, pull the vampire dragon slayers from the prison, defeat the Jorogumo we put there, and return unscathed."

I should have stayed with her.

*Thwack.*

Clia's jaw was hanging fully agape. "Then I watched as her mate nearly tore her apart when she went in to execute the king and queen of Fonsfrick, only to drop her dagger, and that queen killed her own mated king in cold blood."

Camron spoke loudly, gesturing wildly. "Stabbed him and rolled his body to the floor. Then everyone carried on with their trade deals like nothing happened with the major coup that took place in front of their eyes as the queen became a lady and gave her lands to fucking Karma Rexarius, all but ensuring all the borders are well protected."

Clia took a drink and leaned back. "I see," was all she said.

Camron passed the bottle to his mate and sighed.

"And still no idea where Mom is?" Clia asked, almost indifferent. Camron shook his head.

"Not definitively, but they are hiding something big, and I'm sure it's her."

Aleah cut in, "Then, you have to go back and find out what that is!"

Camron groaned and hung his head back. "Yeah, I know, but you know, each time I go, the more likely it is that I will be killed."

Clia laughed. "Brother, we are all dead here. At least you would die after feeling the sky again."

Camron looked at his sister. She was twisted, cold, pathetic, and a spoiled brat. But she was right; they had already died. I should have known better than to let this play out.

*Thwack.*

Ugh, not enough information here. All they wanted was to kill their mother, it seemed. Easy enough. Next, fucking Rexarius. I pulled my shadows back and sent them out to the estate. I should have protected her, my vows—I SHOULD HAVE DEFENDED MY VOWS.

*Thwack. Thwack. Thwack.* Blood pooled around me, showing me my own reflection. Of the wicked beast inside. The twisted truth of my being.

"I hate you," I growled at myself into my silver eyes.

Through the shadows, I saw Karma had flown back to the Otium estate. Alone. He probably had figured now would be a good time to lay into Juniper, and Axl, for that matter. I could only hope. But he hadn't expected them to be on the lawn when he landed.

"You are a piece of work, Karma," Axl sneered. Juniper crossed her arms.

"How could you not tell her? That was your whole fucking job!" she spit out. Karma roared, but his lovers did not flinch. "Get a grip. We both saw what you did to her. How fucking could you?"

Karma shifted back. "How could I? How could I? Easily, that's how! She is supposed to be my mate; she is supposed to trust me to lead her, wield her, use her. She is supposed—"

"She is not like us, Karma! She hasn't been here!" Axl clapped his hands across the syllables of that word.

"She took Cosmos because she thought he was in danger of being with Juniper! She did what she knew was right, and with the lack of information, she made the right call, you arrogant ass!" Axl shrieked, tears streaming down his face. "Now she knows we have lied!"

"Then, why did you panic, Juniper? You only made it worse! You should have talked her down!" Karma spat out at her. She looked rattled.

"Me?" Juniper gasped. "Me? What the fuck do you mean, me? I panicked because I thought you had filled her in! I thought she fucking joined them!"

No doubt she was talking about the dragon resistance I was leading. I am an idiot.

*THWACK.*

Juniper covered her face in her hands and began to cry. Axl was sobbing, but his gaze did not leave Karma's.

"How could you treat her like that, after everything! How could you? You promised it would be okay! You promised I would get my sister back!" Axl's voice broke over every word.

Karma softened. "I'm sorry. I was the one out of line here today. I was taken by surprise at nearly every turn and felt so powerless, so out of control."

I raged. He was an idiot, and so was I. Elsie could end all suffering if we only knew who the actual mastermind was here. We had too many players in this game: Camila, Cliantha, Camron, King Mor, the Rexarius, Canna . . . Who did what first? Who had betrayed whom and plunged this world into wars? Were we really about to kill them all? What would the cost be? Would my kingdom survive? Could I protect Elsie and all of them? Who did this? Who pushed us this far?

WHO, DAMMIT?

*Thwack.* I gagged on the pain.

"It won't happen again." Karma dropped his gaze to the ground.

"If she doesn't come back, I will go to her. I held on, Karma, long after I knew you didn't. I won't let her go again. I will go with her. This time I will go with her, and you will stop me! Not AGAIN! You had your chance."

Oh, so Axl had known Karma considered his sister dead. And knew she was alive? Karma had mourned the girl he loved because he knew the "monster" that was going to take her place.

Axl regained his composure, and just like that, a firm line had been drawn. Good.

*Thwack.*

My vision blurred from the pain, more blood pooling around me. I deserved this. Ripping old scars open, I caused her pain. I would give myself this treatment. I watched as they all silently split off into separate directions; at least they were fracturing at this point. Maybe now the truth would be uncovered. My vision blurred, and my magic faltered as I passed out.

*Forgive me, Elsie* was my last thought before my mind left me, and I allowed the darkness in my vision to take over.

# CHAPTER TWENTY-TWO

## Elsie

"How long do you think till she wakes?"

"Not sure, my love, just let her rest. She's had a hard day—and well, life."

Karri's and Korri's voices were distant but low and soft, at ease. There was the smell of salt and the sound of running water. I didn't want to move, wherever I was. They sounded relaxed. I had to trust them, but who was trustworthy at this point? And frankly, minus the chill, whatever this soft thing I was lying on was more than inviting.

"Do you think we should tell her?"

Without hesitation, Korri's voice clipped, "Yes." I heard a sigh but couldn't tell which one of them it had come from.

"Keeping anything from her is out of the question, my love. I will not keep her in the dark, Karri. She's had enough lies for a lifetime. The moment she even opens the letter her mother left, only more will come to light, I'm sure of it. The journals—who even knows what's between those forsaken pages."

Karri giggled. "Never thought I would consider blood bonding to a dragon. Should be fun." A chill ran up my spine. Blood bonding? What the fuck . . . Yeah, now it was time.

I groaned as I sat up. "The fuck is blood bonding, and why is it fun for you?"

I quickly looked around and found them sitting by a pool of water fed by a small stream of water; the walls were stone. Pleasant, even while everything was damp. Blue algae-covered crystals jutted from the floor and ceiling.

"And while you're at it, where are we?"

Karri stiffened, and Korri laughed.

For once, they weren't in unison, thanks Above.

"And what answer would you like first, my Empress?" Korri flung the words over his shoulder and glanced back at me, his eyes an off shade of orange now matching his hair. Karri had the same orange hue to her. I wondered what they had drunk to do that.

I shrugged in response. I was in a massive bed, dressed in deep blue silk with shells as buttons. The bed itself was a massive shell with pink linens. I looked down at my crown from Juniper around my wrist, with the stone connecting me to Karma missing. Smart of them. I peeled it off and tossed it to the floor. I didn't need that thing. I knew my power. I didn't need a tool. Nothing had been easy for me, and I was not going to take another handout from the Kingdom of Rexarius—the place I had thought was going to be my home.

The vamps stood up from the edge of the pool and made their way to the bed with nothing short of lethal elegance.

"We are in the sirens' territory; this is our suite for when we visit. Orion hung around and came back, opening a Fae gate. The sirens are very kind to us, always have been, and they know far more than they ever let on. Men will confess the most insane things as they are dragged to the sea, their fate to be drowned for sirens' food."

As Karri spoke plainly, her eyes not leaving mine, I nodded. I knew the legends of sirens, but very little of their reality. I was finding this growing world. I now understood not only was I captive in the cell, but I had been sheltered as a royal.

"Blood bonding is what Karri did when we were first turned, locked ourselves together permanently." They sat on the foot of the clamshell bed, locking their eyes with me.

"We both would like to bond to you. It's the lost magic of the vampires, outlawed by our kind for centuries because blood bonding allows the vampire to wield magic."

I felt my jaw drop, then I cocked a brow. *Why would they bond, then?* I thought.

"Karri and I bonded by chance mostly. You could almost call it an accident. Our kind started by chance as well, mutations in a disease that killed humans, leaving our bodies useless and unable to produce blood on our own. Karri, being reckless, stole blood from unaffected humans in sheer desperation, and thus it was discovered that we could live off the blood of unaffected humans."

Korri was talking about the origin, not just theirs, but their whole species. Finally, someone who was going to tell me the whole truth, not just enough to keep me silent. I wanted to know it all; no one had been this blatantly honest with me.

I sat back into the pillows while Karri moved up to my side, pulled me into her cool body, and began stroking my hair.

"From what I was told, terror spread. No one knew what this was; no one could fathom it. Stuck between dead and alive, your body and conscience stayed living, but your body withered. Blood would pour out of you . . . A lot of people died. I fell ill before Karri. But it took her much quicker. My village had been decimated, I was captured, and Karri protected me when I was taken to hers."

Korri got up and began to pace, grasping the back of his neck. He continued, and for once I didn't hear Karri cutting him off.

"Back then, Karri and I had been lovers. We were outcasts, and back then, well, that mattered a lot."

Korri rolled his shoulders, apparently trying to wear a groove in the floor with his pacing. "Because of our status and multiple transgressions, they would not allow us—"

Karri cut in. "The point is, our village would let him suffer instead of gifting him some blood all because we broke a few laws. They would rather see us suffer. The laws of the clan were more important to them than their people dying. Anyway, I offered to save them. Sorry, go on."

Korri cleared his throat, while Karri kept working my hair. "I was dying. Karri couldn't take it anymore. She was and always has been comfortable with killing the people in her village. They were never kind to her. She took a man's life, taking in every ounce of his blood. She came to me, begging me to take some from her. She tore her wrists open and poured her stolen blood into me."

Korri snuck a glance at Karri. The look held adoration but also a certain feeling of regret. Like he still had rather died in that moment. I wondered what they had done for their own kin to abandon them. But those would be questions for another time.

"I felt instantly revived and drank from her. We hunted together that night, and after we each had caught our prey, we drank from each other. It was madness. We could feel ourselves melding together, matching, and then something just snapped into place. It was like drowning and then having air forced into our lungs. Our features shifted, and when we looked at each other, another wave hit, every emotion you could imagine: love, lust, fear, safety, rage, and peace, all mixed into one look, a bond only shared with blood. It's the deepest connection to be born of our kind. Generally, the bonds are for vampires, but over the centuries, Karri and I grew curious and started to bond with other beings just for the thrill of it. That's when more hell broke loose for our kind. We discovered that if you bond with a being with innate magic, such as the Fae, all types high and low Fae, wolves, monsters, and possibly dragons—that bond allows a vampire to wield magic, their magic."

I relaxed into Karri. I knew all of this should scare me. They were ancient, and they had seen so much, but I was enthralled with this story of who they are and how they came to be Karri and Korri, the so-called wicked dragon slayers. Maybe I didn't fear them because I knew they understood the hell that was captivity and endless suffering. I should have feared them, but I was relaxed by Korri's words and Karri's affection.

"Our kind wanted magic so badly, they would get carried away with bonds, bonding almost anything and destroying themselves and going mad with all the layers of emotions. In a vampire's madness, it would wipe out human cities and decimate anything they could. Bonds drove most to insanity, and when a bond was broken, it created monsters, horror stories of our kind. The Fae and dragons finally acted and started wiping out vamp nests. Soon, the only ones left were the smart ones, the ones who didn't dare challenge, who could see our species' carnage, and then the commandments of vampires were brought to light."

"We helped write them," Karri chimed in softly. Korri sat on the bed, staring at the pool of water in this little stone-walled cave.

"The laws for vamps are simple. One, don't infect humans without their full understanding and consent; two, you must be willing to tend to that human for five years before infecting them; three, blood bonding other kinds is forbidden; four, avoid killing humans with blood loss, only take what you need or part of your soul will be lost to Lady Death."

My head snapped up, and I felt the shock cross my face. Korri held up a finger, and I promptly shut my mouth.

"To take the life of another living human being by ripping their blood from their body, to drain that life force, it kills off part of your soul, you survive by killing off your humanity, bit by bit. Lady Death submits to no man, woman, or child. We did not know the cost back then; we only knew the desires we were experiencing, and we acted on them. Only humans can be infected with this disease, and it can only be spread by blood sharing at this point." Korri sighed "That is how we know the lady. We already walked a fine line between Life and Death. We spiraled out of control quickly and lost our souls and humanity."

Korri sank back down on the bed, lying back into Karri's lap, very close to me. "Vampire law is ironclad and punishable by death."

I sucked in my lip as a tear fell from my eye. They wanted my magic. At least they were honest about it, I guess.

"So, you want my magic?"

Karri laughed. "No, silly, not just your magic. Bonds are insurmountable for vamps. Not only would we be far more useful able to use magic from bonding, but it would allow you to feel us: every intention, everything. We would never lie to you, but considering recent events, and with our more than expansive existence, we can understand why you would never trust us wholly unless you could feel it, hear it, and know it. Since you are a dragon, you would not die if our bonds broke, but if you died, in theory so would we. Magic is tricky and this has not been tested, so . . . it may work out fine. You came for us, knowing nothing about who we are. We would be bonding our lives to yours."

Still struggling to understand, I asked, "Why?" my voice colder than intended.

Then, in unison, they said, "You hold the power to change this world. We swore vows, and we will defend our vows till our days' end."

I nodded. "Yeah, and how's that working out for me?"

They laughed and said in unison, "Not very well, Empress."

We sat in silence for a few moments. The pool of water gently lapped at the edges.

"I have questions," I stated plainly.

Korri scoffed. "I am sure of that. Ask away."

"Would I lose some of my magic when we bond it to you?"

"No, if anything, your magic should expand with more training to fill all three of us. Dragons are the only other beings besides the Fae who are essentially limitless when magic is concerned. It is more to do with training your body to handle the vastness of it. Next."

I nodded. "Was my mother bonded?"

In unison, a stern "No" echoed off the walls. I nodded again.

"Would you be put to death if this came to light?"

Small laughs, then Korri's deep, dark voice declared, "Our kind is well aware of who we are and who made the laws. Discussions would be had before they would kill us, or attempt to, anyway."

I nodded. "Why did no one come to save you from the Carcer?"

They shrugged, and Karri said, "I suppose because no one knew we were gone? And only your mother knew where we lived. Assassins do tend to hide in places no one dares go." I nodded.

"You have mentioned vows—"

Korri was quick and surprisingly harsh. "We are not able to discuss the vows we have taken nor anything more about them."

"Why?" I asked softly.

"Peace," they replied in unison. I nodded at that, too.

"Can I think about it?"

They laughed and said in unison, as usual, "You would be stupid not to think it over, Empress."

I cocked a brow at Karri. "Empress?"

Korri sighed. "If you do not know who you are, that is a shame, but it's not our tale to tell nor explain."

I paused and looked at them, then looked at the ceiling coated in reflecting crystals. Empress. Who was I?

I nodded. They weren't going to lie to me, but clearly, there were things beyond what they could share, probably having to do with whatever vows they had in place.

Karri laughed, breaking the silence. "Small detail to think over. When Korri mentioned a flood of emotion while bonding, it's catastrophic. Your body will betray you, and you will want us in ways you never considered. The same would go for us, naturally, so if you do decide to bond with us, you need to know the lust and desire in those moments would be the most intense feelings of your life."

I laughed, and they both raised their brows. "Somehow, this is far less concerning than when I found out Karma is fucking my brother, sister-in-law, and only the gods know who or what else. And mystery vows holding your tongue." Korri and Karri burst into laughter.

We laughed for a good while at the absurdity of it all, while I filled them in on Axl and Karma's love life combined with Juniper, and how I had been so thankful for the freedom, I played right into their hands. They drifted to sleep, and the gravity of what they were offering hit me. They wanted to stay by my side, and they wanted me to know they could be trusted with anything, going as far as bonding their very lives to mine.

Their laws be damned. Their vows were a mystery, but I would be able to feel their intentions and share them, so while they couldn't tell me word for word what was going on, or everything they knew right this moment, they wanted to prove I could trust them. I had little faith in beings. I had been taken advantage of too many times; but my magic, that I had faith in. I knew my magic well, and bonding to something else alive, my magic would consume anything that turned against me.

It had to be both or neither of them. They would die for me if it came to it. I looked over to the algae-covered nightstand, my mother's letter still sealed. Even though that letter could uproot everything, Karri and Korri made this offer. Maybe that held the answers, or at least some of them. A small splash came from the pool, and I looked at it next. Can I ever get a damn break? Why must everything happen so fast? Oh, great, a siren. I let out a sigh. It's fine; I'm fine. Her elbows rested on the side of the pool.

*"I will accept your choice, Empress."*

The voice? But softer, kinder, and no sex joke? Was he okay?

# CHAPTER TWENTY-THREE

## Elsie

She smiled and waved, a dark-haired female with a very full figure, brown eyes like caramel, and a rich brown skin tone; only pink jeweled sea stars covering the sensitive areas of her breasts. It was easy to see why men fell at a siren's hands. She was as sinister as she was beautiful. I tilted my head at her, and she waved me over with a finger over her lips to be quiet. I slipped out of the bed and looked at her. She pointed to the letter and waved me back over to her. I grabbed the letter while Korri and Karri shifted slightly toward one another, still passed out. I stood back from the pool. I was learning I needed to be wary of things.

"Who are you?" I whispered.

"Ithica." She stuck out her hand, whispering her name. "Princess of this territory." She dropped her hand when I did not meet it.

Wary, I whispered back, "Elsie."

She giggled. "I know who all of you are, and I promise I'm not here to drown you. Dragon meat is too tough," she joked, but it did not land the way she wanted. I only cocked a brow.

Her docile voice was still a whisper while a nervousness crept over her.

"The siren's song doesn't work for dragons, my dear, but I hear all the songs and whispers within my territory. The confessions of men and the secrets of the world trapped underwater for eternity—they are mine and my sisters' to hear. I came to talk. You three had a deep conversation earlier. I came to check when your voices had faded, saw you looking at that letter, and, well, I'm offering to take you to a place where only I can hear so you can read in silence. If I'm right, that letter will turn everything upside down, and you have far more power over the world than even you can fathom."

I nodded. "Why would you do that for me?"

She stifled a sinister giggle. "Because the sirens are with you, Elsie. We drag men to their deaths and feed upon their bodies. We are the vampires of the sea, but to survive the war on land, we will be on the right side of history this time."

I whispered back, "This time?" She nodded.

"The wars that ruined the continent when Korri and Karri were still young vamps nearly killed off the human population. Sea trade nearly stopped, and without humans to feed on, our people starved. If I have anything to do with it, they will not face the same fate twice."

Now that made sense. She was kind and noble, understood that life and death had a cycle. Her kind were reapers of human souls, and she would make sure her people were fed, as royalty should.

I walked to the pool and looked down into the crystal-clear water. It seemed to go on for miles, limitless. Her soft pink tail, barely flicking, kept her upright in the pool. She tossed me an open shell.

"Put the letter in there. It'll be safe. Take my hand."

All my better judgment flew out the nonexistent window as I took her hand and climbed into the pool with her. The water was ice cold, so I called my magic to keep me warm, thankful it had returned.

"Geez, don't boil me." She giggled. "Hold your breath."

I took in a gulp of air and was hauled down into the abyss, the water stinging my eyes, and I heard her voice over the water in my ears.

"Close your eyes and listen carefully past the water."

I complied by just bending myself to this princess for no reason at all other than silence and solitude were too tempting. I listened and could hear their song; it was the perfect melody of female voices in all pitches and notes, the most beautiful lullaby. It ended as soon as it began. When we broke the surface, I gasped for air, not noticing how badly I needed it. I looked around, swimming just enough to keep my head above water—when was the last time I swam in deep water?—quickly taking in my surroundings: a coastline, a shipwreck, black sand, and the night sky. She swam toward the wreck and hauled both of us up onto the rock the massive ship was pinned against. A cool, dark mist settled next to me. I knew Death had come to the freaking party as a mist just when I needed her voice.

"This was the first ship I took with my song. It belonged to a nobleman from another continent. He couldn't resist."

She smiled as we sat on the rock. I felt cold, so I surged my magic and nearly was instantly dry.

"He and his crew fed the territory for months."

Her voice, freed from its whisper, was beautiful. Even as she spoke, you could almost hear the melody of her words. She handed me the shell, and I opened it to find the letter completely dry.

"Surprised?" Ithica asked playfully.

I scoffed. "A bit, actually."

"Why did you follow, then?" she asked, turning her body to the rock and flicking her tail up over her, sending droplets like rain over us. It felt refreshing and peaceful.

"To be perfectly honest, the promise of silence seemed worth the risk."

She rested her chin on her hands. "You have had it rough. I don't blame you."

I gripped the letter in my hand. "What if this changes nothing?" I mused out loud.

"Then, there was no harm in reading it," she said softly.

"And if it changes everything?" She gripped my hand, and I locked eyes with her.

"Then everything must change, and frankly, I hope for that. The white king is not kind to us." I nodded.

That was becoming apparent. The trade deals he casually handed out were just well-worded and manipulative deals to bring wealth and territory to himself. He was a lying, power-hungry ass. He had taken a kingdom by just smooth-talking their desperate queen into a coup. Rather than help that queen and her kingdom, he took it from her. He could have helped kill that king, left the kingdom to her, and allowed her to be the first true queen of a whole kingdom, securing her daughters' futures that way, but no, he didn't do that. He manipulated her into killing the king and giving him her lands. I wondered what she had promised regarding her daughters; were they going to mate with Karma? Lords? Would they live as servants or slaves? Did they already know the pain of a collar or bridle?

Karma spoke of equality for all, but when it came time to take some action, he failed to do anything that would not serve himself. Typical.

"He was not kind to me today, either. I was told I his to own."

Ithica sucked her ivory teeth. "I don't like that for you, my dear."

I nodded. She placed her hands back under her chin and began to hum a low, sweet melody. My nerves began to fade. I looked over to Death, and her eyes jumped to the letter.

I scoffed. "I thought your song had no effect?"

She stopped humming. "The song of lure has no effect, but I didn't say a song of peace couldn't bring you some comfort."

I nodded and gripped the letter again, about to open it. "What about Korri and Karri? They will panic if I'm—"

She cut me off. "I hear all, even whispers and breath in my territory. If they wake, I will send a sister to them."

Her humming began again, louder, kinder, softer. I looked at the letter, closed my eyes, took a deep breath, popped the wax seal, and pulled out the single piece of paper. I looked at my mother's shaky writing on the front and back of the page, and I saw tear stains on the side of the paper with a single drop of dark violet in the lower corner. My tears fell, seeing her blood on the paper. Ithica's humming tuned out the world around me, thank the Above for that, and I began to read.

> *Dearest Elsie,*
>
> *If you are reading this, Karrigan and Korrigan have found you. And I can assume I am writing this from beyond the grave. I am so sorry, my darling, sweet daughter. I wrote to your brother as well. He was never a very critical thinker. I hope, over time, that changes for him.*
>
> *I have so many things to tell you. Firstly, I am so sorry I dragged our family into this mess. I truly believed life outside Bellator would be far better. I did not know the other kingdoms were far more ruthless to their people.*
>
> *We made grave errors and put our trust in kings and queens we did not know. I can promise you that if we knew we would accidentally cause a war expanding across continents and possibly generations, we never would have left Bellator.*
>
> *We ran from Bellator and our stations to battle in the tradition of mates, casting us out from Bellator and our families. We never took the Bellator Vows out of fear. We were weak and spoiled, thinking we knew best. We would make our way in the world ourselves without the help and safety Bellator provided. We threw our battles to be officially claimed by each other. A runaway lord and lady of Bellator.*

*We met the new king and queen of Rexarius at that battle and quickly became friends. We seemed to share a lot of the same ideals, and our warrior gear marked us as warriors from Bellator, so our alliance was born. They needed someone to fight for them, and we, not knowing any better, chose to form that alliance.*

*We went back to their estate. We nearly never left that cliffside. We would talk of power moves and freedom among the different beings within the Rexarius kingdom; little did I know at the time it was all a lie. They gave us the manor house after we essentially stole it from Fonsfrick, all in the name of claiming more land, power, and wealth. They want to rule the entire continent!*

*I suppose it's possible, but the human lands of Vitaendara should not fall to more dragon lordship. Humans should be allowed their own space in this world, as should all other kinds. Every life has a place here. To be the hands taking it from so many, it weighed on us.*

*I'm sorry I lied, telling you the manor had been our home for centuries and that we were royalty. The truth is all our wealth and power left us the moment we turned our backs on Bellator. The Rexarius gave us everything, and by the time I knew what they were planning for themselves, it was too late.*

*I had already had hatchlings, and so did the Rexarius. You should know him as Karma; I hope he is different from his parents, but I doubt it based on how they taught him.*

*My last-ditch effort to try to do right by someone in my life was to try and save Camila, Queen of Mor. When I saw her beaten and battered for producing a female hatchling, I couldn't stand it. Unfortunately, I did not know the Rexarius and the Mors had their alliance going, so when I hired Karri and Korri to sneak her out to another continent, I also did not know the other continent I was sending her to also had an alliance with Rexarius. I broke so many deals and hearts that day and betrayed everyone, including my own family.*

*By accident.*

*I'm sorry I did not value you both enough to protect you. I wanted to save her. My old friend from days past, I just wanted to help her. It probably is the Mors who did us in, and if I'm being honest with myself, I doubt the Rexarius tried that hard to save us, or maybe they did it themselves after my betrayal. Hopefully, they took pity on you and Axl, thinking they could raise you both in their homes and keep you both out of Bellator. I hope you find this letter.*

*I am running out of time, and I'm sure things are changing for the worse as I write, so a couple of things. You can trust Karri and Korri with your life. They have so much to offer; trust them. Whatever suffering you have endured, I am so sorry. I was selfish, and I am sure I will pay for this mistake with my life.*

*I am sorry I failed you. I am sorry I betrayed my homeland. I hope with my whole heart this letter is mean-ingless in your life.*

*With Love and Sorrow, Elizabeth Spes-Pax*
*Resigned Princess of Bellator*

I read it several times, then screamed. Ithica's humming could do nothing to comfort me, so she wrapped her wet arms around me. I screamed more, gagging on tears I didn't know were falling.

"It changed everything!"

"And that's okay." Ithica's voice crashed over my screams.

I sobbed, "She lied about everything! Nothing will ever be okay!"

Ithica gripped me tighter as I raged and mourned. I felt Death at my back.

"My entire life is a lie!" A splash of water hit my face, shock-ing my body. Ithica grabbed my face, locking her eyes into mine.

"Okay, she's a liar, and right now, we hate your mother." I nodded.

"Now, what are we going to do about it?" I sniffled, dropping my head onto her shoulder.

"I have no idea," I choked out.

She held me while I gathered myself. I sat back, wiped my eyes, and shoved that stupid letter back in its envelope. Ithica tucked some of my free hair behind my ear.

"You know what I would do?" I shook my head.

"I would take my power back, and I would drown them in it. I would ruin them all, whoever deserved it. I would lay them to ruin and drag their bodies so far into the water they would never know the light of day again. Some may say that's vengeful, but in a world ruled by violence, someone has to be the villain."

I nodded. I understood what she was saying: turn my back on it all, become the villain of their stories, but create my own story, no longer intertwined with this mess. I held a power no one had seen in millennia. I was named Death's Warrior for a reason. "Fuck my last name, fuck my so-called family. At this point, my name is Elsie, only Elsie," I screamed over the water.

*"As you wish, Empress."*

I stood up on the rock, let out a dragon cry, and looked to Ithica, fire burning over my skin, shaken to my core.

"Fly, girl, I can keep up."

Without hesitation, I ripped from my body, letting my wings take flight over the water, and looked down. I lowered myself to the water and stuck out my forearm. She grinned and latched on to it, and I picked her up out of the water.

"What? No WAY!" Her voice crashed over the wind, and I carried her to the sky. I roared into the horizon while she sang her song. I circled back to the wreck, allowing her to see her masterpiece from above. Her voice only grew louder and more poetic.

I dipped back to the water, and she let go while I perched on a massive rock outcropping. I breathed Hell's Fire out over the water, letting all my anguish and despair burn its way out of my body, allowing it to burn out any magic that had touched me. I only avoided my voice, that tiny bit of Cosmos I would carry with me as a reminder. I would free him as well. His childhood did not need to be tainted as mine was. I will finish these wars; I will end them all. I was tired of being patient, tired of being used. I would set an example for him to fight for yourself and those who are too weak. Being weak was not a crime to be punished with suffering; the weak had a right to live as well. Everything had a right to be alive.

While Hell's Fire burned, the redness in my eye came back, clouding it, burning away the magic that was used on me to restore my appearance. No, I would take nothing from them. I let the fire rage, my scars becoming raised and ugly all over again, but they were MY scars, and I was not ashamed anymore. I was more ashamed I had been so weak and desperate for a family that I allowed them to cloud my mind, cover my body, and try to control the fire that raged in my soul. Never again.

*"You are beautiful. In rage and desperation, you are flawless."*

I laughed at the voice and spoke back to it. *"What, no cocky remarks?"*

*"I should have come for you. Forgive me."*

I sighed. *"I will find you."*

*"I hope you do."*

"Are you done with your crisis yet? Korri and Karri just woke up!" Ithica yelled to me. I pulled my body back in on itself. Shifting was getting easier, much easier. I still lacked a fair amount of grace, but I could do it, without anyone's "help."

"Girl, why are you so skinny? Don't those kings feed you?"

I laughed. *Poison. It was always poisoned.* I jumped into the water below, allowing it to crash over me. I swam to the rock where my life was forever changed and took the shell with the catastrophe of a letter locked inside.

Ithica grabbed my hand and hauled me back under the water with such speed and ferocity I knew she was proving she was the dragon of the sea. Sailing upward, my head broke the surface of the pool in Karri and Korri's cave, carved out under the water, allowing just a pocket of peace.

They looked displeased. I laughed, popping up out of the water, turning on the heat, and drying as quickly as if I had never been in the water.

Korri started. "Maybe we should rethink this whole bond thing if you're going to run off without us and—"

"Not a damn chance, babe. You're both stuck with my ass now!"

Ithica let out a beautiful laugh and disappeared into the pool, allowing us privacy. I flicked the shell to Korri.

"Read that shit, then let me know what y'all need for this bonding, because let's be real, you two make up exactly half the friends I got. And y'all are going to need magic, because we're going to fucking war. I will rule over them. I will be EMPRESS of the kings, all of them."

My voice dripped with darkness. It caught Korri off guard while Karri smiled like a child gifted a pony. They exchanged a glance. Karri looked thrilled, and Korri looked concerned.

Both spoke in unison. "I think it broke our empress."

As they opened the shell, I laughed. "There was nothing left to break."

Their faces dropped as they read, much like mine had. Betrayal was the only thing that letter contained.

*"I support you."*

I laughed at the voice and shouted, *"I hope you and your cock enjoy the show I'm about to give you, then. You better watch, and you better not spill any of that seed of yours. I want you to suffer. And know that I will find you. Your ass is mine. You hear me?"*

*"Yes, Empress."*

# CHAPTER TWENTY-FOUR

## Elsie

arri's small frame pressed into my back, her cool body welcoming. Her breath ran across my neck; my skin prickled under it. I made eye contact with Korri, who was as stoic as ever with a cocked brow and angular features.

"Are you sure you want this, Empress?" I gasped as I felt Karri's tongue slide across my neck. Her soft voice spilled over in a moan of desire.

"Yes, I'm sure." Korri cocked his head.

"As you wish," they said in soft unison.

Karri's arm came around my waist. "Ever since that first taste you gifted us, how I have longed for more. I want to be your slave. I want to hear your heart run as we draw from you. I want to be the sin you have run from. Your taste has haunted my dreams in the most delightful ways."

Her other arm came under my shoulder and across my chest, unbuttoning the pearls and shells holding this silk top to my body, exposing my breasts to Korri. She took one in her small but lethal hand, rubbing and massaging and carefully taking my nipple between her fingers. I could feel it peak and harden. I would be lying to myself if I said I didn't find it pleasing. Her other hand started to dip beneath the waistband, trailing to my core.

I was frozen by her words; this was so sensual.

"I thought you said this MAY be lustful," I choked out as she giggled.

Between the licks and kisses, she planted up and down my neck and over my shoulder, she drew her words breathlessly, "Empress, you may be able to control your lust, but even after all my time in this world, no one's blood has sung to me more than yours. You are delicate and a force to be feared. You are a fire that ignites my lost soul."

She breathed, and I could feel it, my body begging, tightening in my abdomen and warmth between my legs, as she softly trailed her hands over my pelvis and breast.

Korri smiled, his fangs coming over his lower lip. "My Empress, the sentiment Karri has shared with you is mutual."

He strode toward us, his face full of excitement. I sank some of my weight back into Karri, tucked my chin down, and closed my eyes. I felt his long fingers sweep some stray strands away from my face and move down my cheek and under my chin. He then tilted my head back into Karri's shoulder, her breath still creasing my neck the same way her hands worked my body. I opened my eyes and found his eyes looking deeply into mine.

"You can tell us no, so I will ask again, are you certain you want this?" His voice was deep and sultry. I placed a hand on his chest, the soft fabric of his red shirt burning away where my skin met his.

"I am certain." In a flash, he scooped both of us up from the floor effortlessly. In the blink of an eye, Karri was on his back, tearing his neck open with her fangs, and his blood dripped onto my exposed chest.

I blinked, and my back was on the bed. Looking up at the crystals that hung from above, I could see them reflected, undressing each other with such grace and care. Korri dipped down to Karri's neck and tore hers open, allowing her orange-tinted blood to flow to her peaks, a beautiful sight to behold; her body was marvelous. I tore my gaze from the reflection and sat up to take the sight of them in. Dripping in orange, the color fading from their hair and eyes, I gasped, fearful of their blood loss.

Karri slid herself up to me, working her hands along my body from my ankles to the hollow of my neck, her face painted in wonder and hunger, her eyes shining. My body shivered in response, the pool of warmth growing hotter between my legs and in the depths of my core and soul. I sighed. Karri tactfully put her hands back over my breasts while her legs settled on either side of my hips. She leaned in and licked over the scar on my neck.

"Ours will be much prettier, my Empress," she murmured as her hands explored my body.

I nodded and sighed. She paused. "Nervous?" she whispered into my neck as her hands found mine.

"Yes," I replied softly.

I felt a quick tug, and just like that, our bodies were pressed into each other. I could feel the coolness and slight warmth of the blood flowing down and coating our sexes as her pelvis rested on top of mine.

"We can go slow." Her eyes met mine. "May I draw from you, Empress?" Her voice was filled with a chime's softness and sultry edge.

"Yes, you may." I closed my eyes and fell deeper into the dark-blue pillows. This felt different. I felt wanted, truly wanted, desired she wasn't holding anything back from me.

Her teeth sank into the side of my neck. I heard her moan as she swallowed. My back arched in response. The piercing pain brought a new sensation across my body. I felt her hands in my hair, her breasts pressed to mine. I felt our weight shift and a third hand on my cheek, caressing softly. The feeling was almost drowned out by Karri's sucking and moaning on my neck, my arousal dripping between my legs.

Korri's voice was kind. "Empress, right now, this is all you, your innate attraction to Karri. When you are ready for more, taste her." I stiffened slightly, and Karri stopped drawing. More?

Yes, I wanted more. I opened my eyes and found her neck so close to my mouth that the orange liquid looked inviting now. I closed my eyes, puckered my lips, and kissed her neck, tasting only salt. I opened my mouth and licked her neck, mimicking the way she had licked mine, the salt coating my tongue. Karri shivered over me and began to draw again, and then like my soul had suddenly been ripped apart, I felt it all, but mostly, I felt the need to have her. Own her.

My arms flew up around her body, clutching her closer. Setting my mind free without an ounce of shame, I spread my legs, begging. My body knew better than I what it was craving at this moment: her. Anything she could give, I would take from her, for her. Her hands gripped my hair tighter as her mouth found mine. I welcomed her within my mouth, allowing her tongue to sweep over mine, a messy clash of saliva and blood. My own hands started to move, one to her hair and the other to her firm breast. I played with her hard nipple between my fingers while she kissed me. This was not near enough of her; more, I needed more. I let out a moan. I sent my hand lower over her perfect body, tracing through the soft curls of her perfect little mound, sending my fingers between her lips, seeking out the tiny bud and twirling my fingers around it. She pulled back and whimpered into my neck, and I used the blood and arousal to push my way into her. I slipped in another, using my thumb to massage her clit as she began to ride my hand. Fuck, I hoped *he* was watching.

*"I am."*

Korri's voice whispered in my ear as I felt his hand trailing to my breasts. "May I take a draw, Empress?"

With Karri's mouth now attached to mine, all I could do was search for him. I unwound my hand from Karri's hair and dropped it next to my body, finding him. He was the more my body was craving. I trailed my hand up his chest to his neck and squeezed.

"As you command, Empress."

The sting of his bite had my body arch, and a moan escaped my throat into Karri's mouth. She broke our kiss and moved down the side of my neck with soft kisses. Leaving me exposed with a vampire at each side. As they both drew from my neck, I turned and opened my greedy eyes to see the reflection of two vampires. I turned into Korri, taking blood from him the same way I had from her, while using my hand, coated in Karri's arousal, to work into his mouth, breaking his hold on my neck. And just like that, everything that I had thought I felt was magnified tenfold. I felt love, lust, rage, and everything in between. Korri began working my clit and sank his fingers deep within me, curling and lifting my pelvis from the bed. Kissing his way down my body, nipping at my breasts along the way, until his breath was on my inner thigh, his bite parted the skin and he drew.

I gasped as my wings sprang from my back. With only their combined grace they not only accommodated for it, but they also moved my small body on top of Karri. She settled between my knees, my wings falling to the side. Korri grabbed my shoulder with such brilliance as he pushed me forward into her breasts, which I happily took into my mouth while his length was sent into my core. A new wave of emotions came over me; tears of ecstasy running down my face. Karri stroked my hair, and I chewed on her nipples. I arched from the sheer exquisite and all-consuming pleasure and found Korri driving deeper into me with one hand on my shoulder and the other holding Karri's pelvis to the bed. Using my hand, I found her lower lips and began to work that bud all over again. His strength and size easily held us together.

Both of us were so easily overpowered by our orgasms that we were rendered helpless piles of flesh, shuddering as each new wave of climax hit us. He sent his cock in and out of me, his hand exploring Karri's most intimate folds while taking my hand in his and guiding me to pleasure her more.

"How does it feel to be worshipped?" His voice was rough.

Worshipped? He drove deeper yet and faster still. Karri had moved silently and with such grace; she was now working my bud in her fingers without mercy while tearing at my breasts. I cried out as my own capturing climax came over me, stealing all my other senses, the world falling to darkness around me.

Worship was the closest thing to love I could wrap my broken mind around. They eased my ravished body to the side, each of them holding me while I searched for my soul that most certainly had left my body.

*"I am thankful, Empress. Allow them to care for you in my stead. Rest now, Firebird."*

*Magnus*

I deserved to sit there and watch, never allowing myself the relief of a split seed. My balls ached as my erection came and went time and time again, day after day. I sat watching, captivated, as my girl was ravished by those vamps. I deserved none of it. I did not deserve her.

I couldn't stand to see her hurt. Could I ever forgive myself for playing with her when she needed a savior, or when the truth came to pass, would she be thankful I was in the shadows? Was I holding her back? Or letting her grow? Damn, this war was exhausting. It was killing me. I needed her, the soul I tied to, by my side at last. I could no longer be satiated in the shadows, taunting her, watching her. I hope she is going to be willing. If not, well, fuck, what was I going to do then?

*Take her.*

NO, damn it, go to her.

She and those vamps needed a place to winter. Well, I could take her home. The court had sent word multiple times over the past few months, letting me know my brother began to spend money frivolously and was getting out of hand. Go fucking figure. Couldn't even keep himself together long enough for me to wrap things up and prepare for the infernal war that was to come. I hoped Elsie would not have to fight in the front lines but farther back, taking the lives she deserved to reap—that Camron bastard, Cliantha, and the fucking king of pigs himself, King Mor.

If we were lucky, if she was able to claim that kingdom in her name, that would allow Bellator to lay claim. Well, and that was if she was willing to accept the vows and my crest. Fuck. I lost my composure and sent a fist flying into a tree, felling it immediately.

Ugh, my damn namesake, my damn destiny. Fuck. I just wanted a simple life, but no, no, Magnus was never supposed to have a simple life. Half dragon, half-demon, I was destined for "greatness." Magnus Bellator, "Great Warrior." Yeah, okay, great spy maybe, powerful shadow wielder, excellent stalker, but a warrior? No, that's what she was, a fucking warrior. She held so much power yet still attempted to use it for good and not just wipe out this whole continent. No matter her heartbreak or torture, she just seemed to want peace. As much as I did. Death's Warrior didn't even crave the violence and bringing death wherever she went, but that was why Bellator's people had assigned her station: empress.

But if you want peace for others, you have to sacrifice some of your own. When this ends, I want to live out my days in the mountains of Bellator, secluded, where my blasphemous ass cannot be bothered. Maybe by then, I will have passed the torch to the next emperor. Kin or not. I did not want this job, but if it meant keeping my mate alive and easing her pain, I would bear it for her. All the pain and suffering she has endured, surely, I will endure while she heals. If she wants to rule the kingdom, so be it. It's hers.

I have given up. I am hopelessly in love with that little black dragon, and she has no idea how I have fallen for her or how long it has been. I had stumbled upon her while gathering intel for Bellator during and after the attack on our resigned princess and lord. I was captivated by the small, frail girl who fought so hard against death.

My father reminded me that she was not my problem. My only job was gathering information, that was it, so I pushed my magic to the brink, trying to keep her nightmares at bay, trying to force my magic to form good memories in her mind, allowing the darkness to call to her and allow my voice to seep into it. I did not care who she thought the voice was as long as she kept holding on.

And she did. My empress. My mate. My love. My Firebird. My soul tied to hers.

I told the people of Bellator of her, a black dragon being held captive, hatched from their fallen princess. They knew Elsie's suffering; they knew her kindness. They chose her. I chose her; there was no one else.

Just her. Empress Elsie. She would claim no last name, and that was fine; it would be Bellator anyway.

Never Rexarius.

That fucking asshole. I slammed into another tree, knocking a druid from it. Whoops. Karma fucking Rexarius just had to show up at the battle of mates. I tried everything to make him late that morning, using the shadows to confuse his staff, changing the clock hours, hiding Fae stones, the whole lot of it, but still, the idiot showed up.

Still should have been able to run his house better; that king had no idea how to manage the chaos.

Then he had the actual audacity in front of all of us to challenge the way he did, allowing nothing or no one. It was at that moment that I knew I was going to have to stalk her like prey and bring her to me. Too bad it all went wrong, and I couldn't just rip her out of their clutches.

I hope she can forgive me. I will tell her everything, leave no detail out. Maybe that will be enough; maybe she will come to love me.

I sank to my knees in the forest and cried.

My mind was breaking. I laughed. The Great Magnus Bellator, crying over a female. Fuck the ancestors; this was a new time, a new era, where queens would rule over kings. She will be the first, but not the last; no, we will change this world.

The Intercontinental Dragon Court would be established by Elsie, backed by Bellator. The empire no one knew anything about would be the only kingdom to uphold the dragons' promise to the gods: protect the world from the menacing magics and gods that wanted to rule it for their enjoyment. The gods named this world for its harmony. All things have a right to live and die in Concordia.

The beings that graced this land were the only ones who should enjoy it. The gods had their chance.

I vowed to protect their peace; hopefully Elsie would also take the Bellator Vows. I stood up, shook off the feelings of despair, and walked to the small town outside the sirens' territory. She would come. She would find me.

And I will give her everything.

# CHAPTER TWENTY-FIVE

## Elsie

I sat with Ithica and Death on our usual rock next to the wrecked ship. Death was in an unusual physical form. Ithica had downed a ship only a few days ago, so that explained why Death was in this form of flesh and bone.

"What is your plan, Elsie? We have been here since you left in midsummer. You need a place to winter." Death spoke matter-of-factly, and I rolled my eyes.

"You need to go somewhere you know as well as I do. You can't stay here."

I sighed. "And why is that? Ithica has offered me a place to stay. I like it here, the sea, the sirens, no one telling me what to do."

That last comment was a jab. Death had been pushy over the last few months, trying to tell me I needed to take some form of action. But what action did she want, exactly? She had about the same ideas as we did, and we had nothing; no good ideas, anyway. Save a theory I had been working on.

"You cannot stay. You have lost more weight. Soon, your magic will suffer."

I scoffed. "Oh, you mean exactly what I want?"

Death groaned, and Ithica giggled. "I know you want to feel love and the feelings they have for each other, but have you ever stopped to consider that a war is tearing apart this continent? Don't you think—"

I cut her off. "No, I am tired of thinking. All I thought of for over a century was freedom and rescue. I got that. I begged for a family and thought I had it, only to find that my so-called family is more corrupt than my wildest dreams, so I ask you this: Why should I think of them and their war when I have found a small amount of peace? Give me some time to figure it out. Damn." I was angry and violently bitter.

Death looked at me with her hard, dead eyes.

"Elsie, I can't force you to do anything, but if you will not think of them, at least think of me."

I stared out to the water and glanced at the beach, where Karri and Korri sat idly and sighed. Death gripped my hand, squeezed, and vanished.

"I see she hasn't let it go," Ithica chirped I ran a hand over my face and leaned back, propped up on one arm.

"I just don't think she understands. This magic, it's all I ever had, and now I have a bond thicker than blood. I have friends who happen to be very much alive and only live, essentially, to worship my very existence. What is the point for me to fight anymore? I never asked for any of this, Ithica. I asked for peace."

She nodded and gritted her teeth. "Els, I'm going to hurt your feelings for a moment. If you choose to winter here, you need to know my sisters and I cannot and will not fight on your behalf. We cannot protect you from him. If Korri is correct, he is waiting for you, waiting for your magic to dull. He will come. He will wreck everything in his path to get back his favorite toy, and we won't be able to stop it." Exactly as planned, he needed to think I was weak and easy prey. No one knew the plan, save for myself and M.

I looked down at the rock. These days, Ithica's words hit harder than my oldest friend's did. She was right; the sirens would be powerless against Karma. He had already told Korri point-blank he would allow me to "play" while they prepped for winter. He felt it was "fair and generous" of him to "allow" me time to be free before being trapped in his home built on death and lies.

"You need to actually think about it, Elsie. How you find the answer you can live with, I don't care. I don't care if you find it under a vamp or at the bottom of a bottle, but you need to take time to consider the facts laid out before you. That is how an empress handles things."

Ithica jumped into the water, not allowing me the chance to say a single word. Maybe that was for the best. What no one understood except M was what I was thinking about. Crying over it. Tormenting myself day in and day out. In the confines of my mind, we spoke; we talked about theories. I still didn't know exactly who M was. He said that keeping his identity hidden was for the best, so I stopped pressing it after a month.

Ithica brought up the fact I was drinking and fucking away my memories of that so-called family. I was not better than Clia at this point, but now I understood how she got there. I missed her and wished I could talk to her. If anyone would understand this pain, she could. Karri and Korri had to shield themselves from my rage, my sorrow, and my deepest feelings. After the first time when the bond was new, the magic almost killed them. The fire nearly burned them alive. We had to stop sharing our full selves and get a grasp on the magic. Now the best we could do was fuck and communicate telepathically—emotions, not words, but I could sense their growing impatience. The rest of the time, the bond was nearly useless. They could make bullwhips of fire and fireballs, but if they drew anything more than that from my unyielding well of magic, it tried to consume them.

The fire was relentless. I loved it still, but damn, sometimes I wish I kept that crown just to tame it in a small way. We needed more time to practice.

Seeing them in such pain after the first time, I wanted the fire to die a bit. I wanted to feel their emotions of love. I wanted to feel wholly loved, and that had been taken from me as well, only to be felt while I lay with them.

*"It's not fair,"* I cried softly into the shadows within my mind as I looked into the sky.

M's voice was soft and kind. *"Take a flight. I know it's not fair. Nothing has been."*

It wasn't that I was refusing the fight; it was that I did not want to fight beside Karma. I sighed.

I shouted to the beach for Karri and Korri, "I am going to town. I will be back before nightfall."

I shut out M's voice and soared into the midday sky. M, who had changed dramatically after I left Karma. He went from taunting and snarky to forlorn and shy. Over the past few months, he rarely spoke unless it was a theory we were sharing, a thank you, or a "Yes, Empress." I kept reaching out to him, taunting him like he had taunted me. Stalker he may be, but a liar he was not. I replayed all the words spoken, and he was never wrong, but I had shut him out anyway, when, in reality, he was trying to help me. I was thankful for that. I should have listened to him at the battle of mates when he screamed for me not to trust them. I should have known myself well enough to see I wasn't crazy, that I had someone on my side trying to guide me this whole time.

The small town sat just to the north on one of the many islands that cluttered the passage; it was a small port town mainly of fishermen and supply shop owners nestled in the Tarrent Sea between Rexarius and Bellator territories. Only a small human-owned place, yet because of all the travelers, you saw all kinds. All in harmony, getting from place to place, selling goods, just existing, doing their jobs. The docked slave ships angered me, but I couldn't afford to draw too much attention to myself.

Even Karri and Korri were normal in this place. If you had coin, you could buy blood here. The only difference between this little place and Otium was that Otium was a wealthy city, but they were not as free as Karma claimed. They thought I was drowning my sorrows in the taverns, and I was to an extent. I was also listening to the beings who gathered here who had traveled. They had a more worldly sense than me or my vamps. We missed a lot over the century. I was gathering information as best as I knew how—lurking in the shadows, appearing poor and displaced. I had not shared the extent of what I had learned even with Death.

If all the pieces fit together the way I thought they did, Death herself would rage for her love of Life. If the theory I had was true, it was worse than any of us had imagined. And it all could have been avoided with some humility among dragons.

As I flew over land and sea, I let my mind wander. Fuck, no one in that wretched kingdom of his was free. I listened to tales in their taverns. To enter and live in the city cost more than most of these men could earn in their lives—for what? Almost nothing in return. Promises of peace and safety. It was laughable. If you defied the laws or held money from the boy king, someone would kill you, whether it was a royal guard or some hired hand. Most of the travelers in this town stayed far away from the Kingdom of Rexarius. Karma had essentially charged all the people in his kingdom to live in a place that only he controlled with fear under the guise of admiration for all kinds. To be fair to the citizens, for most of the creatures with shorter lifespans, that was all they had known. They truly believed the rest of the land, including the human lands, were war-torn with constant bloodshed.

The trade deals were well-crafted gag orders. Why had he been so desperate to take ownership of Fonsfrick? Easy. If everyone lived the same way in both kingdoms, the lies would be easier to control. Why did he want the Mors? More power and territory. He was trying to carry out his family's goals, to rule continents and, eventually, the skies of Concordia.

I never expected my childhood best friend would grow up to be so selfish. Why had he become this way?

It was just the way they knew how to live. His parents had been the same, according to the journals. Karma, well, he was evil. My mother's journals only confirmed everything. She kept notes and details of her meetings with his parents about how to control populations of all kinds, framing other beings for war crimes and heinous behaviors while, in reality, it was all funded by the extreme wealth of the Rexarius dynasty and their sister kingdom on the other continent. Caelum Regandi.

Juniper was just as bad. She was the only heir to that kingdom, and their physical union was good enough in dragon law that she and Karma held most of the power to both. As soon as that sister kingdom's royalty fell, it was theirs. Then it would all be one kingdom, not a court, not anything but a filthy rich king and his bitch wife making the rules for all the others. They would do nothing to support the poor or the weak. Their bloodline would thrive while everything else suffered.

Axl? Well, that was my one wild card. Was he so blind? Or was my own brother also so corrupted?

Out here, all kinds lived side by side. Sure, they all had their own strife and dangers, but nothing like the fear-mongering Karma led his people to believe with stories of blood on every corner. He was just like every other dragon male. Power was his focus, and he would destroy anything to have it, including himself. What I couldn't figure out is this who had grown into by his choice or was it someone forcing him into this depravity?

If I ever got to see Life again, I had a lot to apologize for and a question to ask: Was Karma's second life actually a gift? Or was it a curse? Was it a gift to the world and only a curse for Karma? Or was the Lord of Life contracted to Karma by black magic, forced to give him a second chance, and Karma's inability to take or make life was his punishment?

Karma had faked wars between his subjects, pitting vamps and wolves against each other, elves and pixies, sirens and maids. He would blow it out of proportion in the shadows, then appear the soft, kind king when he was called to act. Controlling the newsletters, controlling everything save the dragons who refused to support them, but I had not been able to figure out their position. And M said he would not tell me until I was certain I was going home.

Dragons did not travel far from the territories they held. But one thing was certain: They were part of the resistance that other kinds mumbled about in the dark. Was the resistance to royals altogether? Or just the Rexarius dynasty being formed by lies in broad daylight?

Well-crafted lies.

No wonder they so badly wanted to bring me into their family as a weapon. They needed my bloodlust. The worst thing I had overheard yet was Karma threatening to unleash the black dragon of death upon the human lands if anyone mentioned this outside his walls after seeing the royal guard kill a man for nonpayment to the kingdom. That man couldn't have paid if he wanted to; he was missing a leg and could not work. The man who spoke about it in the tavern had gone missing only a day later. Karma's claws ran deep, and his wrath and power ran deeper across this continent. Coin, jewels, food, etcetera, all spent the same across dragons. The more you had, the more powerful you were. For him, with his people in fear of each other and the kingdom, the price of life was never too high to be paid. They paid it because they did not hold any power to say otherwise. Most didn't even know better. Everyone was a victim of the dragons greed.

The display of admiration I saw when the four of us flew across the kingdom that day, the day that gave me so much joy? They were forced to do that. The dragon lords knew better; they had seen the outside and had lived long enough to see past it all. The Fae, while old enough to know, also did not act, as a war between Fae and dragon magic would rip the land itself apart. They had allowed so much to go unchecked, thinking it was just a young king trying to find his footing. To dig everyone out of their graves now was an impossible task. I would have to act, but with what army? It was me and my vamps against a creature some would claim to be a future god.

As I came into view of the small town, it was busy as usual. I landed on the ground about a mile away, quickly donned my black cloak, and pulled my hood up. They knew I was a dragon, but no one here knew who I was. The black dragon of death was rumored to have lost the ability to transform due to her insatiable bloodlust. If I had to guess, that was also a courtesy of Karma.

Sick fucking bastard.

My feet were bare, and I had only a small black dress under this cloak. I spent most of the money Korri and Karri made from odd jobs and their savings on food and drink. I couldn't bring myself to waste their money on nice clothes for myself, and I could not work, could not dare bring attention to myself. The beaten, scared, homely little dragon girl couldn't possibly be royal. Karma had at least provided me with a great cover story. Karri and Korri were well connected but not wealthy outside of the kingdoms they had worked for. In the unclaimed lands, we were poor, and that was fine; we had each other. To be fair, those seemed to go hand in hand most of the time, except when a real hard coin was needed in a town such as this little one.

I kept my head down as I walked alone down the path.

*"I see anger and sorrow rising. Are you well?"*

M forced the words into my mind. He had a bad habit of doing that.

Why? Because he was worried. No, I was not well, not mentally, not physically. There was not a possibility of me being any sort of well when the weight of the actual world sat on my shoulders. Life and Death still in unrest, the Mors still fighting a hopeless war, against themselves mostly, and a family of dragons after one thing. To them, to rule was to wipe out all the other kingdoms so they would only be seen as gods and have the world's skies to themselves. And ascend to the Above.

*"I am well. Now, get out of my head. I'm almost there."*

I kept my tone as light as I could and felt the shadows fall silent. A chill crept up my spine. I stopped and saw my breath in the air. Oh, and winter was coming; add that to the list of my growing problems.

Fuck. It. All.

# CHAPTER TWENTY-SIX

## Elsie

I made my way to the center of the town to the largest and most populated of the taverns, the Cat's Paw. It was one of the older establishments, passed down from generation to generation in a human family. It was a clean tavern, with real tables and chairs made from oak wood, mugs carved from bull horns, filled with mead or beer, glasses of Fae wine served in carved crystal, and tainted blood for vamps. It was one of the most expensive places in town, as they also served food, and As Above, so help me, I wanted some of that stew.

I opened the heavy wooden door and was greeted by the overwhelming smells of food and drink. I sighed; at least here, no one knew me for what I was, only what I appeared to be. A displaced dragon traveler, nothing more, and that alone brought me solace among the beings gathered. I passed tables of beings talking about their seafaring adventures, some humans talking about the "tragic loss" that a ship had fallen to the sirens, and cheers of how their comrades had at least died at the hands of beautiful creatures. I kept my chin down and my gaze fixed on the table next to the busy bar but off to the side. At that table, I could hear and see almost the entire tavern, and planted firmly in his seat was the being I had met the first day I wandered in.

I pulled out my chair next to the large being I had grown to know only as M. His voice said male; his size was imposing, but I knew almost nothing about him. But he was my M, my monster, who kept me safe in the darkness of this world. He kept his appearance hidden, black-on-black tunic and trousers, black leather harness filled with daggers, much like my own leather gear I sent off the cliffside. His oversized coat was tattered at the bottom from dragging on the ground, with the frayed hood and high collar covering his face. The few times I managed to see his face, I only glimpsed his strong, defined jawline with a shadow of facial hair. However, he always kept his eyes shielded with a pair of dark lenses.

I knew him, not really, but I knew he was the one I'd started to lean on. I found him here, or he came to me, perhaps both.

"E." His voice, rough like ocean waves crashing on a cliff, nearly undid me every time. His mystery and darkness called to mine ever since the moment I found him in the shadows.

"M." I nodded with my reply.

This being had told me the ways of the world and opened my mind from the heartbreak that was Karma fucking Rexarius. I settled down next to him, fixed my gaze on the far wall, and sat for a moment. The bubbly waiter came by after seeing me take my usual place.

"Hello, E and M, what shall I bring you both today?"

"The usual." His voice was indifferent, with a small wave of his hand.

"The bone stew for me and a glass of mead, please."

"Sure, coming right up!" I could hear the smile in his voice.

M tossed me a sideways glance. I giggled.

"I like its sweet taste."

"You will be leaving soon, no?" M questioned.

"Why do you say that?"

He let out a huff. Clearly, my broody male of whatever was impatient today.

"Dragons typically don't winter at the coast." He paused. "Nor in siren territory."

I mused out loud, "And how would you know where I stay?"

He stifled a laugh. "The shadows, they talk."

I chuckled. "Do they now?"

His tone was serious. "They do." He had never mentioned the shadows prior to this. He only talked about the things he had seen, never about what lay in the dark. I knew it was him; he was the voice, the stalker, my friend. M may not have admitted it yet, but I knew.

The waiter promptly delivered our drinks as we sat in silence. I tuned into a rather interesting conversation between a wolf and a human sailor.

"I'm telling you, you want to sail clear around the Thunder Isles this time of year."

"That will add days to our travel, and my crew cannot handle it."

The wolf stayed firm. "Your crew also cannot withstand whatever monsters that dragon puts in those waters. You will be drowned or taxed for passage."

The human smiled. "My ship is the fastest the world has seen yet. He would have to catch us to tax us."

The wolf growled, "Fine, then, can't say no one tried to save your sorry hide."

I clenched my jaw and gripped the horn so hard it cracked, dammit.

"Easy, E. You can't do anything about it," M said between clenched teeth.

"And if I could?" I questioned in pure defiance from being told I could not do anything.

"Then, I would say you are a coward for not doing anything since you have the power to do something."

He took another sip of his drink and leaned back lower in his chair, crossing his arms over his chest. He spread his knees, allowing me to sneak another glance at the large bulge in his trousers. I sighed and nodded.

"So, what is it, then? Are you a coward? Or can't you do anything?"

I shifted my gaze to the large being at my right. "Neither," I said, my voice cold.

He shrugged. "Could have fooled me. Hiding under the cliffs with sirens and vamps, running away, what a pity. I am quite sure Lady Death had bigger plans for you."

I stiffened. "How do you know that much about me when I have not told you any of that?"

He would never talk of anything except what I thought Karma was up to and the plans I was working on. I let the rage creep in. We were both quiet and still enough that no one paid us any mind, even the waiter, as he dropped his plate of raw steak on the table and my bowl of stew in front of us and turned away as quickly as he came. The tavern was filling, and he was too busy for any of his pleasantries this round, thankfully. I needed him to admit it. We'd spent months playing this game. He seemed to be wearing down and getting more impatient with me. I needed him to say it, own it, admit it, all of it.

"The shadows, they talk."

I groaned, "So you have said, oh mysterious one."

He chuckled as darkness rolled off him. We ate in silence. The waiter came back time and time again, depositing more mead into my cracked horn.

"I am not a coward; I just don't have a starting place," I said after my fourth horn, idly listening to sailors talk about routes to avoid to attempt to trick Karma.

"Starting place?" M questioned, cocking his head.

I nodded. "You know, for war," I said, half joking. He laughed out loud.

"Oh, Firebird, the war has long started. You have come to finish it." He shook his head and stood up. "It is getting late, and if I'm right, you need to be back before nightfall. Let me walk you."

I nodded and reached inside my cloak, but he was swifter.

"Allow me." He placed a large sum of coins on the table. I was not going to argue it. I never argued that with him.

"The vamps, you bonded to them?" M questioned out loud. I nodded.

"Wait, how did you know?" It was a thinly veiled attempt to force him to admit who he was.

M laughed, throwing his head back. "Little Firebird, the sh—"

"Yeah, yeah, okay. The shadows, they talk," I said, mocking him with my hands.

Just say it already, M. Just admit it, just tell me. Trust me. We walked in silence the whole way back over the bridges connecting all the little islands right back to the cliffs. The companionship, even in silence, was nice. I saw no need to fly, leaving my mysterious cloaked figure to himself. If I was lucky, maybe I could persuade him to come to the beach, maybe to the room. Karri and Korri wouldn't mind, that much I was sure of. Maybe then I could coax it out of him.

"Well, this is where I must leave you, it seems," he said to the water, or maybe the shipwreck that sat ominously below.

"Thank you for walking with me," I said nonchalantly.

He sighed. "No trouble, Empress. Perhaps we both need companions who don't feel the need to pry."

I nodded and shrugged off my cloak, getting ready to fly down to the wreck to be picked up by Ithica. I felt his hand grip my forearm.

"Elsie." I ripped away.

"No, you do not get to do that."

"Turn and face me," he ordered, and reflexively, I did. He shoved away his hood and took off the lenses, exposing the most brilliant silver dragon eyes. His black hair with drops of silver running through it, shaved at the sides but long and flowing from the middle, in a long braid passing his broad shoulders, colored bits of leather woven into it. His face was young and aged yet, at the same time, chiseled and forlorn. The age he wore, I knew well—grief.

Silver eyes, talking shadows, IT WAS HIM, I KNEW IT. I hissed while my wings unfurled from my back, and I dipped, ready for a fight. He sighed, removed his own cloak, and exposed a set of wings that rivaled Karma's in size and beauty. Black as the night sky on a new moon with silver dots sprinkled through them, scarred nearly as much as my own were. He stood motionless, holding his cloak and lenses draped over an arm.

"It seems only fair. My name is Magnus."

I nodded and straightened.

I looked him over. Fae stones of red and black adorned his ears, more like fastened in his ears. A large black pendant hung at his throat, black tendrils ran down his face, connecting to his neck and, from what I could see, down his arm. He grinned as I took him in. Clearly, my face was betraying me. Without moving, the tendrils disappeared, and I felt a presence at my back. I turned and looked to find that same shape hovering over my shoulder. Wispy, long shadows.

"The shadows, they talk," I muttered.

He grinned. His fangs and teeth could put Karri and Korri to shame. Who the hell was this guy? I knew him, but this was like meeting him for the first time. Years of his voice in my mind came to life in front of me. The black tendrils returned to his skin, and he offered only a statement. "Hell's Shadows." I nodded.

"Hell's Fire," I offered. That was what came out of my stupid mouth, facts he already knew.

He looked at me with those lethal silver eyes. "I know. I'm sorry."

I just stared at him. What could I say? There was nothing to say. Both our magics were from the Below, granted to us by beings of realms we knew nothing about.

"My life is yours to wield. I don't deserve you. I am pathetic. I didn't save you. I let all this happen. I—"

My cackling laugh cut him off. "No, no, YOU don't get to do that, too. No, you don't get to feel sorry for yourself. You made me feel like I was crazy, like my thoughts couldn't be trusted, like they weren't even my mind talking, only to find out I was right!

It wasn't me in my head; it was you! You stalked me, watched me fuck, and tormented me. You don't get to feel sorry for that."

I turned away, knowing the next words out of my mouth would not only be delusional but impossible to say. I could feel the tears in my eyes.

"Especially when what you did saved my life many times, you can't be sorry, not when I will forever be grateful to you for protecting me and saving me from myself. You gave me courage, protected me from my soft heart, and allowed my heart time to heal and harden on its own. If it was a game to you, consider yourself a winner."

I tossed my hair aside, looking over my shoulder to see the stunned Magnus staring back at me.

"Don't you dare feel sorry for any of it."

Magnus stood, the breeze slightly moving his loose hairs over his eyes. "You don't even know why I did those things."

I scoffed. "Like it matters. The FACT is you did those things to me or for me. I don't care because at least you had the gall to be honest about it; you never hid from me. Even in town, you sat next to me and never tried to convince me of anything. You let me listen and work out my problems."

He stiffened. His hard eyes piercing through my gaze. Taking him in was like coming up for air while drowning. I thought Karma had saved me, but it was Magnus who had kept me sane all those years. He may not have burst into my life a shining beacon of light, but he was part of the darkness that had consumed me for years. He was my savior. In the depths of my despair, he was the monster lurking in the dark, not to hurt me, not for real, but to help me.

"And what if you can't handle me, Elsie?" His voice slightly cracked.

I scoffed and walked toward him, toe to toe. I looked up into his otherworldly eyes, sweeping his stray hairs lightly from his face with the back of my hand. On the tips of my toes, I laced my fingers together behind his neck. The crash of waves hardly drowning out the sound of his breath, I leaned in and whispered against his lips, "When they come for me, watch the hell I unleash. Take it all in, watch me risk it all, then ask yourself again if you think I can't handle you."

Before he could push away, I pushed my lips to his, and his arms circled my waist, dropping his cloak and lenses to the forest floor. I parted his lips with my tongue, and he tentatively met mine. I allowed some of my weight to sink into his massive frame, feeling the bulge of his arousal growing.

I pulled away and gave him a coy smile. He cleared his throat and picked up his things as I turned for the cliff.

"I will come to collect you and your vamps at twilight. I hope to witness the hell you bring. But let me be clear, we leave here tomorrow whether or not they come for you. Let me take you home, Empress."

I smiled and giggled. "They will come; the temp dropped today. I want nothing more than to go home to a real home."

I stepped off the cliff, allowing my half-formed wings to deliver me to the rocks below and to Ithica, who was beaming.

# CHAPTER TWENTY-SEVEN

## Elsie

When I returned to our room under the water, Karri and Korri were packing things into small bags and cleaning up. I got out of the water and dried myself off, walked to the bed, and sat down.

"He will come tomorrow at twilight, and we will go with him."

Korri's voice was tense, and so was his body; he was beyond stressed about the potential encounter we would have with Karma and, officially, Magnus.

"You think they will both appear?"

I leaned back on the bed, letting my dress creep up to my thighs, my hair spilling around my shoulders. I looked at the reflective crystals. I was getting used to it, the scars, thin body, the look of someone near death. At least I didn't feel as bad as I looked.

"I know they both will," I snapped.

Karri flinched; she didn't like it when Korri and I had spats. He ran his hand through his red-and-violet-tinted hair while I kept my gaze fixed on the crystals, watching their moves.

"Magnus, then," Korri amended in a grumbling sneer. "How do you know he's not a contracted assassin for Karma? How do you know he's safe for us to just fly away with? How can you honestly be so unbothered by all of it? You don't know him!"

His voice snapped over that last sentence, and Karri nearly made herself invisible. I sighed.

"Because he has been with me for years. We will winter with him, wherever that may be." My voice stern I was not going to wavier on this. I would be going home, with Magnus.

They did not need to know about him stalking me into Rexarius and out here. Karri would be quick to put it together. I could live with this, running away for now and fighting my way out if need be. What happened with the Mors was different. I was a child. I had no way to fight. Now I did, and I was no coward.

Not anymore.

"And what about us?"

Puzzled, I paused.

"You said you are with me till the end. Have some faith. I have some theories, and to be perfectly honest, if Magnus did go tell Karma where I am," I chuckled, "good. Saves us the trouble of going back to bid our farewells. And if he's not an assassin, truly just a good guy offering sanctuary, then I suppose you could say I finally read a situation correctly."

Karri smiled. She knew better than Korri how my mind worked. She may not be able to read my thoughts, but her read of my intentions was always spot on.

"Korri, we are hers. We need not worry about our empress. If she's trying to trap Karma on neutral territory, then let her, and we will aid her just as promised, and I will remind you we will do so, no matter the cost."

"BUT SHE DOESN'T KNOW MAGNUS!" Korri shouted.

With venom, Karri replied, "And neither do we!"

She spoke softly but with that edge to her voice, "a lot of time has passed with us all in prisons." Making it clear she knew I was up to something I dared not speak aloud.

"Fine then. Tomorrow, we say our goodbyes, grab some supplies, and fly out with Magnus," Korri said, just giving in as his hand gripped the back of his neck.

I smiled. "Now come here, you both. Let us enjoy the night." They nodded, pounced on me, and began their draws, opening the scars on my neck. Delightful.

I sent a whisper into the shadows. *Feel free to enjoy the show.* No reply from Magnus, save for a sinister chuckle.

* * *

I awoke after an eventful night with Karri and Korri to Ithica splashing in the pool that connected our room to the outside world.

"You know, y'all could be a tad more considerate of my virgin ears."

*"Don't ever be more considerate, please, I beg you."*

I laughed. Good, that was the Magnus I knew. I left Karri and Korri sleeping and went to the pool.

"What time is it?"

"High noon. Care to get some sun?" I smiled and jumped into the cold water. I let my wings out. I had been using them to swim with Ithica on our way out, building their strength. Flying underwater was far harder than in the air. We swam quickly, and when we reached our rock, my wings burned with magic and a feeling I had forgotten existed in my body: fatigue.

*"Be safe."*

"You all right? You pushed harder today."

I nodded, out of breath, as I dragged my soaked, frigid body onto the rock.

"It's good to push yourself. Never know when you're going to have to push yourself past limitations."

She nodded, tears escaping her eyes. "So, this is farewell, isn't it?"

I laughed. "As Above, no. I will not say goodbyes. Farewells are for the dead and dying; I will see you again." My words came out confident, but I knew I was taking a gamble.

She wiped her tears and nodded. I sat, taking in the sunlight and the ocean air. The sky was overcast, only allowing small bits of the sun to sneak through. Looking at the shore and tree lines, I noticed the trees had transformed into their auburn colors and the leaves began to litter the land. Winter, a long, hard one, was approaching. If it had been Clia sitting with me in this place, no doubt her healing magic would have warded winter off, at least in this small space of peace I had found. I knew what was coming, yet I still held onto a part of her from long ago when she was kind. If I could save that girl, I would.

"What are you thinking about?"

I sighed. "Honestly?"

Ithica rolled her eyes. "No, lie to me," she said in a voice dripped in sarcasm.

"Cliantha. I can't help but wish I had freed her as well. I regret getting so angry with her, angry enough to blame her for everything when she just needed someone like you and Karri—friends. She needed me, and I allowed her behavior to push me away. I loved her. I think I still do. I know I can't love her, but I need to save her."

*"You are far too kind."*

Magnus was no longer hiding his voice; it was rough, and no matter what I did, I could not pull my mind from the gutter.

"You mean the one who trapped you and tormented you? That girl? You need to save her?" Ithica's tone was dumbfounded.

I nodded. "From herself, mostly. And if my theories about Karma are correct, she's as much a victim of this war as I am."

"Why won't you share with any of us what you have been thinking?"

I laughed. "Because those words are for Karma's ears, and if I'm right, the shock of it will tear his so-called family apart. If it is a true surprise, he can't control anyone's reactions or manipulate them with swift words. Yeah, I have been fucking and drinking away my mind, that's why. Because if I think about this too hard or long, my blood lust becomes insatiable. I want to kill him. What a horrible thing to say. The male I was supposed to find hope in, the one who lit up my darkness, I want to end his life. For someone blessed by Death, I don't exactly love the permanence death brings. Living with your failures and repairing them is harder, more torturous. Death is an easy way out."

Ithaca's big brown eyes were wide as they met mine.

*"My, my, how you have grown, little Firebird. I love the darkness. It's where I found you."*

"I will attempt to reason with him first, make an offer, and if he can't agree, then I will fight."

"But you're weak . . ."

I scoffed. "No, Ithica. I am not weak. I appear weak. I have been channeling all extra resources into my magic. The restoration Cosmos gave me burned away."

Save for only my voice, I had to keep that intact for the time being.

"Every last bit of magic I could spare, has been dormant, waiting for the right time. This simple human body is just one I spent the most time in while I was at the Mors in the beginning, so it's easy. Ugly, but easy. Magic can be used any way the user of that magic desires. I have hidden mine, and let me tell you, the magic within me is just as angry as I am." My mother's journals taught me a lot more than just about the kingdoms and politics. Those journals taught me how to refine my magic.

I took a breath and sighed, looking into the cloud-coated sky. "When he comes, be sure the sirens are far away from here. Karri and Korri will be able to withstand it—but just barely. You guys will need the cool water."

*"A clever, beautiful, dangerous empress you are, my dear."*

Shock and awe were written across her face as she nodded.

"You didn't have to hide this—"

"I did. I don't know all the details for certain. Your ignorance will keep you safer than if I were able to defend you."

She nodded and hugged my arm. "I am glad we are friends."

I nodded and looked at her prized ship. My friends were beings that somewhat needed the death of others, a sad, contradicting existence. We loved life, but we loved what life had to offer, not what we currently had, and we would fight for what was owed to us. The life I should have had, filled with happiness, relaxation, harmony, and quiet, peaceful breezes over my wings. I shed many tears over the life that should have been. The life I was living was no life at all; I would take it back. The afternoon passed, and I took in as much sunlight as possible, waiting for Karma or Magnus—whatever and whoever came first.

As the sun began to dip, Ithica brought Karri and Korri out of the water with their small bags. I shifted, and they climbed up to their usual perches. We soared to the cliff tops, and I shifted back.

"We will wait here. Be ready. And do not call me Empress when they are around. Under any circumstance."

We waited for what felt like an eternity, my magic bubbling with anticipation, Karri and Korri hidden in the trees. I giggled as I let my legs dangle over the cliff edge. The air stilled with the telltale marker of Karma Rexarius—a chill, colder than any blizzard.

*"I am on my way."* I smiled. I knew he would come.

I glanced over my shoulder, and there was Karma, the white dragon with his usual sidekicks, his hands in his pockets, and his fake somber mask over his features. If I didn't hate him so much right now, I would still think he was beautiful as his rainbows fell around us.

*"I don't blame you. He is rather pretty."*

Another giggle escaped me as I turned back to the sea to hide my shit-eating grin from Magnus's words.

"Karma," I said, my voice dripped in venom.

"Elsie?" he questioned.

I whirled and met his eyes. "Who else?"

As I stood, Axl gasped, and Juniper took a step back, my appearance shaking them. Death and despair was marked all over my body in scars and death's markings.

"Come home," Karma demanded, quickly amending it with, "Please, we miss you. And you're not well."

I couldn't hold back the laugh. "No."

His eyes flashed so quickly I would have missed it had I not been waiting for it. They had fooled me long enough; I would see past all of it now.

"Els, please, I want my sister to come home. We—"

"Need me?" I cut Axl off without breaking my death stare into Karma's icy blues.

"Yes! We need you, Els. We need you to help us take down the Mors. We—"

"I never said I wouldn't help you with that. I said no to Otium. There is a distinct difference in those two things, Axl."

Juniper shifted her weight, growing impatient. "What is that supposed to mean?" Her voice grated my last nerves.

"Just spit it out, Elsie," Karma demanded.

I chuckled. "Fine, let me make this simple. You can send word to me if and when you plan to attack the Mors. I will join, happily even," I sneered. "But that's the end of it. I want nothing to do with the lot of you, including you, brother—well, at least for the time being." I shrugged. "I will continue to live my life as I see fit, wild and free as I desire. I will fight them, but I will not ally myself with you. Is that clear?"

*"Well, that's diplomatic of you."*

Karma shook his head. "You know too much; you either are with us or against us. And if this is where you stand, then you are against us, and I will not have it."

I laughed. "So, you will have my own brother kill me? Maybe your son's mother could attempt it, I guess? Pathetic. Your greed for power really has backfired on you, hasn't it?"

He stiffened, eyes growing dark. I stood and took a step forward. He crouched.

"Tell me if I am missing anything here. Your parents held the most power on this continent. They opted to align with Juniper's family in Caelum to eventually take over both continents. Since I was dead by all accounts, they sent you off, and when you returned from your forced mating with Juniper, you found out their true plans. You, Juniper, and Axl have been used as pawns as well. This enraged you; they told you the truth—"

Karma shouted, "Shut up, Els!"

"—That you and Juniper were going to be forced to marry, one way or another, with me out of the picture, but Axl stood in the way of that, so they crafted all this to make sure you also ended up with something—rather, someone worth fighting for, your son—"

Karma cut me off. "Enough, Elsie!" he roared.

"Oh, I'm not done. Shut your mouth, Karma. Let's see how strong your family is when the skeletons come out of the closet."

I let some of my magic escape, turning the ground around me to gray ash. The three of them froze, their eyes wide.

"When you found out about their deal, you killed your parents. That is why it all happened the same day you returned. The royals conspired against you, forcing you to take Juniper and create a son. You didn't emerge unscathed, though. No, no. Your father landed a blow ending your life as well, and then someone used black magic, a curse, to resurrect you, ending up binding the spirit of life to you. Life, with no other choice, left you unable to take another life at your own hands or allow you to make a life. And since they are spirits and not all-knowing—whoops, you already had Cosmos on the way. Maybe after you had seen the damage your family and hers did to the world, you would strive for a better place, one where death was less common, but no, that backfired on Life, and you became a political monster. You needed Axl to carry out your darkness and Juniper to fix any mishaps and injuries. And you, Karma, are still indebted to your in-laws since you, your land, and your son were a prize to them from the beginning, nothing more than that, might I add. Just a male to continue bloodlines of wealth and power."

Juniper stepped forward, and I ignited myself.

"Now you have given them your flesh and blood. You will not agree to MY terms because you're not actually in control, merely a puppet in Juniper's family for conquest. Until the day those poor bastards die. You are at their mercy. Sad, truly sad, Karma." I smiled.

Karma shook with rage. He had no control; all his arrogance was for show, his wings always on display only for show. His entire existence was a bluff, and here I was, calling him out on every bit of it. In front of the two dragons who had either been played mercilessly or were coconspirators.

"How dare you?" Axl shouted. "He loves us!"

I scoffed, "No, brother. He may have at one point, but at the cost of his free will, he has grown tired and resentful. He only cares to usurp the thrones. Juniper, you are no exception. He will take your crown—"

"Liar!" Juniper yelled.

I laughed. "Well, Karma, am I?"

*"Easy, darling. I'm here. Trust the dark."* I smiled. I did trust the dark and the monsters within it. The dark was my kingdom, and I was its empress. I knew the dark, I knew its secrets, I knew how it lied. While Karma was light and airy, there was no mistaking the darkness within him.

My fire consuming my body, I raged, "The only real question I have left is, did you know? DID YOU KNOW I WAS BEING KILLED TIME AND TIME AGAIN? MY LIFE WAS STRIPPED AND ROBBED DAY IN AND DAY OUT, did you know? Did you visit the manor, visiting my grave, because you knew I would never be the same, and the girl you knew did, in fact, die?"

Ice began to creep out of Karma.

"You have never been a liar, Elsie, but you do have one thing wrong."

I cocked a brow.

"I will do whatever it takes to protect Axl, Juniper, and Cosmos because I do, in fact, love them. You are correct. Life is bound to me. I killed my parents when the depth of what they did to break me became apparent. My father did kill me. I knew for a long time that day would come, so I perfected the black magic to bind Life himself to me. Did I see the curse and price I would pay? No. Would I pay that price again? No. You're right. I hold no true power, but, yes, I did know. You are a weapon, Elsie. Come home."

His brow cocked, matching mine, the deadpan stare in his eyes with the faint look of pleading. He continued talking as if I hadn't noticed his tell. I knew it; he would take the fall for it. Idiot.

"But that will change in time. It will be a long, painful process to undo all that our parents did. It was much simpler with you dead. I'll have to agree. No one could stop us before, but now that you're here, let me guess, you are going to overthrow the kingdoms in this order—Mors, Bellator, Rexarius, then you will wipe out Juniper's homeland."

I clapped my hands, "My, my, how quick you catch on is impressive. But you are missing the point. I will only do that if I am forced to."

Juniper and Axl looked cold, sick, and shocked. Except Juniper's was a well-crafted mask; her growing black nails were a different type of tell. I knew it. The fucking bitch.

"How do you know all this?" Juniper whispered, rage coating her voice.

"I have been reading over my mother's journals, I have spent my time here thinking about everything and, most importantly, listening to the people who come and go from this place."

I kept my eyes on Karma, begging that he could read my words.

"You are a master of deception. You knew that if I came into play on my own, I would burn it down. I wouldn't be surprised if the reason you haven't eliminated the Mors yet is that you are waiting to blame it on me, the easy scapegoat. It wouldn't matter if your weapon went on a killing spree, taking more land for your throne, now, would it? Or are you hoping I die in battle?"

"Why would he do that, Elsie? That's—that's—just insane. You have spent too much time with the sirens. They—they must have—"

"Speak of the sirens again, Axl, and I will leave you wingless." I paused, then turned to Karma. "Are you going to tell them, or shall I?"

Karma sent out more ice, and it melted as it hit the smoldering ash at my feet. He cursed under his breath.

"If Elsie is not aligned with us and aiding our goal, my orders are to kill her. The Regandi know if she and I are on the same side, we will overthrow them quickly and without mercy."

Juniper sighed. "Well, we can't overthrow them."

I scoffed, "And why not?"

"Because we don't hold enough power. We are their pawns and will be till the day I die," Karma said.

"Your father is a black magic user. He can strip life from me and leave me dead if I disobey him. And if I kill Elsie myself, then I die because I'm bound to Life. I cannot win this war."

Juniper looked oddly smug for just a moment, and I put the missing pieces together. Black nails, smug look, father of black magic. Theory confirmed. Finally, I had my answers. I knew it was the fucking wholesome bitch. I laughed.

"Juniper, you are the one who bound Life to Karma, aren't you?"

She froze, and Karma jolted forward to attack me. I dodged, silently begging Karma to keep playing this game. He knew I was alive; he let me be tortured, but he came anyway to claim me for his weak attempt to keep me from being killed. Did he know my bloodline? Axl's? He must, he has to know the reason we were targeted first was because we are royals by blood in Bellator. *Keep playing my game, Karma, please*, I begged.

"And Karma, you love Juniper so much that you will even lie to hide her twisted soul. Aw, how sweet." I scoffed.

Using my own sort of tell, I signaled for my vamps, sending my wings out and flexing the tattered webbing, scarred over the bone to show the full extent of my suffering. Karri and Korri dropped from the trees and were at my side in an instant. The shadows twitched.

I cackled. "And they think males are the most wretched leaders of our kind. I think that award goes to you, Juni. You followed your mother's footsteps, trapped a male or two, bound them with impossible circumstances, and ruled from the shadows until you take over and prove your father wrong about us females. Am I right?"

I winked at her, and her rage filled the air.

"Axl, Karma, how's it feel to be played yet again? And you all say I should be less trusting, but let's be real. I sensed it on her the day I met her, just could never figure out why."

*"Uh, you're welcome."*

"So, let's make a deal. We all walk away. You three decide what you want to do and send word to me when you are ready to take some actual action."

"You will die here, Elsie. You will not ruin this for me, not while I'm this close to ruling continents," Juniper snapped.

Juniper raced for me, with gold and black magic radiating from her claws. There it is, the truth behind it all. A scorned woman much like myself, but this one was lost and worse off than Clia. She had led them to believe not only that they had some sort of power but that she loved them.

She didn't; she loved power, and as repayment to her lovely family, she was going to make damn sure only she stood at the end of this. Fucking King and Queen Rexarius shifted in their appearance, dragon scales covering their vital organs, claws from their hands extended and ready to fight two-on-one. I took a glance at my brother, a broken heap on the ground, sobbing. His life was a lie, and he knew it. At least I wouldn't have to prove it to him. He saw it all unfold, as his lovers now were attempting to kill his sister. To save a throne that they didn't even own.

# CHAPTER TWENTY-EIGHT

## Elsie

I laughed. "Wow, never thought I would see the day. Half shifting, really? Desperation looks good on you, eh?"

"Please tell me you have a plan," Korri pleaded quietly.

"Of course she does—"

Karrie sneered as I cut her off. "No, it's more of an abstract idea, actually," I said casually.

They both stopped, open mouths gawking at me.

*"Empress, be safe,"* Magnus whispered.

"You dare talk about me like I'm some low life? Like my entire existence hasn't been to make the most powerful kingdoms and children? I did it, and I will take my parents' throne. I will rule the fucking sky, Elsie, all of it. We will be gods!" Juniper snarled. Karma looked like he feared her for a moment. Interesting and exploitable. I felt the grin tug on my lips.

"Oh, poor Karma, afraid of his wife. Even more tragic, pathetic little ice dragon."

*"What the fuck are you doing?"*

"Be quiet," I demanded loudly, much to everyone's horror.

"I don't fear her, bitch. I owe her my life. Don't you fucking get it? I owe her. She's the mother of my child. Her goals are my own. We will achieve them, whatever she wants, whatever it fucking takes."

I grinned, finally getting under his skin. "And what of your lover at your side, in shambles on the ground? Would you pick him or her to die?"

I hadn't taken a step out of my ash, and I watched as Karma struggled with the answer for just a moment. I knew the lie about to come from his mouth would be the most painful one yet.

"Him. The choice is simple. She is everything."

He shrouded his voice in his usual false bravado while the tears in his eyes spoke a different truth. I tucked my chin and stared at him through my wind-swept hair and lashes.

"I knew it. Too good to be true." A laugh escaped me. "A dragon family who talked of peace and love. What a grand façade, so believable, took me a while to figure it all out. That's what I get, though, for hoping I had found a reason to live."

Karma flinched at my words while Juniper circled, waiting for a moment to pounce.

"Strip Axl of his wings and knock him out. He doesn't need to see them try to kill me. Wait till they aren't looking. I will be fine," I whispered quickly to Karri and Korri.

In perfect unison, the vamps said, "Yes." They spoke aloud and disappeared into the trees.

"Sending your own lovers and bodyguards away? Bold choice," Juniper huffed.

I smiled. "They don't need to fight you, but honestly, what are we even fighting for? You want to rule the world sky the same way you rule your kingdom—with an iron fist? Tax every being for your wealth, force them to maintain separations where not even their children can understand everything has a right to life in this world? Praised as gods of what? Hoping you'll ascend? We don't have any proof worship leads to ascension!"

Karma gritted his teeth. "That is the only way to maintain a kingdom as prosperous as mine."

I laughed again. "It's not even your kingdom!" and Juniper lunged at me. Hitting the smoldering ash, she recoiled and hissed.

"You honestly think everything in this world has a right to live? That there is no point to ruling? How else would balance be maintained?" Juniper sneered.

"Simple. You mind your own fucking business and let them live their own lives without arbitrary rules and dictatorship from dragons who should protect those who are weak."

Karma hissed, "I do protect them! From their fucking selves! They come and go, die and live. There is nothing worthy of living apart from the dragons and Fae. I protect them to feed the dragons' wealth and economy. Their division keeps them honest—"

"Wrong. It keeps them in a constant state of fear, easier to control. And if you are such a smart, complex thinker, doing the right thing, then answer me this: Why the fuck is it okay to make them fear the world and make them pay you for protection, especially with lifespans so short? Why do you not want them to live short but full lives under the actual protection of a dragon? Everyone alive has a right to be and should not be exploited and forced to live only within your guidelines. They should want to follow you, but you have taken that choice away. You, Karma, should know damn better. Look at what you have become."

That did it. Karma soared into the sky. I laughed as Juniper burned herself on the ash again as she looked at Axl. Perfect. His cold wings detached.

"*Excellent. Hold Juniper back while I burn Karma's soul,*" I said to Magnus in the dark. The shadows made quick work of Axl, shielding him from the fire and rage.

I launched into the sky, tearing out of the small body I was in, letting my true monstrous form take hold. I rushed at Karma. His form was just as glorious as it had always been. The redness in my eye that slightly blocked my vision was proving useful, as the setting sun glared off his wings. I felt the cold air and released my magic. It was angrier and hotter than I had anticipated. A scream from below turned Karma's attention from me. it had to be Juniper. I would not be distracted. I soared higher as he dove to evade and then dove further toward Karri and Korri, whose whips of borrowed magic held Juniper tight. With my fire, she was right to scream; that had to be painful.

Karma's back was open. I began to dive, pushing myself harder and faster. My wings burned, not from the heat but from the fatigue of training, but it felt pleasant.

*"Drink in that pleasure. Pain and pleasure go hand in hand. I will show you."*

Magnus knew how to ignite my soul even more with his words. In two wing beats, I knocked Karma from the sky, plunging my talons into his wing and over his vitals and, with my teeth, gripping his neck in my mouth. I was small, but the smallest of daggers can be fatal in the right hands.

Karri and Korri, experienced in dragon fights, dropped their draw from my magic without hesitation and retreated into the trees. More shadows appeared, holding Juniper in place. I grinned. Magnus was very helpful. This would have been very difficult without him. Finally, another ally I could rely on.

I sent fire into Karma as he roared. He thrashed. I gripped harder, sinking teeth and talons into any bit of flesh I could find. With my magic sailing through him, I knew I could find his soul. If I burned it, I could release the black magic hold they had on Life, and with the power Death had granted me, I could offer him the choice, like she did for me. We both may die, but that was not new for me. For him, perhaps, it would be life-altering.

Juniper screamed, rolling in agony on the ground. Gods, she was annoying. Swiftly, Karri threw a dagger from the tress knocked her out with the hilt hitting her skull. I sent more fire into Karma, still searching for his forsaken soul. I was losing some strength between holding him down and focusing on finding his center. It was far more difficult than I thought.

Death appeared. "What are you doing?" I met her eyes, sent more fire into Karma, and gripped tighter. Life appeared next. Well, at least I was getting close. I needed more power. Fuck.

*"Hey!"* I kept the fire. *"You didn't tell me we were killing kings today."* I rolled my eyes. Magnus, right now? Really?

He appeared from the tree line, his cloak and glasses shielding him. As I was stuck in a battle to free Life from Karma, he just had to saunter in here, looking as luscious and dark as my deepest desires. Hopefully, this would work out the way I needed. Just once, let this work out this way. I wanted the chance to go home with him.

Also, great. Just how I wanted him to see me—bloodthirsty and killing myself. At least now, he would have to ask himself not if I could handle him but if he could handle me. Karma stopped moving, but I kept burning. To be free, he had to die, but to die and be offered the choice, I had to burn his essence—his soul. From death springs life; from the darkness, there can be light.

The stars can't shine without the night sky.

Keep burning. "If you are trying to free him from the black magic, it's in his wings!" Magnus shouted. I looked at him, puzzled.

"The shadows."

Of course, the fucking shadows, they would talk. I sent out my wings, only covering a fraction of his, and set them ablaze. Then it all went dark and murky.

I looked around. In full ethereal forms stood Life and Death. I looked down at my body, a blaze on top of Karma, and Karma's soul floated up, also looking ethereal and detached. I looked down at my hands. They had no scars, and they were vaguely transparent. Looking down again, Korri and Karri were running toward the burning dragons. Magnus stood with hands in his pockets, watching the whole thing unfold.

Shadowless.

As the sun disappeared over the horizon, we died. I'd killed us.

# CHAPTER TWENTY-NINE

## Elsie

*I* laughed. "Well, we died, dammit." Death laughed. Life shook his head.

"Honestly, killing yourself to free him?"

Karma looked shell-shocked. "W-What's happening?"

I floated toward him. "I killed you, silly goose, and now, by the power vested in me by Lady Death herself . . ." I joked. Death rolled with laughter; a sound Life had not heard in a very long time by the looks of it. "I now grant you the choice"—I raised my marked arm—"live or die, Karma? The choice is yours. No strings attached."

He looked down and then at me, confused. Life sighed exasperated.

"Live. The lady and her warrior are offering you a choice, a choice your lot forced on me. Very generous of them, and I can't imagine why these women would let you live after all you have done, but here they are, ever compassionate." Life rolled his eyes and crossed his arms.

"Oh, darling, don't be like that. Your side of things will be restored—no more dragon drama. Well, to be fair, I guess this is the start of the end. I still have a few things to clean up on this side of things."

I smiled at Karma while Death embraced Life.

"This is a choice I have faced many times. I am not afraid to die, but I will always choose to live because this life is precious, all of it, from the worms in the soil and the trees to the dragons that soar in the sky. With this choice, you will be free of constraints. It's a truly fresh start. I will still be leaving Otium, but you can do what you want."

Karma nodded. "And if I wanted to wipe Caelum Regandi off the map?"

I smiled. I knew he was in there, the real Karma.

"You would have the power to do so, and I hope you would do me the honor and save some for me."

Karma studied the spirits. "Thank you," he cried, tears running down his face as he bowed to them.

"I will do better." He sobbed. "I choose Life. I will learn, grow to be worthy of this chance and choice you have granted me. I will be more responsible for those in my care."

"Elsie?" Death asked with a sinister little giggle.

I laughed. "You know where I am going."

"Wait, Els—sorry, Empress?" I looked at Karma and cocked a brow. He did know. He had failed me, but he knew. It hurt deeply, but I could understand. At least if I was being tortured, I was alive. Alive and being forged into a weapon for all of them to wield. The truth cold, bitter, and excruciating.

"Take Axl with you, please. Keep him safe. It is my duty to handle her, and I will, just not yet. I need time to plan and try to prepare Cosmos."

I nodded. Life and Death held hands, and I felt myself pushed back into my body. I immediately let go of Karma, whose wounds were closing on their own. I rolled to the side, exhausted.

Back in human form, I opened my eyes to see silver eyes staring back at me.

"You good, Firebird?"

I smiled. "Yeah, never better," I choked out.

"You keep interesting friends," Magnus observed.

I looked around. Karri and Korri were also knocked out, probably from the fact I had died. I had been worried that was going to happen. I couldn't feel them anymore but knew they were alive somehow. Death did not take them. I looked at my marked arm, smiled, and silently thanked Lady Death. Karma was also unconscious but alive and bloody. In the charred mess on the cliff edge lay Axl, curled into a ball, in his typical shade of green when in distress, sobbing. Clearly, he had woken up at some point. Shit.

Then there was Juniper, held to the soil by the black tendrils of shadows on her knees, terror radiating from her very core. Her magic had faded, not a single gold shimmer emitting from her, nor the darkness of the black magic she had imbued Karma and Life with. She was not as skilled in the dark arts as I had feared. If ascension was real, that would never allow her to have any power. She touched his soul and bound it to a spirit whose soul was eternal. Black magic was soul-touching magic. It was disgusting and cruel. If that legend was true, I also had given up the right to be a goddess one day after my death. But I was no longer concerned with the afterlife; I was focused on living.

King Mordryl should have been wiped out as soon as they found out he was a necromancer. Now, it made sense why he never faced death at a dragon's hand. The only thing that should touch souls was the magic that lived in them naturally or the fucking gods. I scoffed. What gods? If the gods existed, they were cruel for thinking a territorial monster such as a dragon wouldn't seek power over its so-called duty: protection.

It was not our place to toy with souls, bending and breaking them. You could learn the dark arts, but why? Why would you learn such things? Could our kind really be that wicked to prioritize power, territory, and bloodline over freedom and peace for other beings to live without fear? The story that had been passed down for thousands of years was that we were the equalizers among beings, granting them safety and prosperity, taking care of them and this world. Our long lives, filled with an abundance of magic, should make this task easy for us. Why? Why did it need to be this damn hard to live?

"What a mess," I said nonchalantly, my voice raspy and tired.

Magnus looked at me with his silver eyes. "You could thank me, ya know?"

I laughed. "Sorry, yeah, thanks."

His mouth widened into a grin. I sighed and coughed, my throat raw.

"I guess we wait for everyone to come to their senses?"

His grin vanished. "You have more to handle with them?"

I paused. "I think so?"

Magnus crouched down next to me, giving me a puzzled look as he slipped his dark glasses on. He dipped them down on his nose and peered over them, a dramatic effect that sent me lusting for him, sending a new type of fire into me with those silver eyes. His long hair was tousled, the colorful leathers in its tangles. His face was defined, and when I looked at him, he was handsome in a dark, in a twisted sort of way. Most would probably see him as dangerous, but I saw perfection. If I had any magic left, it would probably ignite and fuel the desires I was pushing away. Like calls to like, his darkness pulled and melted into my own.

I sighed and looked away. Karri and Korri began to stir, Axl was still sobbing, and Juniper was shaking. I smiled and stood up.

"Would you do me a favor, Magnus?"

He laughed. "Sure, Firebird. What could you possibly need now?"

I looked up at him, craning my head, chin tilted to the sky to look him in the eye.

"Hold her a bit longer?" He chuckled and just nodded as he went to Karri and Korri.

I walked to Juniper and crouched down in my tattered dress. She flinched away. I saw the shadows contort as she gagged.

"What is wrong with you?" I asked, looking directly into her hazel eyes, her hair wild and stuck to her cheek. She gritted her teeth and said nothing. I paused to look around. Good, everyone who would be hurt by this was not looking. I sighed, closed my eyes, and remembered the words Ithica had told me: Sometimes, someone needed a villain. Well, here I am.

I snapped my eyes open as the back of my hand connected with her cheek. I felt her teeth give way, and then I wrapped my hand around her throat.

"I will ask you again, what is wrong with you?" I loosened my grip, and she coughed, spraying me with blood and fragments of teeth. Still silence.

I growled, "Don't make me do this. I promise you, there are things far worse than Lady Death's wrath, and that is me. Your lackeys, the Mors, taught me torture well—"

She broke. "They are not my lackeys; they are my parents' lackeys, just like us. I couldn't watch him die, and Axl was on my heels when I found him. The moment I met Axl and Karma, I knew they were next. I had to try to save them, so I promised my father I would make the most powerful son, and I did. And they lived! Who cares that we must do things their way? At least we are all alive!" she shouted.

"You love them? Or do you love him?"

Her eyes watered. "Him, Karma." She bowed her head. Damn it. Always predictable.

"Fine. On his behalf, I'm willing to make you a deal." Her head snapped up, her gaze locking with mine.

"You and Karma keep running things the way you are for the time being. You will tell your parents I died and took Axl with me to the grave. Karma killed me for going rogue. You managed to rebind Life to him. His wounds—leave them scarred or give them an appearance of scars. I don't care, just make it look good. If I know everything, this will work out just fine and will make Karma their hero. If you have lied to me, it'll be obvious real soon. I will send word when I plan to invade the Mors and take them down. Your sister is mine. You will not lay a damn finger on her. But you will turn up to the fight. No one—and I mean it, Juniper—no one is to know about this conversation. Fuck this up"—I raised my hand marked by Death—"we will come for you, and you better pray she finds you first."

Tears streamed down her face. "And after all that? Then what?"

I smiled and stood. "To be determined. One thing at a time."

She hissed. I returned the sentiment and leaned, growling into her ear, "It would serve you well to remember that revenge has no expiration date. Also, for curiosity's sake, how many times did you try to kill me?"

"Including today, four," Juniper muttered.

I hated her, but that was the truth four times she had tried and failed to kill me. But to take a mother from Cosmos, I wasn't sure if I could live with that consequence. I knew what it was like to grieve for the mother you hated, the painful contradiction; that is a pain I would not send to a child. Karma and I shared this reason to keep her alive. For now. Plus, if her family caught wind of this . . . bitch better keep her mouth shut.

I went to Karma. His eyes fluttered open. "You killed me?"

"No, you killed me. I'm dead as I should be. Follow her lead. I will call, and when I do, you better show up."

His body contorted as he took a breath. "Understood."

That was all he said as he attempted to sit up, coughing up bits of violet into his hands. I looked at Magnus, who grinned as the shadows returned to his body, looking ever so smug. Arrogance flowed as he exchanged a glance with Karma, who quickly averted his eyes. Karri and Korri were weak but standing, and they nodded.

"Have room for another?" I jerked my head toward my brother.

"And if I don't?"

I smiled. "Then, I will say it was nice to meet you in the flesh, but I will not be able to go with you, oh dark and mysterious one." I was not going to use his name aloud in this company; he stayed in the dark for a reason.

I gave him a coy smile and turned to walk toward my brother. He looked worse than any of us. I sighed and knelt next to him.

"We need to go," I whispered.

Sobs racked his body. He wasn't made for this. I had been hardened to heartbreak; this was no different.

"Bring him with us," Magnus said. His voice raked over me with rough yet pleasant kindness.

I felt the sharp wind and watched my brother get snatched by a massive set of talons. Not concealing his true form, Magnus was as perfect as the night sky, speckled with silver dots, mimicking the stars. He hovered above us, wings beating softly, tattered from battles, giving the illusion the sky was ripping to pieces before our very eyes. Karma's eyes went wide as Juniper sank down against him, averting her eyes.

"Karri, Korri." They came to my side, and I shifted, allowing them to climb to their usual spots. I craned my neck back to Juniper, who was standing, shaking, her fist balled up against her chest. She nodded to me. I returned the gesture and launched into the sky, following the wing beats of another black dragon, my brother's sobs escaping into the night. Camouflaged by the darkness, we began to fly, hopeful King and Queen Rexarius would keep their word. If they didn't, I would have to be the one to kill one of my best friends and rip my brother's heart apart beyond repair.

I let my tears fall as we flew. I did it. I freed Life from Karma or freed Karma from Life. However you wanted to look at it, I did it. Did I create a monster dressed in white? Would the winter give us enough time to get ready for a bloody war? Would he stay true? Could he keep a handle on Juniper without her going rogue and forcing my hand? Axl loved her, and his life meant a lot to me. He was lucky, all things considered. His tears fell silently over the life he had lost. Here we were, crying for life, begging it to be kinder; just let us live in peace. Just let us be happy.

I knew the Lord of Life didn't control that nor the so-called gods, but wishing it into the sky felt cathartic. I focused on flying, the wind wiping the tears from my face. I just wanted a chance at a normal life. I would never get it. I would never get to be a normal dragon. I was the Empress of Death and Darkness; I was the monster everyone feared.

Magnus and I had a lot to discuss. If he had been so infatuated with me all these years and had spoken to me all this time, why had he never come for me? Was I so dangerous in my insanity it remained safer for the world if I was locked away?

*"Please, pull yourself together. I hate to even think of your sorrow, let alone watch as your tears fall. Please trust me."*

I stopped my tears, wishing my life would make more sense, wishing I could stop crying for the life I was meant to have. But I would hold back the tears for now.

# CHAPTER THIRTY

## Elsie

It was not long, maybe only a few miles from that little port town, over a few more scattered and vacant islands, that we reached a clearing. Magnus took a sudden dip and landed in it. I followed; my brother had quieted. I attempted to shift but was only able to manage about half of myself. Without warning, my legs gave out, and I was on the ground, Karri and Korri hovering over me. I looked up at the sky, a beautiful night with only the stars providing light.

"Empress, you need to get up. We have to keep going," Korri snapped, still stressed about the situation. Looking at him and Karri, I noticed they were without any color. Shit. That's right, I died; they must have gotten close to death themselves.

"No, we will sit here for a moment. I don't want to arrive till dawn. She needs the sun," Magnus offered plainly. I sighed with relief and closed my eyes.

"Are you two all right?" I asked, my voice fading.

Korri snapped back, "Do we look all right?" I heard a snap and opened my eyes. Karri had slapped him.

"That's enough, Korrigan! We said we would follow her; that included to the grave. Settle down." At least she got it, but then again, she always got it. She may be a wild card half the time, but she always understood me. She was chaos-swayed to evil or good but mainly just a sort of neutral, unyielding chaos.

"Hmm, you're truly bonded to them, eh?" Magnus asked while crouched down, starting a small fire. Even that small amount of warmth was a relief. They nodded, and each one sat at my side.

"Very well, then," was all Magnus said as I fell asleep by the fire Axl cowering by the gentle flames, and my four friends: the lady herself, Karri and Korri, and Magnus.

I woke up from a dreamless sleep moments before dawn.

"Great timing." Magnus smiled. "How are you doing?" he asked as he crouched next to me.

I looked around. Karri and Korri were missing. I sucked in a breath and sat straight up. Massive, scarred hands gripped my shoulders.

"Easy, Firebird. They went off hunting. With the terrain, it will take them awhile. They will return. They didn't have an option with your current state, and I don't share blood."

I looked down; I was still in an ugly, pathetic half-form. "What have I told you about that?" Magnus quipped as I focused and finished transforming to that sickly human look.

Magnus chuckled. "Don't worry about it." He gestured to my body. "Soon, you will be able to take on any human form you desire, but I have to say, I love this look on you. Makes me feel like a hero or some shit," he joked. I went to speak, and nothing came of it. Fuck. My voice was gone again. I had been careful to avoid that tiny bit of Cosmos magic for months, but the after-math of using that much magic and fully resetting my body with rest must have drained every last drop. I'd lost it again. Shit. His eyes widened, then the light silver turned ashy and cold, and his hands draped over his knees.

"Was it him?" he seethed, and I cocked my head.

"That white miserable excuse of a dragon. Was. It. Him?" I shook my head, and Magnus relaxed slightly. "Burnout then?"

I nodded. Voiceless again? Great. Human form? Great. Mysterious giant male dragon who bore the scars of many battles? Also great.

"They will choke to death in the shadows for that, I promise you." I looked away from his beautiful silver eyes.

*Just not Clia, please, just not Clia,* I begged silently. Magnus sat down and gripped my hand.

"We will talk about it if you are so against it, but they will suffer for touching what is mine."

My head jerked back to his gaze, piercing and icy, devoid of anything but rage.

He smiled. "I have met many beings silenced by the Rexarius and Mors. It is, unfortunately, all too common, and in my position, reading a body is as crucial as wielding magic. You, however, I can listen to most of your thoughts. You are loud and coated in shadows veiled in darkness. It's only when you shut me out that I can't hear you. If you keep that wall down, you can talk through the shadows. You have played with it before."

My brow cocked without warning. He chuckled and brushed some stray hair from my face with his hand.

"You will learn a lot about the both of us very quickly, I fear, when we reach our destination."

I sighed. Well, okay, at least he wasn't planning to kill me or worse. At least not right now, it seemed.

"I need you to trust me, then ask all the questions you want after some rest. I will get your brother the best care, and the vamps will be welcomed as well. All I need you to do is stay silent and in full dragon form. After what needs doing is done, you will have more wealth, freedom, and power than you have ever experienced in your tragic life, and I will teach you how to use the shadows so we may always talk within the privacy of our minds. It will be easy and second nature. Just remember you have done it before. You just need to let me in and trust the shadows."

I huffed at him. Yes, my life was tragic, but really? Saying it out loud hurt.

"Shift back now, and when your vamps return, we need to go." I nodded and looked at my brother, still a crumpled mess on the grassy floor, but at least the sobbing had stopped.

I allowed my magic to rip free and sat near the fire, waiting for Karri and Korri, watching Magnus fuss over a long, thin blade. Encrusted in the hilt were red-and-black stones with braided leather, exquisite and, without question, deadly. Just as the sun began to crest, Karri and Korri slipped out of the trees, their eyes bright red. Humans. Well, I suppose it couldn't be helped. I wanted to ask where they even found some humans, but the look on Korri's face told me that would be a bad question to ask right now.

"Load up. We need to go," Magnus barked, and I nodded. Karri looked me in the eye. "What are we doing?"

I looked to Magnus, who was clearly on edge. "It's simple. She stays as a dragon, and none of you say a damn word."

I sighed, but oh well, less was probably for the best for the time being, so I nodded. Without another question, she climbed up while Korri stood in place.

"No." His voice was gravelly. I hissed in response.

"You nearly killed us!" Korri barked.

I hissed again and shook my head.

"Oh, really? You don't think so?" I stood and narrowed my gaze, looking down at him.

"Fine, be ready to explain yourself." He huffed and climbed up, meeting Karri on my back.

Annoyed, Magnus quipped, "You are going to feel so stupid once you cross the gate, Korrigan." That left me with a strange feeling. A gate? What would change for them after crossing a gate?

After Korri's outburst, Magnus wasted no time sailing into the dimly lit sky, much easier to see. I could understand why he opted to fly at night—he was nearly impossible to see, and I doubt anyone could unless they were dragons. Or could look the darkness in the face and live to witness it. As we flew, the only sound was our wingbeats, steady, unhurried, but you could hear and see the malice coating his. Wherever we were going, clearly, he was not thrilled what the next few hours would bring.

I followed; that was my only job right now, just silently obeying. Too easy. I had been trained relentlessly for over a century. I kept my eyes locked on his back and tattered wings. He was a fighter like me but wore it so much better. His scars made him lethal, while mine spoke to the fact I was broken and tarnished goods. He dropped, landing on human feet with my brother in his arms like you would hold a child, his cloak covering his face. I sank my talons into the ground right behind him tucking my wings and chin down. My eyes, however, took in the grave situation before me.

Massive, easily double or triple the height of a well-statured male dragon, were walls of black stone, and before us stood a double door of the same stone but in red across the top, Bellator, and inscribed across the bottom of the doors, in the old language, Memento Mori. Double—no triple—fuck. The Kingdom of warriors and assassins. Knowing this was my home and seeing it were two very different things. You could feel the wards of the walls. It was like having the air pulled from your lungs.

"Who comes to enter Bellator?" a faceless voice called out.

I heard a scoff from Magnus as he spit onto the ground. "Magnus Bellator." His voice rang out, a stern warning. I felt Korri and Karri stiffen. Oh shit, this Magnus was a royal of Bellator. I swallowed back the bile I could feel rising—also not an unfamiliar feeling, but it did not escape Magnus as he slightly turned his head to show me his eye, a wink. Okay, cocky much?

"Along with my soul tie, Empress of Bellator, Elsie, and her bonded, Karrigan and Korrigan." I gagged—his what? Karri and Korri gripped harder, but I lowered my head toward Magnus.

Submission was key for right now. I could trust him. I had relied on him for years without even being aware. I was well-practiced in false submission.

The faceless voice called back, "Welcome home, Prince, Empress, and warriors of Bellator."

The massive black doors opened, displaying the most beautiful landscape I had ever laid eyes on: full grass-covered rolling hills, and the tallest mountains, peaked with snow. The rivers flowed bright and crystal-clear like rainbows in the soil; the sky was painted in a never-ending sunset of color, and everything looked like a more impressive version of the manor, only to be complete with wild roaming unicorns.

It was the manor, my home, only this was a kingdom. My kingdom. I felt the tears welling; the familiar feeling of home was crashing over me as if this land was welcoming me personally like a long-lost friend, a warm embrace full of elegant energy.

*"Those better be tears of joy, Elsie, my Firebird, Empress of Bellator. Welcome home."*

## CHAPTER THIRTY-ONE

### Elsie

Magnus passed through the doors with his sauntering gait, and as soon as he was on the other side, he was flying. I passed through in wonder, my talons sinking into the soil. It was as if the land itself was singing. My magic felt more reachable. Peace and happiness washed over me. The air was warm and a tad heavy with moisture, but I sighed with relief and took off after him. I kept my eyes on Magnus. His dark form and tattered wings spoke to his menacing appearance as he stood apart from this landscape that looked like Life had created it by hand. The colors of spring were bounding from every blade of grass, leaf, and flower I could see before looking back at Magnus. For warriors and assassins, this land seemed too kind, too lush. Filled with peace.

As the sun rose over the land, everything felt light and warm, even the air did not feel thin. However, I knew Bellator was nestled in the mountains. How odd. The magic here felt like the manor; peaceful, abundant, flowing with ease.

We kept flying north, and I peeked around his wings to see a massive building carved from a mountain of that same black stone. High steps and carvings though it, ancient yet timeless, and perfectly devoid of any color; even the sun absorbed into the stone. Magnus kept flying straight for it; this had to be their capital. My capital. As we grew closer, the details of the massive carved black building were more impressive: things of legends and known beasts decorated the walls, from Fae, elven warriors, sirens, maids, and so much more down to the unicorns roaming free as we entered. It was incredible. I had never seen such work.

Magnus descended as he did earlier, becoming human-looking just as his foot touched the dark stones at the front doors, matching the wall. He stayed a good way from those doors. I landed lightly, trying not to damage the stones under my talons. With a knowing glance at me, Magnus snickered. I could feel Korri and Karri clutching my scales as if their lives depended on it. I dipped my head behind him and tucked myself together, as I had been so well trained to do.

His jaw tightened, and he whispered, "I hate that you are doing this so well."

I didn't move, still as death. Obey; questions had to come later. Something was coming. He turned back to face the doors.

"I also hate what I am about to do, Firebird. We are not done killing boy kings, but this one will not be resurrected." I nodded. "Watch him."

Magnus set Axl down and stepped over him. I walked forward and stood over my brother, tucked into my signature stance, ready to defend him or Magnus.

"I know you see me!" He threw his cloak down. "Now, come face me!"

As swift as a bird plucking its prey from the land, a smaller green dragon pounced on Magnus. He ripped into his dragon form, and shadows ensnared the smaller green one. A flawless transition from beast back into man, not even a hint of his clothing disrupted. Magnus grabbed the lenses off his face and tossed them aside as well.

"Do not send your guards, Kavell! You knew this day would come if you did not give up your throne to me. Now get down here and defend it!"

A much larger orange-and-green-scaled dragon appeared from the timeless structure. Magnus ensnared it with more shadows and drove the knife he had been playing with into its eye with a quick flick of his wrist. His ability to wield a dagger with such precision was stunning, much like my own style, but more refined and practiced. Hauntingly beautiful.

A roar escaped it as it became a man the same size and build as Magnus and the same face, but all his features were a deep orange, with hints of green. He was seething, with violet blood running down the left side of his face.

"That hurt, little brother. You will not take a damn thing from me."

Magnus scoffed and held up his dagger, the shadows returning it to his hand. With the eye on the end. "Looks like I already have. Back down. Don't force this on me, brother."

Magnus sounded somber. Kavell growled and lunged at Magnus, who clicked his teeth, and his shadows ran into Kavell's empty eye socket. As soon as it began, it was over as his head exploded. Only a headless corpse remained, pools of violet running over the gray stone. The smaller green dragon bowed and went to collect the body. I was stuck in a state of stunned silence.

"You would think he wanted to die with that pathetic display," Magnus said, flicking the eyeball off his dagger and pulling a cloth from his trousers to wipe the blood from the beautiful blade. His movements were well-rehearsed, like he had done this countless times.

Magnus walked to me, and I did not dare to move.

"You should feel much lighter and better overall. The land calls to the wounded. Are you all right?"

I made eye contact but did not move. His hands shook, then he balled them into fists.

"I am sorry I made you do this, but thank you nonetheless. If you would, please allow me to escort you inside."

I shifted. Korri and Karri fell but landed on their feet. I kept my head bowed.

"Are you able to speak? The magic here may be just enough if you weave it where your vocal cords used to be." I shrugged.

"Elsie, please."

*"I don't want you silenced, not here,"* his voice pleaded in my mind.

I sucked in a breath and focused on weaving a fine line of magic in my throat.

"What the fuck was that?" I seethed, my voice sounding like a crackling fire. Magnus began laughing harder than I had ever heard anyone laugh.

"My older brother. He has been reigning as a stand-in since Dad tossed us the pleasure of the kingdom. The citizens approved my departure to go get you." He rolled his eyes and kept laughing.

"But that's not the king!" I cracked. "I met the king! In Rexarius!" I coughed. Fuck, this hurt.

Magnus covered his face as he laughed harder. "Oh, Firebird, don't you remember me saying 'shame that's not the real king'? You have so much to learn. We never actually send any of the real royals into other territories publicly. Far too risky."

I balked. Magnus kept a shit-eating grin on his face.

"As I said, you are welcome to ask anything you want."

"Your soul tie?" I said, meeting his eyes as they grew dark.

"You don't have to be. However, I think you will learn that I am a far superior choice than the white idiot masquerading around as a god. Or the girl you are in love with whom held you hostage for so many years."

Karri snapped her teeth and hissed, "You did not ask her! She owes you nothing!"

I looked at the ground, the blood and body gone, like the murder of his brother hadn't happened.

"Easy, Karrigan. I know that. However, I also know she won't resist me for long. She is my soul tie. My vows demand it. She still has the choice, Karri, don't you worry."

Magnus turned and picked up my brother with ease. He wasn't wrong. How could I resist him? His darkness, his bloodlust, his skill, his cocky words and full lips. I shook my head, trying to think of anything else.

*"I am in here, too."* His voice sounded in my mind with a chuckle.

One thing was infuriating. "Why is it you and every other dragon have not one ounce of trouble between forms? And what are these vows that you and everyone else are always spouting off about?" I screamed, exasperated, spitting bits of fire out of my mouth. I had practiced to refine my magic, but damn, this amount of control was hard. Impossible on the outside of the walls. Shock and sadness washed over Magnus as he turned away from me.

"Because we were allowed to pass between them at convenience as children and subadults, a grace you did not receive. The vows are something you and I will discuss in private." He carried Axl up the few steps to the massive doors, and I was stuck, frozen in anger and sadness yet surrounded by warmth and comfort. What was this place? Why was I so confused but feeling whole at the same time?

As he approached the door, a small Fae girl opened the door, dressed like a red-and-white mushroom with facial markings to match the girl from my welcome home party. They had come and infiltrated Rexarius to go to that party. A sense of relief washed over me but also anger. Why wouldn't they save me that torment with Karma?

"Welcome back, Prince."

Magnus nodded, offering a small correction to her in a hushed tone, "It's Emperor now, Elowiyn."

She took a hand over her heart. "Emperor, I will inform the others at once."

He looked over his shoulder. "Well, come on." I nodded and followed him in.

Elowiyn stopped us at the door. "And you must be Karrigan? And Korrigan?" The three of us nodded. She was avoiding me.

"Oh, good! Just as Granny said! Welcome home! Empress Elsie!" I gagged a bit as she dropped into a deep curtsy, and Magnus stifled a laugh.

We entered and looked around. The walls were black stone, and the floors black with specks of silver and red running through them. It reminded me of the estate in Otium. Except, the paintings and tapestries were not of the royal family at all, but the land, villages, towns, humans, real paintings of real things in this kingdom, not a trace of their family on anything. Not even a crest.

"Why don't you have anything of the royal family on display?" I asked.

"The land and its people are more important than the royals." It was a statement. No question about it.

I sighed. I was out of my depth here. I came here expecting something small, a normal winter. But I had, in fact, walked right into the heart of a kingdom known for its assassins and warriors, and it was mine. A kingdom that played no political games but seemed far too put together to not be playing some sort of game. What was this place? Were we safe?

*"No harm will come to you within the walls of our kingdom. That, I can promise you. The people are very happy to have you here."*

This was too much to take in as we walked down the corridors of this place. My vision started to cloud. No, not again. I swallowed. After what felt like hours of taking in this place of beauty, we reached a door. A gasp escaped me when I read the name on the door.

"COSMOS REXARIUS," I blurted out, spitting bits of fire from my mouth while coughing.

What in the fuck was happening? Magnus used the bony claw on his wing tip to knock on the door, and the flaky-skinned, green-eyed boy, with his father's white hair opened the door. His bright expression fell instantly as he looked at Magnus and Axl and somberly asked, clear as day without a stutter or delay, "Was it my mom?"

I felt my jaw drop with an audible click.

## EPILOGUE

*Karma*

watched in shocked horror as Elsie took Axl. I was beaten and bloodied. At least I was free from the spirit. Not like that mattered all that much, anyway. I was still trapped with her, the vile creature holding my son hostage. Forcing my hands against everything I loved in this world. Death, I longed for death. So many times, I begged Life to send me to her, end me. End this suffering.

I coughed and sat up, hair matted to my face with blood. Watching as the black dragons faded into the night sky, I couldn't help but wonder, did she know him for who he really was? Did she even know his name? Was it the same one I knew him by? I sighed in slight relief. She at least did what I asked and left Juniper alone. She was my problem, but worse, she was my son's biggest problem. It was my duty as a father to fix this for him. I had to. He was the only reason I chose to stay when Elsie offered me the choice. I couldn't leave him, not with Juniper the way she was. Nor with Axl, who could barely stomach the conflicts I had put him in.

"You tired or something?" Juniper hissed at me. I looked to the ground, unable to find words to respond.

"Say something!" she shouted. I swallowed, wishing I had a drink right now.

"I don't have anything to say, Juniper," I mumbled. I didn't need to pretend in front of her. She knew how fragile I was. Her favorite broken toy. She stalked toward me, blood pouring from her mouth. I hid my smile. *Good work, Els,* I thought.

"You lost her! You are a fucking waste! How dare you?" Juniper's claws met my face, and I gagged on more blood, my wings drooping onto the chilling ground.

"Fifty years, Karma! Fifty years I have spent with you and Axl with the promise you would bring her to me! As a weapon for my family! You said she would be desperate! Then you just admit to her you gave up!"

*I had hoped she was dead, so at least no one could use her the way they had intended to.* Listening to Juniper berate me, I could only think of what could have been if I was allowed to stay dead.

"YOU LIED TO ME! I was supposed to get a submissive little girl with nothing in her heart but fire and rage! You promised if I held out, I would have her to myself!" This time, it was her fist that caught my jaw. I fell to the side, numb. Devoid of any feelings whatsoever.

"You were supposed to give me this whole continent! You had the audacity to die the first time! And now this? Are you really going to do this to me as well?" Juniper snarled as she landed blow after blow into my ribs with the tips of her pointy shoes.

A small sob escaped me as I hugged my arms around myself. "I'm sorry!" I sounded broken.

"You know what is going to happen? They are going to kill us!" Juniper fell to her knees and wailed. "I was supposed to deliver them an entire continent with an impressive bloodline! The best and most powerful dragon line to soar over Concordia!"

Sobs racked her body. "And now, all I have is you!" She sneered. I swallowed back the bile that was rising, finding my words.

"Maybe if you weren't so hell-bent on appeasing your mother, you could have done those things for yourself!" I gritted out with as much venom as I could.

Juniper stopped sobbing and looked at me with disgust. "Our parents sold us off to each other. Do you have any idea what it took for me to allow them to keep Axl alive?" She paused and took a breath.

"You ruined this by killing off your family, Karma. Had you just fucking accepted your fate and married me from the get-go, none of this would have happened!" she shouted, my ears ringing.

"I killed them because of what they did! It wasn't right, selling off their only son! All I wanted was Axl! Why can't any of you just understand that? They died, and so did I! You forced me back! I would have been better off dead!" I yelled, spitting blood onto her dress.

"You would have rather left me with child? A dumb one at that? You—"

"Do not call my son dumb, Juniper, so help me—"

"So help you, what? You'll kill me?" She taunted. "Too bad. If you kill me, you also kill your preciously dumb son."

Juniper stood and walked away. I closed my eyes and sent out a silent plea. *As above, Elsie, save him, forget me, hate me, but please, save him. Save him from the monster that is his mother. Please. Save—*

My eyes snapped open as I felt the cold metal slip around my neck. "You will learn to love me, Karma. Let me show you how a real woman handles revenge."

# Acknowledgments

Wow, we actually made it all the way to the end! I really can't believe we made it here. Thank you for reading. I hope you are just as excited for book two as I am. Okay, okay, now it's time for the sappy, mushy feelings.

First up, thank you to the best partner a girl could ask for. Keenan, I really don't tell you enough how amazing you are. Thank you for everything. From the laptop to the website and listening to me drone on and on for hours about this dang book. You are the man of my dreams, and I am eternally grateful to have you in my life.

Danica, my book bestie, I will never be able to repay you for all the late nights and unhinged conversations. You stuck by me when this book was nothing more than ideas and word vomit on pages. Without you, I could never have made it this far. Cheers to another great year of books and besties!

All right, you know who you are: TRASH SQUAD. You know what you did. And if you wanna hear it again, you guys gave me the delusional confidence to make this a reality. So, thank you. To the burners, ravers, and other alternative lifestyle people I have met in our wonderful community, your continued outpouring of support for artists and dreamers is so appreciated. See y'all at Tribal Roots!

Special thanks to Charlie. My life is forever changed just from having you in it. I love you so much. Thank you for accepting me and showing me new ways to live life and enjoy it. Nothing could have prepared me for the whirlwind friendship I have found with you. Thank you for adopting me into your inner circle when I didn't even know what I needed.

I would be lost without you all in my life. XOXO.

# About the Author

Ashlen Jordan is an author who grew up surrounded by books and teachers, but her love for reading was often misunderstood. Though Ashlen first considered writing in high school, she found herself disillusioned with college and ultimately dropped out.

Today, she writes about tragic love and fantastical worlds, drawing from her own experiences. Living through her share of misguided relationships, she seeks solace in her imagination. It was through this escape that her passion for fantasy and maladaptive daydreaming collided. Allowing her to craft stories that transport readers to worlds full of emotion, chaos, and unforgettable twists.

As the self-proclaimed chaotic friend in her circle, Ashlen balances her love for adventure an creativity with the ability to listen, offering a grounded perspective when others need it. A proud anime enthusiast, BookTok aficionado, a passionate horse owner, and a lover of all things with fur and scales. Ashlen's true joy outside all those things in life is the electric energy of rave culture and embracing the PLUR spirit. Ashlen Jordan is turning her tragedies into fantastical tales and is more than excited to take you on these journeys with her.